THE ANALYST

THE
ANALYST

ANNE OSBORNE

William Morrow & Company, Inc.
New York

FOR D.G. AND I.L.

THE ANALYST

1

THE PHONE WAS RINGING. At first it was part of his dream. An alarm? A warning? Or was he a child again, hearing the late bell at school? Whatever it had been, it had to do with something he hadn't done, had forgotten to do, had neglected, at some time, at some place.

Get away from it then, he thought, climbing out of his bed and walking, naked and barefoot, into the huge living room.

It was still early. The daylight had a mauve tint as it trickled through the tiny, dusty panes of glass in the french windows which ran across one wall of the room, facing out on the long red-brick terrace.

The phone suddenly stopped, and the silence became deafening, frightening. And then, there was something different about the room itself this morning that added to his sense of foreboding. Was it the color? The smell? Yes, it was the smell. He sniffed. Pine needles—remembering the Christmas tree.

A small and sad green triangle of skinny branches, the tree was leaning against the fireplace. It looks as though it were ready for its ultimate fate—firewood.

And the tree looked all the more ready because it was naked, just as he himself was naked on this Christmas morning. The decorations were still in their boxes, lying next to a roll of unstretched canvas, a stack of hollow frames, and an empty bottle of champagne. Had he really drunk it up all himself? He picked up the bottle, saw there was a warm inch left, and finished it off.

The phone started again, its piercing ring making him drop the bottle. His hands were shaking now, and he couldn't stop them any more than he could the phone. The bottle had shattered near his bare feet, and a thin stream of blood was forming on his instep.

Wash it off, he thought, going toward the bathroom. Now it wasn't only his hands but his whole body that was trembling.

Just as the living room was lined with windows, the huge bathroom was lined with mirrors so that, no matter how he tried, he could not avoid seeing himself. Everywhere he turned there were myriads of pathetic, thin, dark young men with charcoal shadows under their dark eyes. They reflected from one set of mirrors to another, moving in unison, slowly, as if following some kind of primitive dirge. There were so many of them, and yet each one looked all alone. Just as lonely as the sad Christmas tree. And just as totally beside the point. Completely unnecessary, clearly a mistake. There was no reason for the tree. What had he been thinking of? What was he trying to prove?

The phone kept ringing, as if offering the answers to his questions. He knew now that it had to be his father. No one else would keep on this way.

"Shut up!" he screamed, grabbing the cup from the bathroom and throwing it toward the sound. The cup hit the edge of the bathroom door. And again, there were slivers of glass around his bare feet.

The phone was getting louder, more insistent, angrier at him for not answering.

He looked down. There was more blood on his feet. It was somehow lovely now, with the red rivulets making an intricate pattern on his white skin.

He bent down, picked up a large piece of jagged glass, and tried to repeat the design on his hands, first cutting one wrist and then the other. But by now he couldn't see the patterns anyway, his eyes were so filled with tears.

I really don't want to die, he thought, but it's the only way I know to stop the phone.

2

THE WIND CAME howling down Riverside Drive, almost stopping Gerson Richler dead in his tracks as he tried to make his way toward Eighty-sixth Street in search of a taxi. He pulled his blue knit scarf over his mouth and then jammed his gloved hands back into his coat pockets. For thirty of his sixty-three years he had battled this freezing gale that raced down from the Hudson River to attack the fortresses of brownstones and apartment houses that lined Manhattan's Upper West Side. And every morning, for twenty-nine of those years, Gerson Richler had bitterly sworn to himself that this was the very last day he would face that treacherous blast. But every morning too, by the time he had arrived at the hospital across town, he had forgotten his plan to call his wife, Leah, and tell her to begin looking for another apartment—maybe something on Fifth Avenue where he could walk to work.

When he got to Eighty-sixth Street, there wasn't a cab in sight. Well, he thought, there wasn't likely to be one at 7 A.M. on the day after Christmas. Leah had told him to call for one and as usual she had been right. He eyed the bus stop. No, today especially, he just didn't feel like taking the bus. Not that he had to hurry. In his line of doctoring there was rarely a cause to hurry and maybe that was what was wrong with it —and that was what was wrong with him as well. His own time was running out, his patience was wearing thin, and his belief in the whole unhappy therapeutic process was wavering. My second crisis of faith, he realized. First Judaism. Now psychiatry.

A taxi pulled up across the street, stopping at the light. Richler hailed it and the driver made a U-turn. "Mount Sinai Hospital," he told the driver as he climbed into the cab, settled back in the seat, and began to rub his hands together, enjoying the warm air. Once out of the wind, his mood changed, and he began to think about work—about his patients—about Paul Kingman. They'd called him from the hospital yesterday to tell him the boy had been brought in—ankles and wrists slashed. Apparently, a cleaning woman had found him in time to save his life. And Richler was sure the boy didn't want it saved. How could Richler go on saying that an attempt at suicide was a cry for help? He didn't believe it for a minute. Instead, he knew it was a try at death. And that boy surely wanted to die. Siegel, the surgeon who had sutured the wounds, told him that one of the incisions—the one on his left wrist—was so deep that although Siegel had kept him on the operating table for hours trying to repair what he could, he was pretty sure the boy would never fully recover all sensation in that hand. Well, he was right-handed, the boy's father had told them. Thank God for small blessings, as Richler's own father would have remarked.

Fathers and sons. Richler sighed, thinking of what he would have felt had it been his Sandy. He knew he would never have had the control that William Kingman had when they spoke on the phone yesterday. Centuries of Protestant training had gone into creating the curbed emotions that Kingman displayed—and centuries of Protestant repression had gone into the making of his son's try at suicide. Richler hadn't even been able to detect any embarrassment in the great surgeon's voice when he asked Richler to see his son and try to help him. Years ago, Richler thought to himself, he would have blamed the proud and unbending tower of Protestant tradition, William Kingman, for not having found help for his son sooner, for having let it come to such an extreme. Certainly, the mother couldn't have been relied on to make such decisions, that self-absorbed woman that she was, or at least seemed to be on the one or two occasions Richler remembered meeting her—at a dinner maybe, some theater benefit. And if years ago Richler would have blamed Kingman for not getting his son to a psychiatrist sooner, today the weary man wondered if it would have made any difference at all. How many attempted suicides, as well as successful ones, happened anyway, even after years and years of analysis? It wasn't only that this kind of therapy took too long but that the pace was always—no matter how hard one pushed, no matter how hard one tried—just a little bit behind the pace of life itself.

The taxi pulled up in front of the huge glass doors of the hospital, interrupting Richler's thoughts. He paid the driver and carefully put on his gloves and tightened his scarf to face the winds that swept the few steps up to the hospital. God, how he hated the cold. He would, he thought smiling to himself, probably end up in Florida like the rest of them.

It was Addie Harris' first week at Mount Sinai Hospital, and what a week to start. There was no time like Christmas, the other nurses in the psychiatric section kept complaining, for bringing out the nuts and fruitcakes. Her first two nights on duty, the pretty sandy-haired young nurse from Carthage, Missouri, hadn't even had time for so much as a cup of coffee, what with Emergency sending up one catastrophe after another. It seemed she no sooner finished hooking up one would-be suicide's I.V. before she was called in to give a shot of lithium to a manic-depressive at the height of his manic phase. One in particular—a fifty-year-old, popeyed, hawk-nosed ex-priest—had been hauled in, according to a lanky intern named Joe Buchbinder, after delivering an oration in St. Patrick's Cathedral, urging Catholics to stone all Protestants. Addie wasn't quite sure that Joe—who had been flirting with her all week and whose prominent Adam's apple gave him an awkward, slightly comical air—wasn't putting her on. But by now, she knew that even wilder things could happen in New York, a place which had turned out to be every bit as frantic as she had always heard it was. Yet this mammoth madhouse of a skyscraper city didn't seem as terrifying to her as it did exciting. She liked the noise and the confusion, and the way everyone walked fast and kept going, whether the traffic light was green or red. Most important, she knew that New York would never allow her to be bored—and boredom was precisely what she had wanted to escape when she decided to leave the Midwest. Even the world of this New York hospital had a fascination to it as contrasted with that of Jackson State, the hospital where Addie had worked for the three years since graduating from nursing school. There the staff had had a bleached sameness, while here, what with the Haitian nurse's aides, the Puerto Rican orderlies, the Jewish interns, and Italian and Irish nurses, it all seemed like a mini-U.N. And where the inmates at Jackson State mental ward had been a bland assortment of drab housewives, mechanics, and clerks, at Mount Sinai the psychiatric section was populated by the rich, the glamorous, and even the very famous. On Thursday, for example, they had brought in superstar Nannette Norton, unconscious from an overdose of Seconal. Addie, checking N.N.'s blood pressure right after her stomach had been pumped, felt a strong mixture of awe and pity as she stared down at the bloated mound of sallow flesh that bore little resemblance to the piquant, vibrant songbird who had been her mother's favorite musical-comedy star. The staff had all been advised that N.N.'s presence was to be kept a secret, but the tabloids got the news anyway, just as they also uncovered the arrival one day later of Adele Munsey, the alcoholic wife of presidential hopeful Senator Thomas J. Munsey. Addie hadn't been on duty when Mrs. M. had been brought in, but the story—this time emanating not from Joe Buchbinder but from the *Daily News*—was that she had arrived completely nude beneath her sable coat, having ripped off her gown in the middle of a party at the Fifth Avenue mansion of the Iranian ambassador to the U.N.

What a party that must have been, Addie thought and suppressed a grin, I wish I could have been there. This was another part of the New York that Addie was searching for, the sexual side of this vibrating city. Back in school in Carthage, and later, at Jackson State, Addie never had to worry about finding lovers. There was always someone, sometimes someone really attractive, but she never found the glamour, the special excitement, that she knew could only come from what was not familiar. Just as five years before she knew she was beyond the dark back seats of cars where the only light came from the glare of a streetlamp or the feeble flicker from the match lighting the inevitable "after" cigarette, now she realized she had also grown beyond an occasional night at the Holiday Inn, where the fluorescent light left everything pallid and ugly. Life, she knew, had something more to offer. She pushed all the sex scenes from the past to the back of her mind. Along with well-done skinny midwestern steaks, these were things to leave behind. Ahead were strange, fascinating objects like lobsters, women whose makeup was like Margaux Hemingway's or who, like Senator Munsey's wife, took off their clothes in a living room full of people. And there were men who made a very special kind of love in a room lit by candles or maybe by the dimmed glow of a crystal chandelier. These were the men that Addie was going to meet. All she had to do was find them.

The next day they brought in Paul Kingman. Addie was on duty when the frail, delicately featured young man was wheeled down from surgery, where the gashes on his wrists and ankles had been sutured.

"God, he's handsome. I don't think I've ever seen anyone who looks like him," Addie whispered to another nurse, Catherine Ripley, as the two stood over the unconscious and ashen figure, Addie checking his blood pressure while Catherine was making sure that his I.V. was functioning properly. "Is he another celebrity? He can't be a mere mortal." Catherine shook her head. A sharp-featured and equally sharp-tongued nurse somewhere in her mid-thirties, Catherine came from Elmhurst, Queens, and so bore the rare distinction of being one of the few native New Yorkers on the nursing staff. As soon as they met, she had quickly become Addie's mentor.

"Well, he's no Al Pacino, if that's what you mean, but he's no Joe Shmo either." Catherine smoothed the covers over the young man's slender chest and then stopped. The white covering sheet had suddenly darkened and turned crimson. "The bleeding's starting up," she said—Addie noticed Catherine's voice had changed to her efficient, professional one. "You'd better get the resident while I stay with him."

Addie hurried to the nurses' station, rang the resident on duty, and finally found herself having to get him from the doctors' lounge, where he was having a winning streak at seven-card stud.

"Why didn't you answer?" Addie asked the plump young Dr. Eakeley, who, at thirty, was already balding.

"Oh, I guess the battery on my bleeper must have worn out again," he said nervously. "Maybe"—he put his arm around Addie—"we can keep this our own little secret?"

Addie didn't answer. She was too amazed. Dr. Eakeley's irresponsibility might even have cost him his job at Jackson State, where the old familiar midwestern types were at least more caring. Besides, she found her first concern was with the patient who was rapidly becoming the image of the special New York man Addie knew would come into her life, take her by the hand, and lead her to some wonderful place where he would take off her clothes and make love to her in some way she could not yet even imagine.

She was certainly not going to have any secrets with that fat slob Eakeley, she told Catherine emphatically as the two were getting ready to go off duty later that afternoon. They were in the nurses' lounge, Catherine sitting in front of the small dressing table, combing out her short, wiry brown hair, and Addie, stretched out on one of those vomit-green couches that seem indigenous to ladies' rooms throughout the country, watching her.

"Look, pal," Catherine said, addressing Addie's reflection in the mirror, "just relax about Eakeley. It's all right to bitch to me but don't go making waves. You can't change the system. All you can do is break up a poker game every once in a while."

"Sure." Addie was still angry. "Just let some poor guy bleed to death."

Catherine turned around and looked at Addie. "Now, you know if it had been a real emergency, we could have gotten someone right away. Besides, the patient in question is no 'poor guy'—wish I were so poor."

"He's a Rockefeller? Come on, who is he?"

"He's a Kingman, that's who he is. You've heard of them in Missouri?"

Addie shook her head. "I don't think so."

"According to *Time* magazine, they're America's First Intellectual Family. I know all about them because I used to work at New York Hospital, where William Kingman, the kid's father, is chief orthopedic surgeon—and probably the top one in the country. Everyone in that family is the top one. Dr. Kingman's sister is a big lawyer who is always in the papers, flying down to Washington and Camp David to give the President her advice. And their brother is the biggest star of all because he's written all these famous books and won the Nobel Prize. And they each have money. And very upper crust."

"And gorgeous," Addie added.

Catherine suddenly became serious. "Addie, believe me, I know just what's going through your mind right now. Every nurse is always looking for a Prince Charming among the bedpans—maybe it's because we're always faced with so much shit, and we have to keep trying to climb out. Anyway, this guy, even if he wasn't in the loony bin, he's not for you. Those Kingmans don't mix with people like us."

Addie smarted at the word "us"—she would hardly have put herself in the same category with the homely Catherine, but she didn't say anything. Besides, Catherine didn't understand at all. She was thinking of Prince Charming and church weddings while Addie wasn't considering any of that. She was, instead, thinking about slender fingers stroking her, of dark eyes traveling up and down her body, bringing it to life. But she was as crazy as the patients here—how could she forget she was thinking this way about someone who had just tried to kill himself? She knew very well that such people frequently repeat their attempts, sometimes with greater success. Well, perhaps there was some way she could help, could inspire. Perhaps they could help each other.

She thought about this again when, some moments later before she left for home, she stopped in his room to look at him. She studied his face closely, engraving it into her mind. She wanted to be able to see it again when she got home that night.

* * *

If Paul Kingman's pale and romantic face had been the image in Addie's mind when she went home, it was also the first thing she thought of when she returned to the hospital the next morning. And so it was frustrating for her, just as she was about to enter his room, to find her way blocked by the small gray-haired chief of psychiatry.

"I'm going to have a brief visit with the patient right now, Nurse," he said in a quiet voice. "You can take his blood pressure later." He closed the door in her face.

"How are you feeling, Paul?" the doctor asked the silent young man whose dark eyes seemed focused on nothing. "I'm Gerson Richler, your psychiatrist."

"My psychiatrist?" the young man asked, looking puzzled. Then his expression changed. "My psychiatrist? But I don't want one." His voice sounded hollow.

"Do you know what you do want?" Richler asked, prodding him to keep him talking.

"That should be obvious."

"Obvious?"

"I want to die," Paul said sharply.

Richler sighed, pulled up a chair, and sat down. His legs weren't what they used to be, and they had to carry around a lot more weight these days.

"If that is what you want, Paul, then you're right. You don't need me or any other psychiatrist. But I think maybe you're not as sure as you think you are. Maybe, like the rest of us, you're confused?"

"But you see, that's it. I'm not like the rest of you." Paul turned and looked directly into Richler's face. "I'm a Kingman, didn't you know?"

"Yes, I know," Richler nodded. "And I think I can understand that having such a name can make you feel different . . . special."

"You couldn't possibly know. Being a Kingman isn't just a burden, it's a whole way of life."

"That's only if you let it be. In fact, being a Kingman is little more than a beginning. You're born a Kingman and then you go on from there."

"Well, then, there you have it. I couldn't." Paul turned his face away. "I'm tired, Doctor. I'd like to be alone now, if you don't mind."

"Of course not. All I wanted to do was to look in on you so I could tell your father I'd seen you and you were all right. We both thought it would be best if I visited you first, before your parents came."

Paul suddenly looked panicked. "I don't want to see them," he almost gasped. "Please don't make me see them."

Dr. Richler put his hand on the young man's shoulder. "Don't worry. If you don't want to see them, you don't have to. I can at least do that for you."

On his way out, Richler stopped by the nurses' station to tell the nurse on duty to administer Valium to the Kingman boy—and to make sure no phone calls were put through to his room.

Addie nodded. She would take care of it.

In fact, there was almost nothing Addie Harris wouldn't do for Paul Kingman. The attraction she had felt for him that first moment she had seen him being wheeled, unconscious, down from surgery kept growing over the next few weeks—despite the fact that she received no encouragement at all. Using her best bedside manner, the cheery smile and soft touch which had always worked so well in Jackson State, she was still a failure. Paul Kingman took no more notice of her than he did of frizzy-haired, overweight Catherine.

"What did I tell you?" Catherine said as Addie came out of Paul Kingman's room carrying some books, having failed again to capture any of his interest.

"Well, he's still under medication," Addie answered. "Even Dr. Richler isn't getting a tumble. I can tell by the way he looks after the sessions."

"And you're so much sexier than Richler, too."

"You noticed?" Addie grinned. "Listen, we girls from Missouri never give up."

But soon Addie began to feel that she might as well forget Paul Kingman. He had only short, almost curt replies to her questions, and he took no pleasure in anything she could find for him—a new book from the hospital library, a special dessert which she had picked up on her way to work. She became more daring, brushing her body against him as she adjusted his tray table down to the level of the armchair where he always sat. He hardly noticed. It was a challenge all right, Addie thought, beginning to accept the notion that she very well might fail.

Dr. Richler too was beginning to doubt any possibilities of success in his treatment of Paul Kingman. True, it had only been a few weeks. True, too, the boy had just been through an extraordinary trauma. But by now Richler had X-ray eyes into cases like this one where the patient constructs an impenetrable fortress around him, daring the psychiatrist to chink away at the surface. Of course one day, like the man in the *Count of Monte Cristo* digging away with his spoon against the walls of the Château d'If, a persistent enough person could get through. But after all, it took that man fourteen years, and Richler knew he didn't have anything like fourteen years to devote exclusively to anything or anyone. Nor had he the patience for one of those old dreadful, formal therapy battles between patient and psychiatrist, where the fifty-minute hour becames an eternity of either silences or sarcastic cuts. The patient refuses to reveal anything. The psychiatrist refuses to prod. Richler hadn't the stomach for such torture—for such waste—any longer. In fact, it was clear to him that he hadn't the patience or the time or the will even to deal with a Paul Kingman. So maybe in four months he would say something revealing . . . maybe in two years he'd have a break-through . . . and he, Gerson Richler, just couldn't wait anymore. Besides, Richler was the wrong age for Paul—too much the image of the patriarch and Paul had had enough of that. There was nothing wrong with bowing out now. After all, there was no defeat when the battle hadn't even begun. What he would recommend for Paul was a younger doctor—maybe even a woman. In fact, there was someone quite specific he had in mind, someone who seemed like the perfect therapist for Paul. He would arrange a meeting as soon as possible.

Isabel woke up in a start, her nightgown soaked through with perspiration. She must have had a nightmare, but it was impossible to remember anything at all except for the panicky feeling that still kept her heart beating loudly. She turned on the lamp on the small wooden night table at the side of her bed, and she looked at her alarm clock. It was 5 A.M. and the pale winter sun had not yet risen. The bedroom was cold, but Isabel could hear the radiators begin to crackle and then, faintly, to chime. Otto, the little bald German who was the superintendent of this small red-brick East Side apartment building, was conscientious about seeing that there was plenty of heat. Isabel, although used to the cold after a lifetime of living in Boston, was grateful. She had had enough of icy mornings, growing up in a drafty old building in Dorchester where it was all you could do to get yourself out of bed and off to school. And even, if like Isabel, you loved school—the neat notebooks with their color dividers, the gold stars, the smiles at report card time, the good feeling when you always knew the answers to the sisters' questions.

Isabel decided to leave the light on. This bedroom, this whole four-room apartment, had been hers less than a month, and she wasn't really completely comfortable yet. "It's just learning what the noises mean," she thought, as the elevator down the hall started humming. Someone was coming in late or going out early. In New York someone was always coming and going, usually in a hurry. Isabel would have to start pacing herself to this new tempo. She got up and walked across the bare floors—the new carpeting hadn't arrived and she had not yet unpacked the rugs she sent down from her Beacon Hill floor-through.

Isabel threw on her white terry robe over her pale green nightgown and walked into the kitchen, the one room she had finished setting up. The old blue coffeepot was sitting on top of the stove along with the copper kettle, both of which she had salvaged from her mother's home. The kitchen, like everything else Isabel gave her attention to, was in perfect shape—neat, orderly, even managing with the help of some yellow checkered curtains to look cheerful despite all the white Formica. The Hospital Look, Isabel thought. After all these years I suppose I should be used to it.

The sun finally came up although the day was going to be dismal. Isabel showered and washed her long shiny auburn hair, drying it and twisting it into a knot at the nape of her neck. It was thick and some curls always managed to get loose, destroying the "woman doctor coiffure" as Isabel's mentor, Arne Larsen, used to call it.

Isabel had arranged through Otto to get the New York *Times* delivered to her door and she now sat, with her coffee cup full and steaming and two more cups waiting in the blue pot, eating a toasted English muffin and reading the paper and thinking that this was a perfect way to start the day, even as dismal a day as this chilly January morning. But there was something wrong—it wasn't a perfect day at all. She remembered—before the coffee or the shower or even the radiators—what started the day was the nightmare. Isabel now began to see a glimpse of it, enough so that if she were one of her own patients, she'd run over to her desk to write it down. But she really didn't have to. It was that old dream she told Larsen about years before and which she had had twice since coming to New York—the dream about the faceless man. She shuddered. But there was no time to think about it now. She had to get to the hospital.

Isabel's secretary, whom she shared with two other young psychiatrists, was already at her desk. A tiny Oriental woman with delicate hands and startlingly small feet, she was also the most cheerful person Isabel had met so far in New York, her round cheeks always puffed up in a broad smile and her black eyes twinkling. She must have been chosen, Isabel thought, to counterbalance the downcast faces which usually filled the waiting room.

"Good morning, Dr. Dunne," Miss Lee smiled. "Dr. Richler just called. He sent the files for the new patients over, and he particularly wanted you to read this one as soon as you could." Miss Lee handed Isabel a manila envelope, adding, "Dr. Richler said he would get back to you in about an hour."

Isabel thanked her and then went into her cramped office, turning on the light. "God, this room is gloomy," she thought as she looked at the gray walls and carpet. To make matters worse, Dr. Richler had gallantly presented her with a print of Mont.-St.-Michel in the midst of a rainstorm, and she hadn't the heart to take it off the wall and put it into the closet, where she felt it belonged. She really had to do something about the decor, but in the meantime maybe just a little more light would help, she thought. She raised the blinds over the one window which, on an oblique angle, allowed a small portion of Central Park to be seen. But since the park these days was in its winter gray rock and mud stage, it offered nothing at all comforting or lovely, and Isabel let the blinds down again. She sat down at her desk and began to look over the file Dr. Richler had sent.

The name on the cover was "Paul Kingman" and Isabel wondered if he could be a member of the noted Kingman family. She opened the folder and saw that he was twenty-three, was born in New York, had studied art, and was the only child of Dr. William Kingman. So he was one of those Kingmans after all, she thought, remembering hearing about the famous Nobel laureate Ernest Kingman, his sister the trial lawyer, and his brother William the surgeon, who was evidently this young man's father. Isabel read further and saw that Paul Kingman had been admitted to the hospital as an attempted suicide. She almost didn't have to go on—these few facts contained much of the tragic story. She herself knew, with painful clarity, the incredible standards such people as the Kingmans impose. The American ruling class, whose existence no one admitted, were not about to be tolerant of any difference, any imperfection, any deviance. Having no external written code or historical precedents like their European counterparts, these American dynasties had developed an internal, and even more rigorous, set of regulations which, along with their Chippendale chairs, their pearl lavalieres, and their midtown real estate holdings, they passed on along with their name from generation to generation. This young man, even though he was born into this aristocracy, obviously could not meet their standards any more, she thought, than she could herself.

She had also been twenty-three when she wished herself dead, she realized. And she had also failed to deal well and wisely with the WASP kingdoms which certainly dominated Boston at least as much as they did New York.

She read on in the Kingman folder, trying to put Boston and herself out of her mind and to concentrate solely on Paul Kingman. But every page, every fact, conjured up her own past and brought back the image of the faceless man who haunted her sleep. Paul Kingman's nemesis—so implied Gerson Richler in his notes—had been his father, William Kingman. Isabel's had been her lover, Bryan Madison.

The buzzer interrupted her thoughts, and she glanced at the clock on her desk. Could an hour have passed? She felt momentarily disoriented as she pressed down a button on the intercom.

"Dr. Richler is on 025," Miss Lee's cheerful voice announced.

Isabel picked up the phone. "Sorry I wasn't here when you called before, Gerson."

"Oh, don't worry about that. It was pretty early. I sometimes forget that the world doesn't get up at six the way I do."

"Well, Miss Lee apparently does. I haven't beaten her to the office yet."

"Look, Isabel"—Richler's voice changed to a serious tone—"I don't mean to rush you but did you get a chance to look at the Kingman boy's file?"

"Yes, but I've only been able to glance at it."

"Well, what do you think?"

"As far as I can see, I totally concur with your diagnosis."

"Then perhaps you'll also concur with an idea I have?"

"Yes?"

"I'd like you to take over the case."

Isabel was taken aback. She had assumed that Richler had simply wanted an opinion. One didn't hand over patients of this importance to junior staff.

"I know this may sound strange to you but you yourself can see that I'm not the doctor for that boy. Not only am I getting nowhere with him now, but I never will. He needs someone younger, and I think he'd do best with a woman, too."

"I'm not questioning you, Gerson," Isabel said. "It's just that . . . well, I don't think I'm the person for it. It . . . it's just not for me."

"Now, there I don't agree. Look, for a fact, Isabel, we know he's just the type you've worked best with in Boston. I heard all this from Dr. Larsen long before I ever met you, and it was what made me want to bring you here in the first place."

"You're very flattering . . ."

"Don't be foolish, it's not a question of flattery. Look, I know a case like this is a little frightening. After all, when you're treating the only child of one of the country's biggest surgeons, it's bound to make you nervous. And it doesn't help that he's actively suicidal. But don't worry about the Kingmans. You won't have to deal with them, at least not in the beginning."

"Thank you, Gerson, but I still feel this case isn't for me. At least not now at this point when I'm so new . . . to the hospital . . . to New York . . ."

"Isabel, do me a favor," Richler interrupted. "Just see the boy. It strikes me that you're not only right for him but that he's right for you. Once you've seen him, then we'll talk again."

Despite her hesitations, Isabel couldn't refuse. And curiously, once this was decided, her nervousness began to change into an excited rush of anticipation.

"All right," she said. "I'll see him. Tomorrow morning?"

She could almost hear Gerson Richler smile. "That would be fine," he said. "Now, tell me, how is everything going? Do you have everything you need? Leah is planning a dinner one of these days to introduce you to all the available men she's lining up. To her, it's a sin when an attractive woman is single."

Isabel laughed. "I hope I'll meet them one by one. Please tell Mrs. Richler I'd love one of her meals anytime."

Dr. Richler said he would and hung up.

Isabel stared at Paul Kingman's folder for a moment. She took out her appointment book and started to write down his name and hospital room number. As she formed the letters, Isabel was surprised to see that her hand was shaking. Why? she wondered. She'd have to think about it later, though. She had a patient coming in a half hour, and she had to review her notes.

* * *

"Visiting hours aren't for another two hours," Addie told the tall, attractive woman who had stopped by the nurses' station. "You'll have to come back later."

"I'm Dr. Dunne. I'm here to see Paul Kingman."

"I think he's still having his lunch." Addie jumped to her feet. "Should I check?" Isabel unnerved her, wearing a fashionable blue wool dress instead of the usual white coat that all the doctors wore when they were on duty. But Isabel didn't seem to mind the fact that she was mistaken for a mere visitor. She smiled at the young nurse. ("Probably a little in love with her patient," Isabel guessed, "probably guilty about it, too.")

The aides came down the long halls with their noisy metal carts, picking up trays from the rooms. "Lunch is over," Addie said, and then could have kicked herself for saying something so obvious. But Isabel just nodded and walked down the hall to Paul's room. She knocked on the door, waited a moment, and then walked in. Isabel had decided against looking through the glass panel in the door, having learned in her Boston hospital that it made many patients resentful that their privacy could be so easily violated. She saw Paul sitting in a large wool tweed chair, next to the window. He was bony, she was startled to see, he must not be eating his meals. Paul's face was as gaunt as his body, the skin pulled tight under the high cheekbones, the black hair hanging lank against the high forehead; the gray smudges, which showed he was not sleeping well, extended from under his dark eyes.

Isabel looked down at the bandaged wrists and ankles. "How is the healing coming?" she asked. There was no answer. "I am Isabel Dunne, a psychiatrist. Dr. Richler asked me to see you." She smiled and reached out her hand. A bandaged, scrawny arm lifted slowly and then dropped.

Isabel pulled up a chair from the corner of the room and sat down across from Paul. She felt comfortable sitting there, and for a while she didn't say anything. Isabel and Paul—sitting silently, like two old people on a veranda or, as New Yorkers, Isabel thought, more likely on a park bench, trying to catch the last of the sun. She turned to Paul and tried again.

"What I want to know," she asked, "is why you tried to kill yourself."

* * *

Addie couldn't stop feeling nervous. "You think she'll make any headway with him?" she asked Catherine.

"I've heard the resident gossiping about Isabel Dunne. She's supposed to be Richler's new pet. A miracle worker."

"I don't care about that. What about Paul Kingman?" Addie spoke too loudly. Joe Buchbinder, the persistent intern who still followed Addie around, walked over.

"Come on," he said, "it's great to be so conscientious about your patient but how about saving a little attention for the interns? Some of us suffer, too, you know."

"Oh, Joe, just leave her alone for now," Catherine said, "she's in one of those moods." Catherine gave Addie a long, meaningful stare, but the young nurse managed to avoid her friend's disapproving eyes.

Addie sat down at the desk. "I wish I knew what was going on in that room. Joe, what do you think of Dr. Dunne?"

Joe cleared his throat at this rare opportunity to have a rapt Addie wait for his words. "Let's see . . . Dr. Dunne. She's supposedly brilliant, has done some outstanding work in Boston, has had some special success with those sad young men who seem to turn you on."

Addie interrupted. "Is she married? Divorced?"

"Single, I'll bet," Catherine said. "Totally devoted to her career."

"Right on the target, lady." Joe, basking now in the attention of both nurses, slowly drew out the few facts he knew about Isabel's fantastic medical school grades which seemed especially to impress him ("Her *average*," he said reverently, "was one of the *highest* ever achieved at Boston Medical School"), her residency under the famous Arne Larsen, and her special rapport with patients. "But we can talk more about all of this later," he whispered to Addie, snuggling up to her ear. "My roommate's on late shift all this week."

Catherine gave Addie a push. She did this every time Joe asked Addie out because, as Catherine kept saying, you don't turn down a doctor, even if he's just an intern with a prominent Adam's apple. Addie, looking at the closed door of Room 43, turned to Joe and said, "Well, maybe I'll stop off for some coffee with you when I get off."

"I'll meet you downstairs in the front lobby," Joe said, beaming.

Addie smiled in return, trying to evoke some of the enthusiasm she knew she should have—and trying to ignore Room 43, where the door remained closed.

* * *

Inside the room, Paul sat on his chair by the window, his body rigid, his eyes avoiding those of the woman who sat across from him.

"I don't know," he had said in answer to that shockingly direct question. And when she repeated it, he had repeated those same words.

"I'm sure you don't," she had said gently, "but what do you remember thinking at the time. Just before you lost consciousness?" Her voice, fluid and calming, somehow seemed to envelop him.

"The phone," he said, suddenly remembering. "I wanted to stop the phone, and I just didn't know how else to do it."

Isabel got up from her chair and walked over to stand behind him. She put her hands on his thin shoulders, massaging them gently. "You knew who was calling then?"

He nodded.

"I know, too," she said. "It was Christmas morning and it was your father, wasn't it?" She felt his shoulder stiffen under her hands. "What do you think he wanted?"

Paul was silent. And so was Isabel. She took her hands from his shoulders and sat down in the chair across from him again, patiently waiting for his answer.

Their eyes met, Paul not averting his this time.

Finally, he spoke. "Whatever my father wanted, I couldn't have given him anyway."

Catherine had given Addie the word—you don't necessarily have to make it with the interns, you just have to learn how to handle them. Some of them, like Joe, for example, were filled with nervous feelings about women despite all their dumb talk. The more you put them off, the more they trail after you.

"But who wants them trailing anyway?" Addie asked, knowing very well that if they stopped paying attention to her, she'd soon start to worry. Still, her idea of an attractive man was the silent figure down the hall, a man with long black eyelashes and a grace of motion, even though swathed in thick bandages, that made Addie think of the ballet ("But not at all faggy," she told Catherine). Catherine kept admonishing Addie to forget Paul Kingman and pushed her toward what Catherine considered to be Addie's best chance ("Obviously, you ignore men like Henry, who only takes blood samples, and Jorge, who is barely white and makes the plaster casts—funny that black people always end up working with plaster").

Addie finally decided that if she were going to make it at all in New York—and why come all the way here from Missouri if you were going to stay home at night—she had better start going out with people like Joe. They certainly weren't beautiful but they might take her to where the really attractive types were. She'd have to be practical, like Catherine. She'd have to stop thinking about Paul Kingman.

Isabel gently closed the door of Room 43 behind her. She smoothed her auburn hair, which had already started to come loose from her barrette, and she began walking toward the nurses' station in the center of the long hall.

The young nurse who had taken her down to Paul's room was still there, staring at her and then looking away. But Isabel didn't have any time to think about her. Her mind was full of the bitter defeat that seemed to make up the whole being of Paul Kingman. And bitter defeat, Isabel thought, was certainly something she could understand.

She was struck by the immediate empathy she felt with this young man. How lovely he was with his handsome thin face, his finely molded features. Might a son of hers have had the same delicate beauty? The same aura of nobility?

Again, just as before when she was in her office, Isabel found Paul Kingman a pivotal force, somehow pushing her back into herself and into her own past, into memories that she had thought had been laid to rest long ago.

3

Boston, 1965

ISABEL DUNNE STOOD in the darkened office, too nervous to even turn on a lamp. The rose-colored light of winter dusk seeped in through the slats of the venetian blinds, throwing soft shadows over the red and blue patterned carpet. In this light, or absence of it, and with the strange, hushed silence of an office on a Sunday afternoon, everything in the room seemed different, unfamiliar, almost menacing. The red-leather chair facing the mahogany desk, for example, looked imposing and formal instead of warm and inviting as it had that first day when she had entered this office for her interview with Dr. Bryan Madison. Dr. Madison, on a National Science Foundation grant in neurology, had recently come from Philadelphia and was looking for a student to work several hours a week as an assistant in the lab he was setting up. Isabel, who was number one in her class and certainly in need of the money, had been told about the position by the student placement counselor and had been recommended by Dean Pierce. She had been told that Dr. Madison was a brilliant and innovative neurologist—Nobel Prize material, even—but she was totally unprepared for the fact that he would also be so young, certainly not more than thirty, and so handsome. Blond wavy hair, clear slate-colored eyes, a tanned face which contrasted dramatically with his even white teeth, he was so wonderful-looking that he startled her. It was unbelievable that anyone who looked like that would ever have wanted her, would ever have asked her to meet him here, would be coming to see her now.

She looked at the gold clock on the desk. It was five o'clock and he was late. She walked to the window and peered down to the shadowed street below, searching for some sign of him. Perhaps he wouldn't come after all. Perhaps that would be for the best, although it was difficult, in fact impossible, to give up something you wanted more than anything else.

And hadn't she waited long enough? She was twenty-two and wasn't it time she had a lover? For all these years she had been the perfect child, the perfect student, the perfect young Catholic lady. She had never missed going to confession, never failed to make her bed and brush her teeth after meals, never handed a paper in late or with the smallest blot of ink on the page. In short, she turned out to be everything her mother not only wished for but deserved. Widowed at twenty and with a two-year-old child, Frances Dunne had had her share of hard luck. The best job she could get was with the telephone company where she could earn extra pay by working the night shift and where she could easily hire a neighbor to care for the sleeping Isabel. And it was a job she was always terrified of losing—sharing this insecurity with Isabel, this fear that maybe next week they would go hungry, that maybe next month they would lose their apartment. The solution was to be frugal now. So Frances and Isabel walked instead of taking the bus, even when it rained. So Christmas presents were always what you needed—a hairbrush, a new pair of shoes—rather than a game or a pretty scarf. There were rarely any treats like movies or even Good Humors. Saturday meant studying and Sunday meant mass and more studying after that. And Isabel never thought to question the strict regime imposed on her. In fact, it became the security that Frances was otherwise unable to provide for her. Good would be rewarded and evil would be punished was the lesson the nuns at St. Matthew's parochial school taught her. And Frances, as sure as they of this truth, reinforced this lesson at home. It was the only thing sure in Isabel's life.

But if the little girl's life was drab and dour in reality, in fantasy it was glorious. And because fantasy time was right before going to sleep, she would cherish those moments, alone and quiet in her bed, when, lights out and books closed, she could shut her eyes and imagine. Here, in this world, rewards were not gold stars or scholarships or a place in heaven—instead they were more tangible, immediate, silky, golden, glamorous. They were a pair of gold figure skates which magically made Isabel pirouette like Barbara Ann Scott or Boston's own Tenley Albright, or a handsome prince who looked exactly like Tony Curtis or sometimes like Rock Hudson and who gave Isabel boxes not only of rubies and pearls but of chocolate-covered cherries as well. And best of all, these wonderful rewards did not come because of Isabel's diligence or obedience. They came simply because she was Isabel, and so all these things just had to be hers.

Frances Dunne was not an unintelligent woman. She was aware that her daughter's life was often bleak and that the child's secret smiles were in answer to something in her mind, rather than anything Frances herself could see. She reminded Isabel that to sin in thought was the same thing as sinning in deed. Frances was disturbed about what she saw as a tendency on the part of Isabel to daydream too much and to sometimes allow these fantasies to obscure the reality that the sensible child would have otherwise perceived. Frances had found a diary in Isabel's room that, had it not been in the child's own handwriting, she would have thought belonged to another person. The girl in the diary spent her weekends at her family's castle in Spain, was a champion horseback rider, and was being seriously considered for beatification by the Pope himself. Frances discussed this with the nuns. How much of the diary was play? How much was it a twisted belief? The nuns seemed to think it was all very simple: A lie was a lie, and liars should be forced to acknowledge the truth. They asked Frances to bring Isabel to Father Moran that Saturday, and the little girl was confronted with her diary, told to place her hand on the Bible and repeat, "I will never make up false stories." But what this translated to was that Isabel would be very careful never again to commit to paper what special thoughts she had. Her dreams were her own, and she would never let them interfere with the work that the good little Isabel of the real world had to do. And her careful strategy all paid off in the end.

Isabel's grades were not only the highest in her class, they were also the highest in the diocese and Bishop O'Connor had given her a full scholarship to college. He had, in fact, encouraged her pursuit of medicine when Isabel's biochemistry professor had informed him she was his most brilliant student. Smarting under the criticism that American Catholics were basically anti-intellectual and that the church encouraged bingo players rather than bookworms, Bishop O'Connor had decided to make Isabel a shining example of American Catholic womanhood. He himself had gotten in touch with his most affluent parishioners, setting up a syndicate to underwrite a scholarship for her. And he had always insisted that her grades be forwarded to him so that the glowing record could, in turn, be reported to those who made all of this possible.

And this was how she was paying them back, showing her gratitude for their faith and efforts for her by offering her body outside of marriage. But there was no way, Isabel knew, that she could possibly give up Bryan Madison. From that first conversation when she applied for the job as his lab assistant, she felt overwhelmed by him. It was as though a thousand schoolgirl crushes she had never had somehow became one immense emotion. And when they started working together and he commended her on her first results, her knees had literally gone weak and there had been a catch in her voice when she tried to thank him. His attention, his very presence, made her suddenly start thinking about herself in a new way.

Busy with her duties and her studies, Isabel had almost forgotten what she looked like. Now she began to scrutinize herself with new eyes. She was not bad-looking after all. Her fair skin was clear and glowing, thick lashes surrounded her bright blue eyes, and although she found the curls in her auburn hair sometimes unmanageable, she had been told by others they were something to envy and admire. In fact, the first time Bryan had touched her, he had brushed a curl off her forehead, and Isabel felt her face get hot.

She looked at her watch again. A half hour had passed. Why was he taking so long? He'd changed his mind. But no, he couldn't have. He'd been so definite, so positive about setting the exact time. And there was nothing about Bryan Madison that was careless, nothing that was disordered. He simply did not make mistakes. Isabel was astounded the first time she had heard him speak into a dictaphone, composing a complex lab report. His sentences were so perfectly phrased, so fluid and concise, that it was difficult to believe he wasn't reading from a prepared text. He ran his lab with a similar easy efficiency. All of his assistants—Isabel and the three fourth-year students—found themselves thriving under his direction, working with startling speed and directness, and turning out some of the best reports that any of them had ever done. Partly because of this, and partly because of his special charm, those who worked for Dr. Madison became extremely devoted to him. And he, in turn, had a concern and loyalty toward them. But with Isabel, there was something more. She had felt it almost immediately on meeting him but knew it for sure when, one afternoon when she was the last assistant to leave the lab, he came up behind her, touched her arm, and asked her if she would like to join him for a drink, to celebrate the fact that it was Friday. They walked over to O'Malley's, a local bar and café that, with its old gaslights, its stained-glass windows, oak-paneled door, and brass handles, had always looked inviting to Isabel. He ordered a kir for her, explaining it was a combination of white wine and cassis, and he toasted her as he sipped his gibson. Complimenting her on her work, he asked if she had ever considered going into research. But of course it was probably best for a first-year student to keep an open mind.

How had she gotten into medicine in the first place? Had she any doctors in her family? He, for his part, came from a long line of doctors —four, to be exact: his father, his grandfather, his great-grandfather, and his great-great-grandfather. Of course, things had changed since the leech and cupping days of his most distant forebears, he said, laughing. So, too, had Philadelphia, where they had lived, although the more recent generations had moved out of the inner city and to the Main Line. Bryan had been born and raised in Paoli, the very last stop on the Main Line, where there were rolling green estates, stables, and tennis courts, and where everything you did ended up on the society pages of the *Bulletin* and the *Enquirer*. Sometimes, he added, things you didn't do ended there as well. He'd find that he'd been at balls he was sure he'd never attended and once was named as the escort of a debutante he'd never even met. There was a lot of foolishness and superficiality in this world, he acknowledged, but a lot that was appealing, fine, and wholesome. In any case, it had been a wonderful place to grow up in and an environment that he would like one day for his own children.

Isabel was fascinated to hear Bryan talk about his background—a background so different from the one she had known. And she felt toward him the way she never had for any man before. Was it her imagination, only wishful thinking, that he returned some of her feelings? Just what did it mean when he rested his hand on hers at the table, when he told her how pretty she looked, especially without her oversize lab coat, when he took her arm as they crossed the street?

The more she saw him over the next month, the more she realized that he really was attracted to her. At least, he certainly wanted to be with her. He invited her one warm sunny day to walk with him along the Charles River, where he was going to check on his scull. He used to row on the Schuylkill River in Philadelphia and now was anxious to try out his scull on the Charles.

Another night he invited her to go with him to the Boston Symphony and to Durgin Park, a restaurant where they had sawdust on the floor and served the thickest slices of roast beef she had ever seen. They had spaghetti one night at Mario's on the North Side. She loved being with him, going to all these places with him, and she was struck by his extraordinary self-confidence no matter where he was. Isabel realized that this assurance was a by-product of Bryan Madison's kind of privilege, of being born into a world you would never want to climb out of. If, like Bryan, you were also genetically endowed with intelligence and fine features, there was nothing you couldn't do, nothing that wouldn't come easily to you. And she saw this ease in his long sure stride, in his lively and fluent conversation, in the way he seemed to know about everything (from the story of *Old Ironsides'* last battle to who held the America Cup record) and everyone (from Dean Pierce, who not only greeted him as Bryan but asked after his grandmother—was her blood pressure finally under control?—to the headwaiter at Mario's).

He also, it was clear to Isabel, took great pleasure in everything he did, whether it was working in the lab, playing tennis or rowing, listening to a symphony. And this great love of life was infectious. Isabel felt herself a different person when she was with him—gayer, lighter, the Isabel not of reality but the Isabel of her own secret night-time childhood fantasies. Was she then fantasizing Bryan as well? Could anyone be quite so perfect? Probably not, but Isabel somehow didn't care. She was, she knew, totally in love with him. And this love gave her the courage to bury her Catholic scruples, to have agreed to meet Bryan Madison here on a Sunday afternoon, to let him know in this way that she was as eager as he to have him make love to her.

And now that she had come here, what if he had changed his mind? Maybe that would be for the best, after all. Medical student or not, she really knew nothing at all about what she was supposed to do. She would make a fool of herself and disappoint him.

The door opened. "Isabel?" His voice enveloped her. "What are you doing, sitting there in the dark?"

She was afraid she had already begun to make a fool of herself. "I guess I was afraid you wouldn't come."

"For a while I didn't think I'd get here either," Bryan said. "Of all days, my parents chose today to arrive in Boston, and they insisted I have lunch with them at the Ritz. I had a hard time getting away but it was worth it," he said, taking her in his arms and pressing his lips against hers. "My God, you're shaking," he said. He held her away from him and looked down at her. She averted her eyes and was grateful for the darkness. "Why so nervous?" he asked.

"I don't really know," she said, but of course she did know and, in a matter of minutes, so would he. She should tell him but somehow it made her seem stupid, foolish. And besides, if she told him now, she might lose him.

"How about a drink, then. I've got some scotch in that cabinet over there. It should warm you up."

"I'd love some," she said, wondering if she could manage to get it down.

Crossing the room in the semidarkness, Bryan reached for a bottle and two glasses. He filled them and handed one to Isabel.

Isabel sipped the scotch. It was very strong, and she felt her eyes tearing.

Bryan took her glass, put it down, and gently led her toward the leather couch, kissing her neck. She felt her muscles tighten. And as he ran his hands over her breasts, she felt her nipples harden and her thighs grow damp. Bryan began to unbutton her blouse and unzipped her skirt, letting it fall to the floor. Her first impulse was to pick it up, fold it neatly, but she felt absurd and, instead, kicked it aside.

He then undid her bra, kissing each breast, and began to slip off her panties. She suddenly felt incredibly free, unconstrained by buttons and zippers and clinging fabrics. She reached down to embrace her lover, but Bryan surprised her, pulling away instead and turning on the lamp on the end table next to the couch. Isabel was mortified and in a quick gesture put her arms over her breasts.

"I just wanted to look at you," Bryan said. "And you're perfectly beautiful." He uncrossed her arms and stared at her. "How could anyone want to hide a body like that?"

Isabel knew she was blushing and hated herself for it. She couldn't bring herself to look directly at Bryan, who stood, leaning against his desk and staring at her. And what was she supposed to be doing, anyway? Medical school certainly hadn't taught her that. Should she sit down? Should she stand up? She felt a fool, naked before this fully dressed man.

Now he finished his drink and began to take off his clothes. His body was, as she knew it would be, perfect. His shoulders broad and straight, his skin taut; he was muscular but graceful, strong yet slender. She avoided looking at his penis and again she felt ridiculous. A medical student, a doctor to be, who would one day look at all kinds of naked bodies, whatever sex, whatever size—her own shyness struck her as ludicrous. But the feeling left her as Bryan took her in his arms and she felt the hugeness and hardness of him pressed against her belly. He lay her down on the couch and bathed her ear with his tongue while his hands reached between her legs, his fingers stroking the sensitive skin which grew moister and moister to his touch. She gasped, the sensation was so extraordinary. But now he was pushing into her and the pain mingled with the pleasure, becoming one sensation.

Suddenly he pulled away. "No one has ever made love to you before?"

She nodded.

"Why didn't you tell me?"

"I didn't know how. I thought you'd think I was some sort of freak . . . some antique." The tears started streaming down her face. She thought she had ruined it.

He leaned over and kissed the tears on her cheek. "Isabel," he said softly. "I think we'd better stop."

"No, please, no." She threw her arms around him and pulled him toward her.

"Are you sure? Is this really what you want?"

"Yes . . . yes."

She felt his hard muscular body pressing against her, his thighs against her thighs, his belly against her belly. Slowly, the weight of him pushed her legs apart and she found herself trembling, her nerve ends tingling. Suddenly he was inside her and she felt, for one brief moment, an excruciating stab. But then warm, powerful waves of excitement began to overwhelm her. She felt herself let go as the pleasure that started in her thighs, then her groin, now undulated over her entire body. She was in a frenzy as, in answer to Bryan's thrust, she moved faster and faster. Her legs were tight around his hips, her nails digging into his shoulders, when simultaneously their bodies began to shudder and it was over.

Bryan threw himself back on the couch and smiled up at her. "I can hardly believe how terrific that was. The mystery is how anyone as passionate as you could have remained a virgin for so long."

She tried to explain. Her life had been so proscribed by her studies, by her responsibilities both to her mother and to her church. She had always known that she was attractive to men—from the time she was a child people always told her she was pretty, joking about her smiling Irish eyes, commenting to her mother that they bet the boys would be lining up at her door as soon as Isabel was old enough to date. Frances had always frowned at these remarks, discouraging anything that might turn Isabel's head. Still, it was difficult for Isabel not to be flattered since the neighborhood boys did start coming around, asking her to dances or to the movies. But Isabel never said yes to any of them. Not only was her every moment occupied, filled with schoolwork, extra projects, chores for her mother, but she wasn't really tempted anyway. A date at St. Matthew's gym with pimply-faced Jimmy Doyle wasn't her idea of romance. In fact, before Bryan, no man had measured up to her fantasies, the image she had constructed as a child of someone she could love, a man who could tempt her to break the rigid structure of her life.

Bryan understood. It was exactly Isabel's aura of aloofness and commitment that had kept him from making love to her before this. He had perceived with the clarity Isabel thought so characteristic of his vision, that he had to proceed slowly, carefully with her. After all, he told her, things that do not easily bend may very well break, and Isabel, positive, determined, not easily yielding of her time and herself, might be similarly shattered. Despite her competence, her stunning intelligence, her controlled demeanor, and fresh and healthy looks, all of which suggested great strength, there was also, Bryan noted, something about Isabel that hinted at an essential fragility. It was this contradiction that fascinated him most. He also found it inexplicable that someone as lovely as she was, and so evidently warm, was so distant with men— so unresponsive to the obvious overtures of her fellow workers in the lab, for example. Surely she must have noticed that the shy little Mark Singer was head over heels in love with her? And she must have had to put a lot of effort into warding off the aggressive advances of Mark's opposite number, the self-confident glamour boy Thomas Ridley. Quite simply, Bryan said, she had intrigued and puzzled him from the start. He had never known anyone like her.

Nor had she, she confessed, ever known anyone like him.

That night, for the first time in her life, Isabel couldn't open a book. She found herself continually smiling at some inner thought and was glad there was no one around to see and question her. She had never felt quite so buoyant. And that feeling was to stay with her for the next few months. Everyone did notice a change in her—her fellow students, her instructors, even her mother remarked on how animated and bright Isabel had become. Bryan told her she glowed, and she knew it was true.

They met frequently. Unfortunately, Bryan's own bedroom was out of bounds. He was staying in the Cambridge town house of his mother's old roommate at Dana Hall, and although Sarah Gooding herself was in Palm Beach, her proper and proprietary housekeeper would have had apoplexy had Bryan brought a young lady into his bedroom. So they always had to meet in Bryan's office which now seemed their private place, an unlikely love nest with its walls filled with heavy medical tomes, its charts and files and intercom—but all this academic paraphernalia became infused with sentiment, the romantic associations of erotic hours.

Usually they only managed to meet when it was late, and sometimes even this was difficult to arrange. There were many evenings when Isabel just sat alone in Bryan's office until it was clear that there was no chance he would come at all. Strangely, she was never angry at him for these absences. Rather, she always blamed some unforeseen circumstance—a special meeting, a troublesome colleague. It never occurred to her that Bryan would prefer to be any place else than lying by her side, on top of her, beneath her. For if their lovemaking was not as frequent as she would have wanted or if their meetings were all too brief, the moments they did have together were filled with a variety and intensity of sensation she had never imagined existed.

Initiating her, Bryan was infinitely patient. He would quietly explain to her the intricacies of that complex web of responses within the human body. It wasn't only that he seemed to know how to bring alive every part of her, playing one tender nerve against another until she felt as though she would explode, it was that he also instructed her on how to skillfully play on his body. She was surprised to find that she was never embarrassed no matter where he put her hand or where he led her mouth, her lips, her tongue. And after a while, Bryan hardly had to guide her at all as Isabel began to be able to anticipate just what would please him and to add some variations that even surprised him.

"Who would have suspected that such a cloistered novice would end up so expert?" He grinned with pleasure and then kissed her up and down her naked body until she felt her skin come alive. At those moments her life became rich in pleasure.

But in her relationship with Bryan there was pain as well. Besides the times that he was too busy to meet her, there were other things that upset her. Long-distance phone calls at the lab which he went into an inner office to take and which she could see through the glass window kept him laughing and smiling. There were letters which his secretary left on his desk and which Isabel saw—letters on linen stationery that were written in a flowery handwriting that was obviously female. When Isabel could no longer keep her suspicions about these calls and letters to herself and summoned up the nerve to confront Bryan with them, he didn't seem to give her doubts any serious consideration. After all, he explained to her, she may have been a nun in Boston but he certainly had not been a monk in Philadelphia. And this attitude made his trips to Philadelphia—as infrequent as they were—extremely difficult for her to deal with. Each time he returned from Paoli to Boston, Isabel thought she sensed a cold and distant air that had not been there before he left. It troubled her deeply that she was never invited along on these weekends. She was especially hurt when Bryan didn't invite her to go home with him the weekend of his nephew's christening. He had mentioned the occasion several times the week before, telling her what a large gathering his mother and sister had been planning to follow the church ceremony—every relative from up and down the Main Line had been invited. He was, he told her laughingly, to be godfather. A fine spiritual father he would make! What struck her most was that he talked about this occasion without ever for a moment considering that Isabel might be included.

As with the phone calls and the letters, she wanted to confront him with his seeming callousness, but this time she somehow couldn't work up the nerve. And partly because this incident pointed up something larger about Bryan that troubled her—the fact that he never really committed himself to her. Despite the intensity of the pleasures they shared, he would never say how much he cared for her, had never told her he loved her or that he always wanted to be with her. Yet, she supposed she could understand this. Bryan came from a world where people did not show or declare their emotions easily. Perhaps the dictates of that world also accounted for the fact that he had kept their relationship so quiet. He was careful never to give any indication of their intimacies in the lab so that none of the other assistants seemed to have an inkling of what was going on between them. And so, their affair remained very much a secret. Especially since Isabel, for her part, was not about to tell anyone. She had never had any close friends and had had only the most casual friendships throughout school. She had even resisted the distraction of having a roommate when she moved into the medical school dorm. And she was certainly not about to bring Bryan Madison home to her mother. Not only because Frances might well suspect that they were having an affair, but because her home had started to diminish in her eyes, now seeming a part of her that she would not like Bryan to see. She had always realized she was poor and had, in her childhood fantasies, wished herself in far more opulent surroundings. But she had always taken a measure of pride in the sparkling cleanliness and order of her mother's tiny apartment. Now, however, she noticed other flaws.

When she looked around, she saw there was not a painting on the wall
except for the garishly colored print of the Sacred Heart hanging next to
the crucifix over her mother's bed. She saw that besides her own school
texts, a Bible, and a world almanac, there were no books. Certainly
there was no record collection, not even a phonograph. How different
Bryan Madison's home must be. He spoke about his father's library,
and she imagined walls of glass-enclosed leather-bound books; he had
mentioned his mother's passion for Impressionist still lifes and her collection of Degas figurines. The point was not simply that the Madisons
were rich and Isabel was poor. It was that they lived in a world rich in
culture, in knowledge, in variety. Contrasting this with her own spare,
restricted background, she suddenly felt inadequate for the first time in
her life, almost as if she failed a test. She could never—no matter how
hard she studied—master the course. It was one that had to be started at
birth, and she had simply entered too late.

She remembered one sunny Sunday having an early dinner with
Bryan in a small restaurant in Concord. He started to entertain her with
anecdotes about the American Revolution, a subject that had always
absorbed his Philadelphia father who felt that Washington was over-
rated, that Franklin should really be called the father of our country.
Isabel wondered what it would be like to have a parent who had any
other interests or any other heroes than Jesus Christ or the Virgin
Mary. Or how it would have affected her own way of thinking to have a
depersonalized, intellectual conversation with her mother about anything
at all. Bryan and his father had debated all their lives—about subjects as
varied as the need for a police review board, Maria Callas' dramatic
power, about the relative merits of Hemingway and Faulkner, about the
so-called American propensity for radical surgery. And his mother and
sister joined in on these conversations, enlivening them frequently with
their own special interests in the visual arts. How could she ever hope
to enter into such talk with the appropriate ease, the appropriate
lightness. It was obvious to her that in contrast to Bryan, she would
always be strained and awkward. And this certainly must not have gone
unnoticed by him. He was polite enough, she thought, not to be obviously judging her deficiencies. For example, when he asked her if she
would prefer seeing the visiting Bolshoi's *Swan Lake* or *Giselle,* and she
confessed she had never seen either ballet—in fact, had never even been
to any ballet—he was silent. She supposed he must have felt something
like disdain or amusement at her lack of experience. And there were not
only the things she had not done, there were also the names she did not

know. She knew he must have found it absurd that she had never heard of Federico Fellini and Michelangelo Antonioni, since once he had explained who they were, she seemed to see articles about them all the time. And how could she have admitted to not knowing where Mykonos was, or even what it was. This time, he couldn't keep himself from laughing when he realized she assumed it was some kind of salad.

And so, though Isabel knew she was in love with Bryan Madison, there was a certain amount of resentment mixed in with that love. For there was something in the way she saw herself reflected in Bryan's eyes that always discomforted her, that gave her a sense of herself unlike any she had had before. She had always been approved of, always applauded, always the best and the first. And with Bryan she was never any of these things. Her conflicted feelings deeply troubled her but because she confided in no one, she had to deal with them herself.

She had also, of course, to keep her absorption with her affair from devastating her grades. She had to literally force images of him out of her mind to make room for details about a cancerous cell, about malfunctioning gallbladders, about the behavior of a dozen Basingis—the mute African dogs the medical school laboratory had just acquired for Bryan's experiments. She couldn't afford to waste a moment now that her time was so full and so precious. She took her books with her wherever she went, using the time spent in waiting for a bus, for a class to start, even for Bryan to show up in his office, to do whatever work she could. Haphazard as it all seemed, fantastically Isabel's grades remained at the top of her class and her work on the Basingis that she was doing for Bryan continued to bring her special notice from the dean.

Her academics going well, Isabel turned to deal with her next problem, her religion. She simply could not go to confession since there was no possible way she could be contrite about her love affair, no way she could promise to be chaste. Without confession, she could not take Communion, and so her solution was to give up mass at her neighborhood church which she had attended together with her mother all of her life, including this last year when she no longer lived at home but in the medical school dormitory. Her habit had been to come home every Saturday night and go to church with Frances every Sunday morning. Now she arranged to visit Frances on Wednesdays instead, telling her that the project with the Basingis required Sunday vigils for taking blood counts and examining feces—this last detail was added to convince Frances that giving up these Sundays at home was indeed a sacrifice for her.

But if Isabel wished to avoid confession and all it entailed, she was not quite ready as yet to give up the church altogether. Partly, this was simply a matter of practicality. If Bishop O'Connor and his wealthy parishioners who were also her patrons discovered that she was a lapsed Catholic, she would also, she knew, be a lapsed medical student since, after all, their support of her depended equally on the fact that she was devout as well as a model student.

But her problem also went deeper. If she argued with the church's views on chastity, she certainly wasn't ready to relinquish heaven and hell and a faith that had been ingrained in her since she could remember. And so she began attending mass at the church near the medical school where the young priest was a liberal, involved in sending students down to register black voters in Alabama, and hardly the type to spy for Bishop O'Connor or to report back to him even were he to pay special attention as to whether or not Isabel was taking Communion or going to confession.

In this way, she still had the comfort of her church—but the routine had been broken. The familiar voice of her parish priest was gone and with it the unquestioning attitude she had always had toward its words. It was clear that she was straying—but she didn't have the time or the concentration to give to the problems of religious faith. Bryan, medical school, and Wednesday visits with her mother took every bit of energy she could summon up.

When she slept at night, it was the complete, black, exhausted collapse from which she emerged each morning, eager to go on with the day. It dawned on Isabel that probably, for the first time in her life, she was truly happy.

This mood lasted, even though Isabel began to suspect that she might be pregnant. After a moment of initial panic, it struck her that this was probably the best thing that could happen, something that would force the issue of her relationship with Bryan. The fall semester was coming to a close, the Basingi project was now completed, and Bryan would be returning to Philadelphia in a few weeks. Not that Philadelphia was the end of the world, of course. But she was too afraid of losing him to allow even that distance between them. Isabel now knew that, more than anything in the world, she wanted to marry Bryan Madison. It was even more important to her, she was shocked to realize, than her church, than her mother, than even medicine. And she realized too that if she did marry him, she would have to enter his world—the world of the Main Line or its equivalent. It was simply that he was too much a part of it, it was too much a part of him, for the two to ever be severed. As for Isabel, who would be a stranger in a strange land, the prospect, while frightening to her, also appealed to her immensely. It was, after all, the contours, the flavors, the shadows of this world that she loved in Bryan—the elements that made him such a golden creature. And the baby she carried inside her would be such a golden creature himself.

She asked Mark Singer, who had been one of her co-workers on the Basingi project and now worked in obstetrics, if he would do a rabbit test for her. Mark, a serious and soft-spoken young man who clearly adored Isabel, seemed shocked at Isabel's request and then looked grave, almost stricken, when he had to tell her that the results were positive. He was dumbfounded at her calm acceptance of this news. He was too shy, however, to say anything more than a few words telling her that he would keep her secret no matter what course she should decide on taking.

Whatever Mark Singer might have thought, Isabel was far from calm; she was thrilled. Her only problem was how to present the news to Bryan. He had left for Philadelphia three days before, promising to get in touch with her next week. If everything was easily settled at Philadelphia General Hospital, he might even fly up to Boston for a few days. Isabel debated. Should she call him or wait for him to call her? Or should she wait to see him in person? It seemed better somehow, she thought, to tell him this exciting news when they could be together. Just as she had been panicked at the initial suspicion of pregnancy, he too would have to be unsettled, possibly even upset, at the first news—but he would see, just as she had, that it was all for the best. After all, their relationship really couldn't go on as it had. It had to grow, to come out into the light.

That Wednesday night, as she was sitting across the kitchen table from her mother, drinking a cup of tea, Isabel told Frances about Bryan Madison for the first time—though, of course, she didn't come close to telling the whole story or revealing anything of her pregnancy. What she did say was that she was in love with the attractive doctor from Philadelphia in whose lab she had been working during the fall semester, that he was in love with her, and that she was sure the two of them would be getting married soon.

Frances was shocked and not pleased at all. "And what about school? Look here, Isabel, I hope you don't think I've been breaking my back the past twenty years so you could marry and have babies.

You could have done that without an education—without medical school, without college, even."

"Don't worry, Mother, I wouldn't think of quitting school. You know how much medicine means to me. Getting married these days isn't the end of your life, the end of a woman's career. I have every intention of finishing school whether as Isabel Dunne or as Mrs. Bryan Madison."

"And what's to keep you from having a baby, I'd like to know?" Frances' voice began to get shrill. "And once you had one, you wouldn't just leave it home with some hired girl, would you?"

"Times have changed, Mother. Women are doing just that all the time. I know it's difficult to combine work and mothering. I know how hard it was for you. But it worked out all right, didn't it? And just think, I'd have it so much more easy than you had."

Frances sighed. She was evidently despairing of the fruitfulness of this line of argument. "Well, whatever you say, it still doesn't sound right to me. I don't understand just why you kept this man a secret for so long. Just why you didn't bring him home to me or why he hasn't taken you down to Philadelphia to meet his parents."

"Don't worry, he will. We've been too busy—both of us. And I'll bring him to see you as soon as he comes back from Philadelphia."

Frances looked startled. "Back from Philadelphia? What's he doing in Philadelphia if he's going to marry you? Are you sure this man's declared himself to you? Is this some kind of daydream, some kind of wish on your part?" Frances reached across the table and put her hand on Isabel's in a warm gesture of motherhood. "Isabel," she started, "you've been so innocent, so unexposed that I worry. And I worry too about that imagination of yours—the way you used to pretend your dreams were real. Are you sure of how this man feels about you?"

"Really, Mother, I'm not crazy and I'm not a child anymore. You'll never let me forget that idiotic diary, those made-up stories of mine when I was little."

"Well, now maybe you're big and maybe you have an even bigger imagination. And that's what I'm worried about. Something in what you tell me doesn't sound right. You can't afford to make a mistake, Isabel, you can't afford it. You'd lose everything you worked for, and you'd end up like me. Worse maybe."

Isabel looked at the pain in her mother's face and felt ashamed. "It's true, I'm not telling you everything, Mother, and I can't right now," she admitted. "But I swear to you, everything will be fine—no, more than fine—it will be wonderful. I love this man, he loves me, and I'm sure we're going to get married, soon, very soon."

* * *

All that week, Isabel waited for word from Bryan—a letter, a phone call, better yet a surprise appearance. She checked at the dormitory desk three or four times a day for phone messages and kept asking Mrs. Dougherty at the mail desk if perhaps a letter for Isabel could have ended up in someone else's box. In the evening, she didn't dare go to the library for fear of missing him, and every time she heard the phone in the hall ring, she ran out to answer—to the point where she felt a fool for having to continually deliver messages to all the other students.

Finally, it was Bryan. He sounded somehow different to her. Maybe it was the distance. And his voice was full of hesitation as he started to explain his schedule. He had far more work than he ever anticipated. His new secretary hadn't worked out and he had to train another. His files had been delayed, and when they arrived, they were all in disarray. In short, it was a nightmare, and there was no way he would be able to come up to Boston for quite a while.

"But you must," Isabel heard herself say, the intensity in her voice surprising her.

It evidently surprised Bryan too. "What do you mean?" he said. "I *must* be down here."

"What I mean is that I have to see you. It's urgent. Trust me, it's urgent."

She couldn't *not* see him. "I'll come down to Philadelphia if that's better for you."

"No, no," he said quickly. There was an uncomfortable silence and then, "All right, if it's that urgent, I'll be there tomorrow. Why don't you meet me in the lobby of the Hilton?"

She changed her clothes half a dozen times that afternoon. Nothing looked right. Did that mean nothing was going to go right? But that was unthinkable. Whatever Bryan Madison touched always went right. And she felt even more sure that everything would work out when she saw him. There was nothing this tall fair-haired man could not do—could not take care of.

He had taken a room for the night. A good sign, she thought. He really wanted to be alone with her, to make love to her. But once they were alone in the room, he did not take her in his arms as she had thought he would. Instead, he sat down on the blue tweed chair and motioned for her to sit on another.

"All right, Isabel, you'd better tell me just what it is," he said, his voice uncharacteristically tense.

She hadn't planned to blurt it out this way but he had given her no choice.

"I'm going to have a baby," she said.

He said nothing at first, showed no reaction. Then he got up and walked slowly to the phone. "No, you're not," he said. "Don't worry, I'll take care of it." He lifted the receiver.

She ran over and grabbed the phone. "It?" she found herself screaming. "It? You'll take care of it? Are you crazy? This is my baby. Our baby."

He put his arms around her and held her to him. "Isabel, come to your senses. You have a wonderful life ahead of you, a lot of things to do, and so do I. There's no way you want to have this baby, I know there's no way I want one."

"Bryan, I can't kill that baby," she sobbed. "I won't be a murderer."

He sat her down. "Look, you're a person of science . . . and a brilliant one. You know that those few cells within you are far from a person, far from anything human, at least yet. You can't possibly let some medieval superstitions destroy your whole life."

"Destroy my life? I never thought of it that way. I thought this baby would be the beginning of a new life—not only its life but ours. I love you, Bryan, you know that. I never would have slept with you if I didn't. And I never would have risked getting pregnant if I didn't sense that you cared for me too—at least enough to do the right thing."

He was clearly shocked. "Come to your senses, you sound like a Victorian novel. In the first place, if you hadn't been so stubborn about not going to the student clinic, this probably wouldn't have happened. Secondly, if you're going to talk about my doing the 'right thing,' let's not make any mistake about what the right thing is. Having a baby is the wrong thing for both of us."

"And what about the third thing?" She was almost screaming now. "What about our love for each other? Mine for you and yours for me?" She was shaking violently now.

Bryan, in contrast, was calm and his voice was steady as he told her, "Listen to me and understand this once and for all. I never told you I loved you. I never made you any promises. I'm sorry this has happened . . ."

"Then you're not going to marry me." Her voice went dead.

He didn't even answer this but turned and got busy on the telephone. Isabel didn't register what the calls were or who he was talking to or

46

even how long it had taken between making them and the arrival of a messenger who handed Bryan a bulky envelope. But it must have been a long time because it was day now, and a white-jacketed waiter was wheeling in coffee, toast, and eggs, the aroma of which made her gag. She ran into the bathroom and started retching. There was nothing to throw up though—she hadn't eaten in almost twenty-four hours. She threw some cold water on her face and tried to smooth her hair with her hands. When she came out into the room, Bryan was eating and the sight of the food almost sent her back into the bathroom.

"Take some dry toast," he said. "That should help steady your stomach."

"No, thanks," she said, walking over and sitting down in the blue chair.

He finished his breakfast, looked at his watch, and turned to her. "I know this is going to sound cold and unconcerned to you, but I've got a plane to catch. I've made all the arrangements for you. In this envelope is the name of the doctor who has your name as well and is expecting to hear from you. He's no quack. He's a responsible, well-qualified obstetrician who has the courage of his convictions and believes that women shouldn't be forced to bear unwanted children. He's in Swampscott and there's a good train that goes out there this afternoon. He'll keep you there overnight or even longer if it's necessary, which I'm sure it won't be. This is, as you well know, a very simple procedure." He paused to take her hand. She was so stony, so silent. "There's also fifteen hundred dollars here. I think that will cover everything."

Isabel said nothing. She didn't even raise her eyes to look at the envelope with the money and the doctor's name. Bryan bent down to kiss her cheek, and the next thing she was aware of was the sound of the door slamming behind him.

It took all her effort to get herself up and out of the hotel, the envelope in her purse. She couldn't see the doctor that day—whatever Bryan had arranged. She had to think but, somehow, her mind wouldn't function. In any case, she couldn't leave it at this. She had to talk to him some more; she had to call him. He had taken the morning plane so he must be back in Philadelphia by now.

She tried the number of his parents' house in Paoli. No, Dr. Bryan wasn't in, would she like to leave a message? a housekeeper asked. Isabel left her name. And then left her name again at his office at Philadelphia General. She had to talk to him and tried again later that night and the next day and the next. But no matter what hour she called, he was never in. And no matter how many messages she left, he never called her back.

4

"I HATE BEING a Kingman," Paul said, staring out of the hospital window into the gray February morning.

Isabel sat across from him in the same chair she had sat in every day for the past week, listening to this sad, sensitive young man struggle to bring his thoughts together, sort out his emotions, and attempt to give her a sense of what was happening inside him. She found herself drawn to him as much as she had been to any patient, as much in fact as she had been to almost anyone she had ever known. His extraordinary beauty—his deep-set eyes, his high cheekbones, and his dark, dramatic coloring—was, she knew, a large part of his appeal. Even more important, though, there was something about his manner and sensibility that touched her in a deeply personal way, setting off long-forgotten feelings, reminding her of a long-forgotten world. This much she understood about her attraction for Paul Kingman. But there was something else, something in Paul that she was reacting to, which kept eluding her. And not knowing what it was about him that so moved her, she found herself more and more intrigued, looking forward each day to her sessions with him—as much, she recognized, for her own sake as for his.

"I've always hated being a Kingman," he continued, now looking straight at Isabel. She nodded. It was better not to say anything and to just let him talk. Today, more than at any other session, he somehow seemed eager to proceed.

"I don't mean that every moment of being in that family was torture. But still . . . I couldn't handle it, even if the others could. And it was always worse, much worse, when we were in Shropshire."

Isabel sat listening, waiting to understand. Oh, Paul, poor Paul . . .

* * *

Shropshire, Paul started to explain, was the Kingmans' special world. Here, in the rolling foothills of the Connecticut Berkshires, was a landscape filled with huge leafy maples and ancient pines and dotted with working farms whose separate fields of corn and oats and clover for grazing transformed the world into the proverbial patchwork quilt. Each of the three Kingman families had a small estate—the one bordering the other. It was Uncle Ernest who, as in all things, had been the family's leader in first discovering the area which had attracted other intellectuals, artists, and writers. These city people, who like the Kingmans drove the two hours from New York to Shropshire every weekend, every holiday, and stayed all summer long, were a strangely old-fashioned sort, people who somehow viewed life in the classical New England way. They respected the landscape and fought to keep it unspoiled—voting against highways, banning billboards, keeping showy shops and restaurants far away, and renovating their houses in style one with the other and with barns and split-rail fences surrounding them. And as they ordered their environment, so too their lives. They clipped their roses and tied up their beans in the morning and wrote their articles, researched their current studies, and painted their pictures after lunch. Always, though, they found time for a swim or a game of tennis at the local lakefront club that the members of the weekend community had all chipped in to build. With its two overgrown, gnat-infested tennis courts, its roughhewn wooden dock, and its simple, overgrown cabin of a clubhouse, the club was hardly worthy of the name. But the people of Shropshire seemed to resist such effete and frivolous amenities as a weeded lawn, much less a manicured one, or outdoor furniture, much less a tufted chaise or cushioned chairs.

Yet, with all its rigors, Paul would have loved Shropshire had he only not been a Kingman. He adored those rich, thick trees and rolling hills, he loved the smell of the cornfields and the chill clear night with its brilliant, starry skies, and the wonderful old houses and weathered barns. But Shropshire, for all its loveliness, was also where the Kingman family seemed to press its hardest on him, and he felt them most of all on holidays. For Christmas, Easter, Thanksgiving, Fourth of July, Labor Day were all a series of rituals—dinners, picnics, games, and contests—with various members of the family taking responsibility for different holidays, each according to age and rank. Christmas Eve, for example, as the most important Kingman gathering, always took place at Uncle Ernest's, which, as befitted the family elder, was the largest Kingman property. Ernest's house was also the grandest of the Kingman domiciles—a sprawling white colonial with a wide center hall, massive stone fireplaces, and a huge dining room in the center of which was a long, dark wood refectory table at which Christmas dinner was always eaten.

The brittle, immaculately groomed Natalie Kingman Rush, the second eldest in the family, was, in the appropriate descending order, in charge of the Thanksgiving meal. In Aunt Natalie's somewhat smaller house down the road from Ernest's, the turkey and ham were served in such thin slices that it became a yearly joke for Paul's father to laughingly ask his sister, had she ever considered giving up the law, going into medicine, and specializing in skin grafts? Aunt Natalie would then counter, in her clipped, almost British voice, with the remark that small slices of food were healthier and led to less waste. Paul, who didn't care about food anyway and spent most of the time at these family dinners hiding a vegetable under his mashed potatoes or slipping bits of meat into his napkin, guessed he agreed with Aunt Natalie. In any case, his smaller appetite certainly made him prefer her meager and simpler offering to his mother's strange-tasting creations. Barbara Kingman, as wife of the youngest, was assigned Easter dinner—the Kingmans, not at all religious, had always been a bit discomforted by Easter and what seemed to them its central primitive theme of bloody sacrifice. And so they gave it lowest priority of the major holidays. Still, Barbara tried to give her dinner some special flair. She was extremely fond of gourmet cooking, to Paul's dismay serving up a quenelle instead of plain fish, a tarte tatin instead of plain apple pie. But Barbara's efforts and time were a waste as far as her ascetic sister-in-law was concerned.

"No need for embellishments," Aunt Natalie would sniff. "Painting the lily, adding sauces to fresh, wholesome food." Natalie also scorned the cornucopia of food which appeared at Ernest's Christmas dinners. Aunt Clara, his wife, would present besides the lavish array of meats, a whole buffet devoted entirely to desserts—apple, mince, and pumpkin pies along with chocolate cake, sherry trifle, and her own candied pears. Paul was always overwhelmed by Aunt Clara's seemingly endless lineup of silver trays filled with so many different things you didn't know where to start. But it wasn't only the food that was too much for him, it was the presence of the entire family, all at one time, all in one place. Father, mother, aunts, uncles, cousins, all of whom were older, bigger, stronger, smarter. As the youngest, Paul had to sit in what he thought had to be the worst seat at the table, down at the foot and next to Aunt Clara, who was, for sure, the most boring of all the Kingmans.

"Are boys nowadays still crazy about baseball?" The gray-haired, round-faced, ever-smiling Aunt Clara must have asked him this same question every year, at every dinner. She would also always follow it with a little speech which began, "In my day, all my brothers ever talked about was baseball. I learned so much myself just from listening to them that none of my beaux could get over how much I knew."

"Hey, Paul, still playing ball?" Cousin Franklin, Aunt Natalie's eldest son, would always call from across the table. Aunt Clara never caught on that Franklin was making fun of her, and she just continued talking about Babe Ruth and Ty Cobb, whose vital statistics she must have learned in order to enchant some young man many years before.

But that young man couldn't have been Uncle Ernest. Not that the eldest Kingman didn't pride himself on his catholic tastes, his Renaissance approach to life. The physical side was important but it was expressed with tennis in the summer, squash in the winter, and skiing for the true outdoorsman like his brother William. In any case, Ernest's main concern, he made clear to all the children, was not their bodies but their minds and something called their "characters." He said about someone he considered unscrupulous or even unimportant, "He has no character." Paul wondered what it was like, having no character at all—did that make you a blank? He imagined a man who was only an outline—no one had bothered to color him in. Maybe character, like crayons, could make you rosy and bright.

Ernest, who with his huge head of gray wiry hair, his strong features, and his booming voice could have easily presided at a feast on Mount Olympus, sat at the head of the table. From this vantage point he could look down and survey his assembled family: his three high-spirited teen-age daughters, Margo, Frederica, and Allison; his three nephews, Franklin, Phillip, and Paul—each two years apart with Franklin the eldest, and Paul the youngest, his brother and his wife, his sister and her husband, and facing him smilingly from the end of the table, his own wife, Clara. His position, both physical and familial, was the perfect one from which to pose the inevitable questions, asked one by one, of everyone assembled to elicit an accounting of their latest accomplishments.

Had the government dropped its antitrust case against Sebastian's client, Salt Lake Copper? Had William published that paper he was planning on the complications in performing bone surgery on hemophiliacs? Had the auction Barbara had organized for the Junior League achieved its target sum? Was Phillip starting on the school soccer team?

Since, like everything else in the Kingman family, these questions assumed a logical, hierarchical order, descending from eldest to youngest,
zigzagging their way down the table, Paul knew his question would
come last. He also knew he would never have the right answer for it.
Paul used to think it was magic the way Uncle Ernest would always ask
everyone else a question to which he or she could answer yes, while in
Paul's case, he somehow discovered just the question to which Paul had
to answer no.

Had Paul made the honor roll? What part did he get in the Christmas
pageant? What? No part? Had he passed his Red Cross swimming test?
And the questions he didn't have to say no to, he usually didn't know
the answer to at all.

There were all those puzzles that reed-thin, hawk-nosed Uncle
Sebastian, a lawyer like his wife, Natalie, loved to test out on the children, so that dinner became a series of questions and answers, a giant
game of "Go to the Head of the Class" in which Paul, the youngest, the
smallest, the least knowledgeable, always ended up the dunce.

"If a bottle and a cork cost a dollar and ten cents together and the
bottle cost a dollar more than the cork, how much does the bottle cost?"
Sebastian asked.

"A dollar," Paul, who must have been eight or nine at the time,
remembered calling out, delighted that here at last was something he
seemed to know.

Uncle Sebastian smiled and shook his head. The sharp-eyed lawyer
seemed to welcome wrong answers.

"A dollar and five cents, Uncle Sebastian," the cheerful voice of
twelve-year-old Frederica, the youngest of Ernest's three daughters,
rang out. Frederica, like her sisters, was an enthusiast.

"That was a good one," said Margo. "Do you have any more?"

Of course, he had. Uncle Sebastian had a battery of such puzzles. But
now, Aunt Natalie, interrupting her husband, took charge of the game.
If her husband's questions always had to do with mathematics and
logic, Natalie's were inevitably concerned with grammar, usage, and
matters of vocabulary. Her bar association committee met bimonthly.

"Now, which of you children know how often that means our committee meets?"

This time, Paul knew there was a trick and he didn't even try to answer. But Natalie's next question was directed at him, and he had no
choice. She had given him a book about poodles for his birthday in No-

vember, since a couple of weeks before, he had received a poodle puppy from his parents.

"So, Paul," Natalie asked, "what does your book tell you about the name 'poodle'?"

Paul had no idea. He had looked at the book, but he couldn't remember if anywhere in it, they even talked about the name "poodle." He sat there feeling stupid. And he was made to feel an even greater fool when his cousin Phillip, only two years his senior, announced shrilly that he knew, even if Paul didn't. Poodle came from the German word for puddle.

"Quite fitting for that little sieve," Barbara inserted. "I guess with all the accidents that puppy's had, he's read your book, Paul, even if you haven't."

Everyone laughed at his mother's remark, the deep guffaws mingling with the high-pitched giggles. Only Paul sat silently.

"Oh, come on," Phillip called across the table to him. "You have to admit that was funny."

"What does it take to get a smile from you?" Margo joined in. The oldest sister, she was the most competitive and least patient with Paul's deficiencies.

Paul would have given anything to be able to smile right then, but he had all he could do to keep from crying. He felt so stupid, so awful. He would never measure up.

By the time dessert came, though, he felt better and ate a big piece of Aunt Clara's chocolate cake. And when they all sat around the lavishly decorated blue spruce that stood in the center of the living room, Paul had forgotten his unhappiness altogether.

As in all things in life, the Kingman family had a ritual for opening presents. The children took turns fishing gifts out from under the tree and reading off the names on the tags. One gift was unwrapped at a time, so everyone could watch and admire. The children, who naturally received a good deal more than they gave, were encouraged to make what few presents they did give to the adults, and so William was not too surprised to receive a knit scarf from his niece Margo, who had given him an identical one last year, nor did Barbara have trouble guessing that her blue box contained homemade candles whose extra long wicks identified them as the handiwork of Allison. Phillip and Franklin, who often worked in tandem, were a bit more imaginative than the girls. One year they made lamps out of old wine bottles, another year three-legged stools, and this year surpassed themselves with shiny, lacquered, wooden chessboards.

Paul knew that his presents were never as good as those of his cousins, no matter how much everyone pretended to be delighted at receiving a painted rock for a paperweight or a bit of felt for a bookmark. This year, though, he had more ambition and had painted pictures for everyone. The biggest was for Uncle Ernest, who was opening his gift right now.

"Well, what have we here, Paul? I'm honored," he said, as he unwrapped the large, flat package. Paul felt himself growing more and more excited. He knew Uncle Ernest would really like this present.

"How nice, Paul," Uncle Ernest said, looking at the colored, petaled flowers. "But it would have been even nicer, my boy, had you been more original and had done a picture that you thought of yourself."

"But I did do it myself. I did," Paul protested.

"Yes, you *painted* it yourself. But someone else painted it first, and a very famous artist he is."

"But it was my idea, it was, it was."

"Paul," William's deep voice called out and silenced his son. "Let's not hear another word from you."

His mother, too, motioned to him to be still. She then sighed and began to toy with a lace handkerchief, smooth her satin skirt, fuss with a curl, all to avert her attention from this scene of humiliation.

Paul felt as if all the chocolate cake he had eaten was coming up into his mouth as he stood, knees weak, listening to Uncle Ernest.

"Paul, this is a small incident but a very significant one. If there is anything worse than lying, it is stealing. And I don't mean stealing unimportant things, material things, like money and possessions. I mean stealing from people's minds and imaginations, stealing their creations. Now Pablo Picasso, who painted your bouquet of flowers long before you did, no doubt wouldn't be upset to learn that a little boy had tried to pass off his work as his own. But it is still a very bad thing for you to do, Paul, and you must learn this lesson right now, if you want to grow up to be a man of character."

"I hope you've listened carefully to your uncle, Paul," his father said. "I'm afraid you've made your mother and me quite ashamed."

It was clear that his parents were not only not going to come to his aid but were on the other side against him.

Paul wished he could disappear. In fact, if it were the only way he could get away from that Christmas tree and from those Christmas presents at that moment, he was perfectly willing to die.

"As Uncle Ernest said, it was a very small incident," Paul said to Isabel. "I don't know why I reacted so strongly, but I did. Every Christmas after that was ruined for me."

"There wasn't anything odd in your responding the way you did, Paul. Your family was incredibly threatening—challenging, demanding, and, as you've described them, almost totally insensitive."

"Perhaps I'm being unfair to them."

"I suspect you're not. You don't have to blame yourself for everything, you know. I, too, would have found that dinner a nightmare, being asked question after question I couldn't answer, being made to feel ignorant and unworthy."

"I can't imagine you ever feeling that way," Paul said. "You seem so sure of yourself, so in control of every situation."

"No one is that sure of himself. Not me, not your Uncle Ernest, and not even your father."

She was wrong, he told her the following day, dead wrong. His father insecure? His father feeling even a hint of self-doubt? Never. William was in fact the most confident man Paul had ever known, a man so sure of himself that he could never even comprehend fear or hesitation in others, much less tolerate such feelings. And insisting that Paul submerge any doubt, any weariness, any trepidation, and be courageous and strong like him, he made life one long struggle for his son.

When the two went on hikes together, Paul had to prove his stamina, never able to admit that he was cold or tired or that the muscles in his legs had begun to throb. When the two built things together—an outdoor grill, a new fence, a woodshed—Paul had to prove his dexterity, hiding the inevitable splinters and bloody thumbs. While when they rode or swam or skied together, he had to prove his courage. These displays of bravado were pure sham. Paul, in fact, was terrified of most of the Shropshire sports. His mouth went dry on top of the ice-covered ski slope. Still, because William would never wait for him, he would force himself to continue right behind him, even though he was convinced that speeding down the perpendicular descent was courting death. As for the lake, its dark waters were always freezing, its rafts placed just a little too far away from the shore. Blue-lipped and shivering, he had to dive in right after William, terrified each time he plunged into the water headfirst that he would not come up again.

The point was that it never seemed to even occur to William that an eight-year-old boy might be afraid of a chair lift, much less of the dark. Or that a skinny child might feel the cold more than a muscular man. Or that small hands and fingers might fumble a task that was simple to an adult.

"Or maybe he did understand and pretended otherwise. I don't know. In any case, he wanted me to be him, and at that I had to fail."

Paul's words gripped Isabel. She reached across to him and took his hand.

"Of course, you had to fail at being your father, but that hardly makes you a failure at being yourself. Still, I understand exactly how you felt. Your father made no allowances for you and so you, in turn, made no allowances for yourself. And when you are so hard on yourself, Paul, when you see yourself as so inadequate in everything, you turn that perception into a self-fulfilling prophecy."

"That's one way of looking at it," he said bitterly. "But how do I ignore the fact that I did fail at everything. In the family, I was always the worst at everything. I was the only one who could never get the hang of a racing dive, never get my horse to take a jump, never master a backhand stroke. Even my grades were lousy, so lousy that I had the distinction of being the very first Kingman who didn't make it to Harvard."

"Even if I were to accept your view of yourself, you still can't deny that there was always something you could do that they couldn't, Paul. You could paint."

"And now I can't even do that." He had begun to cry.

Isabel returned to her office and saw her next patient—Emily Richmond, a worn-looking, red-eyed woman in her mid-forties whose husband had just left her and who had become frightened at her dependency on alcohol and Valium. After Mrs. Richmond left, Isabel went to meet Gerson Richler in the doctors' lounge. They were going to have lunch together to discuss Paul Kingman.

"How about something fancy this time?" Richler suggested. "How about Adele's? That's that new place on Madison."

"That sounds fine. As long as it's not one of those places where you can't hear yourself think," Isabel answered.

"Grant's Tomb, it's not," Richler smiled. "But I don't think it's Grand Central Station either. Let's give it a try."

Richler and Isabel walked down Madison Avenue, carefully skirting the frozen gray puddles that spotted the street. Uncollected garbage stood before the shops and apartment buildings in black plastic bags which could not completely contain the litter that blew around their feet. The cold, the color of the day, the mounds of dirty snow in the corners of the streets, all combined to give the city a shabby and depressing aura. It needed a spring cleaning.

"Here it is," Richler said, indicating the totally unobtrusive entryway to their right. With an unmarked canopy, and a sign the size of a newspaper headline, it was clear that Adele's wasn't planning on getting its customers off the street. Like most of New York's "in" places, the people who went to Adele's went because they had friends who went to Adele's and because they just might see them there. Fortunately, it was a bit early for the literary crowd, who tended to lunch around three, and so Richler and Isabel got a table right away.

The room was a study in cultivated shabbiness. Plain, unvarnished bentwood chairs, unhemmed red checkered tablecloths, and slightly discolored white napkins made for the decor, together with a long bar that ran almost the length of one side of the restaurant. Richler and Isabel sat toward the front, where the light coming through the windows, while it brought no cheer, at least made it possible to read the menu.

"How about the onion soup? That's good on a day like today," Richler suggested.

"That's fine. I'd like that."

He ordered and then, after the waiter had left, assumed a serious expression. It was time to talk business, and he wanted Isabel to tell him how things were going with the Kingman boy.

"So far, so good," Isabel said. "He's really talking to me and I think he's stable enough at this point to be released from the hospital."

"Do you think he'll be cooperative in continuing his therapy as an outpatient?"

"I have no doubt at all. My only worry is that while it's been easy for him to refuse to see his family during the time that he's been here at the hospital, once he gets back into his own apartment, they might all descend on him."

"No, I don't think so, Isabel, not if you ask them not to." Richler smiled to himself as he thought of asking Leah not to see Sandy. He remembered the year when Sandy had been quarantined at summer camp with a case of scarlet fever. Leah had stormed the infirmary, with her baskets of oranges and tangerines—a veritable Brünnhilde. But Leah and the Kingmans were worlds apart.

"Well, I'm not so sure of the Kingmans' reactions as you are," Isabel went on. "Look, Gerson, do you think you could talk to William Kingman and explain that I think it best for the family to continue to keep away from Paul a little longer?"

"If that's what you want, of course I'll talk to him. But I think pretty soon, you're going to have to start talking to him yourself."

"I know, Gerson, but I can't just yet—not until Paul agrees."

"Of course, of course."

The waiter brought the steamy bowls of soup, each covered with a crusty blanket of yellow cheese.

"Delicious." Richler savored the rich brown liquid.

He was in high spirits now that the nagging problem of Paul Kingman somehow seemed on its way to solution. His voice took on a new light lilt.

"You have to admit I was right about you being the perfect doctor for the boy," Richler smiled, self-satisfied. "He's opened up more to you in these few weeks than he would have to me in a year."

"Well, I certainly am beginning to get a feeling for what he's up against as a member of that family. There's no question but that they are the most accomplished group of blood relations I've ever heard of."

Of course, Isabel went on to say, she'd known of other intellectual or highly talented families in the past—the Barrymores, perhaps the Kennedys, the brothers William and Henry James. But not even in these remarkable families had there seemed to have been such a consistency of excellence as among the Kingmans. Everyone but everyone who was a blood Kingman had a gift, a talent, an outstanding ability. And what made the phenomenon all the more striking was that these abilities asserted themselves in such a variety of areas. The Barrymores were all actors, after all, and the Kennedys all politicians. The Kingmans, in contrast, were everything.

And not just the first generation—the Nobel laureate, the famous surgeon, and the brilliant lawyer—that they'd all heard of. It looked as though similar accomplishments would also be coming from the second generation, Paul's generation. Margo Kingman Craig, for example, was currently an editor of the *New Yorker,* while her sister Allison had just won a seat in the State Senate. And Frederica, only four years older than Paul, was already the star of the Anthropology Department at Barnard and seemed destined to be the next Margaret Mead. The Rush boys, the sons of Natalie Kingman, had equally distinguished themselves. Franklin, like Frederica twenty-seven, had a high position on the White House staff and was rumored to have been the author of the Inaugural Address. His younger brother, Phillip, had just been appointed clerk to Supreme Court Justice Taylor.

Richler shook his head. "Poor Paul Kingman. And my son, Sandy, used to complain because he had a father with a Phi Beta Kappa key. He made such a case about it that I was sorry I ever won it in the first place."

Isabel couldn't help but smile. The thought of the big, hardy Sandy suffering any psychic anguish struck her as somewhat amusing.

"Too bad the Kingman boy couldn't have spoken up for himself," Richler went on. "He might have never gotten to the point where his only way of expressing his unhappiness was through self-destruction."

Well, he had made some attempts at asserting himself, Isabel pointed out. When he was eighteen, for example, he had made the bold decision to study art at the Rhode Island School of Design, a choice that went against the grain of his family's Ivy League liberal arts tradition. And more recently, just two years ago, he had taken his own apartment, even making a stab at paying his own rent by doing some free-lance work for an advertising firm—some layouts and designs.

But the family atmosphere had been too paralyzing for these small gestures to have meant anything in the end. At this point, Paul was so terrified of failure that he couldn't do anything at all, even begin work on the canvases which represented, after all, his sole distinction, his possible passport to the lofty realm of the Kingmans. It was almost sure, Isabel added, that he had a similar paralysis as far as sex was concerned but she hadn't gotten him to talk about this yet. It probably was too soon to explore this delicate area.

The waiter brought the dessert menu.

"I really shouldn't," Richler said, as he ordered pecan pie with whipped cream. "But let's just say it's in celebration of your ongoing successes."

Richler felt just wonderful. It was clear that Isabel was hooked on the Kingman case. There was nothing like the clear and unmistakable progress she was making with this boy to keep a psychiatrist involved and committed to a patient.

Yes, Isabel was hooked. But Richler didn't know how deeply, and this, Isabel couldn't tell him. This finely featured young man with his richly complex sensibility and noble aura of tragedy was, as he led her through his memories, taking her inside her own. For when Paul spoke of Shropshire, she somehow saw Paoli, while as he told tales of the Kingmans, she in turn saw the Madisons. And so, in this way, Isabel was forced back to a time and place which, despite her years of therapy, continued to intimidate and obsess her.

Addie Harris watched Dr. Dunne enter Room 43, where Paul Kingman himself opened the door. She hated to admit it, but that woman doctor, who had from the start aroused discomfort and resentment in Addie, was finally accomplishing something. Paul's whole mood had changed in the past few days. He had even given Addie a big smile this morning when she had come to take his blood pressure. She had been convinced it had been a sign of his interest in her until Catherine told her Paul had smiled at her too. In any case, Addie needed some change desperately. Taking Catherine's advice, she had started to spend time with Joe Buchbinder, and he was beginning to drive her crazy.

"He's a bust," she told Catherine in the lounge as they took a coffee break. "No imagination, just in and out, as though he were on call."

"I can do without the sordid details," Catherine sniffed. "Besides, anyone can learn."

"You don't have a shred of romance in you," Addie told her. "Poetry, love, adventure—that's what a young woman wants. I'm tired of these pimply-faced clumsy oafs, even if they are going to be rich doctors one of these days." She left the room, deciding that Catherine and she were too unalike to truly be friends.

Catherine, sipping her coffee alone in a corner, would agree with that.

If Paul Kingman had become central to Addie Harris' sexual fantasies, he had also become crucial to those of Isabel Dunne as well—if in a very different way. It was not that Isabel, like Addie, had a desire for Paul himself. It was that, as he painted the pictures of Shropshire that blurred into those of Paoli and Isabel found herself remembering more and more of the past, she was amazed to discover her body remembering too. So intense in fact was the reawakened sensation set off by Paul Kingman's words that, at times, Isabel felt her palms grow moist, her face flush. It was an acute excitement that overcame her, and though she knew that Paul was certainly not the object of that flurry of feeling, she felt herself more and more unable to separate out cause and effect, stimulus and response.

As disturbing and unprofessional as her feelings might have been, Isabel still could easily rationalize them. Paul, after all, was certainly benefiting from her attention, opening up, mellowing. She could tell others had noticed the change in him too. Besides Richler, who had briefly visited Paul and had complimented her on the boy's progress, there was that pretty nurse who seemed to have such a crush on Paul. The last time Isabel had come for Paul's session, she had found them laughing together in his room. And this time, as she knocked on the door, she heard a rustling before Paul told her to come in. The nurse's face was rosy and her manner agitated.

"I don't suppose I have the right to ask what was going on here?" Isabel said, after the nurse had left the room and shut the door behind her. She was careful to keep her voice impartial, nonjudgmental.

Paul's expression changed abruptly, his manner becoming suddenly withdrawn. "Nothing much. Don't worry," he said dryly.

"What does that mean?"

"Exactly what you think it means," he snapped.

Isabel hesitated. Perhaps the moment had come when she could lead him into discussing that subject he had so assiduously avoided. But she would have to be very careful.

"You never talk about women, Paul," she said, thinking that this would be a start of sorts. Perhaps, if she got him to tell her a little about his relations with various women, she could guide him tactfully, slowly into talking about sex. Perhaps she should start with his mother.

"You've hardly ever mentioned your mother to me, Paul."

"I guess because she wasn't really very important to me. Unfortunately, she wasn't really very important to anyone."

Had she been, Paul went on, it might have been easier for him—he might have found some comfort there. But Barbara, who had obviously resigned herself to the fact that she was unloved by her husband, distanced herself from her only child as well. She hired the appropriate nursemaids and governesses, making sure there was always someone who would go up to Shropshire, and busied herself with long lunches at the Colony, teas at the Plaza, fashion shows at Bergdorf's, openings at the Whitney, facials at Arden's, and an occasional matinee. She hated Shropshire and its lack of these urban amenities and pleasures but dutifully put in her time there, always bringing with her a massive supply of books, magazines, and aspirin.

Barbara spent her Shropshire days mostly in her room, the door closed, and Paul never felt comfortable going into the hushed bedroom with its flowered wallpaper, its huge, old canopy bed, its lacy curtains which had once belonged to Barbara's mother. The room was so carefully arranged—petit-point pillows always placed in the same order on the chaise longue, *Vogue* and *Harper's Bazaar* stacked according to date on the wicker stand—that Paul felt he was an intruder, a blot on the decor. He wondered if perhaps William felt that way too. His father, who had his own bedroom across the hall, rarely came into Barbara's room except occasionally to retrieve the New York *Times* or the Shropshire *Journal* or look for a cuff link.

"Did you ever think about your parents having separate bedrooms?" Isabel asked.

Yes, and when Paul got to be a teen-ager, he even speculated on whether or not his parents had any sex life at all. Not only did they sleep in separate rooms, they never seemed to touch except briefly, with a light kiss, when acknowledging a birthday or a Christmas present. Paul knew that kiss well, since it was the only one he ever got from his mother. His father's main show of affection was a clasp on the shoulder, an imitation of the more powerful clasp that Uncle Ernest gave which often came close to making Paul stumble. But if William and Barbara had now finished with passion, Paul knew with certainty that William was not living a monastic life. And it surely wasn't difficult for him to attract women. William was, after all, the most handsome and the most glamorous of the Kingmans. When Paul and his father went out together, Paul always noticed how women turned around to look at his father. A female clerk in the Shropshire IGA would manage to wait on William before anyone else, and even the sour-faced cook, Bertha, would smile and flutter whenever he came into the kitchen.

William was, in fact, so dashing, Paul told Isabel, that had he not been a Kingman, he would have most likely been a playboy. He loved to dance, to drive low-slung foreign cars, had a taste for rare wines and haute cuisine. But Kingmans didn't become playboys, they became scholars, lawyers, and physicians. And so William's one attempt to break out of the mold was quickly stopped.

Paul had first heard the story from Uncle Ernest and Aunt Natalie when he was a teen-ager. Apparently, William, spending a summer in the Loire Valley at the end of his first year of medical school, almost didn't return. An aunt of Sebastian Rush's, whom the family had had nothing to do with since, had invited William to stay with her at her chateau.

"And I think he simply became besotted on foie gras," said Aunt Natalie.

"Not to mention the charms of his all-too-generous hostess," Ernest added. "I just took a quick trip abroad and ended all that." He grinned at Paul with a man-to-man intimacy. "Well, even a Kingman can be a little irregular from time to time."

"But not when a semester is about to begin," inserted Aunt Natalie. "Your father simply chose to sow his wild oats a bit too late in the summer season."

Isabel was clearly amused by the story. "It's curious to think of," she said, "but though scholar after scholar and psychiatrist after psychiatrist has analyzed Don Juan, no one has ever written a word about the personality of Don Juan's children."

"And I can tell you why," Paul said. "It makes for pretty dull reading."

Addie had agreed to take the night shift when Dolores Mendoza's little boy came down with strep throat. Usually, this shift was active—there was likely to be some hysteric panicked by the dark or awakened by a nightmare, but tonight there was a deafening silence which was making Addie restless. She paced down the hall, her flashlight in her pocket, looking in on Mrs. Rossiter, who was due to be discharged the next day and so was likely to be agitated, checking Francesa Fabrizzio, who had been started on a new drug. Everything was fine, she informed Dr. Eakeley, who was obviously impatient to get back to his poker game.

It was three o'clock when the light went on above the door of Room 43.

"Can I get you anything?" Addie asked as she opened the door.

"A sleeping pill," Paul said. "I've been trying, but there's no way I'm going to get to sleep tonight without it." He was standing by the window, and when Addie looked over at his bed, she saw evidence of just how restless he had been. The sheets were crumpled, the blankets twisted.

"Would you like me to change your linens too?" she offered. "That might help."

"Oh, you don't have to bother. It doesn't really matter," he said.

"No, no, it's no bother at all. Besides, I have nothing else to do." She smiled, went out, and returned with a pill, fresh linens, and a small glass of orange juice.

"Here, I'll get this side," he said, taking one end of the sheet. "I'm an expert at hospital corners."

Each standing on a different side of the bed, they looked at each other and Addie thought she saw Paul reach out his hand. The next thing she knew they were in each other's arms, kissing as they pulled each other down into the still unmade bed. Addie was amazed—this was exactly what she wanted to happen, but she never thought in a million years would.

It was as though life had suddenly given her the chance to write her own script. And emboldened by this sudden realization, she thrust her tongue into Paul's warm mouth and started unbuttoning his pajamas. He seemed to draw away, and she felt a reserve coming over him. Maybe he thought she was unprepared. Maybe he thought she was unwilling. Was that possible? Maybe he was just shy. She took his hand and placed it on her breast. His fingers moved, he began to respond. Now she led him further, taking his other hand and placing it on the damp skin on the inside of her thigh. All the while she kissed him, pressing herself against his growing hardness.

"Wait a minute," she said as she stood up and, in a few expert gestures, managed to get out of all her clothes. Addie had always been proud of her body—it was slender and yet, she knew, sensual. And now as she caught a glimpse of herself in the mirror over Paul's dresser, she noticed that in these flattering soft shadows, she looked even better than usual. She would have liked to have lingered, showing off her body to Paul for a few more moments. But she knew they had better hurry. What she was doing now was insane enough. She could lose her job, her license even. She turned away from the mirror and stepped toward Paul when she realized that he was not looking at her at all but had buried his face in the pillow. He was sobbing, and there was nothing Addie could do to stop the terrible shudders.

As much as she hated to, she had no choice but to call Dr. Dunne, to spill the whole embarrassing story and risk being shipped back to Carthage, Missouri, in disgrace. But to Addie's astonishment, she wasn't fired after all. The amazing Dr. Dunne not only managed to calm Paul down and keep Addie's ill-advised escapade a secret, but she also didn't seem fazed by the idea of sex between nurse and patient. And so, though Addie knew with a depressing certainty that she had lost her chance with Paul Kingman, she was at least cheered by the fact that she hadn't lost her job.

It had taken Isabel a long time to calm Paul down. In fact, she had had to sit up all night with him, talking to him, soothing. As she sat now, looking at his sleeping face with its youthful, almost boyish contours, she thought of the intensity of emotion he had shown. Did you have to be twenty-three to feel so deeply? She thought of herself at twenty-three and of her own overwhelming sense of confusion and anguish. Paul would never forget this night and his feelings of pain, she knew that, just as she would never forget that terrible night in Swampscott and the agonizing weeks and months that followed it.

5

ALTHOUGH THE MAY SUN was strong, the air was still brisk along the beach at Swampscott. A gentle wind came off the sea, carrying with it a fresh and salty aroma. Isabel pulled her bulky gray sweater around her tightly—it was much cooler walking along the deserted beach than she had thought it would be. Still, the sea-filled air felt good on her face, lifting her mood, while the steady sound of the ocean soothed her, lulling her in some hypnotic way and keeping her anxiety from taking hold of her.

But perhaps it wasn't the sea at all that kept her calm, despite what was facing her in just a few hours. Perhaps it was the fact that she had finally made a decision. After months of vacillation, of hoping against hope that Bryan might change his mind and reappear in her life, she had finally reached a point of no return. She was in her fifth month, and there was no way of waiting any longer—in fact, she knew all too well that she had waited too long already. The doctor had looked as if she were insane when she had appeared at his office that morning, asking for an abortion at such a late point in her pregnancy. After all, it had been more than three months since the son of his old friend, Charlie Madison, had called to ask for help.

At that time Edward Lancaster had readily agreed. An obstetrician who had brought too many unwanted babies into this world and had seen the unhappy consequences—forced and bitter marriages, ruined careers, neurotic children—Dr. Lancaster had at one point in his life made abortion his own private cause, his stand against what he believed to be the reactionary and destructive sentiments of the world around him. He was a man with unwavering faith in the ability of the individual to make choices for himself and bristled at the misguided paternalism of a society which set up sanctions and barriers about matters that were not society's concern. But an abortion in the first trimester was one thing. What Isabel demanded was another.

"How could you—an obviously intelligent woman—have been so damned stupid?" the small, balding, sharp-featured man demanded, shaking his head incredulously.

Isabel could find no answer. How could she possibly explain what had been going on within her during these last months? She had been a veritable battleground of violent conflicts, a ravaged field of warring hopes and desires. Part of her planned on Bryan's return and on his assumption of paternal responsibility. Another part of her recognized the total lack of reality in this hope and wished instead for a spontaneous abortion, a sign that God had intervened to keep her from the temptation of committing a mortal sin. All of this tension was reflected in nights of tormented dreams. There was the repeated nightmare in which Isabel had had an abortion only to find Bryan arriving moments later to tell her that he wanted the baby after all. There was another in which Bishop O'Connor, after humiliating her publicly in front of her mother, her professors, and the nuns at St. Matthew's, had thrown her and the bloody infant in her arms into a blazing and bottomless inferno.

Isabel could say nothing of these nightmares and conflicts to Dr. Lancaster. All she could say was, "I'm Catholic. It wasn't an easy decision."

"It's never an easy decision," Dr. Lancaster said coolly.

"I don't know," Isabel said. "I don't know. I only know that I need your help."

"And I could have given it to you easily, had you had the good sense to come to me when Bryan first called. But now . . . No, I don't think there is anything I can do for you."

Isabel was stunned. It had never occurred to her that Dr. Lancaster might refuse her.

"But you can't say no. Who will I go to?" she cried, her voice cracking with panic.

"You should have thought of that before," Dr. Lancaster said, standing up in an obvious gesture of dismissal.

"I can't have this child," Isabel sobbed. "You have to understand—it would destroy my life."

Dr. Lancaster shook his head. "I'm sorry, there's nothing I can do for you."

Isabel didn't move. There was no way that she was going to leave this office without getting Dr. Lancaster to change his mind and help her. But how to do it? Tears, she recognized, the very tears that were now streaming down her face, were hardly enough to move this man who had surely seen too many women cry this way before. What would reach him, Isabel realized in a sudden flash of awareness, was something that touched his sense of himself as a humanitarian, as someone who made sacrifices and took risks for the sake of others and mankind at large.

"Did Bryan tell you anything about me?" she asked, her voice suddenly quite calm.

"Certainly not. Bryan's far too discreet."

"Then you don't know, Dr. Lancaster, that I'm a medical student. And though I suppose that makes my actions seem even more irresponsible, it's also one of the reasons why you have to help me. I'm on scholarship and if I have to drop out now, I'll never be able to go back."

Dr. Lancaster sat down again. He had obviously been struck by what Isabel was saying.

Isabel went on talking. "Medicine means everything to me. You more than anyone must understand that."

"I do," Dr. Lancaster said slowly, "but . . ."

Isabel reached out and grabbed his hands. "Please, please," she entreated.

Dr. Lancaster stared straight at her, considering her. And then he nodded. He was persuaded at last. This did not mean he did not have his doubts, he made clear to her, and he insisted on explaining at great length just exactly what was involved in the operation. At this stage, there could be no ordinary scraping of the uterine wall—he would have to induce labor so that Isabel's own contractions would expel the fetus. The image made Isabel wince. But Dr. Lancaster simply continued, ignoring her reaction. The process would be a lengthy one—it might even take the night. It would also be painful. Furthermore, as Isabel of course must know, even at this stage of her medical education, what he was about to perform was no simple curettage—a procedure with minimal risk. Instead, Isabel would undergo something a good deal closer to childbirth, and the risk would be commensurate. And all the more so because he could not keep Isabel as long as he would like. She could not stay beyond Sunday and, in any case, his small clinic was not equipped for all the possible contingencies. Should anything at all go wrong after she left him, she should go immediately to the hospital. He had found in his experience that few questions were asked once the illegal operation was over and done with.

Had she understood everything? Had she any questions? All right, then, he would see her at about four-thirty. Because it was Friday, his office hours were over at four and his last patient would be out not too long after that. In the meantime, why didn't she take a stroll along the beach, he suggested, cautioning her against stopping in for coffee or, in fact, eating or drinking anything.

This last bit of advice was hardly necessary, Isabel thought to herself, as she now sat down on a gray stone seawall looking out at a jetty filled with raucous gulls. During the entire time of her pregnancy, she had hardly eaten a thing. She had totally lost her taste for meat, had even begun to gag on cheese, and for the past few weeks, had lived almost solely on crackers and tea and an occasional apple. It might as well have been Lent. She might as well have been in prison. The only blessing to come from her constant nausea was the fact that she hadn't gained an ounce and so her condition had escaped notice, even from the sharp eyes of her mother. Frances had, however, remarked continually as to how peaked Isabel looked and how glum her daughter seemed. She assumed it all had to do with Isabel's broken heart, which in a rare display of tact, Frances decided not to discuss.

The only one who knew that Isabel was pregnant was Mark Singer, her co-worker in the lab, and she found herself drawn into a new close relationship with him because of this. Mark, who had always adored Isabel, welcomed this intimacy despite its peculiar basis. He was the kind of unassuming, nondescript person who fades into backgrounds, and Isabel had never paid very much attention to him before. Now, however, he became one of the most important people in her life, the only one she could talk to about her inner turmoil. Mark never said much—at the beginning at least. But as the weeks went by and he saw Isabel more and more frozen into immobility, he became emboldened. He felt called upon to bring a touch of sanity into her unhinged sense of things. It was he, in fact, who finally forced her into coming out to see Dr. Lancaster, clinching his argument with the fact that it was now the conveniently empty reading period before exam week. Mark had offered to go with her to see the doctor, but she had refused, telling him first that he ought to be spending every moment in the library right before exams and second that it was stupid for a medical student to have anything at all to do with an abortion, if he could possibly help it.

But now, as she walked from the beach down the neat suburban streets, she was almost sorry she had refused Mark's offer. She had never felt so alone in her life, and she felt more alone still as she walked up the flagstone steps into Dr. Lancaster's deserted waiting room. The doctor must have heard her come in, for just as she entered, the door leading to the inner office opened. Was she all right, the doctor asked. It would take him a few more minutes to finish up some paper work. Isabel, thankful for the brief respite, nervously picked up a magazine and leafed through it without seeing the pages. Suddenly, she felt a faint movement inside her. A flutter. A kick.

"Oh, God," she moaned. She threw down the magazine and flung open the door to Dr. Lancaster's office. The surprised doctor looked up from his papers.

"I can't wait any longer," Isabel said. "Please, let's get it over with."

The whole process took twelve hours, but it wasn't until another day had passed that Dr. Lancaster felt it was safe for Isabel to leave. Even then, he refused to let her go unaccompanied so that she had to telephone Mark after all. The next two days, Isabel followed Dr. Lancaster's orders, kept to her bed, and took her temperature every four hours. But the third day, she felt stronger and insisted on going to the library. Mark, who had called her faithfully two and three times a day, came along with her. She was nuts, he told her, to be out of bed, but as long as she was going to start marching around, he wasn't going to leave her side. Anyway, being with her right before exams was the best thing that could ever happen to him, he told her jokingly. With Isabel studying every minute, he had no choice but to follow suit, and he knew that if he went on this way, he would be better prepared for these exams than he had been for any in his life. Isabel's diligence was contagious. All semester, as their friendship grew, so had his academic performance. Still, his concentration would never be quite as intense as hers, he thought, as he looked over at her now sitting in an upright tweed armchair silhouetted against the huge, pink-tinged glass wall of the new Bogner Library. The sunlight almost made a halo of her hair, as she solemnly stared down at the heavy volume resting on the arm of the chair. He found his own eyes following the direction of hers, and as he looked down, he started. The green tweed of the chair was glistening with moisture. The tweed beneath Isabel had turned to crimson, soaked with what he realized was Isabel's blood. He rushed to her side, noticing suddenly that her face was stripped of color—ashen—deathlike.

"Don't move," he told her.

She looked at him, not comprehending.

"Stay in that chair. I'm calling for an ambulance."

The glass disk diffusing the overhead light acted as a mirror so that Isabel could see herself—her own abdomen—surrounded by sterile white sheets. Please, she thought, I don't want to see myself being cut open, and if they don't put something in my way, I won't be able to avoid it, to close my eyes to keep from looking at it. A sting in her arm interrupted her thoughts.

"Count backward from one hundred," someone commanded.

She obeyed. "100 . . . 99 . . . 98 . . . 97 . . ."

Another voice, this one a woman's. No, a man's. No, a man and a woman talking to each other.

"You look much better now, Mr. Goldstein," a soothing voice, a warm maternal voice, said. "Your color is fine."

"But my prick ain't," a scratchy old man's voice grumbled. "You should know from such pain."

A searing, hot, stabbing feeling cut across her stomach. You should know from such pain, her own thoughts echoed the old man's voice.

She was out again, and this time, when she came to, she wished she could be unconscious again. The violent contractions made her feel as though a sadistic giant was kneading her, pummeling her from the inside and then from the outside and sometimes both at once. She felt herself covered with perspiration, overwhelmed with nausea. Surely, this was the worst night she had ever spent. She fumbled next to her. The first button merely turned on the light. The second sent for the nurse.

"I'm sorry. There's nothing I can give you beyond a couple of aspirins," the wrinkled crone in the white uniform told her. "There's nothing on your chart, and there isn't a doctor around."

"I'm in agony," Isabel said through clenched teeth. "You've got to do something for me."

"Look, you're not the only one on the floor, and I can't waste any more time." The crone disappeared to comfort someone else.

Isabel wanted to sob, but her stitches made her realize that it would be too painful to cry.

* * *

The crone had been replaced by a cheerful, apple-cheeked cherub of a nurse. Isabel thought how perfect that the crone came by night and the cherub by day. The smiling woman washed Isabel's face, brushed her hair, and gingerly changed her nightgown, chatting all the time about how pretty Isabel was, what a warm, lovely day it had turned out to be, how nice Isabel's flowers looked. Isabel turned around and noticed the bunch of lilacs sitting on the windowsill. The perfume was filling the room. The nurse brought her the card, and Isabel was ashamed of herself and her feelings of disappointment when she saw that the flowers had come from Mark. Who else would have sent them, after all?

The nurse propped Isabel up in bed so that when Dr. Wilcox arrived, she felt she must look a bit more alive, somewhat more human than she had just an hour before. The pain was still there, but here in the daylight and sunshine, everything seemed less harsh.

Dr. Wilcox, a tall, broad, pink-faced man, with closely cropped hair and wire-rimmed glasses, spared no extra time on his patients. He told Isabel—who, he understood, was a medical student, a fact which enabled him to talk to her man to man, so to speak—that her operation had been a hysterectomy. Acute inflammation had evidently set in following her previous operation and by the time Dr. Wilcox saw her, there was nothing else to be done but totally remove the uterus.

"The uterus?" she repeated. She couldn't believe what he had said.

Dr. Wilcox must have been describing the operation in detail for her. At least, she thought that was what he was talking about, but she really wasn't following him. All she kept thinking was that she had just killed the only child she would ever have. It was a punishment and a just one, she might have believed yesterday—another day. Now she simply thought it a dirty trick.

By Wednesday, Isabel was walking and alert enough to realize not only that she had missed her first exam but that it was also her usual night to see her mother. The story she had used to cover herself last weekend—that she needed the hospital reference room to complete a late paper—certainly wouldn't suffice. Exam period was as good an excuse as any, though, she thought, as she walked down the hall to call her mother on the pay phone. She dialed her mother's office and asked for Mrs. Dunne's extension. There was no answer. Could she try another line for her? the operator asked. No, Isabel answered. She would call back later.

As she was walking back to her room, Isabel saw Mark. He told her he had taken it on himself to talk to her professors, and all of them, even crusty Dr. Schacter, had been wonderfully understanding and had agreed to give Isabel makeup exams as soon as she was well enough to take them.

"And I bet they wouldn't have done it for just anyone," he added.

Isabel was relieved. That was one bit of good news, she thought bitterly. Did he want to know what kind of operation she had just had? He knew already. He was sorry. There was an awkward silence which Isabel broke by telling him that she had to try to get hold of her mother. Would he mind waiting while she went to the phone? Of course not. He had plenty of reading to do anyway.

This time, someone did pick up the extension, but it wasn't Frances Dunne.

"Is that you, Isabel?" a familiar voice queried at the other end. "Oh, Isabel, you poor darling. I've been trying to reach you at the dormitory all day and I've left messages all over the medical school. This is Molly, your poor mother's friend. Do you remember me? Molly Herbert."

"Yes, yes, of course I remember you. But what's happened? Where's my mother?"

"Oh, Isabel, you must be brave. Your mother . . . It was her heart."

Isabel must have screamed, because suddenly Mark was there next to her, his arms around her.

Dr. Arne Larsen, a German-educated Dane who had come to this country at age thirty-two, right after the outbreak of World War II, had become one of the key figures in American psychiatry and in the study of human development throughout the world. Endowed with a superior innate intelligence and a first-class imagination, steeped in the classic tradition of Freud, Larsen had become absorbed in problems of individual identity. In fact, it was he who had first introduced the concept of "identity crisis" in his renowned study of St. Francis of Assisi. He was fascinated by the relative effects of secular and religious experience on the formation of personality, and his erudite theories regarding the crisis of adolescence and young adulthood had won plaudits from psychiatrists and social historians both in the United States and abroad. It was a coup for Boston University Medical School to have gotten him on the faculty. And it was while he was on this faculty that he came in contact with Isabel Dunne.

Larsen found himself attracted immediately to this young woman's case. Isabel Dunne seemed to him a compendium of every tension, every conflict, every ambivalence, that he had ever been concerned with. This lovely young medical student was at a stage in her life when she was clearly going through an identity crisis and one of an extremely violent nature. Her mother's recent death had thrust her suddenly into assuming the role of adult—a role that, in Larsen's terms, meant being responsible solely to oneself and not to any authority figure. Her abortion had triggered extraordinary guilt and had set in motion a falling away from the security of her religion. And the love affair that had culminated in her abortion had left her with a devastating feeling of inadequacy.

But it wasn't only the nature of Isabel's anxieties and conflicts or the challenge of treating them that drew Larsen to her. It was that Isabel Dunne struck him as a very special person, a superior young woman who must be allowed, indeed encouraged, to achieve her purpose in life. She was, he knew, a superb student, and Larsen suspected from the first as well that she might have the makings of a superb psychiatrist. But first, of course, he had to bring her out of her present acute depression, to restore her to a fully functioning human being. No, he thought, "restore" wasn't quite the right word. After all, she had never functioned fully. But now she would.

Even though Larsen had been trained as a Freudian, he had gradually become more and more eclectic in his methods. Not for him was the role of silent, unresponsive listener who never raised an eyebrow, ventured a smile, or showed any feelings at all in response to a patient's revelations. For one thing, Larsen himself always had too much to say, and he simply could not repress his need to comment, to evaluate, to direct. For another, he was too active and enthusiastic a participant in his patient's recovery. He was in a position, at this point in his life, to take only those patients he could care about deeply and whose future mental health had a significance wider than their individual well-being, some far-reaching social consequence. Among his patients had been America's most dynamic Secretary of State, a man whose hunger for power had begun to thrust him into bouts of irrational rages; a Harvard-educated novelist who had problems sorting out his creative impulses from his destructive ones and who produced novel after novel, child after child, but almost destroyed in one way or another each of his many wives; and a Russian ballerina, recently defected to the United States and plagued by nightmares of seizure and with guilt at having left her two-year-old son behind, having traded him, in fact, for freedom and wealth.

With each of these patients, Larsen developed not only a close rapport but also a close friendship. With Isabel, he took on the role of parent as well—impatient when she held herself back with self-doubt, proud when her achievements were commensurate with her gifts, and loving and supportive throughout. At the time that he began to treat her, Isabel was in a state of acute neurotic disturbance because of the combined traumas of her mother's death and her own abortion and hysterectomy. But it was not these that she fixated upon—it was instead Bryan Madison. She was overcome with feelings of desperation, inferiority, and inadequacy in the face of his desertion of her. Had she been truly worthy, she kept repeating to Larsen, Bryan would not have left her. She deserved to be punished, she wanted to die, she told him over and over again.

At the outset of her treatment, Larsen was helpless to release Isabel from the iron hold this depression had on her. He was unable to lead her toward any objective viewing of her predicament or to encourage her to examine its deep-rooted causes. For Isabel, at this point, was totally unreachable. She hardly seemed to hear what Larsen had to say during their sessions, much less comprehend and react to it. Her attention seemed to wander even in the midst of one of her own sentences. She tried to explain these lapses by telling Larsen how tired she was. Her nights were sleepless, even after she had begun to use the medication he had prescribed. And she was always so sleepy, dozing off during the day, her eyes closing on her when she tried to read or study. She certainly couldn't attend the review sessions generously offered her by her professors or dare to take any of her makeup examinations.

But finally, as time wore on, Larsen chipped away at her defenses until Isabel found herself responding at last, unable to resist the enveloping affection of the infinitely experienced and profoundly wise psychiatrist. He deftly led her to the shocking realization that the grief she experienced at her mother's death was not so much a reaction to losing her mother as it was to her failure to deeply feel. Isabel may have been everything to Frances Dunne, but Frances Dunne could never have been everything to her daughter. Of course, Isabel appreciated her mother's sacrifices; but she resented the fact that along with them, her mother gave her no real happiness. There was warmth, but never fun of any kind. There was never a giggle, never a laugh, the two never baked cookies or cakes together, never sang songs together, never exchanged a funny story. But why, then, if she did not really suffer at the loss of her mother, did she feel so bereft? she asked. Because, Larsen explained, she had lost something even more crucial—the chance, however remote, that her relationship with her mother might have changed.

As for her father, who died when she was two, she had, of course, no memory of him at all. And her mother never mentioned anything about him, not even his name. It was as if he never existed. Larsen explained to Isabel that it was inevitable that her mother felt a deep resentment at being widowed at twenty and especially since she had no money, no family, and a tiny child. Moreover, it was not uncommon for widows of any age or circumstances to bear grudges against their husbands—even those they most adored—feeling in some subconscious way that they had been deserted, that if their husbands had really wanted to live, it would have been possible to have done so. Such sentiments as these, Larsen said, might well explain her mother's long, unbroken silence about the father of her child.

But now, in any case, the tall, stooped, white-haired doctor, with the faint, lilting inflection in his speech, became to Isabel the father she never had, the mother who had disappointed her, and even the perfect replacement for Bishop O'Connor, who declined in importance in Isabel's life as she found herself growing further and further from the church. She kept up appearances in order to keep her scholarship, she guiltily admitted to Dr. Larsen, and she visited the bishop periodically after her mother's death to continue reporting to him on her progress. If the bishop perceived that she was less than devout these days, he never showed it.

Arne Larsen, in contrast, with his bold open features, was not a man to keep any of his feelings hidden. He had a technique, Isabel remembered later, which was based very largely on shock. Where therapy was in most cases a slow, internalized process in which a patient discovered step by cautious step sides of himself he had never consciously acknowledged, therapy in Larsen's hands was often an attack—a cannon blast in which the doctor told the patient, outright, bluntly, matter-of-factly, things about himself that immediately decimated all the patient's defenses. Like the day he told her that much of what she had felt for Bryan Madison wasn't love at all, but rather jealousy.

"And why shouldn't you have been jealous of him, Isabel? He's rich, you're poor. He has family, you have none. Everything has been given to him, everything you have you have had to earn for yourself. Why shouldn't you begrudge him his privilege and want to snatch it for yourself?"

She was stunned at what Larsen was saying. She had always thought of herself as being above envy and had taken pride in the fact that, although she certainly had little enough as a child, she had never coveted the possessions or advantages of her schoolmates. The only times she had ever allowed herself to express any dissatisfaction at all with her own situation had been in her daydreams. But of course, he was right. She wanted what Bryan had and was angry that it was he who had it and not she.

"You're not only jealous of him, you also hate him," Larsen told her another time, at another session.

And the thought made her burst into tears. It was true, she did hate Bryan and had hated him even while she loved him and even before he had deserted her.

"Do you understand that hatred?" Larsen had asked when she had acknowledged the truth in his perception.

Suddenly, she did know. She hated him because he made her hate herself and what she had come to see as her shabby, ignorant world.

Another day, Larsen did almost all the talking during Isabel's session. He wanted to explain to her something more about her feelings for Bryan and he could do so best, he told her, by telling her about a theory of love he had evolved some years before.

"When we are children, we all make plans for what we want to be," Larsen began, "a nurse, a doctor, a fireman. But we also make these plans in another way as well, for each of us creates what I call an 'ego-ideal'—the person we see ourselves as, that we hope to become when we are fully developed. We build this ego-ideal out of bits and pieces of others. We might take the knowledge of a teacher, the good looks of a movie star, the bravery of a hero in a book we've read, the kindness of a grandmother. Whomever and wherever we take the qualities from, we put them all together to create this ideal, this person we want someday to be. And we carry this image with us into actual adulthood—changing it here and there along the way. Still, sadly enough, we never do become that person. But one day, we come across someone who we believe is, who somehow reminds us enough of this ideal for us to think we have actually met its incarnation. And it is this person we fall in love with."

"So Bryan, you're suggesting, is my own construction?"

"No, not exactly. What I'm saying is that the person you fell in love with was an image of yourself, the person you yourself wanted to be. What I'm saying is that the words 'I love you' translate into 'I want to be you.'"

She *had* wanted to be Bryan Madison, she could realize that now. Not simply to have what he had but to actually be him, to see the world as he saw it, to have the world view her as it did him. But recognizing all these feelings and admitting them to Larsen was not to be rid of them. It was at best to learn how to keep them under control, to prevent them interfering as they had with her ongoing life.

This much Isabel was able to accomplish. And so, though she had been a failure with Bryan Madison, she was nevertheless a success in almost everything else. Throughout medical school, for the next three years, she remained at the very top of her class—with no small help from Arne Larsen, who continued to make it possible for her to keep her mind free and able to absorb the immense amount of knowledge being offered her. She had little time for any social life, any friends, but that in any case had always been Isabel's pattern. Mark Singer, who had been two years ahead of her in school, had gradually moved out of her life. There was the simple fact that he had taken an internship in Providence and got to Boston very infrequently. But more important, about a year after her mother's death, Mark had proposed marriage to her and their friendship had never quite survived her refusal. She was truly fond of Mark and regretted hurting him, as she knew she must have. She had grown, under Larsen's tutelage and because of her own experience, acutely sensitive to the pain of others. It was sometimes almost as if she had antennae the way she could pick up on the slightest vibrations of discomfort. But Isabel had no intention of marrying anyone—not now and probably not ever. Larsen thought she was being shortsighted, not allowing for the possibility of change. But the rigidity of her Catholic background had been hard to dispel and continued to exert an influence on her decisions, often giving them an implacable quality. Well, Larsen didn't really mind Isabel's choice to concentrate all her energies on her analysis and on her work. She would make a great psychiatrist and because of this, a great disciple. His immortality was at stake in the future of Isabel Dunne. And in nourishing her, he was also nourishing his own colossal ego.

Isabel did become Larsen's disciple, and she continually found herself grateful for the guidance of her mentor. If once he saved her sanity, now he helped craft her professional being, directing her, reassuring her, exploring with her the endless problems not so much of the psychiatric patient but of the psychiatrist.

"Of course, you're attracted to Terence Shea," he told her one day when she came to him guilt-ridden, discomforted by the feelings aroused in her by the handsome young man she was now treating in therapy. A former priest who was presently an instructor in theology at Boston University, Terence Shea had come to the clinic because of his growing disgust at his own uncontrollable promiscuity. Isabel, now a resident in psychiatry, had been assigned his case by Larsen, who felt that her experience with Catholicism would aid her in treating Shea. And, of course, it did. As she listened to him describe the strange and dramatic mixture of physical pleasure and mental pain he felt when having sexual relations, she remembered her own confusing anguish. And having analyzed and understood her own conflicts, she was now able to bring these insights to bear on his. She could show him how his pleasure was actually not in conflict with his pain, but was augmented by it, how guilt itself was enhancing. She could share with him too the desire, even the need, for self-punishment. For she too understood the conditioning that anything which was delicious and delightful had to be the temptation of the devil, that the most beautiful rose had the most piercing thorns, and that in order to pluck it one had inevitably to bleed.

But if Isabel could relate to Terence Shea on the grounds of their shared religious inheritance, she also found herself relating to him in another way as well. Sitting across from him in her tiny office, watching his handsome face as he told her of his latest sexual conquest, as he described in great detail the process of his seduction, Isabel had been startled to find herself growing aroused. She had thought until then that all her sexual feelings were dead, buried together with her dead infant. She had assumed that, like the sisters at St. Matthew's, she would spend the remainder of her life in celibacy, her stimulation and satisfaction coming from other sources. If the nuns' came from religion and their work with students, hers would come from psychiatry and her work with patients. But her response to Terence Shea had shattered all that. She knew she wanted him, that she wanted to be the young woman he now described so vividly. She wanted those breasts to be her breasts, those lips to be her own. She wanted to feel his strong body next to hers. And she hated herself for those longings.

"As usual, you're judging yourself too harshly. What if you are attracted to a patient," Larsen observed.

"How can you take what I'm telling you so lightly?" Isabel was almost angry at what she took to be his permissiveness.

"Come, come, Isabel. When will you stop being the little Catholic girl looking for someone to tell you to stand in the corner or rap you on the knuckles? You're a woman, aren't you, even if you are a psychiatrist. You're not a textbook, you're not a machine. And so you have human feelings, human responses. All people ever talk about is the reaction of patients to their doctor, how they love him or hate him, make emotional transference to and away from him. But what about the doctor? Can't he do a little bit of transferring himself?"

"You mean, you've felt this way, too, with your patients?" She was truly surprised. It had never occurred to her that the august Arne Larsen could ever have felt attraction for one of his own patients.

"Of course, I have had such feelings. If I have a very beautiful patient, Isabel, don't you think I notice it? When I listen to the erotic experiences of others, don't you think I'm sometimes aroused? I'm human, I'm not a stone. I find some patients attractive and others in fact strike me in quite an opposite way. And that's the real danger," he said to Isabel. "For if a patient attracts you, you can use those feelings to help him, but if he repels you in any way, there is little you can do. Then, of course, you have no choice but to send him to someone who does not feel the way you do."

"And so you're saying that there is no danger in my feelings about Terence Shea."

"To the contrary. In fact, it's essential. It's what is going to make you a great psychiatrist, Isabel—your capacity to feel."

"I'm afraid in this instance I don't quite see what you're driving at, Arne. All I know is that at the moment, I'm being drawn through this man into my own emotions, into my own being, rather than into him and his problems."

"But that's the point. They really aren't as separate as you think. Terence is awakening feelings in you that, yes, you need to confront for your own sake, but that you also need to confront for his sake as well. You see, what is happening between you and Terence is at the heart of his conflict. He purposely arouses you, flirts with you because you are a woman and every woman must desire him. How exciting that you can live through this experience and understand for him what he cannot understand for himself. Now, you know what his effect on a woman is, and you can also perceive in what way he is inviting it. He tells you he does nothing, that women are the aggressors. But now you know that isn't true, that he has maneuvered their response just as he has maneuvered yours."

With Terence Shea, Larsen had soothed her by absolving her guilt, reassuring her that her reactions were appropriate, positive, useful even. And, of course, they proved to be. Learning to rely on her instincts, to trust and use her own emotions, she ended up being able to guide Terence to a point where he was at last capable of sustaining his first stable and satisfying relationship with a woman, a young assistant professor at the university. Isabel's success with Terence was to be repeated with other patients, and Larsen was clearly elated. He beamed as he described to colleagues the inherent gift that Isabel had for reaching through to a patient—a gift which he had perceived in her and was now helping to develop.

But if Larsen lauded her to others, alone with Isabel he wasn't always so full of praise. Sometimes, and especially when she ventured a move, an idea, that did not follow directly from his teachings, he grew not simply angry at her but, in fact, furious. There was the time, for instance, when Larsen was away on a brief lecture tour and one of Isabel's patients, Phyllis Mitchell, a fortyish unmarried bookkeeper who had recently lost both her parents, went into a state of deep depression. Phyllis was unable to sleep, could hardly eat, and suffered from violent headaches which had no organic cause. Isabel, suddenly terrified at the responsibility for this woman's life, had consulted one of the senior staff members who suggested that Isabel prescribe lithium, one of the mood-stabilizing drugs. Isabel knew how Larsen felt about drugs—to him they were an evasion, even worse, a means of confusing the symptoms so that they were no longer recognizable and thus no longer available for treatment. But she felt helpless now to follow Larsen's rules without the support of Larsen himself standing by her. She could not risk this woman's life.

Larsen did not accept her logic.

"How could you do something so stupid?" he raged, on his return. "I can see others who cannot use their own human insight, who can neither diagnose an ailment nor treat it, resorting to chemicals to solve their problems. But you, you . . ."

"But I was so afraid she might take her own life . . ." Isabel stammered in self-defense.

"And if you were, you stay with her—twenty-four hours, if necessary. You soothe her, you talk to her. What she was going through then might have supplied just the opportunity you needed. But what did you do instead? You put her emotions to sleep so that not you, not she, not anyone, could be in touch with them."

The tears were welling in Isabel's eyes. Of course, it had been the easier way out, and she vowed silently that she would never allow herself to take such a path again.

And she never did, so that conflicts between Isabel and Larsen became extremely rare. Her work was going better and better, and, young as she was, she was beginning to develop a reputation as a brilliant analyst, able to pierce the barriers erected by the most inaccessible of patients, of being able to succeed with them when others had failed. Her directness with these patients, while it was viewed with a certain amount of disfavor and suspicion by the more traditional psychoanalysts on the hospital staff, was continually encouraged by Larsen. He obviously favored her above all his other students and she, in turn, made herself his most devoted disciple. And, as it turned out, she was also his last. Suffering from emphysema which left him in his last year totally dependent on the oxygen he always had to carry with him and which tinged his face with a pale blue cast, he stayed on in Boston to see Isabel through her residency and to secure for her a position on the hospital staff. He then left to spend his last few months in his native village in Denmark.

His departure left a tremendous void in Isabel's life. Larsen had come to occupy the center of her existence, much in the way Bryan once had and her mother before him. Larsen himself had never married and he and Isabel were an odd couple for those last few years—eating dinner together, going to concerts and conferences, continually consulting with one another about their patients and work. She adored him and would, she knew, always. She kept his picture—one highlighting his great shock of white hair and his piercing light eyes—on the wall across from her desk so that her eyes lit on his face whenever she looked up. Once, many years before, it might have been the idol of her religious childhood, the Virgin Mary, which hung on that wall. Later, it would be a picture of the object of her most desperate passion, Bryan Madison.

And now it was the very embodiment of her professional being, Dr. Arne Larsen.

Brilliant, dedicated, Isabel began to develop a reputation of her own —though she was only in her early thirties. She had received all kinds of offers from hospitals here and abroad, and she was just beginning to think that she should take advantage of an opportunity to move on and elsewhere when her old friend, Mark Singer, now married and practicing pediatrics in Brookline, invited her to dinner. His wife, Sylvia, a round-faced, curly-haired young woman who had filled her home with the pottery and weaving she had produced at Bennington College and who was, at the moment, expecting twins, waddled about the living room, carrying trays of guacamole, chick-peas, and stone-ground crackers. Isabel took an immediate liking to her, thinking how much better suited to Mark was the bubbling Sylvia than she herself would have been. Besides, Sylvia could give him children.

Over tequila cocktails, Isabel was introduced to Sandy Richler, an old friend of Mark's who had grown up with him in the same building on Riverside Drive in Manhattan. Sandy, a tall, broad-shouldered man with strong features softened by a good-natured grin, was an internist. But his father, Gerson Richler, was one of the leading psychiatrists in New York—in fact, head of psychiatric services at Mount Sinai Hospital.

"And despite appearances," Mark said, "I am not playing matchmaker. Sandy asked to meet you because his father has heard so much about you."

"My mission," Sandy announced, "in making this visit to Boston is, you see, not only to spend some pleasant hours with a childhood pal but also to try to tempt you, Dr. Dunne, into giving up the land of the bean and the cod and into coming down to the Big Apple. If the thought of a change like that strikes you as possible, I'm here to sing the praises of the big city, of Mount Sinai Hospital, and especially of my father. The latter I can do most sincerely, I assure you."

"Gerson's a great guy," Mark added. "He's not at all like Larsen, but he's someone I know you'd take to a lot, Isabel."

Isabel found Sandy Richler pleasant, intelligent, and wonderfully amusing. All through Sylvia's dinner—meatballs spiced with mint leaves which Sylvia explained she had made according to a Lebanese recipe and which Isabel discovered were not exactly to her taste—Sandy entertained them with stories about his difficulties in juggling his private practice on the Upper East Side of Manhattan and his public health work in Bedford-Stuyvesant, where he had discovered an astounding amount of hypertension.

"De Bakey and those Houston guys should come up to Brooklyn. They could replace all the arteries they wanted."

Isabel noticed that Sandy carefully kept himself from using a hard sell, making New York sound glamorous and Boston provincial. But at the end of the evening, when Sylvia had yawned, patted her mountainous belly, and begged everyone to stay for a brandy even though she had to fall into bed, Sandy pressed his case somewhat more forcefully. At Mount Sinai was one of the largest, most varied psychiatric facilities in the country. And Isabel would surely be fascinated and stimulated by the range of patients a New York hospital attracted.

By the time Mark had gone up to look in on Sylvia, and Sandy had walked her to her car, Isabel had decided to go down to New York. Sandy, she was to realize some months later when she had accepted Gerson Richler's offer to join his staff at Mount Sinai, had inherited from his father not only his charm but an awesome talent for persuasion. She could never seem to say no to either one of them.

6

"I'VE JUST SPOKEN to William Kingman," Gerson Richler told Isabel.

"Did he agree?" she asked.

"Completely."

The two doctors were sitting in Gerson Richler's office on the ninth floor of Gotschalk Pavilion at Mount Sinai Hospital. The room, with its spacious dimensions and corner location, had evidently been built from the start for the use of senior personnel. The phone rang and as Richler signaled to Isabel that he would be just a few minutes—a small staff matter—she occupied herself by reading the series of commendations, citations, and diplomas that in their various-sized ebony frames lined the wood-paneled walls. "A Testimonial to Gerson Richler, M.D., with Deep Appreciation from the Officers and Members of King David Lodge." "With Appreciation for his Support and Diligence in helping our Members and their Families, the Lithographers Guild, Local 423, AFL–CIO." "For his Extraordinary Generosity and Leadership, from the West Side Chapter of the Congress of Racial Equality." There was also an honorable discharge, dated December 8, 1945, from the Army Medical Corps for Colonel Gerson Richler, two diplomas from City College, declarations of membership in various professional societies, and a large picture of Gerson and Sandy at Sandy's graduation from NYU Medical School.

"So who's more handsome?" Gerson smiled at Isabel as he hung up the phone.

"How can I choose between two such dashing types. But I've always been partial to older men."

"Well, then, you'll really be taken with William Kingman," Gerson said as he leaned back in his brown leather swivel chair. "He very much wants to meet you and I gave him your number so that the two of you can work something out."

"I suppose we'll have to," Isabel said. "I certainly can't refuse to see him when he's being so cooperative, but I must admit that just the idea of William Kingman frightens me. Perhaps I've been seeing him too much through Paul's fearful eyes—identifying too fully with my patient."

"Not you, Isabel." Gerson reached over and warmly patted her hand. "Not my Isabel."

Richler now repeated in detail the conversation he had had that morning with William Kingman at Isabel's request. He had explained to the eminent surgeon that Paul's psychiatrist felt it was a good time to discharge the boy from the hospital, allow him to return to his own apartment, but continue in intensive therapy as an outpatient. Richler had then broached the stickier issue—Isabel's request that Kingman and his wife not attempt to see the boy as yet. Richler prided himself on the delicacy with which he had handled the matter, and Kingman had been gracious in accepting this arrangement. All he had asked for was a meeting between himself and Paul's doctor.

Isabel left Richler's office feeling pleased. She had not told anyone—not even the understanding Gerson—about the incident that had occurred last week between Paul and the pretty young nurse. He probably would have felt compelled to fire the girl on the spot, and Isabel thought the experience had been punishing enough for her as it was. More important, though it had been traumatic for Paul, it had also been beneficial, forcing to light a problem that he would have left buried for who knew how long. And the trauma, in any case, had not been severe enough to change anything. Certainly, it didn't force Isabel to alter the decision she had made before it had happened to have Paul released from the hospital.

His physical wounds were on their way to being healed, with the stitches removed and no signs of infection. Of course, he still had to do special exercises with a black rubber ball in order to encourage the return of dexterity in his left hand, but he hardly needed hospital supervision for that. Most important, he was, Isabel felt, in a stable enough emotional state to be able to cope with an independent life—in fact, he would probably benefit from the responsibility of living alone in his own apartment.

He had come amazingly far in his therapy in just a few weeks. It was as if he had been bottled up for the whole of his twenty-three years and

Isabel had somehow pulled the cork, allowing his pain, his anguish, and his fears to gush forth. And this last confession he had made—the one spurred on by the incident with the nurse—was the most crucial of all. It was something he had never told another soul, the story of his first and only friend, his first and only love.

Kirsten Cooper was the most beautiful girl in Shropshire. And although she had lived there all her life, Paul and his cousins had never known her because, as the daughter of a local dairy farmer and year-round resident, she was not part of their social circle. Paul met her the summer he was fourteen, when he had just begun sketching in earnest. He had gone off for the day to do some drawings of the tall silo and red barn that stood near the top of Butternut Hill. And as he sat on a rock just off the dirt path behind the barn, he saw her coming toward him. She was wearing faded blue jeans, a tie-dyed T-shirt, and was slender, tall—just about as tall as Paul, who hadn't as yet reached his full height. Her skin was tanned, her eyes a pale bluish green, and her teeth straight and even. But the most striking thing about her was her hair. Paul had never seen hair that color—it wasn't blond so much as it was silver. And thick and straight, it fell almost to her waist.

This beautiful apparition spoke to Paul, asking to look at his sketch and complimenting him on it. It was her father's barn he had chosen to immortalize, and with a flourish, he presented her the sketch as a gift. For the first time in his life, he had done exactly the right thing. She was delighted. From then on—through the whole of July—they became fast friends and best of all, secret ones, since they both knew, without ever saying anything, that it would be best that way. Each would have been uncomfortable in the other's world. Kirsten loved to watch him draw as if his re-creations of trees and wild flowers and birds were some kind of miracle. She often sat beside him, reading from a book of plays or reciting a poem aloud. She had decided, she told him, that she was going to become an actress. One day, he surprised her with a sketch of her, and she told him that she would always keep it. Maybe, when each of them was famous, it would hang in the lobby of a theater or in a museum: the great Kirsten Cooper, sketched by the great Paul Kingman.

He was completely and totally in love with her. One sketch became fifty, and she was now his only subject. One day, announcing to him that all great artists painted nudes, she took off all her clothes and unselfconsciously posed full front in the sunlight. That first time, he was so flabbergasted he could hardly draw anything. But soon it became a kind of routine. And he came to know that body as well as he knew his own: the curve of her neck, the slender lines that were her arms, the surprisingly large breasts, round and white with their peach-colored up-turned nipples, the smooth flat belly above the silky, golden triangle. But as well as he knew it, as often as he sketched it, he had never touched that body. He knew that he wanted to, just as he knew she wanted him to as well. But neither seemed able to go about making the first move.

But the first Saturday in August everything was abruptly ended any-way. It had been stupid of them to arrange to meet on a weekend, and Paul had forgotten that this was also the one on which his cousins, Franklin and Phillip, were to return from their trip to Scotland. Paul and Kirsten were in a clearing behind the lake, a place that, together with several others in Shropshire, now seemed their own private do-main. Kirsten was lying on the ground, her clothes tossed carelessly be-side her as she read aloud from Poe's "Ode to Helen"—"The glory that was Greece, the grandeur that was Rome." She was Helen herself, and he found himself grow so hard that he ached.

Just then, the nightmare started as that voice—that supercilious, deri-sive, cruel voice that he knew as Franklin's—intruded on them.

"Hey, little cousin, you keeping all of that for yourself? That's not very generous of you."

Kirsten jumped up and grabbed at her clothes, but Franklin was too fast. He took them and, in an expert pass, tossed them to Phillip, who had just come up behind him. A pair of white panties got caught on a branch and a T-shirt got trampled under foot. Kirsten stared at Paul, her eyes frantic.

"Do something, do something," she cried.

Paul's voice had become so choked that he had to stop his story.

Isabel waited, giving him a moment or two to regain control. "What did you do?" she had finally asked.

"Not a god damn thing."

Isabel hadn't had a chance to really consider all the facets of what Paul was revealing—his desertion of Kirsten, his intimidation by his cousins, the invasion of his secret and private individuality. She had gone directly from Paul's session to a consultation with a lawyer who was rounding up expert witnesses for an up-and-coming murder trial, then to see Richler about Paul's release and to find out whether or not Richler had spoken to Paul's father. It was Isabel's strong opinion that Paul was not yet ready to handle a meeting with William—or, in fact, with any of the other Kingmans—and she had asked Richler to discuss the matter with Dr. Kingman. Then there had been the usual sessions with her other private patients, each with his own need for Isabel's thought and attention.

Emily Richmond had just spent her first weekend alone. Her estranged husband, Carl, and his new girl friend had taken all of the children skiing. The two girls and eight-year-old Johnny had looked so cheerful as they left, Emily had sobbed to Isabel, not giving the slightest thought to their poor mother, who for the first time in almost twenty years would be left alone with nothing to do but stare at the four walls while they were all out enjoying themselves. The Valium that Emily's internist had given her, she admitted guiltily to the disapproving Isabel, had helped kill some of the time—but not enough of it. Besides, Emily's drug-induced sleep had been plagued by ghastly dreams. To make matters worse, when Carl dropped the children off on Sunday night, she had seen the look of disgust on his face as he surveyed the unmade beds, the unwashed dishes, her own uncombed hair, her wrinkled kaftan. Isabel made a note that she would have to get Emily off those drugs. Maybe Emily would allow Isabel to contact her internist so that the two doctors could work out some reasonable program for Emily's withdrawal.

After Emily, Isabel had seen a new patient—Gordon Chandler, a forty-seven-year-old bachelor and actuary at Beneficial Life who had just had his first homosexual experience and who had become so fearful of his own identity that he could hardly bring himself to get out of bed in the morning, much less function in any normal capacity in his work or with his friends. Isabel wondered if perhaps someone like Gordon wouldn't benefit from a group therapy situation with others who had similar problems in confronting their own drastically altered self-images. She would look into it.

When Gordon Chandler left, it was past seven and Isabel was weary. Even so, she found herself taking out Paul Kingman's file and thinking over what he had told her that morning. The story of Kirsten Cooper was precisely the kind of breakthrough Isabel had been waiting for. The incident with the nurse had led Paul to admit what she had suspected from the very first—that he was and always had been sexually impotent, and it was now crucial for him to discover the sources of his paralysis. But she had not imagined the initial trauma taking quite this shape. She had always assumed it would be related more specifically to his father. There had to be another story there, she was convinced.

The phone rang, interrupting her thoughts.

"Is this Isabel Dunne?" the voice on the other end asked. "This is William Kingman, Dr. Dunne."

Isabel took a deep breath.

"I hope I haven't called at an inconvenient time."

"No, no, of course not, Dr. Kingman. I spoke with Dr. Richler this morning and I've been expecting your call."

"In any case, I won't keep you long. I simply wanted to set up an appointment for us to meet and discuss Paul's condition."

"There is one problem, Dr. Kingman. I haven't spoken to Paul yet and, as you probably know, a therapist cannot hope to keep the trust of his patients if he talks about their cases with anyone—even a parent—without their specific permission."

"That may very well be. But I should make clear to you that I have only agreed to your rather disconcerting request that my wife and I refrain from seeing Paul on the condition that I keep in close contact with you during this period. I suggest that in view of both our busy schedules we set up an appointment right now. What about a week from today—at five o'clock at my office."

"Six would be better."

"That's fine with me."

"Still, I hope you understand, Dr. Kingman, that should Paul not approve, I won't be keeping that appointment."

"And if you don't, I'm afraid I shall have to see Paul in spite of your concern."

They both hung up.

Isabel felt chilled, terrified at the thought of keeping that appointment.

Paul Kingman was discharged from Mount Sinai the next morning. Isabel signed all the papers, went down with him to get a taxi, and then to Paul's delight and surprise, rode with him across Central Park to his West Side apartment. She wouldn't come up though—she was on her way to a lunch date near Lincoln Center, that lawyer again. She would see Paul tomorrow in her office and if anything at all came up tonight, he should be sure to call her—he had her home phone number.

Isabel hadn't as yet told Paul that she had talked to William Kingman on the telephone. But the next day, almost as soon as he sat down on the large comfortable armchair facing her desk to start his first session as an outpatient, she brought up the subject of his father.

"He's asked to meet me, and I told him I would check with you."

"You mean, to get my permission? What can I possibly say? I don't really have a choice, do I?"

"Yes, you do. If you ask me not to see him, I won't."

"No, I think you had better. If not, I'll have to see him and I don't think I'm up to it."

"Whatever you think," she said, and began to listen as Paul once again started to enumerate his father's strengths and his own weaknesses, his father's expectations and his own failures. Isabel noticed now that there was one subject that he studiously avoided, and she decided this was a good time to press the point.

"Tell me, Paul," she asked, "did you ever see your parents have sex?"

Paul laughed. "See them? I don't think those two ever did have sex with each other. Though—if I'm not an immaculate conception—I suppose they had to at least once to produce me." He paused and his face began to assume a more serious expression. "But I did once see my father making love to someone else."

It was late spring of his freshman year at Glendower Academy—the spring before the summer of Kirsten Cooper. And he had just been informed that he was not to be invited back for the fall term. Two days before, in what Paul even at the time realized was an absurd misadventure on his part, he had been caught red-handed at cheating. It was the first day of the two-week exam period and Billy Whiteman, an honor French student, had slipped Paul a note during their French final.

"Question 18. Subjunctive of *vouloir?*"

Paul, far from an honor student in anything, had been immensely flattered by Billy Whiteman's assumption that he would know the answer. Unfortunately, however, Paul not only didn't know the subjunctive of *vouloir,* he hadn't even mastered the *passé simple.* Even more unfortunately, though, he felt compelled not to keep Billy in suspense and wrote on the bottom of Billy's note, "Sorry, I don't know."

Lacking not only Billy's superior knowledge of languages but also his greater finesse, Paul was promptly caught attempting to maneuver the crumpled paper across his desk toward Billy. And before he knew it, he and Billy were in Headmaster Percy's office, the evidence spread out in front of them. Under ordinary circumstances, the headmaster explained, both would have been expelled on the spot. But since the school year was almost at an end, he would allow them to take the remainder of their examinations so they could at least earn some academic credit. French, of course, was another story altogether. They would simply have to repeat the term's work.

Headmaster Percy, who was always straightforward and aboveboard, dictated the letters to the boys' fathers while the two of them were standing in the room, so that there could be nothing hidden about what he had written. Paul thought he would die, imagining William reading that letter. And however generous Headmaster Percy had been in allowing him the privilege of taking the algebra, ancient history, English, and biology finals, Paul knew he couldn't face them. That night, he packed a small knapsack and left for New York, hitchhiking to the train station just in time to catch the 8:06. He knew that his mother would not be in town, since just two days before he had gotten a postcard from the Golden Door—a health and beauty spa in Southern California. And he assumed that since it was Friday night, his father would be out of town too and up in Shropshire. He desperately wanted to be alone. Sunday night, when his father came back and opened Saturday's mail, would be time enough to confront the humiliation and punishment that awaited him.

It was almost midnight when he walked into the apartment building at Park Avenue and Eighty-fifth Street and the night man had just started his shift on the elevator.

"Hey there, Paul," John, the friendly gray-haired man, greeted him. "School out already? You sure are lucky. You're the first kid in the building home for summer vacation this early."

Paul managed to summon up a smile.

"It's pretty late for you to be out, isn't it?" John went on. "Got your key? I know your mom's away and I haven't seen your dad. Guess he's up at your country place."

"That's okay. I've got my key."

The elevator door opened at the eleventh floor. There was only one apartment on each floor in this building and the hall between the elevator and the apartment entrance was a tiny one, illuminated by an equally tiny brass chandelier. John waited while Paul unlocked the front door and stepped into the dark foyer. As Paul flicked on the light, John waved and descended.

The morning mail lay unopened on the burled wood hall table and Paul looked quickly through it. Percy's letter was not among the bill from Bergdorf's, the fliers from Bloomingdale's and Henri Bendel's, the postcard announcing a tournament at the Racquet Club, the Harvard Overseers' ballot, and the copy of *Sports Illustrated*. He picked up the magazine and went into the kitchen. It was the only totally modern room in the apartment, redone recently by his mother, who collected every kind of new cooking implement and gadget as soon as it came on the market and needed space to house the waffle irons, the lettuce spinners, the crêpe and pasta makers, the espresso coffee machine. Paul opened the refrigerator, found a full container of milk and the remains of a cherry pie. Annie, the cook, had made it, Paul could tell as he bit into it. It was so sweet it made your teeth ache. He poured the milk into a glass and took it and the pie and the *Sports Illustrated* into the huge living room, where he flopped down into the oversize armchair that was usually William's. He could almost hear his mother telling him to get his feet off the coffee table, get his milk glass onto a coaster, and to be careful of those crumbs that were now falling onto the Oriental rug.

He was enjoying himself—so much in fact that he almost forgot the miserable reality that had driven him here. All he needed was some music, but the records in the living room were his parents', which meant that there might be a Judy Collins record, one by Simon and Garfunkel, but certainly no Beatles, no Stones, nothing he would really like to hear. His records were in his room and he started down the long hall that led to the bedroom wing of the apartment.

Suddenly, he heard a woman's voice—throaty, foreign-accented, he couldn't quite make out what it was saying, but it was coming from the last bedroom down the hall, his mother's room. The first thing he thought of was that a band of thieves was in the apartment, trying to steal his mother's jewelry. But as the woman continued to make herself heard—now laughing, boldly, musically, with nothing surreptitious about her voice at all—it was clear that this simply couldn't be the case. Whoever it was felt at home, at ease in that bedroom. Paul couldn't quite explain what made him go down the hall. But he did, tiptoeing all the way, and careful to stand just outside the threshold of the open door so that he could not be seen but could himself manage to see the large bed, with its tufted satin backboard, reflected in the mirrored wall facing it.

There were two people in the bed—both of them naked. One was his father, lying back on the bed, his head against a high lacy pillow. The other was a dark-haired slender woman whose face, buried between his father's legs, was hidden from view. Paul was mesmerized. It didn't seem real, rather as if he were watching pictures on a screen. Even the sounds seemed distant—strange—disembodied—those moans, the sighs, and the immense gasp that must have come from his father. He stared ahead at his father's reflection in the mirror until he started. In the dim light, he could see in the mirror that William's reflected eyes were meeting his. Paul turned and ran down the long hall and would, in fact, have run right out of the apartment's front door had his father not caught him, placing his hand firmly on Paul's shoulder.

He was still naked, and Paul averted his eyes.

"Just go sit in the study, Paul, while I throw something on," William instructed, his voice as cool and collected as ever.

Moments later, he reappeared in a navy blue silk dressing gown, poured himself a glass of brandy, and sat down in the book-lined room facing his son.

"Look, Paul. I know that what you've just seen must have been very surprising for you—maybe even upsetting. But there are some things about men and the world that you will understand one day. Your mother is a wonderful woman—but she and I have different needs. So I'm not really betraying her in the true sense of the word—in fact, I'm actually making things easier for her. In any case, we don't want to cause her the smallest bit of unhappiness by telling her about this, do we?"

Paul shook his head. He promised to keep his father's secret, if not exactly to lie, at least to help hide the truth.

"Must say you gave me a start," William went on. "I didn't expect you home for another two weeks. Are your exams over so soon?"

"No," Paul said, "they're not over."

William's voice went stern. "Then what in God's name are you doing home? You should be up there in the library, applying yourself. Your winter report was bad enough. You keep this up and they won't ask you back."

"They aren't asking me back," Paul said. "That's just it."

William stood up, his face livid.

"Explain yourself," he commanded.

"Well, it was this French exam and it wasn't my fault—this kid ahead of me . . ."

"You got caught cheating?"

"Well, that's what Dr. Percy called it, even though . . ."

"I can't believe what you're telling me. You—a Kingman—caught cheating!"

"Didn't you realize the irony in that incident?" Isabel asked.

"Strangely, not until just now."

Paul looked across at Isabel, and the tension that had gripped his face as he told the story suddenly relaxed and a warm smile slowly took shape.

"I guess I simply accepted it back then, saw it all through my father's eyes. He was a man of the world, doing what men of the world do. And Claudia Monteverde was a very beautiful woman."

"Claudia Monteverde, the dress designer?"

"That's right. She had just left her husband, the Principe, largely it seems because she no longer needed him. She was just beginning to become famous as a designer in those days and I guess also to make enough money to support herself well enough without his help. At any rate, my father saw quite a lot of her over the next few years—at least, until she married that Swedish industrialist. I've forgotten his name. You know, I kind of liked her. I saw her quite a few times after that first night. She once told me in that great Austrian accent of hers about her past. Do you know, her father was a milkman and her mother worked in a sweater factory. To look at her, you'd think that she didn't simply marry royalty, but came from it."

"However likable or elegant this Claudia Monteverde might have been, it still doesn't justify your father's actions."

Isabel was surprised at the harshness of her own voice. She was somehow angry at Paul for going on about this woman. She was, she realized, somehow jealous.

"Of course, I know my father was being unfaithful. And I don't mean to suggest that I was totally calm and accepting of his affair with Claudia. I was devastated by catching the two of them in bed that night. But I guess"—Paul paused—"what really got me wasn't my father's infidelity but what I suppose you'd call his prowess. The point was that he could excite and satisfy a Claudia Monteverde, just as he could ace a tennis ball, perform a brilliant operation."

Paul's voice had begun to quiver and he took a deep breath before he went on.

"He had just given me another area in life where he was a master and where I was doomed to fail."

Isabel, who was now leaning on the front edge of her desk close to Paul's chair, reached out and touched his cheek.

He put his hand over hers and held it there.

The problem, Isabel thought after Paul had left, was that William Kingman was without doubt an impossible act to follow. Paul's perceptions of inadequacy were not simply neurotic, though at this point they had taken on neurotic proportions. Of course, Paul was a highly intelligent, handsome, and talented young man and in any ordinary world, he would have seemed extraordinary—outstanding. But when he put himself up against his father, measuring himself by his father's criteria for excellence, he could not help but come up short.

She too had always come up short when measuring herself against an impossible set of standards. Her mother had wanted her to devote herself solely to work, to her studies, to her devotional duties. But what a dour, impossible existence this was for a child. And what six-year-old could resist thinking about a toy, a pretty dress, a candy bar. Frances Dunne had gone through life wearing a hair shirt, but Isabel could not do the same. As a child she, like Paul, considered her inability to be like her mother a matter of failure, some inadequacy within herself. Now she recognized with a certain sadness mingled in with her resentment that it was her mother's own neurotic drives and denials that set off the illusion of failure.

And Bishop O'Connor too had demanded his own brand of self-denial, also disguised as standards of perfection. Obviously any student on scholarship had to maintain high grades, but Isabel was something more. She had become the bishop's own example of budding Catholic womanhood, not only the unerring student but the modest, self-effacing sexless female. In a strange contradiction, he also insisted that she always look pretty. And so the challenge was how to make herself attractive yet not arousing, appealing yet not too appealing. She was always chastising herself after a meeting with him. Had she been too aggressive? Or not aggressive enough? Had her dress been nice? Too nice?

And if he made it a point to encourage the growth of her intellect and of her reasoning powers, how could he also demand the blind obedience to the very rules that her new curiosity must challenge? Papal infallibility, a doctrine voted on by a group of cardinals? How could she be asked to accept that, given the evidence provided for by history of highly fallible popes? Virgin birth? Logic and science fought such a notion. Heaven and hell? She couldn't work them into the image of the universe her awakening mind was forging. Even in areas where obedience should have been possible, she found herself unable or unwilling to abide by the teachings of her church. She refused its demands for chastity. She ignored its strictures against abortion. The standards of her church, while perfectly possible for so many others, were impossible ones for her.

But, of course, the demands made on Isabel which were most similar to the ones made on Paul were those embodied in the very being of Bryan Madison. How small and insufficient she had seemed when reflected in the mirror of his world. So had Paul, she knew, when faced with the Kingmans. The difference was, however, that where Bryan's demands were unspoken ones that she somehow perceived, the Kingmans' were all too explicit. It was quite clear that they had no tolerance for the less than excellent, no patience with unrealized potential, and appreciation only for measurable accomplishment and visible performance. Such demands had immobilized Paul. She must relieve their pressure, awaken and bring him to life.

That night, Isabel went with Sandy Richler to an Isaac Stern concert at Carnegie Hall. In the months that she had been in New York, she and Sandy had become good friends and he had taken obvious pleasure in showing her the parts of New York that he thought she'd enjoy most —the Cloisters, that wonderful transplanted monastery filled with gems of medieval tapestries and carvings seated on a hill overlooking the Hudson at the tip of Manhattan island; Little Italy, with its street festivals and clam bars and cups of dark espresso; the Regency movie theater on upper Broadway where Sandy always seemed to be able to find some great old movie to introduce her to, like *The Grand Illusion* or *Citizen Kane;* the original Nathan's at Coney Island with its hot dogs and knishes and delicious french fries served in cone-shaped, cardboard cups and covered with salt; and, of course, there was Carnegie Hall.

After the concert, the two went up to Sandy's parents' apartment, where they'd been invited for coffee and Danish. Leah Richler was not too happy about this friendship between Sandy and Isabel—even though Sandy had assured his mother that there was no question of romance between the two of them.

"You never know," Leah had muttered, shaking her head. A gentile daughter-in-law was not what she had hoped for and her only defense, she felt, in the interest of absolute safety, was to play Cupid. Having exhausted long ago her supply of available females for Sandy, she would now have to concentrate on available men for this Isabel Dunne. She would look her over tonight and see who would be right for her— whether she would be more likely to hit it off with Mrs. Monahan's son, Timmy, or Tucker Lawrence, that attractive bachelor on the fourth floor.

After serving mounds of prune Danish, apple strudel, and raisin kugel, together with steamy cups of coffee, Leah just sat and listened. She knew better than to try to get a word in edgewise when three doctors were at it—and especially in such professional talk as they were now.

"If there's one thing I learned from Arne Larsen," Isabel was saying, "it's that you can't always go by the rules. He believed that a great analyst was born, gifted in some way, with instincts that he or she should trust beyond any proscriptions, any textbook utterances."

"That sounds mysterious, mystical, almost dangerous, to me," Sandy said. "I mean, how do you know whether or not you're anointed in that special way, whether or not you're one of the chosen?"

"You know it—that's all," Isabel answered him. "And the success of your patients is an objective enough standard to satisfy even a pragmatist like you."

"But, Isabel," Gerson said, "that success in itself is so hard to measure. Who knows, though? I myself, a stickler for the rules, have so often felt held back by them, kept from doing something, saying something, that might have made a crucial difference. Still, there are just too many risks involved in breaking the rules."

"I understand what you're saying, Gerson. And in some ways, I agree with you. But Larsen, as my therapist, was totally unconventional, and he ended up saving my life. And that, to me, is measurable success."

"You two psychiatrists can go on talking about this all night, if you want. We poor internists have to be at the hospital at seven A.M." Sandy got up and brought Isabel her jacket.

They all said good night and, as Leah Richler shut the door behind Sandy and Isabel, she thought, "Tucker Lawrence on the fourth floor. She'd be perfect for him."

* * *

"Conventions . . . risks . . . sticking by the rules . . . daring to break them . . ." Bits and pieces of her conversation with Richler and Sandy ran through Isabel's mind on Sunday afternoon. What would they think now, she wondered, as she walked through Central Park on her way to Paul's apartment. He had started sketching again, he had told her, and she had been delighted at the news. At least in that one area he was achieving a certain amount of potency. Then he had asked her, hesitating, almost stammering as he spoke, if she would be willing to sit for him. She was, he had explained, the most important person in his life at this moment and he wanted to capture her on paper. Isabel had readily agreed—what better way to strengthen their relationship than through his work. Hadn't Larsen used work in a similar way in his treatment of her? She knew, however, that Richler was likely to disapprove. Encouraging as he was of her direct methods, he would undoubtedly find today's visit to Paul's apartment too radical a gesture or, as he himself would have put it, "too risky."

But she was sure that what she was doing was the right thing for Paul, and the day, an unseasonably warm and sunny one, made her feel even more confirmed in her decision. The bright, clear light would make today a perfect one for sketching. There was, in fact, a man right now, standing a few feet near her off the path, sketching the gracefully arched bridge that spanned a narrow section of the park's duck pond. All around were joggers—some young, some old, some in stylish running outfits, others in torn sweatshirts and shorts, and one man, despite the still brisk March air, bare-chested and sweating.

Sandy had told her that a mere two or three years ago, the Sunday Central Park scene was all bicycles. Now, however, the cyclists were few and far between. Everybody these days seemed to be running, even if their brand of running was hardly running at all, Isabel thought, as she looked at the plump girl coming toward her at a pace that made this particular jogger seem to be jogging in place. Wending their way through the runners and wandering the still brown fields between the park's paths were the dog-walkers, a few of whom seemed to be carrying on quite involved conversations with their pets. One elderly woman, neatly dressed in a gray tweed coat and matching woolen hat and scarf, kept shaking her head at the shaggy mound of white fur at her feet.

"I don't know why you're behaving this way, Muggins, you show no gratitude whatsoever."

Isabel was wondering just how Muggins had transgressed when her attention was distracted by two people, a man and a woman each dressed in tie-dyed purple outfits, who whizzed by her riding purple bikes. Had she seen right? Was that woman wearing purple nail polish, too? And was her hair dyed purple or was that a wig she was wearing? Maybe Paul should take his sketch pad into the park, she thought, as she exited onto the street and walked toward his apartment.

"How lovely it must be to live in a penthouse," Isabel told Paul, as he showed her the view from his terrace.

She could see the whole park stretched in front of her. "Even Mount Sinai Hospital," Paul pointed out.

But it was too windy and cool to linger out on the terrace, and the two went back into the immensely long and narrow living room, with its ornate plaster moldings, its intricately patterned parquet floor, and its wall of lead-framed, stained-glass french doors and windows which faced the sunrise and the park. Like so many apartments in older buildings in New York, Paul explained, this one had its romantic history. It was originally part of a much larger unit, now broken up into four or five smaller apartments, and had been built at the outset by newspaper tycoon Charlie Wheatley for his mistress, Loretta Keyes. Paul's living room had been her formal dining room. Did Isabel want to see the bath? It was larger than most studio apartments and lavishly mirrored as well. The wardrobes hidden behind those mirrors had evidently once housed Miss Keyes' many gowns and were the perfect size, Paul showed Isabel, for storing canvases.

Walking back toward the living room through the bedroom, Isabel noticed some pictures on Paul's dresser.

"Is this your father?" she asked, picking up one of a strikingly handsome man with gray-flecked, dark hair, high cheekbones, and strong aquiline features.

Paul nodded. "And that's my mother, and there's the rogue's gallery of Kingmans," he explained, pointing to a large group photograph of robust children, tanned adults, and assorted dogs, obviously taken at a picnic in the country.

"Let me see how good you've been at describing the family. Here you are and those two boys with baseball bats must be Phillip and Franklin. Oh, this has to be Allison." Isabel pointed to a pretty teenaged girl in a fussy blouse.

Paul smiled and nodded. "You see, I wasn't lying. Allison never appears without a ruffle somewhere about her."

"And this," Isabel went on, encouraged by her success, "has to be Ernest." She put her finger on the leonine head of the man in the very center of the family group. "It's quite obvious that everyone here is in awe of him."

She then went on from figure to figure, not failing to correctly identify any one of them.

"Well, you certainly do capture people well in words, Paul," she said, walking toward the living room. "But now, I suppose, you're anxious to start trying to do it in paint. Where do you want me to sit?" she asked.

"Wherever you'd be comfortable."

"Will this be all right?" She had settled on the dark blue velvet couch facing the fireplace.

"Just fine," he said, pulling up a chair so that he could face her. He began to draw and his concentration was so intense that he became immediately silent, leaving Isabel's thoughts to wander.

How handsome William Kingman was, how evidently assured before the camera. Photographs. She thought of the small, tattered passport-sized one that Bryan had once given her. How many times she had begun to throw it away, how many times she had stopped herself, now and then going so far as to retrieve it from the wastebasket. She knew that if she no longer had the picture, she would lose his image altogether. His reality had long vanished from memory, and she could only recapture his face in her mind's eye as it appeared in that photograph. So too with her mother, whose features remained with her only through a picture Isabel kept on her dresser in her apartment. And all the recollections of what her mother had said and done seemed somehow to spring from that one wavy-haired woman in the print dress who was perpetually thirty-six—an age that seemed younger and younger to Isabel as she herself approached it.

Paul was turning the pages of his sketchbook. "You have such a wonderful jawline. Did you know? It's such a clean curve."

Isabel smiled. "I don't think anyone ever told me that."

She glanced over at the pad.

"Would you like to look?"

"Very much. I would have asked myself, but I wasn't sure what the protocol was between model and artist. I've never been sketched before."

He brought the pad over to her and sat next to her on the couch. She was stunned. The Isabel she saw in these sketches, with her bright eyes, soft curls, and smooth skin, was someone she hadn't seen in years. She was the Isabel of more than a decade ago, and she felt a nostalgia and a great affection for this distant young woman, her long-lost younger self.

"Do you really see me this way?" she asked Paul.

"But that's you exactly." Paul looked at her puzzled, as if he had no idea what she was talking about. And she suddenly realized that for Paul this younger Isabel was the reality. When he looked at her, he had somehow managed—as artists were said to be able to do—to pierce through the surface and get at some essential inner core unavailable to most eyes. That he had seized on her youth was perhaps a reflection of his own young years. But whatever, it was inescapably clear that he was in love with her. His emotions were declared by the intense beauty of these drawings, by the adoration that quivered in every line.

And she knew she was luxuriating in this vision of herself. For to be seen as a girl in her twenties, a youthful, lovely thing, was to somehow become that girl, to actually return to that fresh, green time of life. It was a fleeting time for everyone, that precious moment between childhood and maturity—but for Isabel it had been especially brief, cruelly foreshortened. She had had but a single romance and then for years, forever it seemed, nothing. Oh, of course, there had been flashes of desire, moments of charged attractions. There was a patient like that handsome ex-priest, Terence Shea; an attractive colleague at the hospital; someone she glimpsed at a professional conference, all of whom tempted her but none of whom had tempted her enough so that she had acted on her feelings.

But her response to Paul right now was something different. She wanted him, and she suddenly felt that she had earned the right to want him. She had denied herself for so long; she had in a sense lived up to all the impossible standards her mother, the church, and the bishop had set for her, becoming an expert at abstinence and sublimation. She had in fact become so expert at burying her feelings that she had felt at times that they had disappeared entirely. Of course, they hadn't, and now this beautiful young man before her was arousing them.

But if she wanted him, she was unsure as to how to go about it. How could she let him know without frightening him, without spoiling the other aspects of their relationship? How could she make love to him? More important, perhaps, how could she justify it in terms of Paul's needs, in terms of Paul's therapy? Was it possible that since in drawing her, he had been able to become so alive, so engaged, that he might also be awakened in another way as well? If so, wouldn't that be the best thing for him, more important than anything else she could do, most crucial of all to his well-being?

These thoughts all crowded into her mind as they sat side by side on the sofa. She felt her arm touching his, his thigh touching hers, and she turned toward him as he simultaneously turned toward her. Slowly, gently, she moved her face toward his and kissed him softly on the lips. His arms were around her now, his lips answering hers.

"Oh, God, I love you," he started to sob, "but I can't. You know I can't."

"Don't worry," she said quietly, "I'll help you." Perhaps you can help me too, she thought.

They were in the bedroom now, naked, lying beside one another on the narrow bed. The phone rang, and Paul's body tensed at the sound.

"You don't have to answer it," she told him, as she began to stroke his body, feeling the taut, hard muscles beneath her fingertips.

The phone stopped ringing and slowly, deftly, she managed to release the tension from his back, his shoulders, his neck, until another kind of tension gripped his body. With care not to dispel the precarious balance of that moment, she guided him toward her and into her.

She had forgotten how acute the sensation was, and feeling a wave of physical pleasure from the firm hardness thrusting within her, she closed her eyes and allowed herself to be swept onto its crest. As the rhythm of his movements grew faster and stronger and she knew he was reaching his climax, she allowed herself to join him, feeling her back arch and hearing herself cry out.

She opened her eyes and looked into the face of her lover. For a moment, for a confusing and chilling split second, she was terrified, realizing that it wasn't Paul's face she had expected to see at all. In her thoughts, the man who had been making love to her was instead the man she had heard so much about, pictured so often, and seen for the first time that day in a photograph, the man she would meet tomorrow—William Kingman.

7

WILLIAM KINGMAN SAT in the sunlit living room of his Shropshire home, impatiently drumming his fingers on the low candlestick table next to his green-striped wing chair. The conversation was making him uncomfortable, and he wished this Sunday afternoon was over. Where was Barbara with the coffee? Damn it. The cook moved like a snail and Barbara didn't seem to be able to get her going at all. Neither Natalie nor Ernest would ever dream of leaving without having the several cups of coffee which followed, with the same inevitability as the night the day, any Kingman meal. And especially the long Sunday afternoon dinner in Shropshire which the senior members of the three branches of the family usually shared before they each undertook the tiring drive back to New York. The talk today centered, as it so frequently did, on the absent Kingmans—the children who, of course, were not children any longer—and William knew that soon Paul's name would come up, with the inevitable questions, suggestions, even instructions.

How was it that everything with Paul had gone so terribly wrong? It was a puzzle that tormented him and that he could not solve. All he knew was that it had been this way since Paul was about eight or nine. Maybe he should have seen a psychiatrist sooner. But damnit, other people managed to pull themselves together, so why not him? Besides, it was all so embarrassing. To have to have that kind of talk with a casual acquaintance like Gerson Richler—to have to agree not to see your own son. It was mortifying and would probably be even worse tomorrow when he met with this Dr. Dunne.

"At last, at last," Barbara said, wheeling in the tea wagon, its silver urns of coffee and tea, its Wedgwood cups and saucers, and a small, gold-rimmed platter of lace cookies.

"That smells delicious," Ernest said. "But you always make an excellent cup of coffee, Barbara. Rich and strong. Just what we need to keep us awake on that drive back to the city. By the way, Sebastian, you're not going to try to make it all the way to Washington tonight, are you?"

Sebastian, sipping his tea, shook his head. "No, I'll take the shuttle tomorrow morning. I hardly need my car when I'm there, what with both my sons living in that city."

"How do the boys like Washington?" Clara asked.

"They love it," Natalie answered for her husband. "Not the city, of course. Franklin keeps complaining that everything closes down at ten at night. But he loves working at the White House, being at the center of everything. And Phillip says that clerking for Justice Taylor is invaluable experience, worth three years at the Harvard Law School."

"If only poor Paul could be as happy," Clara sighed, and looked sympathetically at Barbara, who averted her eyes.

"Paul's doing fine, Clara. I'm quite satisfied with his progress," William said in a voice suggesting that the subject was closed for the time being.

"So you've seen Paul, then?" Ernest, either not picking up William's tone or choosing to ignore it, pursued the conversation.

"How does he look?" Natalie added.

"I wouldn't know because I haven't seen him." William was annoyed at the defensive quality he knew had crept into his voice. "But he is out of the hospital."

"Out of the hospital? And you haven't yet seen him?" Ernest looked sincerely shocked. "William, I simply don't understand you."

"I simply don't understand this entire course of treatment," Natalie said. "Just what sense does it make to keep a boy from his entire family, all those who love and care for him, after he has been through such a shattering experience."

William turned to her. "We've been through all this before, Natalie. According to Richler, who, allow me to remind you, is chief of psychiatry at Mount Sinai, Paul's problems, whatever they might be, are inextricably involved with his discomfort with us, his family."

"I think that's a lot of nonsense, and I thought it from the first." Natalie stubbed out her cigarette angrily.

"Come now, Natalie," Clara said, in her all-too-familiar, let's-not-squabble-children voice. "We are laymen, after all, and William is better equipped than we are to understand psychiatry—the special way that science works."

"Science? You call psychiatry a science?" Ernest thundered. "It may well turn out to be the biggest hoax of the twentieth century. A therapeutic process, a scientific sequence so unwieldy, so lengthy in the time it takes to realize itself, that it becomes absolutely untestable. Who knows if Dr. X really cured patient Y? Let's suppose that patient Y started coming to Dr. X when he was depressed and now ten years later, he ends up perfectly happy. But let's also suppose that during that ten-year period, the patient lost his shrewish mother, gained a lovely wife and two healthy children, and inherited a million dollars. The psychiatrist can, of course, claim that without his help the patient would have tossed himself into the grave with his mother, or never would have known a lovely wife from an unlovely one, or would have squandered his million as soon as he inherited it. And we have no way of disputing that claim. But neither does he have any way of proving it. Which takes psychiatry out of the realm of science and places it somewhere between mystical faith and plain old common sense."

"Here, here," Sebastian said. "Think of it from another angle, the rather crass financial one. When you really come down to it, isn't there something a little absurd about a silent listener charging seventy-five dollars an hour for lending a patient his ears. And he can keep lending those precious ears to that patient five days a week for a year, five years, ten years. That's quite an income for a pair of ears." He smiled, evidently pleased at his metaphor.

"I couldn't agree more, Sebastian," said Natalie. She was always in accord with her husband but still, she always felt compelled to score her own points, coming out just a little ahead in the game. "But there's something else about psychiatry that bothers me even more than the financial aspects. And that's the way it encourages people to get so wrapped up in themselves and their own problems."

Clara perked up at Natalie's remarks. "Oh, you're so right, Natalie. There was a long article in the *Times Magazine* section on that very topic. I think they called it the 'me-myself-and-I syndrome,' where you never concern yourself with anything or anyone which doesn't affect or involve you personally."

"That's exactly my point." Natalie's voice sounded like a punctuation mark. "In my time, when you failed you blamed yourself. You confronted what was wrong with you and you shaped up. Now, of course, whatever's wrong is everybody else's fault—your mother's, your father's, your teacher's, the politicians', the President's, the bomb's. Anything or anyone is to blame but you yourself."

"And so your point is that psychiatry encourages this self-indulgence?" Ernest asked.

"That's it exactly," his sister answered. "Instead of helping people to mature, it keeps them infants, each the center of his own little world."

What could William say? He had no more faith in psychiatry than they, but *he* had no choice. Paul, by having tried to take his own life, had placed himself in a position where he, and in turn his father, were forced to deal with psychiatrists. But William certainly wasn't forced, he now realized, to follow the instructions of these doctors and allow them to set their own terms the way he had been doing. Ernest and Natalie were right. Why wasn't he seeing his son? He would take care of that tomorrow when he met with Dr. Dunne. But in the meantime, he had to deal with his family. He did not intend to allow them to think him a fool.

"I'm not sure if all of you aren't being a little unfair—both to psychiatry as a whole and to the way Paul's case is being handled. As far as the field is concerned, there's a lot more evidence on psychiatry's behalf than you're suggesting. And as for Paul, surely you must see the boy's need to be alone, given what he's been through. Gerson Richler is a sensible man, a conservative practitioner, and would never go along with anything that didn't strike him as totally sound, rational in its basis."

William paused, and Barbara took advantage of the silence to join in the conversation. Paul, after all, was her son too. Still, her voice was filled with the tentativeness that somehow always came into it when she had to confront her husband's family.

"I know just how you all feel," she said. "I felt just the same way, being told I wasn't to see my own child. But if it's good for Paul, I'm willing to go along with it."

"But if you can't see Paul, how do you know if what these psychiatrists are doing is, in fact, good for him? Don't you see that, Barbara?" Natalie exchanged a quick look with Sebastian and then glanced over to her brother Ernest. Ernest, as if in response, now took charge of the conversation.

"Think, William. What do you really know about this Dr. Dunne?" Ernest asked.

William was embarrassed. He really didn't know much more than what Richler had told him. He hadn't checked into her at all, he admitted.

"Don't worry," Natalie said. "We all know how hard this has been on you. Sebastian can get someone in his office to find out everything there is to know about Dr. Dunne. They know what to do." She smiled.

During the drive back to New York, Barbara tense and silent beside him, William found himself wondering why he had ever married this vapid woman, absorbed as she was by her superficial concerns with the social sides of charities, her obvious statements which made William inwardly winced and always started off a reaction of surreptitious smiles between Natalie and Sebastian. Ernest, William noticed, did not react to Barbara simply because he chose not to hear her. Ernest had always had a talent for selective listening, for blotting out the foolish trappings and getting down to the essence. He claimed that this ability to keep his mind clear, unlittered by the superfluous, had been crucial in enabling him to write his most important works, the volumes on economic history which had won him the Nobel Prize. And that facility at blocking out distraction, William realized, was how Ernest managed to get along with the often foolish Clara. Clara, he thought, was totally forgivable because despite her banalities, she did produce three young women who were intrinsically Kingmans. William had never been that fond of his nieces—Margo, Frederica, and Allison. Their heartiness was frequently grating, and despite a cultivated air of geniality, they had, he had observed, a strong, even ruthless talent for manipulating people and situations to their own advantage. But likable or not, it had always been clear from their first days in the kindergarten at Brearley to their last at Radcliffe that the three Kingman sisters were, in family tradition, first in everything.

William glanced at the still silent woman next to him. Her profile was delicate, her slender features still youthful, and he thought, that's what she's given her son, his so-called poetic looks. It was not a gift that would go far. To some extent, William was certain, Paul's long string of failures was because Barbara was his mother. And so it's my fault, he thought grimly, for marrying such a woman in the first place.

Her family had been right enough. Dick Wadsworth, Barbara's father, had been chairman of the Board of General Wheat Products and Secretary of Commerce in the Eisenhower Administration. And growing up on a large Lake Forest estate, Barbara had been given the best of everything—her own horse, her own convertible for her sixteenth birthday—and had been sent first to Miss Porter's and then to Finch in New York for the finishing touches. Although Finch didn't offer the academic prestige of a Smith or a Vassar, it did have the advantage of putting one in contact with a group of young women who were to become the nucleus of the New York social scene, including as it did the future president of the Junior League, the future chairwoman of the April in Paris Ball, the future wife of the president of AT&T who would always make sure her old Finch classmates were on the guest list for her Southampton weekends. But if Barbara's family had provided her with all the right connections, they had also provided her with a habit of self-indulgence and petty concern. The single daughter in a family over-whelmed by boys—Barbara had four older brothers—she had only to look pretty and be charming. And from the first weekend when he met her at the Newport races—at the time both were still students—William knew all this about her. Still, sensing in her the makings of a perfect hostess and wife for a famous surgeon-to-be, he had married her anyway and, he thought bitterly, he had been punished for it ever since. At least, in the form of Paul.

He remembered the first humiliation starting when Paul was almost held back in the second grade at Trinity. William had gone to see the headmaster to protest, had hired a special tutor to get Paul through his second-grade reader, had himself spent evenings going over arithmetic with the boy, but to no avail. Paul did not continue on with his class and, in fact, never rose from the bottom quarter of the class he had been put back into—a position the other Kingmans could not help but know about since Sebastian's nephew, himself an honor student, was also at Trinity.

Paul's inadequacies seemed to multiply over the years, no matter how William tried to stem them. Barbara, of course, was no help. Between hairdressers, fittings, fashion shows, and endless, empty-sounding con-versations with her friends, she didn't seem to notice how poorly Paul was doing at school, how his few friends were the class fat boy and the class dunce, and how he had no real enthusiasm for sports and games. To be perfectly fair, William remembered that she did respond the time that Paul was sent home from prep school by encouraging his art, buy-ing him pads of linen paper and thick watercolor brushes. But pretty pictures were about as essential as delicate features. If Paul were going to become a first-rate artist, that was one thing. But since Paul seemed incapable of being first-rate in anything, William could not take too much pride in what would probably turn out to be a minor talent, an ar-tistic flair of some sort.

They knew it, Ernest and Natalie. They knew very well what Paul was and what he was not—how could they miss seeing it? It was far worse for William to have them know and judge, however silently, than it was having Paul's failures exposed to the scrutiny of strangers, of the headmasters, doctors, those psychiatrists, however probing they were, however pointed their questions. For despite William's knowledge that Paul's inadequacies were due to the heritage of his mother, he was not sure that his brother and sister could perceive this as clearly as he could. In fact, he was plagued by the suspicion that they might somehow think that Paul's failures were a reflection of William himself, that William was not enough of a Kingman to produce what the family prized most, their brilliant, accomplished children.

William could feel a rage growing within him, the anger he had always felt about Paul but had struggled to suppress. The boy had not only failed himself but was dragging his father down with him. William had sobbed for the first time since he was a child when he received the phone call that Paul had tried to kill himself, that his cleaning woman, coming by to pick up a package she had forgotten the day before, had found him with his wrists slashed. He was crying for Paul, he knew, but he was also crying for himself. Now he was angry at both of them, himself as well as Paul, for allowing those psychiatrists to maneuver them, to dictate to them. He would telephone Paul as soon as he got back to New York. He'd tell him that he, William, was taking charge now. It was about time he did and the decision made him feel better.

It was early evening when William pulled up to his apartment house. Park Avenue was deserted and the doorman, Pat, noted, as he helped Barbara from the car, that such fine weather must have kept everyone in the country longer than usual. Barbara and the few parcels—some Shropshire jams for the Spence-Chapin auction, some quilts that needed repair from her New York seamstress—were left to be taken up in the elevator, and William went back to his car, guarded from ticketing policemen by Pat. He drove it around the corner to Lexington Avenue and to his garage between Lexington and Third.

"It could use a wash," he said to the attendant who took the keys. William walked to Lexington Avenue, feeling pleased with himself, almost gay. He had made up his mind and was going to act on it. He entered the Wicker Table, a corner restaurant done in turn-of-the-century country style. It was too early for the usual Sunday night crowd of East Siders who came here regularly, attracted by the elegant hostesses— several wealthy young women who owned the place as well and contributed their personal white wicker to the decor—and their specialties, which included dandelion salad, crab meat and spinach pancake, and apricot butter. William found the restaurant amusing, enjoyed the obvious pleasure his hostesses took in his presence, but this time he was there just to use the phone. He had remembered that besides calling Paul, he had another call to make that he didn't want Barbara to overhear.

"All alone?" the slender, striking Nell Parsons, carrying a bunch of menus, asked him. "Are you having dinner?"

"Unfortunately, no. Just need to use the phone."

"Hmmm. I'm suspicious," Nell laughed, her dark blue eyes sizing him up. She was the prettiest of the group, he thought.

He went to the bottom of the staircase where the phone stood, equidistant from the men's and ladies' rooms.

He dialed Paul, knowing exactly what he was going to say to the boy, but although he let the phone ring on, there was no answer. Thoroughly frustrated, William wondered where Paul could be. He was supposed to stay close to home the first weeks, Richler had told William. Obviously the psychiatrist's admonitions had about as much effect on the boy as William's own had had in the past.

Then William made the call for which he had come to the Wicker Table in the first place. The phone was picked up after a few rings, and a breathless voice answered.

"William? That you? I was just out the door."

"Where are you off to?" he asked.

"Where I always seem to be these days, down at Richard's to go over the scene again. Tascha says it needs a lot more work, and we're sure she's going to call on us next class."

"Are you sure Richard's gay?"

"Oh, William, what a thing to ask. If you saw his roommate, Franco, you wouldn't be the least bit suspicious."

"All right, spare me Franco. Anyway, I called to say that I'll be late tomorrow evening. I have an appointment with another doctor to review a rather important case, and I'm not sure how long it will take."

"So you might be very late?"

"I just can't say."

"Well, whatever, you have the key." They both hung up.

Monday was always Isabel's most pressured day. The weekend—with its free time, its lack of structure, and the Saturday night syndrome of pursuit and loneliness—was the most difficult for Isabel's patients, for all patients in fact. And Isabel inevitably found herself spending the first hour of the new week returning the long list of phone messages that her service had collected over the past two days. The emergencies she had already confronted as they occurred.

Yes, she told Emily Richmond, she could see her at three. No, she told Gloria Hooten's mother, she could not discuss Gloria's case with her at this point no matter how much weight Gloria had lost. Of course, she told the lawyer, she would appear in court on Thursday as arranged to offer expert testimony that his client, the now infamous multiple killer Herman Schwartz, was truly schizophrenic and could not be held responsible for doing what his voices told him to. But just now, she was afraid she couldn't talk. Her first patient had just arrived.

"I've had it," Evan Wilcox announced as he sat down on the brown leather chair facing Isabel's desk. "This time I've really had it. I'm leaving."

This was the way Evan Wilcox had started each session since Isabel had begun seeing him three months ago. A thirty-five-year-old fashion photographer who had been married for some eight years now to a former model, Evan kept bemoaning the change in his life-style.

When he and his wife, Ann, were first married, they were each earning over $50,000 a year and with no children or other responsibilities, a house in the Hamptons, a Jaguar sports car, a sailboat, a month in Tahiti, Galanos gowns and custom-made shirts, all were well within their means. Now, however, there were not only four children—two of whom were already in private school at $3,000 each per annum—but the family income was more than cut in half. Ann had decided to be a full-time mother, and Evan's particular, hip, sixtyish photographs had, along with miniskirts and bell-bottoms, gone out of style. Not that they were starving by any means, but the pressure was on and Evan couldn't bear up under it. As clear as the situation might have been to any objective viewer, Evan was blind to the causes of his problems. The villain, the one responsible for his current unhappiness, had to be Ann. No longer a cadaverous 112 pounds, the 5'10" Ann, who at her current 135 might seem pleasantly curvaceous to others, to Evan took on the dimensions of a cow. She disgusted him, he hated her, he wanted out, he told Isabel day after day.

"She's simply not the same person. She's no fun anymore. My God, it's always the children. I asked her last night—let's take off for a week or two together. Go up to the Cape, just get away. And what do I hear? Adam's open-school week, Jan's in a play, Jenny and Susan, for God's

sake, have interviews at nursery school. There's no end. I can't stand it."
"You may not be able to stand it," Isabel said, "but just what are
you blaming Ann for? Should she ignore the children? Would that be
better?"
"Sure it would be better. Fifty thousand a year better, if she went
back to work. She's a goddamn compulsive about these kids."
"Is it compulsive to go to see your son if he's in a play? To visit a
teacher during open-school week?"
"No, that isn't what I mean, but . . ."
"But what?"
"Oh, Christ, I don't know."
"Yes, you do," Isabel insisted.
"Look, I just can't hack it. And I hate the shabbiness of having to
worry about cash, about whose turn it is to pick up the tab, about how
long you can get away without buying a new car."
"So is Ann really to blame then?"
He shook his head slowly, hesitantly.
This time Isabel was silent. It was clear that Evan Wilcox was grop-
ing toward a new awareness and she did not want to interfere. It would
come to him soon enough.
Isabel's next appointment was Gloria Hooten. A twenty-year-old
from a socially prominent family, Gloria had spent her teen-age years
as a compulsive eater. An elephant of a girl, her father had told Isabel,
her closets, her purse, all her pockets and dresser drawers were filled
with Tootsie Rolls and Hershey bars and any other candy she could get
her fat little fingers around. Then, at Bennington College where she had
taken up Zen, brown rice, and amphetamines, Gloria had lost 150
pounds. The problem was, however, she told Isabel, she had become so
entranced with her new silhouette that she kept losing and losing. And
now she found she couldn't stop. The very thought of food made her
gag. In fact, the only time she could eat was when she knew no one
could possibly see her. Eating in public became a revolting and humiliating act. In her weakened condition, she was constantly exhausted and
slept an ever-increasing number of hours. Her dreams, moreover, were
always centered predictably on food.
"This morning's dream was horrible, horrible," she said, fighting
back the tears as she spoke. "I can't tell you how awful it was. I was in
a room. It was at college, but no, it couldn't have been, because my parents were there. They were sitting across from me passing me great
bowls of noodles and I was eating them, gorging myself on them. When

suddenly, the food wouldn't go down my throat. It was stuck. I was gasping, I couldn't breathe. And my mother and father didn't notice that I was choking to death. They just kept on eating and eating. I woke up terrified."

"I know your terror was the strongest feeling you had, but was there anything else?"

"What do you mean?"

"I mean, how did you feel about your parents?"

"How can you ask that? I hated them. I hated them," Gloria screamed.

After Gloria left, Isabel was exhausted. Miss Lee brought her a cup of tea and a sandwich. Usually, she went down to the cafeteria to lunch, but today she needed this quiet time. All morning, Paul had kept intruding on her thoughts and the effort to push him and last night out of her mind and concentrate fully and wholly, first on Evan Wilcox and then on Gloria Hooten, had drained her to the point where she just wanted to be alone. Gloria was the most pressing problem right now. Her weight, while beginning to rise again after reaching a dangerous low, was nevertheless still not in the comfortable range of normalcy. True, she had made the great breakthrough—she had come to understand that her starvation was an act of self-punishment, and the very frequency of her many vivid dreams indicated a desire to come to terms with this new understanding. But eager as Isabel was, she had to be careful not to push Gloria too quickly. But what was too quickly? There were no hard and fast rules. That was what was so intriguing about psychiatry and so frustrating as well. Time, that was Gerson's theme. Over and over, he came back to it. She agreed, the process was too long. Yet she knew as well that it could not be too short.

The buzzer rang. Isabel glanced at the clock. It was time for her next patient. Another special referral from Gerson Richler, Leslie Chester was a former tennis star who years before had broken both her legs in a ski accident and had to give up her career. Her daughter, however, fourteen-year-old Pinkie Chester, had become the top junior tennis champion and was presently considered to be the next Chris Evert. Pinkie, who had just made the cover of *Sports Illustrated,* had during the last six months moved in with her father—long divorced from her mother and now a well-known if infamous member of the jet set. Pinkie now refused to see her mother at all and Leslie, overcome with grief, blamed herself for Pinkie's estrangement. She had failed Pinkie, she was a bust as a mother.

"But what about Pinkie's successes?" Isabel had suggested. Could Leslie take no credit for that? Competition was draining. A child had to be strong to bear up under it. Surely Leslie had provided her offspring with enough inner strength for that. So she wasn't such a terrible mother. And wasn't it possible that Leslie was not to blame for her daughter's desertion. Might not Pinkie herself, no longer an infant, have some responsibility for the tension between them? Would Pinkie agree to see Isabel? In this case, it might help.

Mothers and daughters, fathers and sons, parents and children—psychiatry's everlasting themes, Isabel thought as Paul Kingman came into her office. How different he looked, unlike the Paul she had seen on any other occasion. He smiled, he glowed, and when the door was shut behind him, he grabbed her up in his arms.

"I know you understand everything," he said. "But I don't think you can ever know how happy I am at this moment, how happy I've been since last night."

"I'm glad," she said and kissed him. But when he responded so strongly, making clear that he was ready to make love to her right there and then, she pulled away from him, shaking her head.

"Not here, not now," she said softly. Although she was careful not to show it, she was acutely uncomfortable, more uncomfortable than he could imagine. And not only because she was his doctor, he her patient, and she not sure how to guide their relationship back to those terms, but also because she knew she did not feel toward him as he felt toward her. The image of his father that had come to her at the climactic moment of their lovemaking had made that all too clear. Yet she herself was at a loss to understand precisely what that image meant. It was this that she had wanted to think about all day. It was this that she had to think about later. Now, above all, her responsibility was Paul.

"Come now," she said. "Sit down and start talking to me. After all, this is your session"—she smiled—"and I am still your therapist." She sat down behind her desk as if to prove the point. He, however, refused to take his usual place on the other side of the large walnut barrier and, instead, perched himself on the edge of the desk nearest her.

"Shall we talk about yesterday?" There was a challenge in his voice.

"If you want to."

"Yes, but I want you to talk about it too. I want to know what it meant to you."

"Shall I be honest with you?"

"Please."

"Then I have to say that I just don't know."

He stood up and looked at her. He was silent for a moment and then he said, "Okay, that's honest. But can you tell me this? Did you do it just for me?"

She shook her head. "No, Paul. No, I didn't." What she said was true. But if she acted just for herself, her feelings still remained unclear. Just what did she feel for Paul? He was very important to her, she knew, but what of William Kingman, the image she had seen as Paul made love to her?

She suddenly remembered. Last night she had had another dream about the faceless man who haunted her sleep. She was walking down a long hall, the wind forcing open its many doors, tearing down the moldy muslin curtains that hung on its long row of windows. When the ferocious wind slacked off for a moment, she heard the sound of footsteps behind her. She whirled around but closed her eyes, wanting to confront, not wanting to see. Then she forced herself to open them. It was the faceless man she saw, but suddenly, he wasn't faceless anymore. He had features now but she couldn't quite make them out because they kept shifting, fading. First Bryan Madison's, then they were William Kingman's, then Bryan's again. Then the face remained William's face, the face from the photograph, and Isabel knew, even though she would meet William Kingman in person that afternoon, she would always see his image as the one she first had seen in Paul's apartment, the one that now completed the form of the faceless man in her dreams.

Paul interrupted her thoughts. "Isabel, I love you . . . and I think it must show."

"What do you mean?"

"Remember that nurse Addie Harris?"

"I remember. How could I forget?"

"Well, I ran into her on my way up here. She's working in pediatrics now."

"A better place for her, I'd say."

Paul grinned. "Exactly. Anyway, she said that being out of the hospital must really agree with me. She said that I looked as though I were in love."

Isabel saw that the nurse was right. The vividness in Paul's face, in his whole bearing, was unmistakable. "We'd better go on with this session. We've got a lot to go over."

"More family?"

"Your father might be where to concentrate this morning since I'm going to meet him this afternoon."

Paul was startled. He had evidently put it out of his mind. And for the first time that morning, he looked again like the old uncertain Paul.

Isabel arrived at William Kingman's office at a quarter to six. She hadn't planned to be this early, but after she had hailed a cab in front of the hospital and had the driver take her to the Madison Avenue address, she discovered that Dr. Kingman's office was only a few minutes away. She could easily have walked and still been there in plenty of time. Standing on the corner of Madison and Eighty-fifth, in front of the street entrance to his office, she was annoyed at herself first for her own excessive promptness and then for not entering just because it wasn't precisely the moment to keep this six o'clock appointment. She was being absurd, letting her nervousness get the best of her, she thought, and decided to ring the bell.

An attractive gray-haired woman in her fifties opened the door. "Dr. Dunne? Please come in. I'm Dr. Kingman's nurse. Doctor just called to say he was going to be held up, but he should be here in ten or fifteen minutes. Why don't you make yourself comfortable?"

Isabel sat down in the small, dimly lit waiting room with its rust carpet, brown sofas, and small tables holding lamps and ashtrays. There were also several hassocks around—supports for the leg casts that would inevitably be worn by many of the patients of an orthopedic surgeon.

"Can I get anything for you? I'm going to go and change now, if you don't mind." The nurse's voice was so cultivated, her speech pattern so educated, that somehow she seemed an unlikely type for this kind of job. Only a Kingman, Isabel thought, would find the sole nurse in New York who had her name in the Social Register.

And only a Kingman would have this selection of magazines. Instead of the usual *Newsweek, Time,* and *Saturday Review,* there was a copy of *Horizon, Partisan Review, The Manchester Guardian,* and London *Times Literary Supplement.* On the walls were several prints and lithographs—a Prendergast of Central Park, a Whistler portrait of a young woman wearing a Gibson Girl blouse and black velvet ribbon around her neck, and a Marin watercolor of sailboats in what Isabel knew had to be Cape Cod. She examined the paintings and prints, looked through the magazines, but kept returning her attention to her watch. It was now 6:30, and she felt like leaving. The whole situation was making her uncomfortable, sitting around in a doctor's waiting room. She had done that quite enough when she was twenty-three—she would have thought she was past that now. In any case, she had enough trepidation about meeting William Kingman to begin with without this unnerving delay.

The nurse, now dressed in street clothes, was sitting at her desk, typing up some records.

"I don't think I can wait any longer," Isabel said, getting up and walking over to where the nurse sat. "Please tell Dr. Kingman I waited as long as I could."

The nurse looked shocked. "Doctor wouldn't like you to leave. He is expecting to see you."

Isabel felt reprimanded and sat down again.

How had she allowed herself to be put in this position? First, she had agreed to come to Dr. Kingman's office rather than have him come to hers or to meet on some neutral ground. Then she had allowed him to gain the upper hand even more decisively by coming early while he came late, and now he had, in some way, put her under the control of this officious nurse who had just reduced her to a schoolgirl.

The front door opened and a tall, distinguished man in a navy blue blazer entered the office. He did not look as though he had just come from performing an operation or indeed from any other professional duties.

"Dr. Dunne?" He looked at his wristwatch. "I'm so sorry. Please forgive me, but it will take just another five minutes for me to get ready. I have to make one quick call." He rushed off to another door, saying to his nurse as he went, "You can leave now, Mrs. Gregory. I'll go through my messages myself."

He closed the door behind him and Mrs. Gregory walked out the front door. Isabel was again left alone. She began to wonder if all this had been carefully planned when William Kingman opened the door and said, "By way of atonement for all this delay, would you allow me to take you to the Carlyle for a drink. It's quiet there and we can talk. This office can be a bit gloomy at this hour, and we both could use some cheering up."

Of course, she would go to the Carlyle. He was, as she knew he would be, as charming as he was assured. She felt vulnerable, afraid.

A man in a tuxedo greeted them at the entrance to the Carlyle's Bemelmans Bar. "Dr. Kingman, we haven't seen you in a while. Glad you could stop by."

"How's your knee, George? Still doing those exercises I told you about?"

"I keep forgetting, Doctor, but the knee's a little better," George said, as he guided them across the room to a corner table directly beneath one of the brightly colored murals of Paris that decorated the bar. "What will it be?"

William looked inquiringly at Isabel. "I think I'll have a kir," she said, startled to hear herself order this drink which she had not had or thought of in over a decade.

"Chivas Regal on the rocks?" George asked William, who nodded. He brought both drinks and left.

Isabel sat there looking at the murals, at the few other people, at her own drink, at anything to avoid looking directly at William Kingman. She was so struck by his appearance—his tanned face that would have been rugged had it not been so refined, his quick broad smile, his regal and yet relaxed bearing—that it was almost as difficult to look at him as it was to stare up at the sun.

"I think perhaps I should come right to the point, Dr. Dunne."

"Please do."

"I wish to see my son."

"I can understand that, but as Dr. Richler . . ."

"I am completely aware that both you and Gerson Richler feel that it would be detrimental to Paul to see me, but I have to tell you that I am in complete disagreement with that conclusion."

"It's natural for you to disagree."

"Look, Dr. Dunne, don't patronize me." His voice had become sharp.

"I was not about to. I was only trying to tell you that I appreciate how uncomfortable your position is, and the additional strain that this estrangement from your son must be putting on you. However, you must understand that Paul's total well-being has to be my primary consideration."

"And you don't think it is mine?"

"Of course, it's just that I don't think, in this instance, you can see the situation as clearly as an outsider."

William looked furious. "I think I know my son as well as anyone could. And I think I know what's good for him as well."

"Let me remind you that your son tried to kill himself, and unsuccessful suicide attempts are frequently followed by others which may well be successful. I don't think any of us can afford to take risks with Paul."

"I don't see the risk as you see it. To me, it's just the opposite. Suicide attempts are made by the estranged, the people who have no families, no close ties."

Isabel wondered how much she should tell William Kingman at this point. Many parents of troubled children were racked with guilt, highly sensitive themselves to any statement that might imply they were responsible for their child's suffering. But this man exuded such self-confidence, such assurance, that Isabel felt she could talk plainly.

"Yes, some suicide attempts are made by people whose mental anguish comes in part from their loneliness. But, in Paul's case, it is quite different. You, your family, all of you, are the source of Paul's agony. And he needs to be stronger before he can deal directly with you and the pain you represent."

"I appreciate your frankness, brutal as it is." William's voice was icy. He took a large swallow of scotch.

Isabel wondered, Had she made a mistake in saying as much as she did, as strongly as she did? He was clearly not the man of iron she had judged him to be. She would have to do something now to appease him.

"Dr. Kingman, would it be any help at all if I told you that Paul might be able to see one or another of his cousins? I really do think it would be too much for him to handle his uncles or aunts or his mother." She consciously avoided mentioning him.

William abruptly looked at his watch. "I'm afraid I have another engagement, Dr. Dunne. Perhaps we can talk about this more over the phone."

Isabel, startled, could hardly answer. At any rate, there seemed to be nothing left to say.

Moments later, outside the Carlyle, William put her in a taxi. "I know you'll think this a chauvinist remark," he said before he closed the door, "but somehow, talking to you on the phone, I never thought you'd be so feminine."

Isabel, an hour later, was lying in a warm bath. She could not stop thinking about William Kingman and his last remark. He was a Jekyll and Hyde—harsh, almost cruel one moment, charming and warm the next. Paul had said nothing about this mercurial aspect of his father's personality, and she wondered if she were up to the task of dealing with it. She would have to keep some distance between William Kingman and herself. No one in a very long time had made her feel so weak, so frail, so conscious of herself as a woman.

William Kingman told the cabdriver to drop him off at the corner of Twelfth Street and Fifth Avenue. It was a one-way street going east and he would walk the short distance west, past the gardens of the First Presbyterian Church, the row of wide graystones, and then the narrow brownstones. It was up the steps of one of these last that William walked, opening the heavy front door with one key and the inside parlor-floor door with another.

He entered the large high-ceilinged room with its ornate moldings, small-paned windows, and carved fireplace, all from another era. On the mantel was a note with a "W" written on it. William picked it up, opened it, and read. "Was exhausted, up since 6 A.M., so am napping. Wake me. K."

William walked into the darkened bedroom. The light from the living room streamed in so that he could see the sleeping young woman on the bed, her long blond hair covering the pillows. He pulled the sheet back carefully so as not to wake her as yet, and he stood staring at her naked body.

It was her skin above all, he realized, that was most perfect. It was like mother-of-pearl in its luminescence, its smoothness. She was lying on her side, her body curved into a silken S. Her right hand was flung across her large breasts with their soft pink aureoles. Her left hand was stretched out across the bed, almost beckoning him to join her. He felt the blood pulsing toward his groin, his arteries dilating, his heart rate increasing, his organ stiffening. He quickly took off his clothes and lay down next to her, placing his lips on her stomach. She began to stir as he moved his lips down her belly, his tongue tracing a line from her navel down to her mons veneris. With his thumb, he found her clitoris, beginning to massage it until he felt it grow erect, while his fingers separated her labia and reached into her vagina. She was moist, ready for him.

"William," she sighed, coming to life. "I've been wanting you in my sleep."

"Sh-h-h, go back to sleep," he whispered, stroking her thighs, her buttocks.

"Okay"—she grinned—"I'm sleeping."

He slipped one of the pillows under her hip and began to straddle her, now moved his penis into the warm silky tunnel he had prepared moments before with his fingers. As he looked at her body, her back arched beneath him, her nipples erect, her face flushed and rosy, his excitement grew more and more intense until he reached a plateau of pleasure where he waited for her to join him before exploding into orgasm.

"Cigarette?" she asked, offering one from the pack on the night table. He shook his head, as she lit one for herself.

"What a day," she began. "Can you believe a six o'clock call in New Jersey? My agent said it was worth it, though. This commercial is definitely slated for network prime time."

"And that means some Hollywood producer will see you washing your hair and call to offer you the lead in his next movie?"

"Would that he would. But all I have in mind is paying for my rent and food plus next year's acting classes. The rest is all gravy, and I'd give it up in a minute for a juicy part."

"I could always help you, you know," he said, kissing her neck.

"Don't even talk that way. For one thing, I manage very well by myself even if washing my hair, dabbing perfume behind my ears, and leaping around in pantyhose is an idiotic way to make a living. For another, playing the role of rich man's mistress is just not my scene. What you can do for me right now, however"—she paused and kissed him on the cheek—"is buy me some dinner. I'm famished."

She sat up and got out of bed, leaning her weight on her right arm in the process. "Hey, that hurts," she said, rubbing her wrist.

"Is that fracture still bothering you? It shouldn't be," he said, reaching out to examine the injured joint.

"No, not really, only when I lean on it. I'll be fine. Do you mind waiting while I take a quick shower? I'll be ready in a few minutes."

William lay back in bed. He really should have her come into the office and check that wrist out again. It had been a tricky fracture and she would probably always have some residual discomfort. Too bad, but then had she not had that fracture in the first place, he never would have met her.

It had been a Sunday morning in Shropshire. He was driving back from the small village grocery where he had gone to pick up the Sunday papers when state trooper Dan Matthewson had flagged down his Porsche. There had been a car accident and Dan asked the doctor if he would take a look at the driver, a local girl. A tennis ball had rolled under the brakes and she had, responding to the wrong instincts as she had explained, bent down to pick it up on a turn.

William was frequently called in to help out in emergency situations—the time Josh Hall's tractor had overturned, splintering his femur; or the time Rick Turnbull's son fell out of the apple tree. But never had being a Good Samaritan, he smiled to himself, paid off quite so well. The girl leaning against the fence near the ditch where her red Volkswagen lay stranded was one of the most striking young women he had ever seen. And he wanted her from the moment he had seen her. There was something familiar about her and though she had, she told him, been born and brought up in Shropshire, he was sure he knew her from somewhere else.

"It's your hair," he said, with sudden recognition. "You're the girl in that shampoo commercial on television—the one who's always tossing her head. I'm surprised you haven't dislocated a vertebra."

She admitted that she was indeed the shampoo girl, adding that she also recognized him. When she had been younger, she had been acquainted with the younger Kingmans. Now, however, she only visited Shropshire on weekends to see her father and was living in New York.

Yes, he thought, she must be in her early twenties, just the age that most of the young people left Shropshire.

"Well, since you live in New York," he said, "why don't you come into my office there tomorrow and I can X-ray that wrist then. I'll splint it for you in the meantime."

She agreed, and the next day, she agreed again to have dinner with him. She did so, however, only after making it perfectly clear that she didn't quite see herself as "the other woman" and had no intention of either coming between William and his wife or, in fact, becoming anything important in William's life at all. William found her outspokenness incredibly refreshing. Furthermore, her view of what form their relationship would take—a casual if exciting interlude which would interfere with nothing in either of their lives—was precisely the same as his own. He assured her that whatever should happen between them, his marriage was and would remain a thing apart. He also relieved her conscience, which he thought he sensed troubling her, by making it very clear that she was not setting some sort of evil precedent. He had had affairs before and would have them again in the future. Besides, their May and September romance, should it ever blossom, he laughed, was hardly the kind with a great future to it anyway.

So they had had their dinner and several after that until, as they both knew from the first, they ended up in bed together. It was incredibly exciting for both of them. Her openness and frankness characterized her lovemaking as well and gave it a rare and delightful lightness. Very early on in their affair, she gave him her key, telling him that he could come and go as he wished. It surprised him until she explained that she had had very few love affairs and felt herself quite incapable of having more than one lover at a time. She was an incurable monogamist, she admitted, even though it might be out of fashion these days.

But monogamist or not, she had no intention of committing herself on a truly important level. She was totally absorbed by her career—not commercials, of course, but acting. She took classes three times a week from Tascha Yaslovsky at the Berghof Studio and had voice lessons once a week at Carnegie Hall. A tap class, a fencing class, and a mime class completed her week, which, together with learning her parts in Tascha's group and her work on commercials—she was an extremely successful model and much in demand—kept her so busy that she had little time for other men. It was hard enough to make time for William. But she did, and he had had the key to her apartment for more than half a year now.

It was a perfect place for "secluded rendezvous," he thought, but something else as well—a place to escape to, to relax in. He found himself going there sometimes even when he knew she wouldn't be home for hours. Sometimes he would read, sometimes he would listen to music, and sometimes he would just nap.

It was a dramatic apartment, not only because of its fourteen-foot ceilings and nine-foot windows, but because of the way it had been decorated. Richard, her homosexual actor friend, had really put the place together for her, with the help of his roommate, Franco, a window dresser at Saks. The two, she told William laughingly, had come in for a week and with a flurry of hammers, thumbtacks, chintzes, muslins, a bolt of charcoal-gray felt, a staple gun, and even some old lace tablecloths, had transformed her rent-stabilized three-room floor-through into a production worthy of Saks Fifth Avenue windows at Christmastime. She had just stopped them, at the last moment, she told William, before they had mirrored the ceiling of her bedroom. That, she said, would have simply been too much.

"Hmmm, I'm not so sure about that. It might have been fun now and then with the mirrors, having four of us in the room at once. And I don't mean you, me, Richard, and Franco."

Now, lying on the paisley-patterned sheets of the queen-size bed, staring up at the gray felt ceiling, William thought about the mirror again with a sort of wry amusement. At least so far, they hadn't needed the added stimulation of an overhead reflection. In fact, as she came back into the bedroom wearing a lime-green silk blouse which clung to the curves of her full breasts, he thought he would have preferred to forget about dinner altogether.

She laughed, knowing what he was thinking without his saying a word. "Come on, now, I'm starved. I give you just ten minutes to shower and dress."

He got out of bed, kissed her on the neck, and then went into the bathroom and turned on the shower. The stream of warm water felt good as it hit his back, rolled down his thighs, spilled over his toes. The tinge of desire he had felt before transformed itself into a sensation of satisfied well-being. It had been a good evening, a good day, in fact. He would have no trouble at all with that Dr. Dunne.

8

ISABEL SAT on the brown velvet couch in Paul's apartment, watching him squeeze thick ribbons of shiny, flesh-toned oil paints onto his palette. With a slender wedge-shaped knife, he folded one color into the next, stirring and spreading samples of each of the mixed tones on the canvas before him. He was trying, he explained, to capture the color of her skin, and flesh tones were always the most challenging to reproduce. He had begun her portrait some days ago, after he had finally been satisfied with the last of the dozens of preliminary charcoal sketches, pastel drawings, watercolor studies he had done of her. Sometimes she would pose for him as often as two or three evenings a week, and she had sat for him an entire Saturday while he produced a full eight sketches. Invariably, their posing sessions climaxed with the two of them making love, Paul growing more and more secure, adept, and passionate.

Isabel loved lying in his arms, aware of her own naked body in a way she hadn't been for years. She was seeing herself, as it were, through Paul's eyes, and so part of her pleasure was a newly aroused vanity in her own lines and dimensions. The rest, of course, were the reawakened sensations, a chain of sharp, unbelievably pleasurable reactions, that moved from one part of her physical being to the next. She marveled that after a decade of quiescence, her body was still capable of responding in this way, that the delicate structure of signals and messages had not broken down, had not completely atrophied.

The sensations brought her back in time and she felt young again, a sense of herself intensified by the youthful body that lay next to her. And sometimes, when her eyes were closed, she could almost not sort out the past from the present. There was something delightful in this confusion of time.

She took pleasure too in the pleasure she was giving him, in the look of near ecstasy that gripped him while they were making love, in the look of rapture which came over his face afterward. That apparent joy was part of her evidence that what she was doing was the right thing. After all, before knowing her, he had never experienced anything like this, and his failure in this aspect of life was crucial to his denial of life itself.

But it was not only that she was leading him from impotency to virility where sex was concerned, it was also that she was encouraging a potency in him in other areas as well. Certainly, it was because of her and their relationship that he had begun to paint again after almost a year of artistic immobility, a year of empty canvases and dried-out palettes.

Yet she knew that despite all of this proof that what she was doing was the right thing, much of the world would condemn her. And she could not help but be terrified of such condemnation, knowing that along with it would come the destruction of everything she had built—her career, her sanity. Her debt to Larsen could never be fulfilled. She could never carry out the work he had always believed she would. What would William Kingman do if he knew about her and Paul? A shudder came over her—it was almost too frightening to think about. He would humiliate her publicly. He would destroy her. And he would have no sympathy, no leniency, and neither would anyone else. The world would see her as the corrupter. She remembered as a child seeing an illustration in a textbook of a vicious-looking serpent—a monster with claws and scales and fangs—one of the servants of Satan, it had said below the drawing. Would the world envision her this way? Of course it would. The doctor and the patient, the older woman and the young boy. How could she seem anything but evil to anyone looking at her from the outside?

But that wasn't the way it was. That wasn't the way it was at all. She wasn't leading Paul into corruption. She wasn't leading Paul into sin. Oh, God, she started. What was she saying? She had slipped again, fallen back into the images and terms of Catholicism. When she was terrified, she realized, when she felt herself insecure, she slipped back into the punishing strictures of what had been her religion. Together with her guilt came the bloody nightmares of her childhood, the dreaded images of pain and hell.

But when she was sure of herself and the correctness of her actions, she thought in other terms, those terms psychiatry used to encase human motives and actions. Here there was no sin, no evil. At worst there were destructive instincts, obsessions, and compulsions. And one didn't punish them, one cured them, one healed them. Larsen had cured her. More, he had given her faith in herself and in her own instincts. And if her instincts told her to make Paul her lover, Larsen would have believed her right. If only he were here to tell her this, how much easier it would all have been.

But even without Larsen, she could see how she had done the right thing. Paul was so delicate, so fragile. Sensitive, introspective, brooding, he needed her to bring him out, to clarify his sexual ambivalence. Had this in some way accounted for his impotency? Isabel wondered. Had he ever had any homosexual relations? she had asked him one day.

No, he hadn't, though on several occasions homosexuals had made overtures to him. Once, falling asleep on the New Haven railroad going back to Rhode Island, his classmate who sat next to him started stroking his cheek. Paul had awakened with a start to see the other's face coming closer and smiling. "I'm sorry," he remembered himself saying.

"And I was sorry. Crazy as it might sound to you, it would have been a relief to be a homosexual, to have some sexual relationship after all. But I was nothing, neuter. I couldn't have sex with him or with any man or with any woman. That is, until you." He went to embrace her, but she held him off. "You don't know what you mean to me. What you are to me."

But she did know. What puzzled her, what plagued her instead, was what he meant to her.

Of course, he aroused her. Of course, she loved the physical pleasure he gave her. But if it were truly Paul she wanted, why had she seen the face of William Kingman that very first night he made love to her? And why was it William Kingman who occupied her thoughts, who overwhelmed her dreams, even more than Paul. In her dreams it was always William who was her lover, just as it was always his office which was the scene of their lovemaking.

And there was the other dream she had had too, the dream about the faceless man. She had performed an operation, grafting onto him Paul's eyes, nose, mouth, chin. But when she removed the bandages, she discovered that the operation was a failure, that the features had all slipped off and that he was faceless again.

Isabel shuddered at the thought and then felt she couldn't sit still any longer. "I'm beginning to creak," she said. "Is this a bad moment to stop?"

"No, it's fine."

"Can I look?" she asked.

"Yes, but you won't see much change from the last time. It seems to be slow going at this stage."

Even in this incomplete form, the printing had the grace of Paul's line, the subtle contrast of dark and light, the delicate interplay between shades and color that were all characteristic of his work as a whole. He had captured something vital.

"You are really very talented," she said to him. "I think you ought to seriously consider working toward a show. You've never exhibited those wonderful seascapes you did of Watch Hill Beach when you were in Rhode Island or that series of etchings of trees you did in Shropshire."

"I'm not sure I'm ready for, good enough for, any show. I think I'd rather wait."

"You ought to get someone else's opinion on that, someone more objective than either of us. If I come up with the name of some gallery owner who might be interested in looking at your work, could he come up here?"

"Would you be with me?"

"If you want me to be."

Who of all the people she knew would know about the art world of New York? Isabel wondered. Sandy Richler, of course. And as usual, he came through. It seemed that Mark Singer had a classmate at the High School of Music and Art, Marcel Block, whose family owned the Block Gallery on Fifty-seventh Street and who had, five years before, opened his own gallery in SoHo which, Sandy said, "I'm embarrassed to tell you is named 'Mental Block.'" Marcel, reacting to the dour atmosphere he grew up in—his parents, wealthy and cultured French Jews who narrowly escaped from the Nazis, were filled with a tragic sense of life that permeated their home and, inevitably, Marcel's childhood—had developed an Oscar Wilde flippancy. "Overcompensation," Sandy said to Isabel. "If you can stomach his dandyism and the fact that everything he says is derived either from Oscar Wilde or the latest movie, he has a fine eye for art and his gallery is considered one of the best in the city."

Isabel laughed. "You needn't prepare me. I meet lots of odd types in my work."

"I guess you do," Sandy said. "Listen, if you can wait a couple of weeks, Mark and Sylvia are coming to town, without the twins this time, thank God, and we could all have dinner together along with Marcel. Then you could talk to him about your artist friend. It should be an amusing evening—that is, if you don't mind going around New York with a man who only wears white suits."

"As you must know, I am accustomed to men in white suits."

But Marcel Block not only wore a white suit, he also wore a white tie, white shoes, and even a white beret. Yet no one in the SoHo Delicate Essen seemed to notice or care. Either Marcel was a familiar sight to these denizens of SoHo, Isabel thought, or among so many idiosyncratic costumes, his was hardly noteworthy.

"You must be invisible in a snowstorm," Mark observed. "You sure have come far from the plaid shirts and corduroys you used to wear at Music and Art."

"However do you keep those clothes so clean in the city?" If everyone else in this restaurant was blasé, Sylvia was wide-eyed.

"I polish them," Marcel answered. "I've always thought in my profession that if you couldn't create a work of art, you might as well be one yourself."

"You didn't think that." Mark grinned. "Oscar Wilde did."

"I guess I owe a lot to old Oscar. But then, so do many others, at least those cultural Robin Hoods around here who are always stealing from the witty and giving to the dull."

Sandy and Isabel exchanged glances, and Isabel laughed. The evening was turning out to be an amusing one. Even without Marcel, SoHo had a distinctive charm. Isabel had never been down here before, and she particularly enjoyed walking through the narrow side streets, one of which led to the SoHo Delicate Essen. It was the variations in this neighborhood that struck her, the contrast between a newly renovated Federal house with shiny brass doorknobs, its redwood window boxes filled with sweet peas, trailing ivy, and geraniums, and the plumbing supply store next to it with displays of toilets, sinks, and pipes. Or the contrast between a Mom and Pop candy store, with its long soda fountain counter populated by the under-ten crowd, leafing through the store's supply of comic books and licking their cones or sipping their egg creams (at least, that's what Sandy called the concoction of chocolate syrup and soda water which contained neither egg nor cream) and the elegant boutique next to it in whose window stood a dramatically posed mannequin garbed in a filmy chiffon evening dress, spotlights on her and a hidden fan making the chiffon billow.

Marcel's charms were infinitely less varied than those of SoHo and verged on being as monochromatic as his outfit. He seemed, Isabel thought, an odd choice of friend for serious, studious Mark Singer.

"How did you two ever become friends?" Isabel asked.

"Bertolt Brecht brought us together," said Marcel. "In our senior year in high school, Mark did the musical arrangements for the senior production of *Mother Courage,* and I did the costumes and sets."

"What sets?" Mark asked. "As I remember, we played *Mother Courage* on a bare stage."

"And you don't think that was a genius inspiration?" Marcel said with a flourish of both hands. Isabel noticed he wore three rings on his right hand—a coiled snake on his pinky, a huge amethyst on his ring finger, and what looked like a class ring on his index finger. He really was rather ridiculous, she thought. His thin light brown hair was parted in the middle and hung in a carefully executed pageboy, his glasses were little round spheres surrounded by silver wire, his face was scrubbed pink, and he exuded the strong aroma of spice, giving Isabel the faint sensation of sitting next to a cinnamon bun.

"Of course, I'd be delighted to see your young friend's lithos," Marcel was saying to Isabel. "But don't expect me to be polite. And I hope he's not the 'sensitive artist' type. The last thing I'd like is to receive a severed ear in the mail. And especially"—he turned to Sylvia—"since our New York mail comes so late that putrefaction would surely set in before it arrived."

Sylvia, her first time away from the twins in many months, was clearly enjoying herself immensely. Marcel, if he was ridiculous, was also very funny, and Sylvia was a perfect foil for him, feeding him lines almost as if she were his straight man.

"Hmmm," she had said, "I just love this pâté. Marcel, do you think they'd ever tell you the recipe?"

"Not only wouldn't they tell me," he said in an ominous voice, "but if I were you, I really wouldn't want to know."

"Oh, Marcel, that's not very kind," Sylvia went on. "Just think, if you were in that chef's shoes . . ."

"Impossible," said Marcel. "What do you think he used to make the pâté?"

Whatever Marcel might have said about the customers and cuisine at the Delicate Essen, it, nevertheless, Sylvia told him, served as a delightful backdrop for him, what with its immaculate lightwood floors, its butcher block tables, and its gleaming counter displaying an assortment of cheeses and mixed salads.

Marcel made it clear that he would have preferred a more baroque and less mundane setting. He really didn't relish the idea of taking stage center on a butcher block.

Sandy, growing tired of all this silly banter—after all, it was not Marcel's wit but his keen appreciation of art that had made Sandy arrange this meeting with Isabel—decided to change the subject and began to question Marcel about current trends in painting.

"You see," Marcel answered Sandy's complaint against the new photographic realism, "what these painters are doing is not merely copying reality. They are, whether you accept it or not, transforming it. And that's where the art lies. They take the most common thing—garbage, a cut of meat, a typewriter—and force you to appreciate, as they have, the uncommonness in it."

Of course, he was right, Isabel thought. So this walking confection called Marcel Block who seemed all frosting had, in fact, some substance. He was, however, quite easily distracted, she saw, and preferred to affect superficiality than to risk failed profundity. Now, for example, having made his comments on contemporary realism, rather than pursue such a potentially pedantic topic, he abruptly shifted his focus.

"Good God," he said, indicating the crowd gathering at the Delicate Essen's entryway. "The place is getting to look like a suburban shopping center."

Isabel glanced around her. The Delicate Essen clearly was a very popular place. There were people waiting by the counter for tables, and a tall slender black hostess, wearing blue jeans which showed off what Marcel termed "*the* perfect ass," was taking their names or checking them off her list. She escorted one couple down to a table that had just become available across the room. It was the girl who caught Isabel's attention at first. Tall, slender, and with a long mane of shiny silvery blond hair, she was so beautiful, she seemed to attract everyone's attention.

"Oh," Sylvia said in an excited voice. "Isn't that the girl in the Belle Chevelle shampoo ad? You know, Mark, the one who's always tossing her head and flashing her teeth?"

She might indeed have been that girl but Isabel had stopped thinking about her, even stopped seeing her, for the man next to the girl, now holding her chair, was someone whose face was much more familiar to Isabel than any girl in any ad: William Kingman.

The rest of the dinner was excruciating for Isabel and must have been, she thought, excruciating for William as well. She knew he had noticed her although he did nothing to acknowledge this, and she carefully refused, in return, to let her eyes meet his. Still, he must have been aware that she had caught him with someone who was clearly his latest affair.

She was struck by her own reaction, for what she was feeling, she realized, was something akin to jealousy. No, more than that. She was as jealous as she had ever been in her life. She was so miserable that it was all she could do to summon up the appropriate words and manner of appreciation when Marcel made a date to go up and look at the work of her young artist friend.

"Did you see that man in the white suit who just left?" Kirsten asked William. "That was Marcel Block. He owns the gallery where Christopher exhibits. I'm sure he'll be at Chris's party, too."

"Too?" said William. "I told you I didn't think I was up to any party tonight after the day I've had in the hospital."

"What's the matter with you?" she asked. "You've been acting so odd since we came in here. Don't you like this place?"

Her voice was grating on him now. He only wanted her to stop talking, stop pressuring, stop asking him what was wrong. It was her fault that he had been put in this position, being seen having dinner in this pretentious and coy restaurant with someone so hopelessly flamboyant that she couldn't help but be noticed. Why did she always have to be on stage, always in costume? What female over twelve years old wore her hair down to her waist that way? But of course she wanted to be noticed. Wasn't that what her career was all about? More and more, he found himself arriving at her apartment, ready for a quiet drink, an intimate dinner, only to find himself being dragged off instead to some party or other. There was an opening of a new play on Broadway with a cast party at Tavern-on-the-Green. The producers of a movie musical were throwing a bash at Studio 54. The Museum of Modern Art was having a party in its garden to inaugurate its festival of silent comedies. And she had to go to each and every one. Mike Nichols might be there, Dino De Laurentiis might be there, David Merrick might be there, Lee Guber, Dick Cavett, Barbara Walters, Arthur Miller. You never knew when the chemistry might be right, when the big break might be coming. At first, William had to admit, he found himself enjoying those parties. Even given his own stature as a Kingman and noted surgeon, there was something appealing about this glamorous world of Beautiful People—of movie stars, high-fashion models, and high-priced designers, best-selling novelists and modish painters—that spoke to a part of him he had long since put away, that had been left behind in France that summer he almost didn't return to medical school.

But it didn't take long before these evenings became a bore and he began to see Kirsten's whole social world as hopelessly superficial and ludicrous. With few exceptions, the people at these functions were totally predictable. Their looks were stereotyped, their conversations banal, their sensibilities essentially vulgar. What was most ridiculous was the false intimacy they brought to even the most casual of relationships. Everyone at these parties made a point of hugging and kissing everyone else, always fawning, always flattering whoever was in sight. Yet while they smiled at you, they were busily glancing over your shoulder to see who was standing behind you. They were careful not to waste a moment, not to throw away a chance, not to miss an opportunity.

William made his view of Kirsten's world clear.

Did he think of her that way too? she asked him.

Sometimes, he had to admit.

She was hurt, more hurt than she had been the time she had heard that Paul was in the hospital and she asked William just what was wrong with him. William had acted as if she were peering through keyholes or reading his mail. She had meant only to show concern, but his attitude seemed to be that anything to do with his son or the Kingman family was too sacred for her to know about.

She had chosen to overlook this, though, realizing that he was upset at the time. This current attack, however, was directed precisely at her. He was being an elitist, putting her down, putting her world down. He was assuming, she told him, the old-fashioned New England view of show business inherited from the Puritans. He was being as arrogant and prejudiced as Dorothy Parker when she had summed up Hollywood as a white-gloved hand leaning out of a Cadillac, holding a buttered bagel with a bite taken out of it.

How literary of her, he had answered. He hadn't thought she'd had the time, partying as she did, to have read Dorothy Parker.

That argument had ended with William not coming to see Kirsten for a week. He had kept her key, though, and one night he dropped into her apartment after leaving the hospital, offering no explanation for his absence and no apologies. Kirsten was happy to see him and told him how foolish she thought they both had been to argue about their different tastes and different worlds. It made no sense for them to fight this way. After all, theirs was a relationship with no ties and no responsibilities. All they owed one another was pleasure.

With this last observation William agreed and for a while he simply refused to join her at her various parties, using a different argument, when he bothered to use one at all. With everyone asking "Who are you?" or "Who were you?" all the time, there was the possibility, although slim, that he might run into someone he knew. Of course, he had planned from the outset that should such a thing occur, he would pretend to be alone. But he had never been convinced that this would work, and he was now less convinced than ever.

Why then had he ever agreed to join her tonight? The occasion wasn't even one of her glamorous all-star fetes but instead, one of those parties which to him were even worse, those given by her "pals" in acting class, parties that didn't even have the allure of the rich and famous, or the elegant locale, or the tasteful cuisine. And they were usually in the kind of primitively furnished SoHo loft he was being dragged to tonight.

What was he doing here? Dammit, this place was ridiculous with its ridiculous name, Delicate Essen, the foolish people sitting around, staring at each other, that absurd man in white that Kirsten had pointed out. And what was that man doing with Paul's psychiatrist? A patient perhaps? Would his own son end up in a white suit or something equally idiotic, surrounded by sycophants and idolators? Damn that psychiatrist. What was she doing here? He hated to see her have the edge over him this way. Wasn't it enough that he'd had to give in to her as much as he had? He'd agreed to the additional month of grace that she had begged for on the telephone the day after their meeting at the Carlyle. For despite Ernest and Natalie's admonitions, William realized that Dr. Dunne was right, the risk was still too great to take at this point. He would not insist on seeing Paul yet.

"Listen," Kirsten interrupted his thoughts. "Let's leave. You obviously don't like it here, and we can get coffee at Christopher's loft."

"Kirsten, I'm not in the mood for any parties, especially in a loud crowded loft filled with a bunch of fairies smoking dope."

"Some of those 'fairies,' as you so quaintly put it, happen to be my friends, I'd like to remind you."

"I wish you wouldn't remind me. That's one side of you I'd just as soon forget."

She took out her compact and started to put on some lipstick, a gesture he had made clear many times that he detested. "Thanks a lot, William. I think that if you're tired, you ought to go home and get to bed. I'm going to Christopher's. He's expecting me."

William was stunned. He admired her independence, it was part of her appeal. But this wasn't independence, it was more in the order of rebellion. A woman didn't simply pick herself up and leave the man she was with and take herself to a party without him. It was rude, it was self-indulgent, it was inconsiderate. He was furious but he said nothing. He hated scenes, especially in public.

He simply got up, left a startled Kirsten with a fifty-dollar bill to cover the check, and walked out of the restaurant.

There was something funny going on between Paul Kingman and that Dr. Dunne, Addie Harris told Catherine during their lunch break. Since Addie had started working in pediatrics, there were no chances for those nice relaxing cigarettes in the nurses' lounge together. Instead, they had to make more formal dates to meet and have lunch, dinner, coffee breaks, depending on their schedules.

"You're nuts," Catherine said. "Do you think any doctor would risk her career just to screw around with a patient? He might be irresistible to you but there are others who have more sense."

Addie jumped. She had never told Catherine about that night with Paul, so how would she know? But of course she didn't. Catherine was just talking about Addie's crush on Paul, not her secret and disastrous attempt at seduction. Catherine was obviously not as sharp as she thought she was. There were a lot of things she didn't see or know about that Addie did.

"I tell you," Addie said, "I saw them together in the hall, and the way he looked at her was a dead giveaway."

"Then that Dr. Dunne must be a pretty busy lady. I've heard that she and Richler's son are a big number."

"Well, he sounds more her speed. But I tell you, whatever is going on with Richler's son, something's also going on with Paul Kingman."

And whatever it was, Addie didn't intend to just let it happen. Dr. Dunne may have saved Addie her job, but there was a limit to what Addie owed her for that.

* * *

William Kingman seemed to inspire sexuality, Isabel thought. And it was not only the effect he had on her. Paul had spoken about the response of women to his father, and she herself had seen just the night before the beautiful blond woman who was with William at the restaurant in SoHo. Surely they were lovers. Paul's own sexual problems, his analysis had already pointed up, were tied to his father's allure and evident capacity for making love. What was not yet clear was the moment at which those problems had manifested themselves to Paul.

"Tell me," she encouraged him to speak as the two sat in her office, starting the morning session. "When did you first think of yourself as impotent? Can you remember a particular incident?"

It took Paul some minutes to answer. "Yes," he said softly. "I guess I can. But I never really think about it that way. I think about it as the other time I almost died."

It was the year that Paul was eighteen, the year Uncle Ernest won the Nobel Prize, making the family name, if not a household word, at least known to those who read the front page of the New York *Times*. For many years a leader among conservative economists, Ernest had finally come out with his lengthy historical study of Marxist economic theory, proving that the traditional view of the relation of capital to value was based on erroneous assumptions. He put forth a brilliant case for looser controls in monetary economics and reasoned for the necessity of floating exchange rates, arguments that impressed the members of the Swedish Academy enough to give him the edge over German economic historian Hans Gottlieb.

The entire Kingman family went over en masse for the ceremony in December, almost filling the first-class section of the SAS plane, since they now included in their numbers the husbands of Margo and Allison and Margo's infant daughter. They all stayed at the Grand Hotel across from the Royal Palace, where they were treated like royalty themselves. Paul would never forget the ceremony. It began with a blast of trumpets and the explosions from rows of cannons on the battlements along the harbor, while it seemed that every church bell in the entire city rang out. Then there was a huge ceremonial procession from the cathedral to the Swedish Academy. The cortege included gray-haired distinguished gentlemen in white tie and tails with medals across their chests, stately women in long satin gowns, and young girls all dressed in white, carrying bouquets of flowers.

When the bells stopped and everyone was seated in the great hall, there was a series of pronouncements and long speeches, some in Latin, some in Swedish, and a few, fortunately for Paul's uncomprehending ears, in English. And then there was Ernest, looking as though he truly belonged in this company, receiving his award and giving his acceptance speech, copies of which had already been sent to leading newspapers all over the world.

There was a banquet that night, and all that week the family was invited to luncheons, dinners, and parties. One evening, they all were at the home of Max Dahlbeck, a member of parliament and the scion of Sweden's leading steel manufacturing family. Max, it turned out, had four children between the ages of eighteen and twenty-five, and one of them, pretty twenty-year-old Anne-Mari, was very much taken with Franklin. Whether or not Max was aware of Anne-Mari's feelings, he ended up inviting Phillip, Franklin, and Paul, all of whom were planning a European trip that summer, to come and spend a few weeks on his island Ulfland, about a two-hour sail from Stockholm in the Oestsjon. A large group of young people would be there during the summer season, and he was sure the boys would have a wonderful time.

Franklin leaped at the offer, but it did not hold much interest for either Phillip or Paul. Phillip had planned to spend most of that time mountain climbing in Switzerland while Paul had registered for an art course in Florence. But these plans were quickly abandoned as Ernest made clear that Max Dahlbeck's invitation was not one to be turned down.

The boys arrived in Sweden, Paul recalled, the second week in July so as not to disrupt the annual Kingman July Fourth festivities in Shropshire. One of Max Dahlbeck's staff met them at the Stockholm airport and drove them in a huge black Mercedes straight to the marina where a launch was waiting to motor them out to Ulfland, one of the larger of the thousands of islands which made up this archipelago. Max was standing on the dock to greet them. He was a large, stocky man whose skin had been burned pink by the sun and was surrounded by an army of tall blondes. All in their teens and early twenties, they seemed so healthy and vigorous that they could have been the Swedish Olympic team. The boys were given a warm welcome, their young hosts—Max's two sons—even bursting into song.

The island was exquisite, Paul thought, with its steep stony paths leading to the sea, its fir trees and birches and low brush covered with blueberries, lingonberries, and raspberries, its constant canopy of gulls, its raccoons which darted out from woods and ran across the meadows. Ulfland in July still had the long days of midsummer, and the evenings were washed in a cool, almost blue light. Paul was fascinated with how clear the air was, how well defined everything seemed—the sharp outlines of the rocks, the fringed branches of the trees, the huge frame of the Dahlbeck house which stood on a bluff facing the sea. Paul's room was on the seaside, off a huge hallway filled with doors leading to the other bedrooms. There were so many doors that Paul had trouble finding his own room after dinner that first night. The house must have had fifteen bedrooms, and it needed them. Besides the Kingman boys and Max's two sons, Olav and Ivar, and his daughters, Anne-Mari and Gunnel, the house was filled with nephews, nieces, cousins, school friends, who kept coming and going in one or another of the Dahlbeck boats.

"What's funny," Franklin said to Phillip and Paul two days after they arrived, "is that you can't tell these Vikings apart."

"Come off it," Phillip answered. "I notice you can even find Anne-Mari in the dark."

That was all Franklin needed to start him off on one of his lengthy and detailed accounts of his latest adventure with Anne-Mari. These Swedish girls, Franklin assured Paul, were everything they were cracked up to be. Yesterday he and Phillip had gone sailing with Anne-Mari and her sister, Gunnel, and the girls had guided the boat to one of those small deserted islands that made up a large part of the Skargarden archipelago. The girls had told them it was a great spot for picking wild berries.

"But if there were any there, we never saw them," Phillip inserted. "As soon as we anchored, would you believe they both took off their clothes, jumped into the water, and swam to shore, daring us to do the same. And so"—Phillip shrugged with a broad grin—"what could we do?"

"The water was freezing, and the ground was as hard as a rock," Franklin took up the narrative now. "But with a soft warm girl under you, you hardly noticed. Well, not that they were always under you. Christ, those girls screw like acrobats."

"You're an ass, Paul, if you don't get some of that for yourself," Phillip said. "What a place to finally get a piece. The sky overhead, the waves beating on the shore. It's right out of a movie, for godsake."

"And that Inge really has the hots for you," Franklin added.

Of course, Paul would have liked to have a go at it. Inge wasn't exactly his type—she was a little pushy for his taste, and he found her somewhat unfeminine, she was so big and strong. But still, she was a nice-looking girl with her silky brown hair, her big toothy smile, her smooth tanned body, much of which he had already seen since she wore the briefest bikinis of any of the girls. She wasn't a Dahlbeck but a friend of Anne-Mari's younger sister, Gunnel, and, she told him, she had spent much of the past three summers at Ulfland. She knew the waters well. Why didn't he come sailing with her? There were lots of little islands to explore. Staying on Ulfland sketching or reading all day was all right for old ladies like Mrs. Dahlbeck maybe but what a queer thing for him to want to do.

If Paul didn't much like Inge, he liked sailing even less. It made him queasy, and everyone was always shouting orders at each other. "Tie that rope." "Watch the dock." "Don't step there." Sailing seemed to bring out the most officious side of everyone's personality. When Franklin and Phillip were sent to sailing camp one summer on Cape Cod and Paul was offered a chance to join them, he declined with rare forcefulness. His few experiences on Sebastian's nephew's boat sailing on Long Island Sound had turned him off masts and topsails and spinnakers for the rest of his life, except perhaps as subjects for sketches and paintings. He told Inge as much, with the vague hope that she might stay with him while he sketched instead of sailing off with the others. But she apparently didn't want his company enough to give up a sunny day on the sea.

"That's where all the fun is," she said.

He knew she was probably right, that the others did have fun together on those islands. Yet he rather enjoyed these long lovely hours by himself, sketching on the rocks, trying to capture, with his pastels, the strange foreign tonalities of the Swedish light while he listened to the mesmerizing calmness of the lapping sea. The arrival of his father, however, brought an abrupt end to all this. William had been in London, a guest of the Royal Medical Society and a lecturer at St. Mary's. And he had been invited by Max Dahlbeck to join the boys at Ulfland. William's schedule would only allow him to stay a few days, and so he arrived on a Friday morning, planning to take the boys back with him to London Sunday evening.

It took William only a few hours to size up the situation and express his disapproval to Paul. The point was that Paul, unlike his cousins,

Phillip and Franklin, was not entering into the spirit of things, not only the spirit of Ulfland but the spirit of young men everywhere. For this was the time in your life when you had the vitality, the opportunity, and the freedom to play out your passions. Never again would the moment be so right, and Paul was being a fool, throwing it away, wasting it. Good God, had William himself been eighteen, he would have been berry-picking up and down the archipelago and with every pretty girl in sight. What in God's name was wrong with Paul?

Besides, that Inge wasn't half bad. Paul could have done a lot worse than a pretty, athletic Swedish girl like that, who surely knew the score.

Saturday morning, when Paul and William were sitting at the long breakfast table, sipping the rich dark coffee and finishing off the last of their kippered herrings and boiled eggs, Inge stopped by. She was wearing a turned-down sailor hat and a white T-shirt with a peace sign on it. The T-shirt came only slightly below her waist, leaving a smooth brown band of skin showing between its hem and her bikini bottom.

"Morn . . . morn," she said with her big wide grin. "Hey there, Paul, how about you coming sailing today. The wind is fine, the weather is clear. That is, if you don't mind my taking Paul away from you, Dr. Kingman?" She turned to William.

"Of course not. Max and I are going to try our hand at some fishing today. You two go right ahead," William said.

Paul stood up. There was no way out of it now.

Moments later he found himself on the dock, in the midst of what seemed to be a horde of Vikings shipping out to sea in their longboats, ready to invade the coast of Scotland. No fewer than seven different vessels were tied up at the Dahlbeck marina, and the young Dahlbecks, their friends, and Franklin and Phillip and Paul were all being assigned, it seemed, their separate posts. The Kingman cousins were allotted a Ballard and a Folkboat, the former accommodating four, the latter only two.

"Why don't you and Inge come with Anne-Mari and me," Franklin offered. "Phil . . . you and Gunnel can take the Folkboat and we'll all meet at our Little Island of the Wild Berries."

"Fine with me," Phillip answered, untying the Folkboat as Gunnel proceeded to climb in.

"We can spend the day," Anne-Mari shouted out to Gunnel and Phillip as they sailed off. "I've brought lunch." She held up a large straw basket. "And I've got some beer, too," she told Franklin.

The very thought of beer made Paul ill as he felt the first push of the waves beneath him.

"Hey, don't just sit there, Paul," Franklin called out. "Roll up the chain from the anchor. It's all over the place."

If he moved, he might just be sick. But if he didn't, Franklin wouldn't shut up. He had to take the risk and fortunately managed this task without disaster. But it did seem hours before they arrived at the famous Island of the Wild Berries. Phillip and Gunnel were already there, their lighter craft pulled high on the beach. The Ballard, however, was too heavy for such maneuvering so they anchored it instead. The tide was low enough to wade to shore, and they carried the basket of food, some blankets, and the case of beer over their heads.

"Hey, Paul," Franklin yelled at him, "you're dragging that blanket in the water. That'll be yours, pal."

"Thanks a lot," Inge said.

The six of them ate the hastiest lunch Paul could remember, then grabbed a few beers apiece and disappeared, two by two, in opposite directions.

Inge led Paul away from the beach into the shrubbery, warning him to look out for the nettles which seemed to grow all over these islands. However, she knew a lovely spot, she told him, no nettles and a lot of privacy.

When they arrived at the little clearing and sat down on the damp blanket next to each other, Paul felt terrified. He really didn't know how to proceed. He finally reached over to kiss Inge and was surprised by the enthusiasm of her response. She held him tightly at the shoulders, pressing her body against his, and returned his kiss with such intensity that both their bodies tumbled back, prone, onto the ground.

Paul began to stroke her tanned skin, feeling the hard muscles of her sturdy thighs, of her tight stomach. He felt himself growing excited.

"You can make love to me," she whispered in his ear. "That's okay."

Well, then he would, he thought. Why not? Franklin was right. Except for the lack of a more resilient surface beneath them, everything seemed perfect. Inge was willing, helpful, and would also be knowledgeable enough to be on the pill or be using some sort of birth control.

Inge started to take off her clothes as Paul removed his own. Then he looked at her as the sunlight came through the trees. Suddenly he realized that he was seeing someone else, another naked body outdoors, on a blanket, under a tree. He grabbed Inge and held her to him, trying to blot out any memory. She held him too, no doubt mistaking his quick gesture for a stir of passion. But from then on, nothing seemed to be able to happen. Paul felt himself grow soft. The moment that never really arrived was over.

"That happens to everyone, you know," Inge said. "Come on, I can help you." She took his penis in her hand and began to rub.

He pushed her away abruptly. "No," he said. "It's no use, I know it's no use."

"Oh, how do you know?" she asked, her voice becoming impatient. "You're not giving yourself a chance. Or me either."

"I know, Inge. I can tell."

"Well, this certainly isn't turning out to be much fun," she said, getting up, putting her bikini back on, and starting to fold up the blanket. "You could help me, you know," she said. "You don't have to just sit there like that."

Paul stood, put on his shorts and shirt, and helped her carry the blanket and beer back down the beach.

He could think of nothing to say and just stared ahead at her angry back.

"You know," she said, "I am very bored here today. And I think I am going back to Ulfland. If you wish to join me, you can. Or you can wait for the others and pick berries. But I must warn you, from what Anne-Mari has told me, they will take awhile. Your cousins and you have very little in common in that department."

Her sarcasm knifed him, and Paul, in turn, could have killed her. He wanted to get away from her as fast as he could but he really felt he had to go back with her. It would be much worse to face Franklin and Phillip, and then his father. At least, if he returned with Inge, it might fool someone.

They walked down to where the boat was beached. The sea had gotten much rougher, the sky grayer, and it looked as though a storm was coming up.

"We'd better put on our life jackets," Inge said as Paul nodded. "I hate these clumsy things but it would be foolish to leave them off right now."

"Help me push," she told Paul, who did as she instructed, and both climbed into the small Folkboat which Inge expertly turned around, carefully avoiding the sharp rocks near the shoreline.

By the time they got out to the open waters, the sky had become almost black and the air was frigid. They were still quite far from Ulfland but also far, by now, from the tiny island they had left behind. And there was no safe harbor in between.

"Damn this weather," she muttered. "But I think we'll be all right."

Paul said nothing. He was thinking that if everything had turned out different before when they were back on the blanket, they'd still be on that island where they inevitably would have waited out the storm.

Now the rain started, coming in huge pellets which began to fill up the bottom of the boat. Inge gave Paul a can, and he started to bail as she maneuvered the sails. The boat listed so hard that Paul saw the mast almost parallel with the surface of the sea. He was terrified now as he watched Inge, white-faced and grim, struggling with the tiller and the ropes. She shouted instructions to him which, because of the furious winds, he could hardly comprehend. He was given ropes to pull, told to move his weight as the boom flew over his head, and then given the tiller to pull as she grabbed at a rope.

Just then an enormous wave slapped against the side. It was a powerful blow which made the little boat recoil and then jump. Paul looked up just as Inge, her own face registering disbelief, was knocked over the side.

He crawled to the edge of the boat and reached out into the churning water. He could see her, bobbing up and down like a tiny cork. Thank God they'd worn the life jackets.

"I'll get you," he shouted, and she shouted something back he couldn't hear.

He grabbed the tiller and tried to steer toward her, but the wind had shifted, flattened the sail instead of filling it.

Paul finally succeeded in getting the boat to tack up and back, hoping that in one of these passes he could bring it close enough to Inge to reach her.

As he maneuvered the tiller and ropes, he never took his eyes off her. She waved at him for a while but then her arm was down. It looked as though she was trying to float on top of the waves that kept dashing at her, dashing at him, and covering them both. Had he fallen overboard, she would have been able to get him. He, for his part, seemed only to get the boat farther from her.

The sky had become so dark now that he could barely make out the small figure, not much more than a shadow on the sea. He tried to run again but this time a wave lifted the boat, flinging it on its side. Paul felt everything slip out of his hand, his whole body dashed into the stern. When the boat again sprang into an upright position, Paul looked out to see if he could find Inge. The sea had become calmer now as he stared out, searching with his eyes for any form on the now smooth surface.

Paul screamed her name but he heard nothing. The storm was almost over now, and he could handle the boat. He carefully turned it to the direction where he thought he had seen Inge, but without any landmark to guide him, he couldn't even be sure if he was heading toward her or away from her. His mind was racing. If only he had been able to make it with her on the island so that they would have still been there and missed the storm, if only he knew how to handle a sailboat, they would have been all right; if only he were different, everything would be better.

Paul combed the waters for hours, aided by the fact that the sun remained so late in the sky. He kept thinking about the life jacket. That might have kept her up, despite the heavy waves. Then he tried not to think at all, just sailing up and back, peering into the dark blue water.

He stayed until the motor launch from Ulfland came up. The Dahlbeck boys had been looking for them since the storm. They tied the little sailboat to the launch, hoisted him aboard, and then radioed the sea patrol to send a helicopter. The search went on all night, with all the boats from Ulfland along with the ship and the helicopter from the patrol, Dahlbeck himself arriving to join the search for his young guest. But it was no use.

The next day a fisherman found her body, which had been carried by the current almost three miles away from the accident.

Max Dahlbeck was sympathetic and cooperative about keeping the Kingman name out of the papers. As far as the report went, Inge had been sailing alone. William was grateful to Max and was tender with Paul. He understood, he told him, what an awful experience this whole thing must have been.

Phillip and Franklin were sympathetic too, although Franklin couldn't resist an off-color remark or two about how at least Inge's last moments had been happy ones.

Everyone felt for Paul, everyone understood. And that was just the problem.

So this, Paul thought, is what "entering into the spirit of young men" was all about. So this was the "freedom" his father had talked about. A freedom from responsibility, a freedom from scandal, a freedom to do damage and run.

Why didn't they blame him? Screw them all, he was guilty.

9

IT WAS A COOL dry June day when Franklin Rush arrived in New York from Washington. It was his first vacation since the Inauguration in January, and he was anxious to get up to Shropshire. But first there was the compulsory visit to Sebastian's office which, this time, Franklin looked forward to with special enjoyment. His job as a White House aide was precisely the kind that would win him new approval and prestige from the members and employees of Stevenson, Goddard, Carlson, and Rush. And indeed, when he gave his name to the receptionist, he noticed a new reaction, a more concentrated interest in him than even the son of a name partner might expect.

"How are all the President's men these days? Still the best and the brightest, I can see," she smiled.

"Better and brighter than the last batch, I hope," Franklin answered. Had he seen her before? He couldn't quite remember. With her perfect teeth and her shiny hair, she looked exactly like every other young woman who ever sat at this desk—pretty, well bred, and, he thought as he glanced at the gold band she wore, married. The firm seemed to have a policy for the hiring of receptionists. They were always desirable and, at the same time, unobtainable and working to support a husband who was finishing up a doctorate or some kind of internship. This made these overqualified young women poor enough to grab at the job, steady enough to keep it, decorative enough to go with the abstract paintings and rich fabrics on the furniture, and yet perfectly safe, conservative, and presenting no real distraction to either clients or young associates.

She buzzed Sebastian's office and Mrs. Petrie, who had been Sebastian's secretary for as long as Franklin could remember, came out to greet him.

"Well, here's *our* man in the White House," she beamed. "We're all so proud of you, right there at the pulse of the nation." Mrs. Petrie, Franklin thought, was never one to be disturbed by clichés. "Your father's in with Mr. Goddard," she went on. "Would you like to wait in his office?"

Yes, he would, Franklin told her, and followed her to the large bright corner office. Windows made up two of the four walls and looked east across the river and south down Park Avenue up to the Pan Am Building, an edifice that Sebastian had frequently complained about to his son. It was always blocking his view, he maintained, whether south from the office or east as he left from the Harvard Club. Franklin could understand his father's feelings about the hulking aluminum structure which sat astride Grand Central Station, just as he could also understand his father's discomfort at the firm's decision to move from its original Wall Street location to join the many clients who had moved uptown. It did seem somehow less solid being a Park Avenue law firm than a Wall Street one. Still, wherever you were in New York, it was great compared to sleepy Washington.

"Well, there, son," said Sebastian, walking into his office accompanied by a tall, stooped gray-haired man. "Seward just wanted to say hello to you before he left." Seward Goddard, seventy-five and semiretired, only spent half days at the office.

"Actually, I just wanted to get the lowdown on what that man you're working for thinks he's doing. That speech about the legal profession . . ." Seward Goddard shook his head and sighed. "I know we're fair game but attacking us that way is my idea of poor politics. Wins nothing, loses everything, doesn't make a bit of sense."

"Franklin had nothing to do with that speech, Seward," Sebastian said hastily.

"That's true. Please don't hold me responsible for everything the President says."

"Don't worry, my boy. We don't." Goddard clapped Franklin on the shoulder and sighed. Democrats in the White House always made him sigh, Sebastian told Franklin after the old man walked off. So did much else in life. Sighing was Seward's own special punctuation.

"You look pretty glum yourself," Franklin said, noticing the deep ridge that was forming between his father's brows, a sign he had long ago recognized as inner stress.

"The IRS is giving Consolidated Packers a rough time these days, and we're getting an even rougher time ourselves from Consolidated

Packers. But beside that, there's also this business with your cousin Paul."

Sebastian sat down behind his large rosewood desk, motioned to Franklin to take the rust-colored leather chair across from him, and proceeded to tell him about the last family gathering. Paul and Paul's therapy had been the questions at hand. The point was, the boy's treatment seemed unorthodox, even suspect, and worst of all, no one really knew anything about the psychiatrist treating him.

"She's at Mount Sinai, and your mother remembered, or at least thought she did, that your old roommate at Harvard, Erich Hausmann, was a resident there."

"Yes, I think she's right. I haven't seen Erich since he started his residency, but I'm sure Mount Sinai is the hospital." Franklin smiled to himself. Erich was a hard man to forget in any situation, the old cocksman himself. "Did you want me to talk to him about this doctor of Paul's?"

Sebastian nodded. He hated to ask his son to give up any part of his vacation or to get involved in any snooping, but he was, as he explained, under considerable pressure from Natalie and Ernest.

"You know how your Uncle Ernest is. He always has more questions than there are answers."

"So does the President," Franklin said.

Sebastian smiled. He was looking older these days, Franklin thought, and as he heard his father emit a quiet sigh, beginning to sound more and more like old Goddard.

Anyway, Franklin assured his father, it would be no trouble at all to spend an extra day or two in the city getting in touch with Erich before going up to Shropshire. He'd like to do whatever he could to help, find out whatever the family wanted to know. Poor old Paul. And besides, being in town wouldn't be so bad. The weather was cool and that was some recompense for giving up time in Shropshire.

If the cool weather was refreshing in the city, it was a bit too brisk for Shropshire, and the only ones in the lake were the youngest children, protected by their layers of baby fat from the frigid water. Frederica, the youngest of Ernest Kingman's daughters, sat wrapped up in a blanket near the lakeside court, watching the tennis. Her sister Margo and her husband, Whitney Craig, were playing against her sister Allison and Frederica's own husband, Mitch Harvey. Allison's husband, Jonathan Everdon, did not play tennis. Indeed, Frederica thought, he didn't do very much of anything. Without his four-million-dollar inheritance, he'd be a complete cipher. Her husband, on the other hand, did things with a vengeance. Not only did he play tennis but he had even been the captain of the Duke tennis team, which made him practically a professional. Still, Frederica had to admit, Whitney, even with his extra poundage, was giving him a good game, getting balls past him, returning his powerful first serves. And Margo, who stood five ten in her bare feet and had a commensurate reach, was always hard to beat at net. She did have trouble, though, with Mitch's top spin as one of his serves whizzed by her at the moment. The next serve, however, she managed to return with a low cross-court slice.

"Out!" Allison called.

"Oh, come on, Allison. That was right on the line," Margo insisted.

"I'm telling you it was out," Allison repeated. "Look, Margo," she started walking over to the tape. "There's the mark the ball made and it's right outside. Not by much, I admit, but it is outside."

Margo walked across the court. "That mark was there before. What do you think, Whit? Wasn't that last ball in or am I crazy?"

"Looked in to me. Looked like a terrific shot, in fact. What do you think, Mitch?" he called across the net to his brother-in-law.

"From this side, it looked out," Mitch answered. "But let's do it over."

"That's all right with me," Allison said. "The score is forty-fifteen."

"Forty-fifteen? It was thirty-thirty." Margo was now furious. "What was the score, Freddy?" she called over to her youngest sister.

"I wasn't paying attention," Frederica said hastily. In fact, she hadn't been. But even if she had, she was not about to take sides in Kingman family arguments. And she especially was not going to take sides against her sister Margo. Margo, more like her father than the other girls, had inherited more fully the Kingman assurance that whatever they did was right. Look at her this moment, Frederica thought. She was wearing torn jean shorts and a faded T-shirt and yet she somehow managed to make the others look inappropriately overdressed in their whites. And especially Allison, in her scoop-necked tennis dress with the pink trim, her long straight hair tied back in a matching pink ribbon. Allison certainly was the prettiest of the three of them, Frederica had to admit. Margo, at thirty, was already beginning to get a matronly quality, saved only by her athletic look—she would never lose the aura of having just gotten off the hockey fields at Brearley. Allison, though equally tall, was certainly more feminine and fine-featured like their mother. Frederica had always envied Allison's grace. She herself often felt awkward, all knees and elbows. People would never call Frederica pretty although she had been told in recent years she was a handsome woman.

"Hey, Freddy," Allison called out. "Want to take over for me? I'm bushed."

If Frederica knew better than to take sides in a Kingman dispute over who was winning a game, she also knew better than to ever serve as her husband's tennis partner. Mitch did not tolerate errors. She shook her head.

"Well, then," Margo called over. "If you can get out from under that blanket, why don't you go up and get some food ready for us? We're going to be starved."

"Don't forget the drinks," Mitch shouted.

"Do you want me to feed all the children too?" Frederica asked, not bothering to disguise her annoyance at this command performance. The last thing she felt like doing was going back to her cottage and fixing lunch. But she knew she had no choice.

"No, that's okay. Jenny will take the children," Margo said, resuming her game and oblivious to her sister's sarcastic tone. Jenny was Margo's mother's helper, a chubby and officious little English girl who not only cared for Margo's daughters, Posie and Abbie, but also, reluctantly, now included among her charges Adam, Allison's young son. It was Adam's name that Jenny had shrilly been calling out at regular intervals all morning as, indulging in his favorite sport, he continually attempted to jump off the dock and land directly on each of his cousins' heads. Boys, Jenny had complained, were twice as much trouble as girls. And in Adam's case, Frederica had thought, she was probably right. But whatever the sex, children were still a bother and Frederica, an anthropologist with a lifetime of travel to primitive places facing her, wondered if she'd ever have any of her own. Well, if everyone was coming to her house, she had better get it in shape. She drove from the lake in her new Toyota, paid for out of her first salary from Barnard, and parked it in front of her cottage, one of the three on her father's extensive property. Then she started to straighten up the tiny barn-sided living room, the country kitchen with its hanging clumps of herbs (she only used Spice Island herbs from jars but these, tacked up to a string across the ceiling, always made her guests praise the flavorsome soups and stews she served, and the new bedroom that had been added by

Mitch, who, though he shared a love of authentic rural charm, believed in wide beds, modern bathrooms, and bright lighting fixtures. Frederica grabbed up her blue nightgown, Mitch's pajamas, the box of Wheat Thins next to the bed, the bottle of scotch, and made sure that if anyone wanted to see the new bedroom, it would look as if inhabited by nuns or chambermaids.

But what was there for lunch? She found some cheese, bread, ham, and hastily tossed together a tuna salad, and put them all on platters. She filled the ice bucket, found some Fritos and the last unopened box of Wheat Thins, and felt grateful that Mitch had somehow left a full bottle of Hankey Bannister along with beer for her sisters. With some fruit she had taken from her mother's kitchen, there would be enough for everyone.

A car honked outside. It was Phillip, still tan from an anniversary weekend in Bermuda with his wife of a year, Pat, the daughter of Senator MacIntyre. Frederica hadn't seen Phillip for months. The six-hour drive from Washington to Shropshire was a long one for weekends but now that the warm weather was coming and Washington would soon be so uncomfortable, Phillip was probably getting his cottage ready for the summer weekend ritual.

"Just thought I'd say hello," Phillip called out.

"Where's the bride? Did she run off already?" Frederica came out to the driveway.

Phillip laughed. "She's taking a nap. I guess I wore her out."

"Want to stay for lunch? Everyone else is."

"I have received more gracious invitations but I'll accept anyway. I have an hour before my match with Fletcher Conroy."

Phillip entered the tiny kitchen just as the rest pulled up in front, led by Mitch in his old red Austin Healy which had held up since college days. Whitney Craig drove Margo and Allison in his new Mercedes—investment banking paid off these days, especially when you had a brother-in-law like Jonathan Everdon with four million dollars to invest. Jonathan, they explained, had to drive Jenny and the children home for lunch at Margo's, where she was sure to serve them her specialty, canned ravioli.

"Hi there, Phil." Whitney shook his hand and embraced him simultaneously. How was he? How was Washington and Justice Taylor? How was Pat? Pregnant yet? And when would they be seeing Franklin? Not this weekend? How come?

Phillip started telling them about Franklin's mission, finding out about the therapist treating Paul.

"She sounds crazy to me," Mitch said. "And I think you're all nuts to go along with her rules about your not being allowed to see your own cousin." Frederica managed to land a sharp kick on his instep but it didn't stop him. "I think you ought to do something instead of just sitting here." He poured himself a large scotch, an act which did not escape anyone's attention.

"There is something we can do," Margo said, looking sternly at Mitch. She clearly found him presumptuous and he, for his part, found her overbearing. Her strong features were getting broader and more blunt, and he thought she looked more and more like her father every day. "I had lunch with William this week and apparently Paul's doctor feels that he is well enough to see one of us, one of his cousins. She still thinks it's too much for him to handle the older generation. So the only question now is, which one of us shall it be?"

"Why not you?" Whitney said to his wife. "You seem the logical choice as the oldest."

Mitch interrupted. "I nominate Allison. She's the most gentle of us all." Mitch could have added, the silliest too. For if Margo was her father all over again, Allison was her mother, simpering and sentimental. Thank God Frederica, with all her moods and Kingman impatience, lacked such parental resemblances.

"Well, whoever it will be, it certainly shouldn't be me," Phillip remarked. "Paul never did like me."

"Did Paul like any of you?" Mitch had finished his drink and was pouring another. The cherubic freckled face was becoming more and more florid. It was this boyish look that had originally attracted Frederica when she had met him at a faculty tea at Columbia, where he had looked more like Baby Face Nelson than a noted linguist. And it was this very same look that now was beginning to give him a callow and weak appearance. Nobody bothered to answer Mitch, who no longer noticed or cared.

Phillip was getting impatient. "Look, I don't care who we choose and I don't think it matters much." Phillip had little tolerance for anything that didn't touch directly on him. Besides, nothing the family had ever done for Paul had accomplished anything anyway, and he was convinced that this latest bit of solicitude on the part of his cousins was simply another meaningless gesture. He had heard sad tales about Paul ever since he could remember. This youngest cousin was such a natural-born victim, so much the type Phillip shied away from with instinctive distaste, that it always seemed a burden to have him in the family. For his part, he would just as soon leave Paul alone, and he was annoyed at his cousins. "In any case, I have to leave. I promised Fletcher Conroy I'd play singles at the lake."

"Oh, don't let us keep you, Phillip," Whitney Craig glared. "You'd think you could spare a few moments for the family."

"Jesus, Whit, you've become more of a Kingman than any of us, you're more Catholic than the Pope," Phillip said.

Sensing the harshness of Phillip's tone, Frederica interrupted hastily. She wanted to end this conversation before an open rift developed. "Margo is clearly the best choice, let's leave it at that."

"You'll go easy, Margo, won't you?" Allison looked pained. She was all too aware of her sister's most frightening quality, the breeziness that could turn itself into a gale, mowing everything down in its path. Paul, frail as he was, never did well with Margo, never lived up to her no-nonsense philosophy, and Allison felt sorry for him having to face her once again.

"Margo will be properly affectionate, don't worry," Frederica said before Margo's husband could again rush to her defense.

Just then Allison's husband, Jonathan Everdon, walked in. "Sorry I'm late."

"There doesn't seem to be any more lunch," Allison said. She rarely showed annoyance but Jonathan's mysterious disappearances, his constant offers to drive Jenny, the baby-sitter, places, had stretched even her tolerance. "I hope you've had some of Jenny's ravioli."

Jonathan was an extraordinarily pale man, and so it was difficult to ignore the fact that he was now beet red. The millionaire playboy, Frederica thought to herself. She had never liked him, she never would, and he was just the type, she thought, to be tasteless enough to have an affair with a baby-sitter. But Allison, who surely was the last person in the world to marry someone just for his money, apparently saw something behind Jonathan's vacuous light eyes, narrow shoulders, and sunken chest that Frederica missed.

"Well, now that everything is settled and Jonathan has joined us, how about another drink?" Mitch asked.

" 'Fraid not." Allison stood up. "I'm going to pick up Adam. Unlike his father, I don't think he likes Jenny all that much."

"You know, Allison," Margo said, "you might consider getting your own baby-sitter one of these days." She certainly could afford it, Margo thought.

They all left, and Frederica began washing glasses and sweeping up crumbs. There was something wearying about her family, she thought. And Margo certainly was among the most difficult. Maybe she'd made a mistake in supporting the choice of Margo as emissary to Paul. Poor Paul.

Margo, as her father always said with a mixture of pride and amusement, was one of the "no sooner said than done" school. Monday had been a busy day for her at *The New Yorker* what with a proposed outline to check over for a profile on Hendon Oakley, a modern Renaissance man. A blue blood with sufficient income so that all his work could be play, he spent his time living out other people's fantasies—becoming a lion tamer, an acrobat, a movie actor, a deep-sea diver—and kept writing intelligent, witty books about his experiences. After Margo wrote her comments on the outline, she rushed off to a lunch meeting with a young Puerto Rican member of the State Senate who her sister Allison felt could add special insight to a Talk of the Town piece on a welfare alternative movement. Allison, new to the State Senate and committed, as of course she would be, to day-care centers, minority problems, drug abuse legislation, and work training for the unemployed, had become fast friends with Luis Mendoza and felt he could use the publicity.

But despite all that Margo had to do, she nevertheless managed to clear her desk by four o'clock and take off for Paul's Central Park West apartment. She had decided against phoning first since it would appear more casual to just drop in. Why had she taken on this responsibility, acting as William's surrogate and surrogate for all the Kingman cousins? She'd said she'd do it because, as in all things, she did what had to be done. But what if Paul were really unbalanced? However would she tell his father? Whatever the situation, she had already decided that she would be totally honest.

Paul, as it turned out, was too excited about another visit to register much surprise or even interest at Margo's appearance at his front door. He had just finished showing his paintings to Marcel Block, who was clearly enthusiastic about Paul's work ("You may be lacking a bit in experience and sophistication but you've got real talent," Marcel had told him), and had just poured Marcel a drink as Margo rang the bell.

"Margo, how are you?" he said warmly, taking her hand. "Let me introduce you. This is Marcel Block. My cousin, Margo Craig."

"Are you Craig's wife? Or his other wife?" Marcel asked.

"Actually, his first and only one," Margo answered in an annoyed tone. Marcel was clearly not her type.

An awkward silence filled the room. "Look, don't let me interrupt you," Margo said.

"Actually, that's precisely what you did, Mrs. Craig. I was just talking to your talented cousin about his work. And since I'll be leaving in a moment or two, you won't mind if I continue?"

"Go right ahead," she said. "I can amuse myself." She eyed the stack of canvases standing against the wall. "You don't mind if I look at your paintings while you talk, do you, Paul?"

"Of course not," Paul answered.

"Anyway, Paul, what do you think?" Marcel asked as Margo went off to look at a stack of paintings. "I'd really love to offer you a one-man show, but it would be a mistake at this point. Would you consider being part of a group exhibition in November? I could definitely promise you an excellent wall, the best of critics, the richest of patrons, and a write-up in *Art News* and the *Times,* although how favorable they'll be remains to be seen."

Paul felt a smile cover his whole face. He must look like an idiot, he thought, but he was so happy that he didn't care.

"November will be perfect. How many oils?" All business now, Paul managed to find his voice.

"Five oils, as many drawings as you want for the bins, no prints this show. Okay?" Marcel was equally professional, showing the side of him that was responsible for the black figures on the ledger of Mental Block.

It was all perfectly agreeable to Paul. Would he have to add more? Give indications of greater variety? He could manage that. Should he take a look at current shows? There were no hard and fast rules? That was fine with him, too.

He would do anything. His career was about to start, and all he wanted to do was to throw his arms around Isabel and thank her for everything. He would do that later.

"Anyway, Paul, we'll talk later in the week," Marcel said. "So sorry I can't stay, Mrs. Craig. I was so enjoying our conversation." Marcel bowed and walked out the door.

"Whoever is that man in the white suit and hat?" Margo asked. "He's insufferable."

"He, you ought to know, is the man who is going to make my whole career. Did you hear him, Margo? He thinks I'm talented, very talented. And he's going to show my paintings."

"Of course I'm glad for you, Paul, but I'd also be very careful about letting someone like that handle my work. He doesn't strike me as stable. But," she quickly added, "your work is lovely, simply lovely. Tell me, who is that woman in all your portraits? There seem to be dozens of her."

"That's my doctor," he said. "My psychiatrist."

"Your psychiatrist?" Margo looked surprised, even amazed. "She models for you? I should think she'd be too busy."

"She's very interested in art."

"I see." Margo put her hands in the pockets of her skirt and with her long strides, began to walk across the living room.

"Well, just how are you, Paul?" she asked suddenly, peering into his face as if to see more of the truth than he might be willing to reveal. "We've all been so worried—not being able to see you, getting every bit of news by hearsay."

"I've been in good hands," he said with a smile. "Well cared for, as you can see. I understand Gerson Richler talks to my father frequently, and I'm sure my father has talked to the rest of you."

"That isn't like seeing you ourselves. This enforced distance is so . . . well, so unnatural, peculiar, really."

Paul looked surprised. "Do you really care so much?" He had always felt unimportant in the family, the most insignificant of Kingmans and one whose absence would hardly be noticed.

"We're family, Paul. How can you ask if we care? I care, Allison cares, Frederica cares—we all care. And your parents care most of all. You should see them, they've been so upset."

So this was why Margo had come, on a scouting expedition. "Margo, what goes on between my parents and myself is my own business." Paul's uncharacteristic forcefulness seemed to startle Margo. "Anyway, you're the cousins' delegate, aren't you?" He smiled at her, aware that he was at last capable of putting her on the defensive.

"I suppose I am," she admitted. "We were told that one of us could see you."

"And so you picked straws and you lost?"

"Come off it, Paul." She was clearly beginning to get impatient. "You can't go through life feeling so defensive, so sorry for yourself."

"I don't feel sorry for myself, at least these days I don't. And you can tell that to the others."

Margo looked at him appraisingly. "That doctor has certainly given you self-confidence, anyway," she said, kissing him on the cheek. "I wish I could spend more time with the new Paul, but it is getting late and I promised the children I'd see them before they went to bed."

"Sorry you can't stay, Margo," he said, walking her to the door. He couldn't wait for it to close behind her. Would he ever feel comfortable with his family? They certainly didn't make it easy.

Franklin had stayed in New York over the weekend, but he couldn't get in touch with Erich until Monday. In the meantime, he had amused himself with a night at Regine's after seeing the musical *Annie* (what a disappointment that was), by stopping into Brooks to pick up some summer suits, and finally, by a hastily arranged meeting with a checkroom girl at the Pierre who had left her phone number on his raincoat check. If it had been better weather, he told her, they might have never met. That night he had rushed home, hoping he hadn't been foolhardy and risked some disease. After all, being prudent was a Kingman trait.

Erich Hausmann fortunately still had a spirit, a way of viewing the world or at least viewing his world, that gave everyone a lift. *Joie de vivre* was a perfect phrase for describing this special way of Erich's which made everything come to life. Besides, as he had confided to Franklin when they first met as juniors at Harvard, Erich had made a science of successful fucking. Women sensed this special interest, he claimed. Franklin had to admit they certainly seemed to, clustering as they did around the small, blond Swiss boy who, with his money alone, could have had most of them anyway. Erich was almost as rich as an Arab, he had told Franklin, an admission Franklin had promised to keep secret.

Now Erich was in the overwhelmingly serious endeavor of becoming, of all things, a pediatrician.

"But I've always been fond of children, Franklin," he protested when Franklin found his area of specialization amusing. "It's the one field where you get to see nice healthy bodies, so neat, so seemingly simple, and yet so fascinatingly complex." Franklin found his mind wandering as Erich grew poetic.

He was struck with how his old friend looked these days. Erich's hair was beginning to bald and he had developed a small paunch. Franklin, whose strong features suited his twenty-seven-year-old face far better than they ever had and whose erect posture, inherited from his father, gave him an imposing, rather grand, aspect, was more handsome than ever. Although, he realized, he would never be as attractive as his younger brother, Phillip, whom Washington hostesses referred to as "Phillip the Fair."

When Erich stopped rhapsodizing about his profession, Franklin explained his purpose in visiting Mount Sinai. He wanted to find out about the doctor who was treating his cousin Paul. Did Erich know Isabel Dunne?

"Of course, I know the name," he frowned in thought as he had coffee with Franklin in the lounge. "I'll ask around of course, but I seem to remember that one of our nurses worked with her, perhaps even at the time your cousin was admitted. I'll ask her. She's extremely agreeable, extremely nubile—the nurse, not Dr. Dunne, of course."

"Let's do that right now," Franklin said. Erich couldn't be counted on not to forget his quest if a new, complex case came along or a new, complex female.

"God, what efficiency. You haven't changed a hair from Harvard days," Erich sighed, getting up to look for the nurse. "Or perhaps I shouldn't mention hair," he added, patting his thinning head. "Come on, we'll find her."

The pediatric floor was far more upsetting than Franklin had been prepared for. There were babies with enlarged heads, semiconscious children with tubes running through their arms and noses, and some scurrying along the corridors, ignoring their missing limbs or comparing the zipperlike scars down their chests from open-heart surgery. Franklin thought about his own work. The responsibility and challenge of the White House seemed small in comparison.

"*Et voilà!*" Erich said ecstatically as he held up the arm of a pretty young nurse who was comforting a sobbing ten-year-old wandering down the hall. "I'll find someone else to take care of this young man. Milly, could you take Tommy down to his room?" he asked another nurse who was walking by. Amazingly, Tommy agreed to leave without protest, and the sudden quiet was like a surprise vacation.

"Addie Harris." Erich sounded formal. "This is Franklin Rush. He'd like to talk to you. Can you spare a moment?"

"How do you do, Dr. Rush," Addie said in a voice that sounded like she had rehearsed those words for a play.

"I'm not a doctor," Franklin said.

"He's a speechwriter," Erich told her. "In fact, he writes the very words your President has said."

Addie was impressed. "You're visiting from Washington?"

"Actually, yes," he told her. "But my family's from New York. In fact, it's my family I wanted to talk to you about. Erich tells me you used to work in the psychiatric section, and we think you might have been there when my cousin was a patient. Paul Kingman?"

Addie's expression made it clear, even before she spoke, that she knew Paul. "Yes, I remember him very well."

"And did you work with his doctor at all?" Erich asked.

"Isabel Dunne?"

Erich nodded.

"Yes, I did," Addie said.

"Look, Addie"—Franklin smiled, making an attempt to be his most charming—"I was wondering if you could tell me something about her. I don't want to do anything that would make you uncomfortable or have you go against your professional ethics. But I did want to ask you a few questions, if that would be all right."

"Well, I'm not sure what you want to know. Or even what I could tell you that might help," Addie answered. "But of course, I'll try to give you all the information I can."

"I have a terrific idea," said Erich, glancing at his watch and putting an arm around Addie. "Why don't we all have dinner together. I know a little French restaurant just a few blocks away."

Addie agreed to meet them in front of the hospital at six-thirty.

Le Ciel d'Or was one of the few French restaurants which could really prepare a perfect martini, Erich told Addie. They ordered one for each of them and Franklin, claiming that six months in Washington had made him immune, ordered still another.

By the time they were finished with their cocktails and several glasses of Médoc, they were all feeling relaxed. Addie, indeed, was in heaven. Here she was, having dinner with Erich Hausmann, the most appealing doctor in pediatrics and rumored to be the most versatile in bed, and Franklin Rush who, though not as poetic as his cousin Paul Kingman, was certainly as great-looking as anyone Addie had seen around in New York. Catherine would never believe it. Neither would anyone in Carthage, Missouri.

"God, I needed this," Erich said. "There's nothing like the combination of a martini and Médoc to combat hospital fatigue."

"I'll have to remember that," Addie laughed. She was feeling good too, almost sloshed in fact. She'd have to watch it.

"Of course, sitting next to such a lovely lady helps too." Erich's accent always got more pronounced when he talked to women, Franklin noticed. "That hospital staff has really been getting on my nerves." Erich went on, "I keep having to change my schedules, my team arrangements . . ."

"I can't see you bowing under hospital pressures," Franklin said. "Even bending."

"Well, then, you haven't met our chief of pediatrics. I can see our going along with demands for equal opportunity by appointing a woman chief, but this one is no credit to her sex. In fact, I doubt if she has one." Erich then looked at Addie, suddenly remembering her as part of the hospital context. "Oh, my dear young lady, you will be quiet about this, won't you? I shouldn't be talking about Dr. McLeod in front of you."

"That's all right. None of the nurses like her either. She's always forgetting what she said before, giving new orders so you don't know what to do."

"And her orders get progressively more confusing after lunch, which I understand is largely a liquid one," Erich added. "*Your* boss has to be an improvement on that," he said to Franklin.

Franklin took another sip of wine. He too was feeling the effects, despite his professed ability to handle martinis. "It's not so easy in Washington these days either."

"The President seems so nice, so friendly," Addie said, looking surprised.

"Then we're doing a good job in the pressroom if we're pulling off that miracle of subterfuge."

"He's not so nice? That big smile is pasted on?" Erich asked.

"He has a terrible temper, he's suspicious of everyone, and if you think he likes the Vice-President, you're dead wrong. He's so jealous of that guy's popularity that every time a poll comes out, he locks himself into his room for hours. One of the reporters said he's probably putting pins in the V.P.'s old campaign pictures." Franklin stopped himself. He hadn't wanted to tell this to anyone quite yet. You never knew how the situation might turn, whose side you would or should end up on.

Erich shook his head. "It's a dreary world, all right. Here, eat these wonderful filets, and we'll all try to forget our troubles."

Franklin turned to Addie. "With all our complaints about our work, I'm afraid we've been neglecting yours. Pediatrics under Erich, I'm sure, is a ball, but what was it like in psychiatry? Was it difficult working under Dr. Dunne?"

"No, not really. She was okay, just different."

"Different, how? What did she do?"

"It's hard to say exactly," Addie began. "She seems very direct, very close to her patients. Not like a doctor at all, especially with your cousin Paul. The two of them seem, somehow, more like . . ."

"Lovers?" Erich filled in the blank with a wink.

"No, I don't mean that. Well, I don't know. It's just that Paul seems so much happier. Well, whatever she does, it works."

"I'd say," Erich winked.

What had Addie done? She hadn't meant to hint about anything, although she knew she was right about Paul and Dr. Dunne. But she had no proof. Besides, she didn't really want to prove anything anyway. She certainly didn't want to cause any trouble. The evening was not turning out the way she thought it would. "Maybe I'd better go home," she said, starting to get up.

That was all Erich needed. Franklin watched in fascination as the Swiss doctor used words to soothe this silly girl, making her smile again, inspiring that look of adoration to again light up her pretty face. Franklin joined in wherever he could, and by the time they had eaten their raspberries in Cointreau, Addie felt just fine.

It was a warm, clear night as they walked down Madison Avenue from the restaurant. Addie lived in the sixties, near First Avenue, and Erich and Franklin insisted on each taking an arm and walking her back. Her apartment was on the first floor of a tiny apartment house, each unit little more than one room with a long narrow hall leading to a bathroom and tiny kitchen. The sink had to have come from a dentist's office, Addie joked. It was so small she could only wash one teacup at a time.

And besides tea, what else did she have to drink? Erich asked. She had a bottle of scotch which she opened for them as the two men sat on her Salvation Army tan couch. She came in with the drinks, and with exaggerated gallantry, Franklin and Erich moved apart, allowing her to sit between them. They were looking very handsome and sitting so close, she could feel their legs against hers. She was getting more and more aroused, and she wasn't at all sure how to handle this situation. Who would stay? Who would go? It was an impossible choice.

At first, it seemed as though they were making the decision for her. Erich grabbed her shoulders, turned her head, and kissed her, his tongue inside her mouth and his whole body pressing against hers. She saw Franklin get up and felt a pang of disappointment, knowing whichever of them left, she would have felt the same regret. But no, Franklin was not leaving. At Erich's signal, he had begun to turn down the bright overhead light and switch on a small lamp across the room.

"That sofa, Franklin," Erich said. "I am certain it can become a bed. Get up," he commanded.

Addie stood up as Erich pulled off the loose cushions, pulled down a metal bar, and revealed a double bed. "Only tonight, triple," he laughed and grabbed Addie.

It was crazy. But what could she do? It was also wonderful. They had all taken off their clothing slowly, laughing as though they were children playing strip poker. They threw the clothes into the air, looked at each other's bodies, and made admiring comments. Then Erich and Franklin placed all the cushions on the bed and put Addie on top of them, like a queen.

Soon it became more serious, starting with Erich's head between her legs, then her head between Franklin's, then someone's hands caressing her breasts, then someone (which one?) stroking her ass. She was gasping, doing whatever she could to whatever was within her reach. Whose was what? Everyone was so beautiful, it didn't matter. And everyone was incredibly aroused. There were moans in increasingly fast tempo, thrashing legs, wetter and wetter skin. Someone had entered her, fiercely pounding her as she used her lips, her mouth, her tongue on someone else.

It was a miracle but it all worked out. Not in one explosion, of course, but in several rapid-fire ones, each just after the other.

While the two men got ready to leave, Addie poured them each another drink. It had been great, they told her. They had tried this in Cambridge, but it hadn't worked out well at all. It was tricky, all right.

After they left, Addie collapsed on the bed. Finally, she thought, she had had her romance, the one she hoped to find in this wild city. And what a romance. No one would believe it. But, of course, there was no one she was about to tell.

*   *   *

162

Franklin woke up Tuesday morning to a phone call from Margo. She had heard from Phillip that he was in town and she had to talk to him. It was urgent, she told him. He agreed to stop by her office that afternoon. It would take a few hours, he thought to himself, to summon his energies.

How perfect Margo fit in, Franklin thought, as he entered the rather shabby offices of *The New Yorker,* gotten up with the express purpose of flaunting their chic. Just like good old Margo whose wardrobe always had the look of having been bought five years before and probably would be around in some store or other five years from now, Margo's office had a defiant "clothes don't matter" quality, and her office furnishings indicated that decor was equally unimportant.

As soon as Franklin sat down on a frayed chair in the gloomy room and Margo closed the door, she began to talk. "I don't quite know how to begin, Franklin. I'm just sick over this. I've seen Paul, and do you know, he has dozens of paintings of his psychiatrist? She's been posing for him."

"In the nude?" Franklin asked.

"Oh, really, Franklin. Do be serious. It's bad enough. I know you're going to think I'm mad, but do you know what crossed my mind?" She reached out and put her hand on her cousin's.

"I know exactly what crossed your mind because it crossed someone else's mind too." He began to tell her about Addie Harris' observations, and before they were through talking, they had both concluded that Dr. Isabel Dunne was Paul's lover. And miracle worker or not, she was, in that capacity, a threat to their cousin. How could an analyst have the proper objectivity when she was intimate with her patient? And how could a patient deal wisely with his analyst when he was not only under her care but her lover as well? Franklin and Margo both suspected that Paul's affairs with women had been extremely limited. If this were so, then his relationship with Isabel Dunne would hold even greater significance for him. Therapist and lover, a frightening combination. Paul would be trapped, anyone would be. And while it wasn't clear what this entrapment entailed or what Dr. Dunne wanted of Paul now that she seemingly had full rein, this very lack of clear-cut motive made the situation even more ominous.

After talking for only a half hour, both Franklin and Margo realized that William had to be informed, in fact, told immediately. They called him at his office and told him they had something very important to talk to him about, something to do with Paul. Could they see him that evening? It would have to be after nine if he didn't mind. Margo always liked to be around for the children's bedtime.

No, nine would be just fine. Since it was about Paul, it was just as well that Barbara would be at the ballet where she religiously spent every Tuesday night. It would be easier to speak frankly if she wasn't there. Margo agreed with her uncle. It was best for William to confront this problem alone so he could do whatever had to be done without anyone looking over his shoulder. Besides, all three of them—Margo, Franklin, and William—although they said nothing to each other, knew instinctively that Barbara would just as soon not be aware of this latest mess in which Paul had gotten involved.

William was in his wood-paneled library when they arrived, his voice calm as he asked after Margo's two children and about Franklin's new job. He listened attentively but his clenched jaw gave away his agitation and impatience. Franklin realized he had to get right down to the pressing subject of Paul.

"What we've turned up is what my father would surely call circumstantial evidence," Franklin started. "Still, we think it's significant, which is why we're here. I spoke to my old classmate Erich Hausmann, who works at Mount Sinai, and he tells me that Isabel Dunne is considered brilliant but unorthodox. In other words, she's likely to do things other doctors would not do, take actions which might well be described as controversial, although Gerson Richler, a conservative himself, is always defending her as more effective than the traditionalists, who complain about her from time to time."

"The nurse," Margo prompted. Franklin could sometimes go on too long.

"I was coming to that. The nurse who worked under Dr. Dunne when Paul was in the hospital and has seen him since, thinks something is going on between him and Dr. Dunne. She was reluctant to say anything, but I put two and two together."

William seemed to take this news with amazing calm, and Margo, relieved, felt free to describe her visit. After a short preamble about her distaste at acting the spy, Margo told of the dozens of sketches and oil portraits of Dr. Dunne that Paul had done. Furthermore, her face had been re-created with an evident spirit of idolatry.

William thanked them both for coming straight to him. He'd handle the situation, and he was sure he could count on their discretion.

Of course he could, they assured him, and they left his apartment feeling unburdened. There was no question in their minds but that their uncle, with his icy calm and strong will, was capable of cleaning up this whole unpleasant mess. It was going to be fine, they told each other.

After William escorted them to the elevator, he went back into his study, locked the door behind him, and began to shake with rage.

How dare she, this meddling bitch. How dare she start in with his son. He'd ruin her, he'd devote everything toward doing just that. She was finished.

Ernest and Natalie had been right to suspect her, and William had been a naïve fool. Gerson Richler too had been deluded. William would tell the old man just where his advice had placed Paul, had placed William.

What did this Isabel Dunne want of Paul anyway? Why was she doing this? William felt certain she hadn't been overwhelmed by any passion for his son. Besides, even if she had been, she was a doctor after all, with professional responsibilities. Was it to get at William? At the Kingmans? Was it just a sign of a sick, demented mind?

It didn't matter, though, because whatever it was, it was over as of now. He'd see that she was through, he'd ruin her, he'd do it with pleasure.

William felt a sense of release. At last he had a focus for the rage he had felt since that awful Christmas morning when they called him about Paul.

Natalie and Ernest had been right, but William would show them how he could rectify the situation. Paul was a Kingman and had to be restored to his place within the family. With Isabel removed, William could easily accomplish this. He'd go to Gerson Richler, to the Mount Sinai Board, to the County Medical Association. But first, William realized, he'd have to be sure. He would have to go and see Paul.

William started to walk down Park Avenue and then grabbed a taxi. He had too much to do tonight to waste any time. Brushing past Paul's doorman, an ineffectual little Cuban who never succeeded in getting anyone's name, he took the elevator up, rang the bell, and found that he was breathing audibly, was actually sweating, as he heard his son's footsteps.

"Dad, how are you?" Paul stared at him. William stared back at the thin young man whom he hadn't seen in six months.

"May I come in?" he said. "I know it's against your doctor's rules and regulations."

"Please, Dad, come in. Please come in." Paul took his father's jacket, hung it up, and the two men walked into the huge living room, its french doors open to let in whatever breeze stirred in the park. "Would you like a drink?"

"Scotch and water," William ordered, and stood while Paul went off to the kitchen to get the ice.

As he waited, William looked around the room. There was artwork everywhere, paintings, sketches, crayon drawings. And many of them, as Margo had described, showed the same face. Isabel was sometimes smiling, sometimes looking rather solemn and sad, but always beautiful.

"You've been doing quite a bit of painting, I see," he said, taking the drink Paul had brought him from the kitchen.

"Yes, and it looks as though I'm going to be part of a group show in SoHo this fall."

"SoHo . . . I see. And do they go in for sacred pictures there?"

Paul looked startled. "What do you mean?"

"Well, it looks to me as though you've joined the cult of the Virgin. Don't tell me that's not Jesus' mother you have all over your walls? Or is some other female worthy of all this worship?" William took a long sip on his drink. His son was silent. "Can't you answer me, Paul?"

"I can answer, but what's the use? It's obvious you know all the answers."

"Speak up." William's voice was one Paul remembered from the past.

"You know who this face belongs to. I know you know, because she told me you had met each other."

"Not the most pleasant of meetings, I'm afraid. It looks as though your experiences with Dr. Dunne have been far more genial."

"She is a wonderful person." Paul's voice was getting choked. "She helped me when no one else could. I owe her everything."

"So that's why you're giving her so much."

"What do you mean?" Paul jumped.

"I think you know what I mean."

"Maybe you'd better say what you're thinking." Paul felt the tension growing, he had to get it over with.

"Shall I be blunt? You're screwing your doctor, aren't you?"

"And what if I am?" Paul was amazed at his own words.

William looked at his son. "Because, you little fool, you're getting screwed too. Getting royally screwed."

"How can you say that?"

"It's quite clear that she's using you. What kind of psychiatrist anyway would be part of such an affair. It's unhealthy, it's wrong. Can't you see that?"

"No, I can't. Look, Dad, I love Isabel. And she loves me. And we have something very important between us, no matter what anyone else may think. No matter what you may think."

There was no way of getting through to Paul right now, William thought. And no use in continuing this confrontation.

"I think we'd better wait and talk another time," William said calmly, going to get his jacket. "Good-bye, son. It was good seeing you, even for just a moment."

"Good night, Dad." Paul watched as William left.

It was over, the meeting he had been dreading. He felt relieved, strong, proud of how he handled it, and filled with love for Isabel. She had made it all possible.

10

ISABEL, HER HAIR brushed loose around her shoulders, her body cool and limber after a long bath, sat in the red leather armchair that stood near the window of her small study. Open at several of the seams, worn through here and there on the arms, the old chair should have been thrown out years ago—she certainly never should have bothered to move it from Boston to New York. But it was one of the few pieces of furniture that she had saved from her mother's home and, as she sat now, her bare feet curled under her loose-fitting cotton robe, a book spread open on her lap, she felt herself completely relaxed and ready to tackle the symposium on family therapy that Gerson Richler had given her to read that day at lunch.

"Look it over," Richler had told her. "It seems to be the wave of the future."

"Another new wave." She smiled. "You're always coming up with the latest wrinkle."

"Well, this isn't really such a new wrinkle. Once they used to say there were no illegitimate children, only illegitimate parents. So now, instead of illegitimate they substitute neurotic."

"I'd go along with that in either form," Isabel said. "I've often thought many of my patients weren't really reacting neurotically so much as they were reacting to a neurotic instead—a father, a mother, a sister, some other family member who was really the disturbed one."

"Yes, but you're still thinking in terms of *your* patient, the individual whom you treat. The difference is that in family therapy, you think in terms of the whole gestalt. You treat the family itself, all of its members together, to get at the source of the problems."

So instead of Paul, she might be treating the Kingmans instead. What an image—that of Ernest, Natalie, William, and the others sitting around in one room being led by Isabel. It was positively surrealistic. There were some families, whatever these therapists might say, that you didn't lead into open confrontations. There were some families that you didn't ask to make adjustments themselves, but that you simply had to encourage the patient to adjust to himself. Stand up to the Kingmans? Tell them that they had to change, that they had failed in any way? Their record said otherwise. If Paul didn't make the grade, they surely would never accept that it had anything to do with them, with any possible pressures they themselves had created.

But if much of what was outlined in the pages of this symposium didn't seem to have anything to do with the Kingmans or with Isabel's own way of working, as she sat now reading of the use of one-way mirrors and video tapes, much also seemed valid and very much to the point. Yes, she agreed, the therapist should not be a silent and impartial listener but rather a responsive and active guide. Yes, he must even be a participant in the process of a patient's cure.

The phone rang, interrupting her thoughts. She glanced at the clock on her desk. It was almost eleven. An emergency? Emily Richmond in one of her recent attacks of hysteria? Or Paul?

"Hello," he said. "I love you."

She was too absorbed in her reading, too weary to begin one of their almost nightly discussions about his feelings toward her. But she didn't have to say anything anyway, for Paul just wanted her to listen. He had something exciting to tell her, really exciting.

It struck her as he spoke that his voice was somehow different, though she couldn't quite describe the changes. All she knew was that she wasn't quite sure she liked what she heard.

"I've just seen my father," he began. "Remember, I told you my cousin Margo was here. Well, I guess she began to suspect something after her visit and told my father as much because he came here to ask me outright just what was going on between us."

She felt an uncomfortable flutter in her chest, a tightening in her stomach.

"You didn't say anything, did you?"

"Anything? I told him I loved you."

"You told him what?"

"I told him everything." He paused. "Why not?"

She was too numb to speak.

"And Isabel, it was all right. I really stood up to him. I wasn't afraid of him. I told him that I loved you and that I didn't care what he thought."

She still said nothing.

"Isabel? Are you still there?"

"Yes, I'm still here." She felt her voice breaking. If she tried to say anything more, she would begin to cry. An analyst bursting into tears before her patient. What irony.

Paul kept on talking. He was telling her not to worry, assuring her that everything would be all right. At least, that's what she thought he was saying, but she couldn't quite follow him. What struck her most was that he was saying it all in that new voice of his, that surer voice, that firmer voice. What was it about that voice? She suddenly knew. Paul sounded like his father, and the recognition panicked her completely.

"Paul, listen to me. You've got to tell your father that what you told him was a lie."

"A lie? What's the matter with you? Why are you acting like this?" Couldn't he understand?

"Isabel, don't worry. I love you. I owe you everything. I'm telling you I'll take care of everything."

She wanted to scream, but she swallowed the sound. Somehow, she managed to keep her voice steady enough to tell him she couldn't speak to him now, she couldn't listen anymore. Tomorrow, tomorrow, she would talk to him again. Her head was throbbing, her hands were shaking, and she knew that she was going to throw up. She ran into the bathroom and leaned her head over the toilet bowl, vomiting so violently that her stomach muscles ached and her throat burned. Finally, she stood up, ran cold water into the sink, and splashed it onto her face and into her mouth. She felt better now, but still queasy, and sat down on the edge of the tub. Oh, God, what had she done. She had sinned and was being punished for it. Isabel was jarred by her thought. She had to pull herself together, had to get a hold on her terror. How absurd. There was no sin, and even had there been, what she had done wasn't wrong. She had cured Paul, she had helped him.

It was the intercom. It might have been ringing for a long time, she wasn't sure. All she thought as she picked up the receiver was that she must be calm.

"Yes?"

"There's someone named Kingman here to see you, Dr. Dunne. Shall I send him up?" She heard the voice of Henry, the night doorman.

How dare Paul come here now. What was happening?

"Tell him I can't see him now," she said, hanging up the receiver. She not only didn't want to see him now, she suddenly realized that she wanted him out of her life.

The buzzer rang again. "He insists it's very urgent, Doctor."

"Oh, all right, send him up, Henry," she said wearily.

When he came through that door, she thought, she would tell him it was over. He was strong enough now to do without her. And even if he weren't, she would have to tell him anyway that he was dismissed. These words ready, she turned the doorknob. But it wasn't Paul who was standing on the threshold—it was William.

What struck William Kingman most when Isabel Dunne opened the door of her apartment was what a damned attractive woman she was. He hadn't really noticed before. But now, with that great shock of red hair curling around her shoulders, in that pale blue, flowing robe, he could understand Paul's feelings for her. But Paul's feelings weren't the issue, he reminded himself. It was this woman's behavior—this woman's betrayal of medical ethics, of her profession itself.

He didn't apologize for the late hour, he didn't even wait to be invited in. He simply walked into the apartment, turned to her, and told her, "I have something very important to talk to you about. But first," he added, as she closed the door behind him, "I'd like something to drink. Scotch, if you don't mind."

She nodded and walked over to a small liquor cabinet. William, in the meantime, looked over the room. It was neat and efficient but without distinction or personality. Filled with one of those assortments of Danish modern furniture that almost seemed prepackaged, it was the kind of room that belonged to someone either who cared very little about furnishing or who had very little taste.

She handed him his drink. Was her hand shaking or did he imagine it?

"Let me come straight to the point, Dr. Dunne. I've spoken to Paul and I must say that I was horrified by what he told me. It would be an understatement to tell you that your behavior has been grossly unprofessional."

"Not everyone would agree with that." Her voice was steady, but why was she avoiding his eyes?

"The Medical Board might. Why don't I ask them?" He had her

now, or so he thought, until she said quietly, "That wouldn't be the wisest move to make."

"Why not?" he asked.

"Because," she said slowly, an unmistakable quiver in her voice, "Paul is in love with me."

"What makes you so sure?"

"Among other things, because I am your son's analyst. In any case"—she breathed deeply—"if anything were to happen to me, especially anything that Paul was in any way responsible for, he would be extremely upset. So upset he might even do something drastic."

"We'll just have to take our chances," William said coldly.

"You can't mean that. I find it hard to believe that you're so lacking in concern."

"Dr. Dunne, your opinions don't interest me in the slightest."

Isabel looked pained. "I'm sorry to hear that, because there's a great deal I could tell that might help Paul and that might even help you. But however you feel, it doesn't really matter. The point is, there is nothing at all you can do to me. And mainly because there is nothing you can prove. Paul would never testify against me."

"How can you be so sure? Remember, you won't have very much control over him once he's no longer your patient, and as of tomorrow, he won't be."

"Perhaps so. But even if you do take Paul out of my care, there is no way you can affect his feelings for me. You see, I've given him more than you know." There was almost a sob in her voice.

"What are you talking about?" William asked.

"The relationship you considered so unprofessional," Isabel paused. "You see, before me, your son was sexually impotent."

William was startled. What was she saying? "Really, you can't expect me to believe that."

"Whether you believe it or not, it's still the truth."

"And I gather, then, that you managed to work some quick magic on him then."

"Hardly magic, hardly quick."

He looked at her, and for a moment, a picture of her naked body caressing his son appeared before him. It was so vivid, he could almost feel her touch. Could she actually be telling the truth? Was it possible that Paul, his son, had been impotent?

"You're lying."

"If you would only stop to consider just who your son is, who he was, you'd know I'm not. If he failed in everything else, don't you think he would fail in that too? If you were always setting examples for him that he couldn't live up to—and you always were, Dr. Kingman—don't you think when he saw you, for example, with Claudia Monteverde that that incident too would provide him with an example he would be too fearful to try to imitate?"

Claudia Monteverde. William hadn't thought about her in years. He suddenly recalled the distant memory of a boy standing at the threshold of his bedroom watching him through the mirror. How strangely exciting it had been. But if this Dr. Dunne knew about that and about Claudia, what else did she know? She must know damn near everything or, at least, everything that Paul knew. Curse that boy. He was always making him ashamed.

"Dr. Kingman, I know this all must be very difficult for you," Isabel said, as if reading his thoughts. "But Paul is all right now and if you leave us alone, he'll continue to be all right in the future. It's just that being part of your family has been so burdensome, so painful for him. And from what Paul has told me, I imagine it must have been painful for you, too."

Her voice was soft, sympathetic. How dare she patronize him this way.

"You really mustn't feel guilty either. No one could possibly blame you," she went on. "The more I understand what being a Kingman involves, the more I see that you, like Paul, have been a victim."

He could have killed her. He, a victim? He, like Paul? He, impotent, powerless? William Kingman felt a fury rising in him unlike anything he had ever felt before. He reached out and slapped Isabel across the face. And again. And again. The third blow started her sobbing and he felt a pulsing in his groin. She had turned away from him and he grabbed her by the shoulders, forcing her to stand facing him. Then, suddenly, his mind a blank, his whole being overwhelmed with furious sensation, he ripped open her robe. Instinctively, it seemed, she threw her arms across her breasts, hiding them, protecting them. But he forced her arms open, holding her by the wrists, pressing them, squeezing them with all his might until he felt the pulse throbbing beneath his fingers.

She was wearing a cream-colored nightgown with a gathering of lace at the bodice and he could see her nipples, her hips, the lines of her thighs, traced beneath the clinging fabric. Fiercely, he began to tear at the gown until first her breasts were exposed and then she was completely naked. She was struggling, trying to pull away from him, but he kept a strong hold on her left wrist, twisting and pressing until she screamed with pain. Her body seemed the color of the gown, the texture of the gown—silky, flowing. It was an exquisite body, and he wanted to tear into it. He was, in fact, so overcome with desire that he felt weak in the knees. He pushed her back against a wall, pressing her against it and pressing himself against her. Her legs were tight together, and with his knee, he forced them apart, then reached into her crotch with one hand, his fingers almost tearing into her vagina. With the other, he undid his trousers, freeing his penis and then pushing it between her legs, forcing it into her. But though her body, parched and tight, had almost refused him at first, suddenly it began to respond. And as he thrust harder and harder, she began to ride him. Her thighs became moist and she lifted her legs, wrapping them around him. She pressed harder and harder as he held her in the air, pressing harder and harder into his thrusts.

"Oh, William, oh, God," she moaned.

Isabel's reaction had stunned her, and she could not stop thinking about it as she lay sleepless on her crumpled sheets. The smell of William was all over her and she luxuriated in it. Before tonight, she would have sworn that violence held no excitement for her. Before tonight, the thought of a man taking her by force would have repelled her rather than filled her with the most incredible pleasure she had ever experienced.

And he? What did he feel? She would never know. Had he ever at another time broken through that calm facade, those centuries of training, as Gerson always put it. Now she had seen him let loose an anger of incredible ferocity, a sexuality of breathtaking intensity.

Afterward, he hadn't apologized. He had not said anything at all, in fact. He had merely picked her up and carried her to her bed and made love to her again—this time, less violently, even at moments gently. Then, after he had washed and dressed, smoothing his hair and clothes so that he once more appeared the prestigious and respected surgeon, he bent down and kissed her, not passionately but almost fondly, lightly brushing her lips. She made a feeble effort to get out of bed, but he gestured to her to remain still.

"No, stay where you are. I can let myself out," he said, adding as he stood by the bedroom door, "Isabel, you'll take care of this business with Paul, won't you? What's done is done, but let's have it over with. I think he's had enough therapy, don't you?"

She wasn't sure. As an analyst, she doubted that Paul was quite ready to stand alone without her support, to deal competently with his anxieties, to tackle his own depressions. But she knew too that once having experienced the original, she herself could never again close her eyes and pretend that the frail and delicate boy was his father. There was, quite simply, no way that she could continue to see Paul—either as therapist or as lover. But she had to release him gently. How, though? Walking to her office that June morning, feeling the heat begin to gather around her, she realized that the season could be her accomplice. She would tell Paul she was going away for a few weeks in order to take a brief vacation. No, better yet, she would send Paul away to Shropshire.

He was surprisingly agreeable when she brought the idea up at their session. She had begun that morning by apologizing for her abruptness of the night before. She had, she admitted, overreacted to the news of Paul's talk with his father. Thinking it over more rationally, she could see the importance of that revelation to Paul. Still, she admonished, he must understand that whatever the relationship between him and herself had meant to the two of them, whatever it still meant, very few people were likely to be sympathetic or even tolerant of it and least of all, Paul's family. The point was that to say anything at all about what had passed between them was more than indiscreet, it was dangerous. And he must promise her, whatever comes, that he would never mention it again.

Paul understood. He was contrite. He had, he now saw quite clearly, been thinking only of himself, so surprised and thrilled had he been at his own emotional strength. She too, she told him, had been surprised by his control. And perhaps—and she made this transition very carefully, tactfully, slowly—having discovered that strength, he should now attempt to test it not only in relation to his father but in relation to the Kingman family as a whole. The time was ripe. It was June, beginning to get hot and sticky in the city, cool and inviting in the country. It would be the perfect time for him to go to Shropshire, to face his aunts, uncles, cousins, mother, and to do so alone without Isabel by his side.

"I'm not sure I can manage it," he said slowly.

"But you must try, anyway," she encouraged. "Besides, I'm confident that you'll handle it all very well. Remember the Paul of last night, the courageous, independent Paul who felt he could take care of me, himself, of everything?"

Paul smiled. "Yes, I guess you're right. I do have to face them sometime and so, why not now?" He reached out to take her hand. "But I'll miss you terribly."

She said nothing, only placed her hand in his, pressing gently as if to assure him.

"I can call you, can't I, if I need you?"

She nodded. Of course.

But she didn't want him to call. Not that she didn't care about him—of course, she did. She would always love him a little. And she was somewhat afraid for him in Shropshire. But she had to believe he would be all right and that this first and seemingly temporary separation would make the permanent separation that would, that must, follow easier and more acceptable to him. For it had to be finished, even if she never saw William again. But that was unthinkable. She had to have him again, at least one more time.

Strange, she had never felt quite this much desire, even for Bryan Madison. Strange, too, that it was Bryan, not William, she had dreamed of last night. She and Bryan were in her mother's parlor and she was sitting on his lap. What was strange was that she was very small—her legs didn't reach the floor. Of course, she was small, she was a child. And Bryan wasn't Bryan at all. He was her father. She sat up with a start. My God, the faceless man in her dream wasn't Bryan either. It was a man who never really did have a face for her because she couldn't remember it. And that man was her father.

The phone rang. It was Sandy.

"Hi, toots. How about a movie?"

"I'd love to, but I've really been exhausted the last few days."

"I hope you're not getting that flu that's been going around." He laughed. "Maybe I should come up and do a culture?"

"If I don't feel any better tomorrow, I just may take you up on it. I think I just need a good night's sleep, though."

"Okay. I won't press the point. I guess I just have to call one of the other women in my little black book. Call you later in the week."

Isabel had just put the receiver down when the phone rang again.

"Isabel? It'll take me less than an hour to finish up here. I'll see you at your apartment."

* * *

Although mostly it was William in whose arms she found herself, sometimes—even now—it was Paul. It had been a month since he promised to go up to Shropshire, but still he hadn't left. He kept calling her, insisting on seeing her, and there was no way she could refuse him. It would have been too cruel, too traumatic, perhaps even dangerous. And when he came to see her, she found it impossible to deny him the intimacy they had shared in the past. What could she tell him? That she was sleeping with his father? There was probably no man in the world who would be a more devastating rival for Paul. The thought of him finding out about William filled her with guilt. The thought of William finding out about Paul filled her with terror. What if the wrong name slipped off her tongue? But that was unlikely, she could never confuse them. Not only were they so different, one from the other, but she was completely different with each of them. If in bed with Paul, feeling the closeness of his young lithe body, she felt a girl again; with the sturdy maturity of William's muscular, seasoned form, she felt herself a woman. What was startling too, although she never could have anticipated it, was that the guilt she felt was solely in terms of bringing Paul pain, of betraying him. She felt no guilt at all at the idea of having two lovers, even though they were father and son. Or was it, she wondered, that her guilt was so enormous she could not begin to let it surface into her consciousness? Whichever, as pleasurable as each separate moment was, she could not let the situation go on much longer. For while it might hurt to lose Paul, it would be worse to lose William. In fact, it would be unbearable.

William reached over the night table and looked at the clock.

"Dammit. I'm going to have to go. Christ, I'd like to spend the night with you." He bent over and kissed her on the breast. Her nipple grew hard at the touch.

She placed her hand gently on his neck.

"No, don't start again," he said. "I really have to go."

He got up, put on his suit, and took the pile of change he had put on the dresser back in his pocket. Kirsten's house key lay among the quarters, dimes, and nickels. He glanced at Isabel, as she lay naked on the bed. She was all he wanted, he thought, at least all he wanted right now. He would mail that key back to Kirsten this evening.

* * *

It had been weeks since Kirsten had seen William, and she had been too busy to think too much about it. She was in the midst of working on a television pilot for a new prime-time series. It was a comedy about two single girls who shared an apartment in Greenwich Village—a kind of updated "My Sister Eileen," except that here the girls weren't sisters, they were office mates. Kirsten had the "Eileen" role, while her new-found friend, Lynnie Lambert, had the fast-talking, wise-cracking part that once would have been Eve Arden's or Rosalind Russell's. Kirsten knew that Lynnie had gotten the better role—whoever remembered the actress who played "Eileen"? Just another pretty girl who sank unnoticed into the background. But it was big money and if the show was a hit, big exposure, her agent had persuaded her. Richard and Franco had encouraged her in it too. Well, if it wasn't Shakespeare, at least it was better than washing your hair in public, they had told her.

It had been three grueling weeks already. She was exhausted and glad the whole time that William hadn't been down to her apartment—she wouldn't have been much of a partner for him. But when she received her house key in the mail, she realized that it wasn't only that she had been too busy for William, it was also that she wanted their affair to be over. For whatever sophistication she had gathered in her brief two years in New York, whatever dreams she had had as a young girl of being a famous actress living a fabulous, glamorous life, there was still a streak of romanticism, of sentimentality even, in Kirsten that made her uncomfortable about her relationship with William. Not that she thought their affair important enough that William would ever cast her in the role of home breaker. But there was something basically wrong, something basically immoral, in being part of someone's deception and dishonesty. A casual interlude with a man as unattached as she was herself was one thing—an affair with a married man like William Kingman would always be another. And as much as he had appealed to her—he was a remarkable lover, an exciting, seasoned man who always gave her great pleasure—she wanted nothing more to do with him. With his wife, his son, his world, he had made her feel guilty and somehow unclean. But Shropshire would take care of that. When the pilot was finished, she was going to spend some weeks at her father's farm and she knew that after a few days there, she'd feel better again. Of course, there was always the chance of running into William in Shropshire, but their worlds were so separate, it seemed quite unlikely.

*   *   *

It was foolhardy to go away together like this, William had told Isabel, but circumstances made it too tempting to resist. He was spending a weekend at one of the seminars held by the Institute for Cultural Research in Aspen, Colorado, during the last week of July and then, that coming Friday, attending an AMA convention in Salt Lake City. It seemed foolish to return East for those few days between commitments and especially since Barbara, who was meeting him in Salt Lake City, would be spending that time at Main Chance in Arizona—he would never understand Barbara's passion for spas, for the wasteful, sybaritic existence they offered. If Isabel could only come out West and spend those four days with him, it would be an ideal interlude. The only problem was a hotel. Places like the Broadmoor at Colorado Springs, anywhere at all in Vail or Aspen, were quite out of the question—much too much risk of running into someone you knew.

But he did recall one place they might try, the Wildwood. A large Victorian structure, it might have been in Ocean Grove, New Jersey, had it not been situated on a bluff, overlooking Crater Lake in Rocky Mountain National Park. Built in the century's teens, just before the area had been turned into a national playground, the hotel—with its spacious foyers and wide halls, its large high-ceilinged bedrooms, its game rooms and sun-rooms and breakfast rooms—had turned out to be ill-suited to the simple and hardy tourists the area soon attracted. Arriving with their tents and trailer trucks, these families—if they wanted a place to stay at all—wanted it cozy, small, unimposing.

Still, Hotel Wildwood managed to survive until the Depression. Then it had been boarded up, its gazebos let fall to ruin, its paths allowed to grow over, until some twenty years later, two English sisters had bought the place for back taxes. Closing down about four fifths of it, Ethel and Flora Ankerson had made it a mildly profitable resort that attracted aged professors of botany who walked its trails collecting samples of flora and fauna, quiet fishermen who each year raided its trout stream (though according to park rules, they could not go beyond the limit of ten pounds for a day's catch) and groups of mountain walkers who would set out each day from Wildwood's heights to explore the dramatic moraine. True, the food at the hotel was only tolerable, simple fare that was much too plain for William's sophisticated palate, and the place was a little shabby. But with its magnificent views, its exquisite landscape, and its cool and pleasant Rocky Mountain summer weather, the Wildwood would be a perfect place for the two of them to spend a few days. Here, most important, they were unlikely to run into anyone William might know.

Isabel loved the idea. It would be wonderful to be able to spend some real time with William, instead of being inserted between the other commitments of his life—professional, social, familial. For the first time, she would be able to spend a whole night with him, wake up in the morning with him beside her. But what was important too was that this would be a way to finally make a break with Paul. If she were gone, if she were actually unavailable to him, perhaps then he would go up to Shropshire.

And it was important that he go not only for his health and her safety but because his failure to appear in the Kingman nest continued to be a sore spot between Isabel and William. Over and over again, she had assured William that Paul would soon be able to make the move, and William was growing more and more impatient—probably under pressure, she thought, from his brother and sister. She didn't dare mention this, however. There were many things one didn't dare mention to William.

Isabel had still another reason for looking forward to the trip—a much simpler one. She had never been out West, and having traveled little, the idea of travel itself was especially exciting to her. She was elated when she got off the airplane and saw William, tanned, in blue cotton shirt and white pants, with a jacket slung casually over his shoulder, waiting for her at the entrance to the terminal. But her feelings of elation quickly disappeared when he greeted her coolly, shaking her hand rather than kissing her, behaving as if they were little more than colleagues meeting for a conference. She said nothing, only followed him as he took her bags and began leading her out of the terminal toward the car he had rented for the week.

"It's Dr. Kingman, isn't it?" A bald, bland-looking man in a seersucker suit reached out and put his hand on William's arm. "Henry Wheelright. Remember me? You fixed my knee up for me about five years ago. Not a drop of trouble since."

"Pleased to hear it, Mr. Wheelright." There was an awkward silence as Isabel and William stood facing Mr. Wheelright. There was no way William could avoid introducing her to his ex-patient. "Mr. Wheelright, this is my colleague, Dr. Dunne."

"Pleased to meet you. Well, what brings you two out to these parts?"

"A conference," William answered.

"Don't say. Well, how about coming over for drinks or dinner. The missus is away but she never does any of the cooking anyway," he said with a laugh.

"It would have been delightful, but I'm afraid we're moving right on to Aspen."

"Sorry to hear that. But you'll like that part of the country, and good running into you anyway."

The encounter made William sullen and it wasn't until they were out of Denver, driving toward the Rockies that loomed before them like a giant wall, that he reached over, placed a familiar hand on her thigh, and smiled. How different he seemed to her, she thought, realizing that except for their first meeting when she had been to his office and he had taken her out for drinks at the Carlyle, she had not seen him outside her apartment. She had hardly seen him dressed, so intensely sexual was their relationship. Unlike Bryan—and certainly, unlike Paul—William was a thoroughly unpredictable lover, at one moment gentle and generous, at another relentless and demanding. With William, she did things that had seemed unimaginable to her before. Not that she had lacked passion, but with Bryan she had been too naïve, with Paul too careful. Besides, it had always seemed to her that the great stress on variation in the recent years of the so-called sexual revolution, the emphasis on alternatives, was less a matter of liberation from taboos than from heterosexuality, an apologia for making the sex of your partner irrelevant. In other words, though she knew that in psychiatric circles such terms were not used, these current practices had seemed to her perverse, symptoms of a confused sexual orientation. With William, however, almost everything seemed exciting and part of one's inherent sensual being. And she was as overwhelmed by his imaginativeness as she was by the extraordinary intensity and strength he brought to the act of love. She, for her part, was always ready for him. Even now, his hand on her thigh, she felt herself grow moist.

"I missed you," she said.

He smiled. "I'm glad."

"How was the conference?"

"Tiring, but fascinating. They'd brought in Ilya Prokosh, who opened up the conference with one of those long tirades he's been publishing about all the damage that the medical establishment has been doing to American society. He dredged up all those statistics again that he's been bombarding us with on the relationship of the decline of health to the increase in the health service. It was challenging to respond to him, though, and mostly, I suppose, because most of the members of the Institute share Prokosh's view. But I think I gave them some serious grounds for reconsideration." He glanced over at Isabel. "Afraid I didn't have much opportunity to think about anything else—even you."

She smiled back at him, then glanced at the winding road. "Right now, I think you'd better concentrate all your attention on the driving. It's dizzying out there."

They were deep in the mountains now, climbing steadily, and the road had grown more precipitous. Isabel had never imagined the landscape to be so spectacular. To the east, the Great Plains stretched endlessly, it seemed, toward the horizon, while to the west, the mountains reached up to jagged, frightening peaks. She could see bits of snow here and there on the highest ridges.

"Is it much farther?"

"Another couple of hours."

The time passed quickly, as Isabel filled her eyes with the sights of the narrow canyons, the exotic rock formations that seemed a part, not of this earth, but of some distant moonscape, the walls of brilliantly colored stone that met them now and then as they followed the curve in the road. Finally, they were at Wildwood, standing before the huge, white clapboard hotel whose wooden porches and railings and wings and eaves seemed to embrace every imaginable style, while stretching endlessly in all directions. Only a very few of the windows were lit. Much of the hotel was now closed off, William explained. Years ago, when he had spent some days there, fishing with a colleague, more of the rooms had been open. He led Isabel into the brightly lit entry hall, with its long, white wooden counter behind which was a row of empty mailboxes. Off to the left, Isabel could see a spacious parlor furnished with white wicker chairs and flowered chintz sofas. Several gray-haired women sat about in the room, and two of them, on seeing William and Isabel, got up to greet them.

They were Flora and Ethel Ankerson, sisters who, though not actually twins, surely could have been. Small and slim, one with a hearing aid, the other with thick glasses, both in prim white blouses, tweed skirts, and sensible shoes, they were as out of place in the Rockies as was the Hotel Wildwood itself. Indeed, the Misses Ankerson were as British as the high tea they made it a practice to serve each afternoon at five.

"We do hope you'll join us, Dr. and Mrs. Kingman," Flora Ankerson chirped after them as they started up to their room, accompanied by a wizened, gray-haired bellboy of the Ankerson sisters' vintage.

"Do you think it was wise to use your real name?" Isabel whispered in William's ear. She was surprised but somehow enjoyed the idea of being called Mrs. Kingman.

"Why not? And I had to make you Mrs. Kingman or those little old ladies would have had a stroke. But whatever you're called," he continued, once they were alone behind the closed door of their large square room where shepherdesses danced about the walls on soft blue paper and where organdy-curtained french windows opened on to the lake below, "I'm glad you're Isabel and even more glad that you're here."

Unfortunately, William was not to repeat such a sentiment for the rest of their stay at Wildwood. The very next day things started going badly between them. It was bright and clear, as were all the days that week, and William took Isabel on what he referred to as a mountain walk. The Ankerson sisters supplied them with backpacks and a lunch, wishing them a lovely day as they started up a gentle green incline that grayed to rock at the top. She recognized that it should have been an easy climb, up that gentle hill, but she nevertheless immediately felt the strain in her legs. William, in contrast, seemed to feel nothing at all. His stride was long, his pace was fast and steady, and she found it difficult to keep up with him.

"Come on now, if we go at this snail's pace, we won't get anywhere," he called back at her.

She was too winded to answer. How could she tell him that less than an hour into the climb, she wanted to rest. She knew, without his saying it, how annoyed he would be. So she forced herself on until the sloping field was behind them and she found herself climbing up a narrow path where at least there was the relief of some shade from the unrelenting light of the summer sun. Suddenly, there was the smell of cool air, of distilled mountain water.

"Let's stop here," she suggested, sitting down beside the rippling stream, cupping her hands in the freezing water and throwing it on her face.

"What a fool thing to do," William said.

"What?" she looked up, puzzled.

"You'll blister, that's all. You're a doctor, aren't you?"

"A doctor, yes. A mountain climber, no."

"So it seems."

He looked up, considering the mountain that loomed ahead of them, chose a path, and started walking again. Isabel followed. Up and up they climbed, and the higher they went toward their goal, a snowy peak, the farther away it seemed. Suddenly, Isabel lost her balance and began to skid over some crumbling reddish rock. She screamed.

"Let out another shriek like that and you'll really start an avalanche," William called back, laughing. "The stimulus, as they say, was hardly worth the response."

She felt ridiculous. But the ground kept feeling more and more unsteady under her feet, more and more rock seemed to slide beneath her until she was facing the steepest incline yet—a path that went up at such a precipitous angle that some helpful ranger had screwed metal pegs into the rocks and stretched a wire rope along them as an aid to climbers.

"Just hold the wire loosely," William instructed from overhead.

She couldn't handle it at all. Her hands were perspiring and her feet shaking. She looked up at him, helpless.

"Well, if you can't manage it, there seems to be another way around," he said. He climbed back down to her and taking her hand in his, led her around a bend until they came to a narrow ledge. It was impossible to walk two by two and William let go of her, seeming to almost lope ahead, mountain-goat style. She looked down—the drop seemed bottomless, filled with sharp rocks and thorny brush, and she couldn't make herself move.

"I can't," she cried out to him, "I can't."

She couldn't see him, but she could hear him, and his voice was harsh.

"Why don't you just go back down then, Isabel. This is hardly Mount Everest."

She would go back down if she could—but she was unable to move. She was stranded on that terrible ledge, her legs trembling so that she was sure she would fall. What was worse than falling though, was the thought that William just might leave her there.

"William, I can't make myself move in either direction—forward or back. Please. Come and help me, please."

He did come for her, but that was the end of their walk. It was simply no pleasure, he told her, to spend the day with a whining, complaining piece of femininity. He hated people who started things they couldn't finish. He walked down the mountain ahead of her, sullen and angry. Isabel was angry too. William was being unfair. At the time she had started out on this climb, she had had no idea of her own physical limitations. Never exposed to athletics as a child and even less exposed as an adult, she had never really known anything at all about her stamina or about her courage in the face of physical challenges.

And it was not only heights that terrified her, she learned in the next few days, but speed, water, and the physical dangers they threatened. William took her with him water skiing on Crater Lake one afternoon, and though, after great effort, she did manage to pull herself erect and stand behind the speeding boat, feeling proud and self-satisfied at her accomplishment, she nonetheless realized she was so tense, so full of fear every moment, that there was no pleasure in the sport. She was, she now knew, one of those people who hated the sensation of having their entire body in motion, of being suspended in the air even for the briefest moment. She needed the physical security of the ground touching her feet. She didn't dare tell William about these feelings, since he was obviously the kind of person who loved the very things that terrified her—diving, sailing, skiing. Besides, he had been so incredibly impatient with her on their mountain walking expedition, so irritated as well that she took so long to get up on her water skis. And then, when to avoid a trip on horseback he had planned, she had feigned a headache—she was shaken at the thought of even trying—he grew absolutely furious with her.

He had taken her to one of the most exquisite stretches of landscape in the United States, he told her, a place with Alpine lakes and rushing falls, where glaciers still stood blue and diamondlike at the head of gorges, where the wild flowers and wildlife were incomparably varied. And she clearly felt such little appreciation for it all that rather than explore, she would prefer to laze about on the hotel veranda, that instead of fishing in the cool streams, she would rather sit, sipping tea and reading one of the ancient dog-eared novels from the hotel shelves. Had he known this would happen, he never would have brought her here.

What could she say? How could she tell him that in these few days she had not only encountered a new set of fears but had also come to realize, having never had the chance to know it before, that she wasn't comfortable with those glaciers and streams, with that incomparably varied wildlife, with the great outdoors itself. She was a city person, and though William may have been both town and country, it was a privilege that had not been afforded her.

If she told him she hated the bugs, he would find her finicky. If she told him she was horrified by the snakes that roamed the mountain paths, he would laugh at her and find her overly delicate. If she told him that she grew tired in the clear, thin air, that she was satisfied to view the landscape from the window of their room, he would tell her she was being self-indulgent, unappreciative, unadventurous. She felt helpless, inadequate. She felt herself a weakling, a coward. Good God, she started, what a negative image she had of herself. Here, with a Kingman, she was another Paul.

A profound depression came over her at this realization, and she found herself trying to make up to William in the evening for her failures during the day. But even here, her efforts were useless. Unlike William, she could not make charming small talk with either the Misses Ankerson about the inns and gardens and manor houses of the beloved Surrey of their youth or with the retired Reed College professor and his wife about the ornithological wonders of Rocky Mountain Park—Isabel didn't know a grouse from a rosy finch. Nor could she feign interest in Indian history, in the lengthy descriptions of the Pueblo culture offered them by the two young men from California out here studying cave drawings and artifacts. She was even unable to join William in a bridge game with the group of Norwegian geologists here at the park in seach of fossils—the only card game Isabel had ever played in her life was casino with her mother.

She was thrust back into her youth, face to face with her bitter past with Bryan Madison. Again, she saw the endless stream of sophistication and knowledge that were the birthright of these wealthy white Protestant Americans. With all her schooling, with all her knowledge of medicine, or psychiatry, she had, ironically enough, nothing to offer William but her passion. And even here, she sensed that something had been lost. The moments of gentleness, few and far between as they had been, were gone completely. William was as impatient with her in bed, as gruff and irritable, as he was on their walk. It had been a mistake to come here. Their affair obviously could not survive beyond its small private world—the confines of her apartment. At least, she comforted herself, it would be all right when they returned there. In the meantime, she would at least make their very last evening at Wildwood a lovely one.

It was July 28, William's birthday, and she had asked Flora Ankerson if she wouldn't mind making William a small cake. Isabel, having had as a child such meager festivities surrounding birthdays and holidays, tended to look forward to such occasions with considerable excitement, and so too apparently did the sisters Ankerson. Not only did they have a cake ready but just before it was to be served at dinner that night, they turned out all the lights in the sparsely filled dining room, providing a dramatic context for Ethel, who walked across the room carrying the candle-bedecked mound of white, encouraging the other hotel guests to join her in a hearty chorus of "Happy Birthday, Dr. Kingman."

But William wasn't pleased or touched. He was, although he certainly hid his feelings from the Ankersons, quite annoyed with the whole business. Birthdays, if they were celebrated at all—and at fifty-one, one generally preferred to forget them—were family matters, not occasions for public celebrations in hotels and restaurants. But if William was irritated at the small festivities Isabel had arranged, he was even more disturbed by her sizable gift. She had noticed that William wore no watch and bought him one as a present, bringing it with her from New York. She had been careful not to engrave it, but she had made it special anyway—quite simply, by buying it at Cartier.

"I simply can't accept it," he told her as they stood in their room after dinner. She had waited until they were alone to give him the watch.

"What do you mean? Why not? Don't you like it?" She couldn't understand his reaction, and she was furious at her own incomprehension.

"For one thing, Isabel, it's much too expensive."

"But I want you to have it," she protested. "I have a large enough income, I—"

"Look, I don't want to discuss it," he interrupted coldly. "You'll simply have to return it." And that was that. He handed the watch to her and began to undress.

"What do you mean, I'll have to return it?" Her confusion was now turning to anger. "You'd better explain yourself," she said in a voice as frigid as his.

All right, since she had insisted, he would explain. Not only was the present too costly, it was inappropriate. Watches of any price were too intimate, too special a gift for her to give to him. A wife might give her husband a watch, a fiancée her affianced, but not a mistress her . . .

She raised her hand to slap him, but he grabbed her wrist and held her arm in midair.

"You wanted me to tell you and so, I am telling you." Kingmans didn't go about *buying* watches, he continued. They *had* them, inherited them. In his vault right now, for instance, lay his great-uncle's pocket watch and that of his grandfather as well.

So like everything else, a watch was part of family tradition, a tradition from which Isabel was always to be excluded, a set of rites and rituals which she would never be able to learn. Deliberately, she released her wrist from his grip, took the watch, and placed it in her drawer. She knew that if she said anything further in protest, William was likely to walk through that door which broke the pattern of the pale blue shepherdesses and refuse to ever see her again. And besides, as she somehow knew he would if she gave him the chance, that night he made love to her more fiercely than he had on any of the preceding nights they had spent together at Wildwood. Anger, Isabel thought, was clearly his aphrodisiac.

William Kingman had always liked the Hotel Utah—the elegantly appointed lobby with its balustrades, velvet drapes, brocade upholstery, and huge crystal chandelier; the rooftop restaurant with its intimate little side rooms, suggesting a day and age when gentlemen ordered private dinners for their ladies; and the spacious, finely furnished suites. But if he had always appreciated the Utah's luxuriousness, he felt it even more keenly now after four days at the Wildwood. Wildwood's setting might be spectacular, the Ankerson sisters amusing and charming, but the service they provided was minimal, the food bland, and the beds—well, at least, he was fortunate enough at his age to still have a good strong back.

Barbara, William saw on signing the register, had already checked in. No doubt, he glanced at the clock above the desk, she was at the hairdresser's, preparing herself for the cocktail party and dinner that would launch the AMA convention. She really was the most self-absorbed creature he had ever known, what with her massages, her exercises, her saunas, her health spas, her hairdressers, and her dressmakers. But, as she walked with him now into the grand ballroom of the hotel, dressed in a classic cream-colored gown, her hair looking well worth the three hours and forty dollars she had spent on it, he had to admit that sometimes it all seemed to pay off. She definitely was the most stunning woman in the room, and the approving glances of his colleagues, the jealously appraising gazes of their wives, made it perfectly clear. What's more, as she moved gracefully from one person to another, a charming smile across her face, her eyes registering an expression of intense interest in what he knew had to be a dull story, he was truly appreciative of her social ease, her absolute perfection at dealing with occasions like the one tonight. She knew, as if by instinct, precisely whom to talk to, what to say, how long to stay with each and every one of her conversations. If he had often forgotten why he had married her, he remembered tonight. More than once, she had made an important contact for him, more than once she had charmed a hostile colleague. She had even put the finishing touches on a crucial appointment.

"Your wife really is a most charming woman, Kingman," remarked Ernest Liggett, confirming William's feelings. Liggett was professor of internal medicine at Stanford Medical School, and William hadn't seen him for a couple of years.

"Thanks, Liggett. I agree."

"She was telling me about that new hip operation you're trying. Listen, I've got about four patients who'd be willing to give it a go, if you're interested."

Barbara sat at the mirrored dressing table, carefully removing her makeup, using what seemed an enormous assortment of creams and astringents she had brought with her for the occasion. William leaned over and kissed her neck.

"You were wonderful tonight," he said, in a rare expression of appreciation and affection. She had been wonderful and so had the champagne. William was uncharacteristically high.

"What's come over you tonight?" Barbara asked coolly. "A tinge of guilt?"

"What do you mean?"

"You know precisely what I mean." She turned around to face him. "Listen, William, you're getting careless in your middle life. I've never cared, as you well know, just what slut you've decided to take to bed as long as you've been discreet about it. But I'm afraid discretion's a gift you may be losing."

William was jarred. They hadn't had a discussion on this order for a decade.

Barbara continued. "I want you to know I almost didn't come here. While I was at Main Chance, another guest at the spa—a Mrs. Henry Wheelright—happened to get a call from her husband who mentioned that he had bumped into you at the Denver airport and that you were with a very good-looking redheaded woman."

"All right," William said calmly, "what do you want me to say? I hardly expected to run into Henry Wheelright, who, I assure you, I hadn't even recalled lived in Denver."

"But that's not all, William. Over the past few months, I've received several reports of your having been seen in the company of—do I have it right?—a tall, statuesque blonde who is young enough to be your daughter."

William turned away from her. He detested being put in this position. What good would it have been to say he was sorry or to explain that it was over with Kirsten?

"You've made my life hell enough, William, don't make a fool of me, too. Why didn't you bring your redhead with you here, since you bothered to travel all this distance to be with her anyway? Believe me, if I hadn't been at Main Chance, I really wouldn't have come."

Isabel here? Instead of Barbara. Right now, he wanted to assure her that he wanted no one but her, but William had long since forgotten the way of offering that kind of assurance—that is, if he had ever really known it.

"Forgive me," he said.

She would never have suspected how sincerely he meant it.

For someone who rarely traveled, she was really getting around these days, Isabel thought with some amount of bitterness as she stood, unpacking her small suitcase in the medley of lavender hues with which the guest room had been decorated in Mark and Sylvia Singer's Brookline home. Her black dress unpacked and hung in the closet, her underwear and nightgown laid neatly in an empty drawer, her cosmetic case placed on the dresser top, she took off her shoes, pulled back the spread, and lay down on the cool sheets of the freshly made bed to rest for a few minutes. She was exhausted. She had gotten back to New York from Denver only yesterday, her anxiety and tension at what she now thought of as the Wildwood fiasco aggravated by the heat and humidity, to find a telegram waiting for her.

"It is with deep sadness," it read, "that I inform you that Bishop O'Connor has entered into eternal life. The funeral will be held Friday, at noon, at St. Mary's Cathedral."

It was signed Matthew Dowd, and for a moment Isabel couldn't recall who he was. Then it came to her—the small, red-faced man who was Bishop O'Connor's chancellor. Friday at noon. Today was Wednesday and the telegram had come yesterday. Bishop O'Connor had died, she thought, while she was in Wildwood, probably while she was in William's arms.

Her life somehow seemed punctuated by ill-timed, ironic deaths. In fact, by death itself. How was it that she who had begun with so very few who had mattered to her in life had lost everyone. But it struck her too that though she had lost everyone, Bishop O'Connor's funeral would be the first one she would ever attend. She had been too young to go to her father's, too sick to go to her mother's, and Arne Larsen had died in Denmark, miles and miles away. Boston too seemed far away right now.

She looked at the clock on her desk. Nine o'clock. Too late to leave tonight, she would go instead in the morning. But she didn't want to be alone whenever she went, and so she had called Mark Singer to see if he and Sylvia could possibly put her up for a couple of days. He was delighted to hear from her, even under the circumstances. They'd love to have her. The house was big, she'd have her own room. It would be ready for her in the morning.

She had caught the 10:30 shuttle and then took a taxi from Logan Airport to Brookline, arriving just in time to watch the twins, each in her low feeding table, pushing bits of banana and American cheese into their mouths. Two round-faced, smiling creatures with sparse, fair hair and bright blue eyes, both wore little gold loops in their newly pierced ears.

"They look just like grapefruits with earrings, don't they?" Sylvia laughed.

The twins laughed with her. The fluffy white puppy barked. The phone rang. Rhoda, the cleaning lady, started the vacuum. The phone rang again. And the scene grew even livelier once the twins were out of the confines of their tables and crawling over the beige tweed living room carpet. Between the twins and the puppy, it was an obstacle course, just getting across the room.

"You bought some new artwork?" Isabel asked, looking at something made out of heavy rope and bits of bone which was hung above the long brown sofa. She wasn't quite sure what label would suit it. Sculpture? Collage?

"It's an African fertility symbol, just what I need," Sylvia said as she rushed to pull a straw flower out of the mouth of one of the babies. "Isabel, it's so great to have you back in Boston, even if it is a sad occasion."

Just then the phone rang again.

"See that they don't stick their fingers into electric outlets, will you?" she said as she ran to the phone. "I'll just be a second, I promise."

There always seemed to be someone calling Sylvia in need of advice as to how to add egg yolks to boiling stock, how to keep an avocado plant from looking cadaverous, how to make diaper rash disappear without doing away with diapers altogether. Sylvia had time for all these calls and time too for the kiln Sandy had given her for her birthday. She was really serious about her pottery, she told Isabel, when she got off the phone. She'd send her something soon—maybe a fruit bowl. She'd already sold some of her work at the Faneuil Hall market. Had Isabel been there? The old market had been renovated with arcades, restaurants, shops that not only sold Sylvia's ceramics but furniture made out of baskets, hand-woven caftans, everything you could want, Sylvia said. Maybe they'd have time to go there. Sylvia was addicted to the Papaya Smoothies they sold at the Juicerie.

Just watching Sylvia had made Isabel weary. She yawned and Sylvia suggested a nap. She'd try to keep down the din, she said, as she unplugged the phone in Isabel's room and moved the twins down to the sunny family room which was on the other side of the kitchen. The vacuum was still going right outside her door, but Isabel had no trouble sleeping.

Now it was six and Sylvia awakened her. Mark was home and offered to drive her to the cathedral for the wake. Bishops, Isabel explained, did not have the drunken Irish brawls that everyone thought of when they heard the word "wake." This wake was far more dignified, simply the time when the body of the bishop, garbed in clerical vestments and laid with his head to the altar, could be viewed by mourners who brought their flowers and said their private prayers before the funeral the next day.

Isabel and Mark stayed only a short time, just long enough for Isabel to leave a bouquet of lilies at the bishop's throne and to look down at the ashen face above the white silk vestments. How much smaller he looked, she thought. It seemed wrong to pretend to say a prayer, and there really was none she could offer. Her feelings about this man were as mixed as her feelings about his church, the church that had once been hers as well as his.

When she was a little girl, she remembered, how she loved the beautiful blues and reds and ambers of the great stained-glass windows, especially the huge rose window above the carved wooden doors. She loved the cool within the cathedral door, the quiet, almost crisp, darkness that enveloped her even on the warmest, most oppressive days. The tiny flickering candles seemed to her like little fairies, though her mother told her that it was wrong to think of them that way. The smell of the incense, while it sometimes turned her stomach, especially when she was taking Communion and hadn't yet had anything to eat, nevertheless fascinated her with its exotic aroma, its exciting sense of long ago. And the tinkling bell, the chanting of the priests, the swell of the organ, the murmur of the little old ladies who invariably sat in the front rows, kerchiefs covering their gray hair as they recited—all of this was the poetry and the beauty that Isabel's life otherwise lacked.

For a while, like all little Catholic girls, she dreamed of becoming a nun, marrying God himself in the church, and with a golden band on her finger to prove it. Sometimes too she thought of becoming a saint— of hearing angels, like Bernadette, and having a shrine dedicated to her, maybe a shrine like the one at Lourdes. But best of all was imagining herself as a little girl in heaven, surrounded by rosy-cheeked cherubs, listening to golden harps, and sitting at the feet of a sweet and smiling Virgin.

Thus, the aesthetics of the Roman Catholic Church provided the pageantry and color so needed in Isabel's dreary existence. Its doctrines, in contrast, supplied material for nightmare. If she daydreamed about heaven, at night she was haunted by hell. Horrible monsters with pitchforks, pointed tails, and with slanted eyes behind which fierce flames blazed, attacked her in her sleep; emissaries of the netherworld, they came to punish her for her misdeeds. And if she complained that they were being unfair, that she had been good and pure and obedient, they would laugh. It was for the misdeeds that she might have done they were punishing her. And such fears carried over to Isabel's waking hours—especially those she spent with the nuns at school. For though she did everything right, she was always terrified that one day she might slip and that the nuns, kind as they were, might be transformed into punishing ogres, acting toward her as they did toward other less perfectly behaved children—the ones who didn't get A's and forgot their homework.

More terrifying than the nuns, though, was Bishop O'Connor, because he was the most exacting. The more he gave her, the more he was capable of taking away from her; and the more power he had over her life, the more she felt enslaved and eventually resentful. Even the very last time she saw him, when she was moving from Boston to New York and had long since broken her ties with the church, she still felt compelled to justify herself to him, telling him every honor she had recently won, enumerating every success she had had in the last few months. Yet, she left him as she always did feeling that nothing was quite enough.

Now he was dead. But would she ever get over the desire, the instinct almost, to report to him whatever she had accomplished, to tell him about all her gold stars?

The next day she got up early, had breakfast with Mark and Sylvia, and watched the twins expertly maneuver bits of scrambled egg not only into their own mouths but into each other's.

"If people on communes were so cooperative," Mark noted, "the whole world would be a kibbutz."

Isabel laughed and then, looking down at her own black dress and remembering the occasion, became suddenly very sad.

"I think I'd better start for the cathedral. Can you call a taxi for me?"

"Mark will take you," Sylvia said. "It'll cost a fortune to go by cab."

No, Isabel protested. She wouldn't let Mark take her. She really wanted to be alone, to concentrate on the ceremony with all the pomp and ritual which had once signified so much to her.

There were at least fifty celebrants, priests led by a bishop who, dressed in white, was offering the Mass of the Resurrection. A small, thin priest read the Epistle, another read the 23rd Psalm, still another a verse from Lamentations, followed by a passage from the Gospel of St. John—"Woman, why weepest thou? whom seekest thou?" The eulogy was delivered by the bishop in white, a lengthy speech about all of Bishop O'Connor's good works in this world and his glorious eternal life in the other. Finally, there was the hymn that Isabel remembered so well—"I Am the Resurrection and the Life"—and as the music swelled within the great Gothic walls, she was as moved as she had ever been, although the feeling now was fleeting and quickly passed. She did not go to the cemetery but decided, as she left the cathedral with its altar boys swinging their incense and the organ music filling the air, to walk through Dorchester again. She had a sudden urge to see the old green and tan wood frame houses with their open back porches filled with laundry, tricycles, and cats.

She took a taxi, instructing the driver to go past University Hospital and the medical school. The area was still grim with empty lots, shabby cars, the truck terminal, and the lumber company. The driver—from Polish stock, he told Isabel—was relieved to leave this predominantly black area and head for the somewhat less shabby Dorchester with its colorful bars and their equally colorful names—the driver's own favorite was a place called Bear Feet Aloud.

Isabel left the cab at Dorchester Avenue and Kimball Street. She wanted to walk past her house. The narrow road was filled with small children on roller skates, tricycles, and skateboards. That was the only thing new, Isabel thought. She couldn't remember skateboards when she was growing up.

The sacred statues were still in the overgrown front yard of the house next door to the one she had lived in. Her house, three stories high and called in Dorchester vernacular "a triple-decker," was still the same bilious green, its shingles a dark brown. Someone was living in her apartment, she could see laundry hanging out on the porch. There were baby clothes, a man's pajamas, some slips. She wondered if these tenants liked the stained-glass bathroom window as much as she had. Her house was the only one on Kimball Street to have stained-glass windows and she had always been proud of them, feeling they somehow made the house sacred, although these windows depicted flowers instead of saints at the Immaculate Conception.

She walked back to Dorchester Avenue, past Woolworth's, where she had, as a child, bought her few Christmas presents, the dry cleaner's, the podiatrist's office—she always used to wonder just what a podiatrist did—John Shea's funeral home where her mother had been laid out, the Glocca Morra Bar where the men used to call out to her when she got to be a teen-ager. At Ronan Park, the children were still playing softball, the fathers still cheering them on.

She hailed another cab. She was lucky to get him, the driver told her. Cabs didn't usually cruise around Dorchester. She wanted to go to Brookline? Funny, he would have guessed that she did. She grew up on Kimball Street? He was surprised. She certainly had Irish eyes, all right, but she still didn't look like she belonged here. That was just it, she thought, she didn't belong anywhere. Not in Wildwood, not in Shropshire, not in Bryan Madison's Paoli, and certainly not on Kimball Street.

11

THE DELICATE FUCHSIA geranium plant which hung from a brass chain in the corner of the sun-filled screen porch was one of the largest, most beautiful Paul could ever remember his mother having. Somehow, in the way that rooms resemble their inhabitants and pets their owners, the rich, exotically colored flowers seemed to match her, Paul thought as he sat across from her at breakfast this August morning. Like the geranium's petals, Barbara's hair fell in soft tendrils. Like them too, she was a perfectly designed and decorative object in her cool white organdy dressing gown, her smooth skin taut and golden. And so it was fitting that she alone among the Kingmans would dare to display such an obviously store-bought plant. The others in the family grew theirs from pit, seed, or cutting, and they concentrated not on lush and ornamental indoor flowers but instead on hardy, practical crops. Their flowers came on their strawberry and potato plants, on their cherry and apple trees.

"I'd like to paint a picture of that plant just the way it looks right now, with the morning sun on it," Paul told his mother. "How would you like to have your geranium immortalized?"

Barbara smiled. "Yes, it is beautiful, isn't it? I just couldn't resist it when I saw it in the window at Christatos."

"I can't blame you," he said. "But I suppose I'm the only one in the family who wouldn't. It certainly is the kind of purchase that wouldn't go over very big around here." He looked at her as he sipped his coffee. "You're really so different from the rest of them. Now that I think about it, it must have always been very difficult for you."

Barbara averted his gaze and busied herself buttering a hot biscuit. "Mary has really outdone herself with this morning's breakfast. She must be pleased to have you home. With all our comings and goings, she's hardly had a thing to do."

Yes, Mary really had put on quite a show, Paul thought as he looked at the round table filled with porcelain dishes of sweet rolls, homemade strawberry and blueberry jam, candied grapefruit and orange strips, and soft golden puffs of brioche. "Aunt Natalie's cholesterol count would go up just glancing at all of this. There isn't one whole grain on the entire table."

"Well, what are your plans for today, Paul?"

His mother's question seemed abrupt, somehow out of nowhere. "I don't know. Why?"

"I was just asking."

"There are other questions I wish you'd ask instead." Paul's tone was suddenly serious.

Barbara looked puzzled.

"I mean questions about what these last few months have been like, about why I tried to kill myself. You haven't asked me anything about it. Don't you want to know?"

"I didn't want to disturb you, Paul."

"Are you sure it's me you didn't want to disturb?"

"What do you mean?" Barbara looked startled.

"I mean that in the two days we've been together, our conversations have been nothing but polite trivia. And every time I've tried to make it more personal and meaningful, you've cut me off completely."

Barbara stood up, her hazel eyes beginning to fill with tears. "I don't think I feel too well, Paul. I'm going to lie down." Her voice had the same tremble he had heard so many times before. Whenever a situation became difficult for her, she always sounded like that, on the brink of sobs. Paul and his father knew better than to ever pursue a topic that brought her to this state. She would go upstairs to her bedroom, draw the flowered curtains, and stay there silently, only opening her door to get the trays of tea Mary would leave for her. Sometimes she would spend as much as an entire weekend this way. Barbara was an expert at avoiding the problems set before her, and much of this expertise came from her experience as the mother of a child with lots of problems for her to avoid. Paul had thought, even when he was a child, that if he fell from the barn ladder or the high branches of the apple tree when his mother was around, she would close her eyes to avoid the sight of him rather than try to catch him. And here she was, closing her eyes again.

Would it always be like this? he wondered now as he sat alone at the round glass table, sipping the last of his coffee. Looking out through the screen porch and onto the field of Shropshire that stretched green, square, and orderly before him, he thought of the rest of his family who were part of this very landscape. Would his encounters with them be as predictable as those with his mother had been? Probably. And that was partly why it had taken him so long to get up to Shropshire.

It was now more than four weeks since Isabel had first suggested to him that he leave New York to spend time with his family in Connecticut. At first, he couldn't leave Isabel, and then, he couldn't face them. But he forced himself, in a way he had never forced himself before, to do what was discomforting, distasteful, even frightening. Of course he had hedged his bets, choosing to arrive in Shropshire during the time his parents were out West. And the three days before Barbara's arrival were lovely. He saw no one but Mary the cook and Ned Hutchins the gardener. He had gotten up early each morning, had one of Mary's huge breakfasts, and spent the rest of the day in his tiny studio by the stream that ran behind his parents' home. He hadn't used that studio in more than a year.

He remembered when he was sixteen. His mother had surprised him by having the old one-room cabin by the stream redone for his birthday. She and Foster Richardson, a local architect and good friend of the family, had designed the studio, cutting out a skylight on that part of the roof that sloped north, putting in heat, plumbing, and electricity, and constructing special racks for canvases, shelves for paints, and a rough-hewn silver birch easel.

When Phillip and Franklin heard about the cabin, they were ecstatic. It was, they concluded after inspecting it, the perfect place for making out, and Paul's painting was frequently interrupted by a bobwhite whistle which was a signal meaning, "Clear out." Obediently, he always did. In the last few days, though, the studio was his alone, and he made good use of the unaccustomed privacy.

"Paul, you little stinker." Frederica burst onto the porch. "When Ned Hutchins told me you were here, I couldn't believe it. What do you mean by not getting in touch?"

Thank God it was Freddy. The youngest of Ernest's daughters and the one least bent on always winning, most tolerant of other people's losing, she was the easiest of his relatives to get along with. If he had to break the ice, and he did, Frederica was the best place to start.

"Hi." He kissed her on the cheek. "Have some coffee?"

"Mary's coffee? Of course." She sat down across from him. "Paul, you look absolutely terrific."

"You do too."

She was wearing her usual Shropshire uniform—cutoff faded blue jeans, a blue denim work shirt, and a pair of dirty Tretorns. Oddly enough, shabby as it was, the outfit did flatter her or at least show her off to her best advantage. Frederica, like her sister Margo, always looked best when most informal and worst in the dresses and high-heel shoes that her profession often demanded of her.

Frederica sat down, and in moments she was chatting away as if Paul's separation from her had been caused by a happy journey or a high-spirited vacation rather than a suicide attempt followed by hospitalization and intensive therapy.

Scooping up the last of Mary's blueberry preserves on a baking-soda biscuit, she gave him the rundown. Margo had interviewed the British Prime Minister, Allison had gotten a bill passed giving free prenatal care to needy unwed mothers, Ernest had just given a lecture at Glasgow, Phillip's new wife was a perfectly lousy tennis player and couldn't cook at all, three-year-old Posie had just had the chicken pox which she had passed on to her father.

Paul wanted to talk about other things. Frederica had expressed an interest in seeing Paul's work, and as they walked down toward the studio, he began to tell his cousin the facts about himself and his family that he had discovered in these last months.

"What I don't understand is that no one else seemed to suffer the way I did," he continued as they walked across the field. "Take you, Freddy. Wasn't it hard on you? After all. You were the youngest, like me."

"I was never like you, Paul."

"Obviously not, you don't have any scars on your wrist. But you don't seem to have any scars anywhere else either. How come? How come?"

"You know, I think when people analyze things too much, they start working themselves up into a basically unhealthy state."

"I think I was unhealthier before."

"Maybe because you always looked at things too closely and right now you're trying to get me to do the same, share some of the unhappiness that your kind of scrutiny has brought you. Paul, I don't want to look at my life while wearing your particular pair of magnifying glasses. Nothing, and no one, can take that kind of scrutiny. Enlarge anything, study anything that closely and you see every wart, every vein, every imperfection. Remember what Gulliver saw when he looked at the giants? Well, that's how you are looking at the world right now. I'd give you other advice on how to see things. But don't ask me, ask your analyst."

"Don't worry, I won't ask you. I'm sorry I said anything at all."

"Well, you don't have to get so up in arms. Margo might be right that you're more self-confident these days, but you sure are as touchy as ever."

"And you're as blunt as ever. As an anthropologist, do you constantly use shock tactics in dealing with your tribes?"

"Sure," Frederica said. "I just walk right into a cannibal ceremony and order them to eat carrots instead."

Paul laughed and then shrugged. What was the use of trying? There was no way any one of them would ever understand him. In fact, he realized after Frederica had given his paintings a rapid look and then left, there was only one person in the world, at least at this moment, who could understand. He went back up to the house to telephone her as he had found himself doing almost every day for the past month. Sometimes she didn't answer. But he always had to try.

It was evening before he could get her on the phone. Her service had taken his message in the morning, explaining that she would be tied up most of the day. She had never called him back so he decided to finally try her at her apartment.

"Hi, I miss you. I missed you all day."

"Oh," she said. "Sorry I couldn't call you back. It's been frantic." Her voice sounded funny, far away. "Nothing's wrong, I hope?"

"No, just the usual. Missing you, wondering why I was such an idiot not to insist on seeing you and to agree to coming up here where everyone's the same as they always were."

"Well, look, if nothing's wrong, do you mind if I'm a bit short on the phone. I'm really exhausted."

"I do mind, but I guess there's nothing I can do about it. Are you sure there's nothing wrong with you? You sound different."

"No, no, I'm just tired. I'll speak to you later."

Isabel hung up the phone.

"That was Paul, wasn't it?" William said in a cold voice. "How often does he call you?"

"Every day. I'm sorry, I can't make myself totally unavailable to him. I'm doing all I can."

"You'll have to do better, and so will he." He took her in his arms. "I can't stand the idea of sharing any part of you."

He lifted the sheet and rubbed his cheek against her naked belly.

Natalie Kingman Rush had never kept her political ambitions a secret. The walls of her study would have given her away in any case. There were dozens of framed photographs of her at various ages and with various political luminaries, each of whom had left his salutation scrawled over the lower right corner of the picture. A young Natalie in a tweed suit with short skirt and heavily padded shoulders, her hair in an upsweep, stood next to a dapper, mustachioed Thomas E. Dewey. An older Natalie, in white slacks and a Liberty silk blouse, stood between a smiling Nelson Rockefeller and his equally cheerful wife, Happy, at the Rockefeller Westchester estate. Still another Natalie, this one in a full calf-length skirt, stood shaking hands with Dwight D. Eisenhower when he came to address the New York State Republican Committee in 1956. There were also pictures of Natalie with a series of exotically garbed foreign dignitaries whom she had come to know during the time when she had served on the staff of the United States ambassador to the United Nations. A very large photograph of Natalie with a group of men, all of whom at various times had clerked for Justice William O. Douglas, hung next to a photograph of the justice himself. And finally there was an even larger picture of Natalie among her predominately male law school class at Yale. In those days, Harvard didn't take any women, Natalie always explained to her younger visitors. And sex notwithstanding, she had been first in that Yale class, a rank which recommended her as clerk to Justice Douglas, and this combination in turn led to her being hired as the first woman associate in Lashley and Gorham, "one of the most prestigious on Wall Street" as the New York *Times* never failed to describe it when it figured in a news story. After eight years, she was offered a partnership and became the chief litigator in charge of antitrust cases.

Having conquered all these worlds, Natalie had a new challenge before her now. She was determined to be appointed by the President to the United States Court of Appeals for the Second Circuit. If that woman in California could make it, so could she. And her boys' new contacts in Washington were going to help her. In fact, it was likely that

every single member of her family could do something, she was telling
her brother Ernest as he sat in the leather chair in her study, smoking
an after-dinner cigar.

"You absolutely must show up at that cocktail party, Ernest. Manny
Rosenkrantz is really getting a run for his money this time around. He's
been sitting in that Senate doing nothing but smile for the last six years.
I think the Democrats are about to wipe that smile off his face if we Republicans don't do something for him."

"If Manny can't manage more than a smile, maybe we'd do better
with the other fellow," Ernest suggested.

"I'm not trying to argue Manny's merits, or demerits for that matter.
However, the other fellow and his party are not about to get the President to appoint me to the bench, lest we forget what this is all about."

"I can't see where I come into this. You know how I hate cocktails,
parties, and New York in August."

"Oh, you can leave your beloved garden for two days. I'll even treat
you to the theater," Natalie offered. "But you have to be there. You're
the big draw, my brother the Nobel Prize laureate."

"You make me feel like a movie star. All right, I'll come. But no au-
tographs. And no promises that I vote for Manny."

"I don't care whom you vote for, just as long as you keep quiet about
it."

"Keep quiet about what?" Sebastian said as he entered the room,
Clara beside him.

"Oh, we're just talking about that cocktail party for Manny Rosenkrantz. You'll come with Ernest, won't you, Clara?"

"Of course, Natalie, and if I can do anything to help, please let me
know. Allison will certainly be glad to do what she can, and I think
she'll make a real contribution as the representative of the new frontier
of young Republicans. They're really so involved, those young people,
socially conscious, caring."

"Not a Herbert Hoover among them," Ernest smiled. "Well, Clara,
what did you think of Sebastian's famous cauliflower. I think he's going
to cast it in bronze if it wins first prize at the Shropshire Fair."

"Well, he certainly ought to be proud. Most people can't grow cauliflower at all," said Clara.

"Most people simply wouldn't want to," said Ernest, glancing down
at his watch. "William should be here at any moment."

"Yes, and I think it's about time Clara and I left," Sebastian inserted.

"I don't see why you can't be here," Natalie said. "After all, you are as much William's family at this point as I am. And if it weren't for you and your prodding, we might not even have uncovered what was going on in the first place."

Clara shook her head. "I still can't believe it. How could any doctor have done what that woman did with Paul, have an affair with her own patient. It's just so shocking."

"What's even more shocking," Ernest added, "is what Frederica turned up today when she went over to borrow something from Barbara and overheard Paul leaving a telephone message for Dr. Dunne. According to William, it was all over with. Paul and that doctor weren't supposed to be seeing each other at all anymore."

"I just don't know what's happening to William. He doesn't seem to be on top of anything these days."

"I couldn't agree with you more, Nat," Sebastian said to his wife, "but I really do think Clara and I should be off. With Barbara left out of these talks—and of course she has to be or we'll have another breakdown on our hands—it simply looks better if Clara and I are excluded too."

"I guess you're right," Natalie sighed. "I'll give you a ring up at Clara's when we're finished."

As late as it was, William didn't arrive at his sister's for another hour. Traffic leaving the city this Friday night was horrendous—two accidents on the Major Deegan, and one involved a trailer truck full of bacon. It was so damn hot, the bacon was frying on the highway and cars were skidding in the grease.

"I haven't even been home yet," he told his brother and sister.

"Here, I'll fix you a scotch, William," Natalie offered. "But we really do have to get down to business."

"Fine," William said, wondering what the two of them had come up with this time. The last occasion on which they had summoned him to one of these meetings was to discuss the suspicions of Franklin and Margo, suspicions which William felt compelled to inform them were indeed well founded. It was simply too risky not to tell them the truth and above all because Paul, given his present instability, could not be trusted to keep his affair a secret. Still, he had told them, there was really nothing they could do, however distasteful the whole business was. There was Paul's frame of mind for one thing and the lack of evidence for another, he had said, using Isabel's own arguments for why it would be harmful, even impossible, to force her to end her relationship with Paul. And then, William had added his own bit of fuel, there was the possibility of scandal. Morality and medical ethics be damned, the family's reputation was at stake. He would do what he could, though, take Paul out of therapy, take whatever steps were prudent to assure the fact that Paul would have nothing more to do with Dr. Dunne.

"What we wanted to talk to you about, William, was Isabel Dunne," Ernest began.

Good God, they knew. Somehow they had found out that William himself was sleeping with Isabel. What could they possibly say, what would they possibly do? Oh, Christ, he had always been their secret black sheep, the Kingman who couldn't quite live up to the family's standards, who couldn't quite play by the rules.

"We are under the impression from something Frederica overheard this afternoon that Paul is still seeing her, or at least speaking to her," Ernest continued.

So that was all, Paul calling Isabel. Thank God.

"Now, William," Natalie joined in, "we know you've told us there's very little we can actually do, but you did promise, as you might recall, that you would see this Dr. Dunne and make sure that she would have nothing more to do with Paul."

Yes, he had said that, hadn't he? He'd assured them he would settle the affair, make a trade-off of sorts. He would tell Isabel that if she stopped seeing Paul, everything would be forgotten. Dammit. Why was Natalie always exposing his sins of omission this way. He could never please her or Ernest either, never do things exactly the way they demanded things be done. And damn that Isabel, he was letting her make a fool of him. The best he could do now was try to save some face.

"I've known about Paul's phone calls all along, but the situation has turned out to be a good deal more complicated than we'd all imagined."

"You knew about them?" Natalie sounded sincerely shocked. "Why didn't you tell us this was going on?"

"Now get this straight, Nat." William's voice was now firm and steady. "Nothing is going on."

"Nothing?" She was skeptical.

"That's it. Nothing. The two of them are merely talking. You see, there was one part of this affair I was able to take care of, the most important part, the sex part. It's over, completely over."

"How can you be so sure?" she asked.

William again felt panic. That was the problem, he couldn't be sure. Damn Isabel. If she was still sleeping with Paul, he would kill her. But that was impossible. She wouldn't have dared.

"Well, William?" Ernest prodded.

"I'm sure because I've seen this Isabel Dunne and I have her assurance."

"Really?" Natalie's sarcasm was piercing. "You accept her assurance."

"Yes. The only reason she is still in contact with Paul is that he must be handled carefully. I'm getting her to let him down gently, that's all. She'll do it, don't worry."

"Sorry, William, we are worried, whatever you say," Ernest said sharply. "You simply haven't done your job."

What was he, some child, that they were talking to him this way?

"You two are simply not getting the point. Paul is still a sick boy and he's so involved with that woman that it might be too much of a shock for him to break off with her completely. She believes—"

"I don't care what she believes," Natalie interrupted. "The point is, why should we trust anything this woman thinks or says?"

"Here, here," Ernest joined in, approving his sister's words. Trust was exactly the issue, Ernest said. Besides, while there was still contact between Paul and Dr. Dunne, the chances were all too great that their affair might rekindle.

Ernest was right again. What William felt for Isabel, Paul might feel as well. Good God, hadn't he himself wanted to stop seeing her and wasn't he still drawn to her, unable to free himself of those incredibly intense yearnings that even the thought of her excited in him. What was it about her? Whatever it was, that desire was also mingled with hate.

"Well, William, I don't think there's any more to be said, do you?" Ernest was wrapping things up. "Natalie and I will simply rely on your taking care of the whole matter first thing Monday morning."

Paul sat in the living room, watching a late movie on television. Barbara, complaining of a headache, had taken a Valium and gone up to bed. And Paul, feeling depressed and edgy himself, too restless to concentrate on either sketching or reading, had turned on the television and was now watching a movie he'd seen bits and pieces of before, a 1940's opus, *Now, Voyager*.

"Don't ask for the moon when you've got the stars," the dashing Paul Henreid told the mousey Bette Davis before her transformation from a bespectacled ugly duckling into breathtaking sophisticate, turning down other suitors because she couldn't have the man she truly loved.

Sure, you don't ask for the moon when you yourself are the star, Paul thought, but he had to admit with all its contrivances, it was great melodrama. What woman could resist Paul Henreid as he lit those two cigarettes at once? And who, man or woman, could resist the fantasy of one day discovering you were a swan? Maybe his day for such a metamorphosis would come too. Come to think of it, Bette Davis did have it easier than he. She was only traumatized by an oppressive mother, he was traumatized by an entire family. Speak of the devil—his father's car pulled into the driveway.

"Hi, Mother's asleep. She said to tell you she waited up as long as she could, but she had a bad headache."

"I'm not in the mood to discuss your mother's headaches," William said harshly. "I've just had a very unpleasant talk with your Uncle Ernest and Aunt Natalie, and the topic happened to be you."

Paul was startled by this hostile tone. He hadn't seen his father in weeks, since before William had left for the trip out West, and their last couple of meetings before that—over lunch at the Edwardian Room, dinner at the Palm—had been surprisingly enjoyable. He wasn't sure what prompted this new outburst, although his father's caustic tone was hardly unfamiliar. How many times had he heard it before?

"What have I done now?" he asked.

"I'll tell you once you turn off that blasted television."

"Well?" Paul sat down again once the set was off and waited for the attack.

"I've been told that you are still in touch with Isabel Dunne."

"Not really in touch, at least not literally. I haven't seen her in weeks. I've talked to her, that's all."

"Even talking to her is too much. I think I made my wishes very clear to you that you were to have nothing at all to do with her."

"Yes, you made yourself clear, and not only to me. Ever since that night when I told you about Isabel, something's been wrong between her and me. She's started pulling away from me, closing up." Paul wasn't ready for this confrontation, he didn't feel emotionally up to it, but once having started it, there was no turning back. "And I always suspected you had something to do with it, that you'd gone to see Isabel, threatened her with something. She denied it but I always sensed she wasn't telling me everything, the way she'd tense up whenever I mentioned you."

"Don't you think she might have just gotten tired of your relationship? It does happen, you know."

"Maybe. After all, I know I'm not the Don Juan my father is."

"How dare you talk to me like that."

"Well, it's true, isn't it? Come on, Dad, what was it you once told me? That when I'd get older, I'd understand those things?"

"We're not discussing me. We're discussing you and your disobedience."

"My disobedience? William Kingman commands his son to fall out of love and his son obeys? Come off it."

"Paul, you're not only being disrespectful, you're being unfair. I've only had your own interests in mind from the start. Your relationship with Dr. Dunne is an unhealthy one, whether or not you realize it. Not good for you, not good for anyone. I also made clear to you that if you felt you needed to continue in therapy, that you were perfectly free to do so. Gerson Richler would surely agree to take you on again, and I don't have to tell you again how solid an analyst he is, even if he was mistaken about Dr. Dunne."

"How generous of you, Dad. Christ, don't you understand? I love her." Paul felt his control slipping away.

"You'll love a lot of women in your time."

"No, I don't believe that." His voice started to crack. "I want her."

"Good God, Paul, don't start slobbering."

But he couldn't help it. Why wasn't Isabel here with him, holding him, telling him how to be strong. He needed her, how much he needed her.

Paul had avoided seeing anyone all the next day, taking lunch out to his studio and skipping dinner altogether. But by Sunday, his mood had lifted and he felt capable of facing his father and the rest of his family again. Besides, there was really no way to keep away from them on this Sunday. It was Ernest's birthday, a day even more enshrined in family tradition than any of the national or religious holidays they celebrated. And the festivities—the picnic, the softball game, the fireworks— were to take place this afternoon.

All the cousins had assembled near Ernest's pond, where, at the moment Paul arrived, the littlest Kingmans were rehearsing their original birthday skit. Five-year-old Abbie, Margo's oldest daughter, and her three-year-old sister, Posie, were dressed as Pilgrim ladies in outfits sewn by their nursemaid Jenny. Adam, Allison's four-year-old, was happily chewing on one of his grandfather's cigars and calling out, "Puff, puff." He had the honor of portraying Ernest himself while the girls were evidently intended to embody the spirit of his ancestors, Paul surmised as he heard Abbie announce in her piercing soprano, "I am the ghost of Kingmans past."

Just what we need, Paul thought as he made his way over to the table where Franklin and Phillip, both up from Washington for the occasion, stood sipping some of Clara's cranberry punch. Flanking them were two striking women. One, of course, was Phillip's wife, Pat, the senator's daughter, who was holding on to her husband's arm in a proprietary manner. Nearly as tall as Phillip, slim and long-necked and with sharply defined features, Pat could have been a fashion model except for her large bosom. The other woman, as tall at Pat, had almost a boyish body, what with her flat chest, long legs, and narrow hips. Her streaked blond hair, large mouth, and heavily lidded eyes struck Paul as familiar-looking. He had seen her somewhere before.

"Hi there, Paul," Franklin called out. "Let me introduce you to Peggy Flynn. Peggy, my cousin Paul."

So that's who she was, the Washington *Guardian*'s gossip columnist who was always on late-night television with her flash reports of cabinet payoffs, congressional alcoholism, and senatorial homosexuality which she always had a way of making seem more significant than the reports of a new Mideastern crisis or a bombing in Northern Ireland.

"Hmmm," Peggy almost purred as she looked Paul over. "If your uncle is the ultimate Kingman brain, this must be the ultimate Kingman beauty."

Franklin, Phillip, and Pat all turned around to look at Paul.

"Funny, I never thought of you that way," Franklin said to his cousin. "But I guess maybe some day you will get to be the best looking of us."

"Get to be?" Peggy said in that husky voice that was as much her trademark as the audacity it always carried. "I think you're a little behind the times. He's perfectly gorgeous right now." She turned to Paul. "Come on, gorgeous, let's get to know each other."

She put her arm through Paul's and started walking with him toward the summer house by the pond.

"And what do you do?" she said, sitting next to him on the painted wooden bench.

"I paint."

"Really? What perfect typecasting. You do look artistic. And those long-fingered artist's hands . . ." She reached out and turned both his hands toward her, palms up. "My God, what are those scars?"

"Just what you think they are, Peggy Flynn. In your line of work, you must have seen them before."

A look of sympathy came over Peggy's face, and for the first time this afternoon, Paul thought she seemed human.

"What are you doing, reading his palm?" Franklin came over to the summer house and started to join in their conversation with evidently forced joviality.

"No, not his palm. His wrists have a good deal more to tell me."

Franklin scowled and Paul looked at him. "Well, I couldn't exactly claim I got these opening tin cans."

"Hey, come on, the softball game's starting," Phillip called up to them. "Hurry up, Peggy, you're on my team."

Paul, though far from a softball fan, was glad to have this interview interrupted, and he ran out to the field where the playing members of the family were warming up.

Counting husbands, wives, and at this moment girl friends, the players numbered an even fourteen. Clara and Barbara never joined the game, but Natalie, who prided herself on her good legs and strong heart, often played when the teams were uneven. Today, however, she was umpire while Margo and Franklin, the eldest in their respective families, served as captains.

As always, Ernest was the first chosen and one of the two awarded the starring role of pitcher, a position which, in Ernest's case, made everyone progressively more nervous as the years went on. For one thing, Ernest couldn't pitch and so had to stand so close to home plate that it became dangerous for him and intimidating for the batter. For another, as he puffed redder and redder throughout the game, everyone worried more and more about whether he would survive. The other team, not succumbing to such sentimentality, bypassed their oldest member, William, and chose Phillip as pitcher instead. Phillip was by far the best ballplayer in the family, even better than Frederica's letterman husband, Mitch Harvey. Paul, who wasn't really chosen at all and ended up on Franklin's team by default, had the good fortune for once to be on the side destined to win. He stood now facing Uncle Ernest, who kept adjusting his red baseball cap in between his extravagant windups.

"Strike three!" Natalie shouted as Paul walked away from the plate.

"Listen, you're swinging too soon, I keep telling you that," Phillip said.

"It may be my old man's birthday but to let him strike you out seems like too much of a present," Frederica joined in. "You don't have to be *that* generous. Now, next time, just step into that swing."

Christ, he thought. Wasn't there anything you could do in this family that didn't require lessons, instructions, a whole Kingman methodology?

But if Phillip and Frederica were unpleasantly didactic, Franklin was icily unfriendly. He avoided looking directly at Paul and said not one single word to him during the entire game. When it was finally over, Ernest's team losing despite Paul's unbroken record of no hits and no runs, Paul saw his cousin go over to his uncle. It was obvious that they were talking about him, and from their frowns in his direction, he knew it was nothing flattering.

What in God's name could they be talking about? How lousy he was at softball? Dammit, he was tired of these stupid games. Why did he go along with them? He hated softball, he had always hated softball, and he didn't give a damn whether he was good at it or not. Even if he ever did have any taste for it, he certainly would have grown to hate it by now with everyone carping at him.

He looked around at his family assembled on the green grassy field. There was his father in a navy blue LaCoste shirt and white duck pants, miraculously unsoiled after the game, deep in conversation with Peggy Flynn and Pat Rush. He was obviously entertaining them since both young women were continually breaking into laughter. There was his coolly elegant mother, sitting on a lawn chair, listening to a beribboned and chatting Allison, while a few feet away from them Margo and Frederica were helping their mother and Aunt Natalie put out bean salad and fried chicken. Whitney and Mitch were bringing out a keg of beer and tapping it under directions from Sebastian, and on the other side of the field Franklin and Phillip were stringing up the badminton net. Jonathan was helping Jenny set up for the play, the three little children doing their share by dragging out painted fruit crates for extra benches. Ernest, as guest of honor, was not allowed to do a thing and just sat in a chair, resting up from the taxing exercise of having pitched a full nine innings.

Paul thought about himself. What was he doing? He didn't belong here. He didn't feel part of them and he didn't have a real friend among them, a person who could understand how he felt. But how did he feel? Sorry for himself, that was it. He thought he was done with that self-pity that he knew could drown him. He couldn't make it, couldn't keep on without some help. He couldn't manage without Isabel, and they all wanted to take her away from him.

"I'm not at all happy with what I've been hearing about you," the crisp voice of his Aunt Natalie broke into his thoughts. "You must promise me never to have anything more to do with that terrible woman."

"Terrible woman? What are you talking about?"

"Keep your voice down, Paul." She was almost hissing at him.

"I just wanted to get things straight, Aunt Natalie. Isabel Dunne is . . ."

"I don't want to hear another word about her. Or about you and her." Natalie walked off.

"The children's play," Allison announced. "Everyone sit down. You, Daddy, come sit in the place of honor."

Jenny stood in front as everyone took a seat on one of the boxes or rough wood benches. The plump nursemaid, wearing a much larger version of the little girls' Pilgrim dresses, banged a huge wooden spoon against a metal baking pan to call for silence. Paul sat there long enough to hear Abbie repeat her line, "I am the ghost of Kingmans past," and then he realized that he was far too restless and upset to just sit there. He got up as silently as he could and walked toward the woods, aware that everyone would notice and be annoyed by his departure. But he couldn't help it. There was no way he could stay there a moment longer.

He heard some sounds of laughter and then a burst of applause as he stood, his back to the field, his eyes fixed on nothing, his mind unfocused as well.

Another burst of applause and then silence.

How he had lied to himself these last few months. He could deal with his family but only when he didn't see them. Here, with them now, he knew he couldn't make it.

There was an arm on his shoulder and he turned around. It was Ernest.

"Paul, what is this Franklin tells me about what you've been saying to Peggy Flynn? Really, my boy, you must know she's a gossip columnist and although our family is not as newsworthy as the Kennedys, she would still love to spread us all over her shabby column."

"What could I have said to her? After all, she did notice my wrists."

"I'm sure you could have made up something. I think you don't realize the importance of discretion and the responsibility entailed by membership in this family."

"Not realize the responsibility? It's been the burden that's weighed on me all my life."

"Then you should have known better than to take the risk of appearing pitiful, of exposing us all to the suspicions and judgments of others."

Paul was as angry now as he could ever remember being. "To hell with what others think, to hell with appearances and the Kingman name. How about a little human feeling, for a change? Let's hear it for some heart, some concern."

"We're all concerned, Paul." Ernest was obviously startled by Paul's outburst. No one had ever spoken to him like this before.

"Are you? Aunt Natalie didn't ask how I was, she just came up and passed judgment. And you, you didn't give a damn if I was standing here planning to try to kill myself again. All you cared about when you walked over here was to deliver a reprimand for my failed protocol. And as for my cousins, some are informers and the rest wouldn't even take the trouble to be that. You've made me sick and I'm sick of all of you."

He didn't want to hear whatever his uncle had to say in response. Stunned by his own behavior, Paul walked quickly away, down the edge of the field and toward the road where his old M.G. was parked. He got in and drove off, in what direction he didn't care.

As Paul drove, he thought to himself that Isabel would have told him that what he had just done was a sign of health. He had confronted his uncle, the most frightening and august member of the family, and had demanded his rights as a human being. Whether or not this would accomplish anything was not the point. What Isabel would stress was Paul's ability to recognize injustice and speak up for himself, to protest in a way other than self-destruction. But despite what Isabel would say, he didn't feel very healthy right now. Just exhausted, used up.

He pulled the car over to the side of the road and lay his head down on the wheel. He must have fallen asleep because the next thing he knew, a small Volkswagen was stopped at the side of his car.

"Hey, there, can you move it? I can't get by," a voice shouted.

How stupid of him. He had pulled over right across the entrance to a small side road. "I'm sorry," he said, and started up the engine and began to drive forward, allowing the other car to pass, when the voice yelled, "Stop! Is that you, Paul? I can't believe it."

"Kirsten?" It was she. Of course, he was just outside Butternut Farm on the Old Avon Road. He couldn't remember the last time he had been on this road. Some years before he could drive, he knew that. Sometime that summer when he had met her.

She was just as beautiful, her hair slightly darker but still a surprising silver tone, her skin now tanned, her smile as broad. Her voice was deeper though, her tone more assured as she asked him to follow her down the dirt road that led to the farm. Why not come in for a cup of coffee? she asked.

Fine, he said. He wondered what she was like now.

"You sound different," he said as he got out of his car and she out of hers. "Acting classes?"

She laughed. "Had to get rid of my hayseed speech, only I hope that now I don't sound like an elocution lesson."

She didn't, he assured her. He followed her into the small white wood frame house, the front door leading directly into a kitchen which was filled with open shelves containing what seemed to be hundreds of jars of preserves and huge tins labeled oats, rice, corn, flour, beans, and nuts.

"I keep telling Pop he's part squirrel," Kirsten said. "We could have a blizzard and be snowbound for months, but we'd never starve. Right, Pop?"

Paul shook hands with the square bald man who sat at the kitchen table, reading the paper and drinking tea. His only resemblance to his daughter showed in his bright bluish-green eyes. For while Kirsten gave the impression of lightness and grace, her father was so sturdy that his very fingers felt thick and muscular as he gripped Paul's hand. "Kirsten has always liked my preserves, whatever she says. And all her New York friends seem to love them too." He looked at his daughter with obvious affection and then turned back to Paul. "Are you spending the summer in Shropshire too? Seems to be the year for homecomings."

"Yes, it's been years since I've spent a whole August here, but I had planned to spend the month painting. I'm having a show in the fall."

"How wonderful, Paul. Where?" Kirsten asked.

"At Marcel Block's gallery in SoHo. It's not my own show, I'm going to be part of a group called New America."

"But still, that's fabulous. That's one of the best galleries in the city."

"What about you, Kirsten? What's happening with your career?"

She sighed. "I'm afraid I'm a bit of a sellout." She poured the now-warm coffee into a mug for him. "I've done some commercials and I've just had a crazy hectic month working on a pilot for a new TV series. It's a dumb situation comedy, and I had to forget everything I'd ever learned about acting. But who knows where it will lead, to quote my greedy agent. Anyway, I haven't had a moment to breathe. Have you ever been like that, going so quickly that you think if you don't just squander a few minutes sitting on the edge of your bed and staring, or reading something totally meaningless for you, like the social notes in the *Times,* you'll crack up?"

"No," Paul said. "My life doesn't seem to be so frantic."

"Well, mine won't be either, at least for the next couple of weeks. I refuse to put a toe in that city until after Labor Day."

Paul looked at Kirsten. How perfect that she would be here while he was. He smiled, and the same thought must have crossed Kirsten's mind because, at the very moment, she smiled back at him.

"Well, while you kids talk, I'd better start tying up the tomatoes before the wind gets to them," Mr. Cooper said, picking up some twine.

"I'll do that tomorrow, Pop. You just sit. It's Sunday, you know."

"I know. But I still think I'll start now. You've got me feeling sorry for you with all your work."

"Oh, come on. Now you feel sorry. Before you didn't even think acting was work at all."

Her father looked at Paul and smiled. "Hard for a farmer to think that pretending is working. But I'm willing to learn. Painting too can seem silly, unless it's barn red on wood. Still, I've changed crops, changed methods, changed in more ways than you can imagine after Kirsten's mother died. Why not change when you learn something new? Right?"

Paul nodded as the old man walked out, not waiting for an answer. His step was quick and Paul saw in his spirit of physical assurance some of Kirsten's own positive gestures as she moved her arms. "Oh, it's so good to be home. Don't you feel that way?"

"You can't imagine what a day you picked to ask that question." Paul's bitter tone, he realized, was more evident than he had intended it to be.

"I'm sorry. I obviously said the wrong thing."

"Don't be sorry. It's really funny." He paused and, determined not to allow himself to dwell on his pain, changed the subject abruptly. "Why haven't we seen each other all these years?"

"You're in the in-crowd, that's why," she said quickly.

"What? Me?"

"Sure. You go to that club to swim, not to the town beach. And you play tennis there, not at the high school."

"I don't play tennis at all," he said.

"Well, your cousins do."

"Speaking of them," Paul started, "someday maybe you'll be able to understand that day when you were posing . . ."

Kirsten put her finger over his mouth. "Sh-h-h, my poor innocent father might be right outside. Listen, Paul, I do understand. Franklin and Phillip Rush were big bullies. They probably still are. And nothing really happened, as horny and grabby as they were. We country girls learn fast about strategic kicks and scary threats."

"I'll never forgive myself for not helping."

"As my father would put it, don't be so dramatic. Sarah Heartburn he'd call me when I said anything like that."

"Are you really going to be here all summer? Can I see you?"

"Paul, you're just like an old movie, so polite. Sure, I'd love to see you. It's peaceful here but sometimes life can be too peaceful."

"Not mine."

"Tell me?" she asked, walking him to his car.

"Only if we can compare situation comedies."

"I'll show you mine if you show me yours. Oops." She laughed. "That wasn't the best thing to say, was it, considering our previous relationship?" She leaned over and kissed his cheek. "Paul, I'm so glad you're going to be around. Come by tomorrow, you can work on the tomatoes."

Paul got in his car and drove down past the field where Mr. Cooper was planting stakes. The old man waved a hefty arm and then got back to his work.

Paul turned at the roundabout, following the road which led to the Kingman part of Shropshire. He realized that he still had the smile on his face that he formed for Kirsten's father. His change of mood, he thought, was dizzying. It suddenly struck him that for the first time someone other than Isabel had been able to distract him from himself and to eclipse the harsh Kingman glare. For the first time in months, someone other than Isabel had made him feel happy.

12

As SECLUDED AND unspoiled as Shropshire seemed, it was nevertheless close to the center of the great festival of cultural events New England traditionally presented every summer. Less than an hour away was Tanglewood, that vast grassy estate where the Boston Symphony came in retreat from the hot city, giving to other urban refugees the pleasures of their music in great outdoor concerts. Next to Tanglewood was Jacob's Pillow, where various dance troupes came to perform at the small wooden theater in its sylvan setting, while just a few miles south, at the Berkshire Festival in Stockbridge, both new and established playwrights had a chance to showcase their wares, having the advantage of the top directors and the big-name stars this particular summer theater attracted.

The Kingmans supported all of these institutions and their programs and others in the area as well. They had contributed to the restoration of the Hancock Shaker Village, an authentic replica of an eighteenth-century Massachusetts town; had helped in the development of the Stockbridge Gallery and the Old Corner House, both small museums for the display of local art; had been instrumental in the building of the Nathaniel Hawthorne Berkshire cottage, a facsimile of the writer's nineteenth-century home, and in the development of the Stockbridge Historical Society.

But it was the Berkshire Music Center at Tanglewood that received their greatest support. Clara was on the Executive Committee of the Tanglewood Council, while all six of the elder Kingmans numbered among the Friends of Music at the center and had two choice season boxes in the great shed under whose huge roof the Boston Symphony and other visiting groups performed. Paul, from the time he was a young boy, going to those concerts with his family, wearing jacket and tie, always wished he could have been, rather than in the shed, among those barefoot young people casually dressed in dungarees who lay on the surrounding lawns, sprawled on their blankets under the stars with jugs of wine and wedges of cheese. But somehow, before tonight, he had never been among them, he told Kirsten, as they spread an old faded summer quilt on the grass outside the shed. Kirsten had a straw basket in which was the picnic dinner she had volunteered to prepare—cold ham, macaroni salad, and peaches and homemade oatmeal cookies for dessert. She had also brought some beer and offered one to Paul.

"Would you believe it. I'm ashamed to admit it, but I've only been here once before. And don't laugh, with my Girl Scout troop," Kirsten said.

"I promise you'll like it more this time," Paul said, putting his arm around her. "Of course, you don't hear as well on the lawn as you do in the shed, but if the acoustics are no good, the atmosphere makes up for it."

She looked around at the tall leafy trees silhouetted against the darkening sky, at the twinkling hurricane candles which stood here and there on neighboring blankets. Sounds of violins being tuned, of a horn and a flute, filled the air.

"You're right," she said. "This has to be the most romantic place I've ever seen in my life. Of course, I didn't realize it when I was here with the Girl Scouts." She leaned her head against his shoulder.

A huge burst of applause came from the shed before them. The Japanese-born music director of the Boston Symphony, Seiji Ozawa, was conducting tonight and must have just assumed his place on the podium, Paul explained.

"It really is a shame you can't see him from here, he really is fascinating to watch," Paul said. "His movements are so completely different from those of other conductors, so Oriental somehow—as silly as that sounds."

Kirsten smiled. "I wouldn't know what I was seeing anyway. I'm an absolute ignoramus when it comes to this kind of music. I guess I never graduated from the Beatles."

"I don't think you'll have any trouble understanding tonight's program. It's Richard Strauss and Ravel and they're both easy to take—as romantic as the atmosphere."

The music started, rich, melodic, and full of energy, with horns and strings announcing *Ein Heldenleben*'s majestic themes. As the orchestra repeated and varied these phrases and motifs, the sound growing progressively fuller and louder, night fell and the sky grew black. Kirsten and Paul lay back on the blanket, facing up at the star-studded sky. Paul felt Kirsten's hair brush against his cheek. It was cool and silky, and he loved its fresh smell. He could feel her breathing, almost to the rhythm of the music, it seemed at times. Their shoulders touched, their hands brushed, even their bare feet moved against each other. Now the symphony was dominated by an ornate violin solo. The playful melody was the heroine's theme, and it suggested the coy teasing of a shy and reluctant mistress. But the hero, whose musical motif was played by the full orchestra, finally overwhelmed the delicate violin, making it part of a grand harmony.

Paul lay there listening, allowing himself to be swept up in the great sentimental wave of this romantic music. At this moment, he was the hero, vanquishing his enemies, winning the heroine, and carrying her off. The appeal of this music, he thought, was that it embodied the daydreams of every little boy, fantasies that the adult male had never really put away. Now, as he looked at Kirsten lying beside him, he realized to what a great extent she was a part of his fantasies as well, the heroine to his hero.

The great, swelling final movement came to a close, and the audience suddenly burst into applause. The big spotlights went on. It was time for intermission.

"Let's stretch a little," Paul suggested, helping Kirsten up. They both slipped on their sandals and began to walk down the gravel path toward the souvenir shop.

Whatever the people around them wore—whether cutoff jeans or cotton flowered gowns, whether bearded or clean-shaven—they still had a similar look about them, Paul thought. They could all have been part of the faculty or faculty family of one or another of the many New England colleges in the vicinity. And if not on the faculty, at least one of the students at those schools. Their conversations were animated, their voices modulated, their tones fluent and facile, and they had a look about them of thoughtful intelligence. The children among them were, for the most part, well behaved, silent during the concert, but now taking advantage of the hubbub of intermission, they ran around chasing one another and laughing loudly.

"Hey, aren't you the girl in the Belle Chevelle ad?" a small boy in a Snoopy T-shirt asked Kirsten.

She smiled back. "And aren't you the boy in the Snoopy T-shirt?"

"No, yes." He was flustered. "Hey, stop kidding. Are you or aren't you?"

Kirsten nodded.

"Can I have your autograph then?"

"You really want my autograph?" Kirsten was truly amazed. "Sure, why not," she said as she wrote her name on his program.

"Hey, Kirsten," Paul said as they walked back to the blanket, "you're getting as famous as my Uncle Ernest. Thank God, the resemblance ends there."

Intermission was over and the music resumed. Now it was a chain of waltzes bursting forth from the shed, the rhythmic, graceful, delicate *Valses Nobles et Sentimentales* of Ravel, and Paul once again felt the warm presence of Kirsten's body. She was lying with her eyes closed and he found himself staring at her. She really was so beautiful and he knew that he wanted her. But he also knew that the chances were he would never be able to have her. And not because she would refuse him —her gestures during the past few days had indicated to him that she was at least fond of him, that perhaps she found him appealing—but because his body itself might refuse. For though he had been able to make love to Isabel, he had no way of knowing if he would be able to have sex with anyone else. And with Kirsten, his first love and one of his most dramatic failures, perhaps least of all. It was simply too frightening to try.

He decided to put it out of his mind and concentrate instead on the music. But the sensuous rhythms, the vivid, almost tactile sensation of hearing waltz after waltz after waltz, forced him back into an acute physical awareness of the body next to him. He felt a stirring within him as the music swelled to a turbulent crescendo. He held Kirsten tightly, almost clutching her, until the melody subsided and the rhythms grew faint. The orchestra played one last waltz, and then the concert was over.

Two nights later, it was Kirsten's turn to act as Paul's guide. Not that he hadn't been to the theater at Stockbridge many times before, but he had never been backstage as he was going to be tonight. Richard Farrow, Kirsten's scene partner from her acting classes, was in a new play being premiered this summer. It was a musical version of Dostoevsky's *Crime and Punishment* called, simply, *Crime*. Richard had told Kirsten, when he called to invite her, that he thought the title deplorable.

Punishment, even, would have been better, he had suggested. At least that would have brought in the S/M crowd, though best of all of course would have been to have called it *Borscht.*

There was no one, Kirsten agreed, who could possibly have resisted going to a show called *Borscht*—though who knew whether *Crime* would pay off or not. In any case, even if the title was lousy, Richard said, the score was really terrific—especially the recitative between Raskolnikov, the murderer, and Zamyotov, the police inspector. And the staging of the final number—a love duet between the repentant Raskolnikov and the pure-souled prostitute Sonya on the steppes of Siberia—transformed the entire theater into a winter wonderland. The wind machine was a bit strong, but it was the only one the company could get hold of to blow around the snow. And they could always pass out mufflers. Richard had about the best part in the whole thing, he said modestly. He was the pawnbroker whom Raskolnikov, the starving student, was driven to bludgeon to death.

"But isn't the pawnbroker an old lady?" Kirsten had asked.

"Mais oui," Richard answered. "Don't be narrow-minded. Wait until you see my death scene in the second act. Ketchup all over the place. Better eat a light dinner," he advised, "it can be pretty upsetting."

Kirsten, however, didn't think it was quite necessary to follow this advice. Besides, Paul was anxious to take her to the Fox and Falcon Inn before the performance and standing rib roast was not only their specialty but Kirsten's favorite dish, she told Paul.

The restaurant, which made up nearly the entire first floor of the large colonial inn, was to Paul's way of thinking the epitome of New England style rigidity and for that reason alone, amusing to visit. Here, in the middle of a country village and during vacation season when people came to unwind and relax, the Fox and Falcon maintained strict rules of dress and decorum. Men were required to wear ties and jackets, women were not allowed in the dining room in pants—no matter how dressy or fashionable—and children were banished altogether, forced to take their meals in a separate room in the rear and at a separate hour. The children ate from five to six, adults from seven to eight, and anyone delayed and missing this brief hour would simply have to go elsewhere.

The menu was a limited one and featured, besides the roast beef, Indian pudding, which in its Fox and Falcon version was so thick in molasses as to threaten the patrons' dental work or give cause for it in the first place.

"You're right," Kirsten laughed with Paul. "This place really is detestable. But I understand precisely what makes you want to come here. It's so much a stereotype of the Puritan way of life, with its stuffiness, its silly rules, its demand that you eat when or what they tell you, that it really ought to be enshrined. How do they get away with it?"

"I guess because people like us keep going, and it does serve the best roast beef of any restaurant in New England."

If dinner at the Fox and Falcon paid homage to tradition, the musical *Crime* at the Berkshire Playhouse paid homage to anything but. Never, even in this day and age when nothing was sacred, was anything so profane. Richard had failed to mention that the finale was played in the nude, making the snow and the prospects of Siberia that much more cruel, or that *Crime* had a rock score, delivered in deafening amplification. It was so loud, in fact, that the lyrics were mostly distorted into unintelligibility—something which both Kirsten and Paul decided afterward was probably a blessing. They were careful to say this in hushed voices, to avoid hurting Richard's feelings. It had been a bad enough evening, the audience having been distinctly unresponsive, with many leaving after the first act.

"If we could only get this play to New York, I know we would find our audience," the director, Bob Greenglass, attempted to comfort himself both with his rationalization and with the joint he was now smoking. It was after the performance, and Richard had taken Paul and Kirsten with him to this party Bob was throwing. Unfortunately, the party had taken on more the spirit of a funeral than that of a festivity, everyone in the cast feeling the dampening effects of the audience's chilly reception, not to mention the chilly blast of the Siberian snow in the finale.

"Oh, cheer up, guys," Richard said. "It could be worse. You could all be back waiting tables again, and I could be back teasing hair at some shopping mall in the suburbs."

To help brighten everyone's mood, he began to sing "Let Me Entertain You." The actress who played Sonya ran over to the piano and began to accompany him—they had obviously done this number before. And Richard, as he sang the stripper's song from *Gypsy* in a falsetto, proceeded to deftly remove all his clothes.

Kirsten was convulsed in hilarious laughter but then, as if suddenly remembering Paul's presence, she caught herself and turned to him. "Are you uncomfortable? I keep forgetting, everyone isn't as used to crazy actors as I am."

But Paul was laughing too. "I can't see Richard making anyone uncomfortable. He's just too funny."

"Oh, you'd be surprised," Kirsten said. "A lot of guys don't enjoy being around gays like Richard. You must be very sure of yourself."

He didn't know, but he was sure that Richard was one of the funniest men he had ever seen, and several times on the way home, they both burst out laughing as they recalled one of Richard's gestures or jokes. The laughter brought them closer together and when they arrived at Kirsten's house, she leaned over and kissed him warmly, affectionately. At that moment, all he could think about was that he wanted to make love to her—but he was still too frightened to try. The irony of her observation struck him. She thought him sure of himself; she would never understand his total lack of assurance. And not understanding, she would soon grow annoyed at him and at his inability to make a move, weary of the situation, static, incomplete, and ultimately unsatisfying as it would soon become. No matter what he did, he was bound to lose her again.

If Paul was terrified of making a move and losing Kirsten, Kirsten was equally terrified of losing Paul. He had fascinated her as a boy—he was so different from anyone she had known and, somehow, so much better. He was the one person who had ever understood her ambition to become an actress, who didn't either laugh or put her down in some way. Even her father, who was forced to be doubly attentive to the ten-year-old Kirsten after her mother had died, was merely humoring her.

Kirsten loved the way Paul saw things too, with his painter's eye, the way he noticed the colors of shadows and showed her how what she thought was gray was really purple or green or deep blue. He also taught her to look for patterns, to see how the shape of a rock would be repeated in the shape of a cloud, how the veins in one's hand would be repeated in the veins of a leaf. But what appealed to her, above all, was his delicate touch. Unlike the boys in her high school class, unlike the young men who helped her father on the farm, Paul never made vulgar comments, never pressed himself on her in any way. He always watched and waited for her signals, and so he became for her in those years the one boy she was ever the aggressor with. Something in him invited her to lead the way, although their relationship had abruptly been broken off.

This time, she would have liked it to be different. But if his cousins had interfered before, now it was his father, or at least the idea of him. What if Paul ever found out about the affair she had been foolish enough to have with William? He would have to be disgusted, unforgiving. And so having had the father, was she now prevented from ever having the son? But she wanted him, and Kirsten was not one to deny herself. Whatever she wanted, she usually got—at least, that was what her father always used to say.

"But are you sure it's a Kingman you want?" he said now as the two worked together in the vegetable garden. "They're a snobby, stuffy lot, Kirsten. They all have ramrods up their rears."

"Paul isn't like that, Pop. You can sense that, can't you?"

"Yes, I can. He is a nice boy, but you'll have to deal with all the rest of them and I wonder if it's worth it. You're not their kind of people. All these years, have they ever invited you and me or any of us who live in Shropshire year round into their home, except maybe to do some handiwork? Did they ever invite any of us to any of those big parties they always give or to any of those dances at the lake club? No. They dig a deep furrow between us and them and don't you ever forget it."

"Come on, Pop. You're being very old-fashioned," she said as she pulled some weeds out from between the carrot plants. "Granted, the Kingmans aren't exactly bombarding us with invitations, but who cares anyway. The kind of class distinctions you're talking about went out with the horse and buggy."

"I'm not so sure," he said, tossing some beets into a basket. "Why do we plant beets, Kirsten? We both hate them. And your mother used to hate them too."

"Tradition, Pop," she laughed. "We plant beets and the Kingmans belong to clubs. We're not so different after all."

"Maybe you're right, you usually are. Somehow, kid, you always come out on top. Sent you to New York, you didn't know anyone, and in two months you had a job, an apartment, friends—such as they are. They're a little sissy for me, but if you like them, I'll try to."

"You're beautiful, Pop."

"You're not so bad yourself, kid." He smiled at her. "Guess I don't have to give any of this Kingman business a second thought. Guess I don't ever have to worry. Everything always works out for you anyway."

Kirsten's closest friend from high school, Maggie Webb, had a tiny cabin on Mt. Mohecan. Her family had moved up to Vermont, finding the Berkshires too built up and expensive for their taste. But though they had sold their farm to a New York writer, they had held on, at Maggie's insistence, to the isolated cabin. Maggie used it most weekends, driving up from Hartford, where she now worked for an insurance company. But during the week, it was always deserted, and she had invited Kirsten to use it whenever she wanted to. Kirsten loved Mt. Mohecan. The highest point in the Connecticut Berkshires, it had a great plateau at its summit in the midst of which was a large crystal lake. Mt. Mohecan had once been the site of a thriving village. Ore deposits having been found in the area way back before the Revolutionary War, a large forge had been built on the spot to process the iron which was used to make such implements as anchors, caldrons, and plows. By the time of the Civil War, however, the community had begun to disintegrate. The ore beds ran dry, and by the turn of the century, almost all of Mt. Mohecan village lay in ruins with only a few stragglers, called Roamies, living there. Some said that the name of these dark, shabbily clothed people came from the fact that they were wanderers, roaming the Connecticut countryside. Others said it was a shortening of Romany, or in other words, Gypsy. But whatever, even the Roamies finally disappeared from Mt. Mohecan village, leaving the forest to take over, burying everything but a few stone walls here and there, the foundations of a house, and the hollow of the forge.

Maggie Webb's cabin was one of the few that had been built around the lake right after World War II. Mt. Mohecan, with no electricity and primitive plumbing, never attracted too many tourists, and these simple cabins remained isolated and few.

"What a great place," Paul said as they walked into the single large room built out of roughhewn pine planks. It was furnished with a Franklin stove, two beds which doubled as sofas, a small table, and four ladderback chairs. The only hints of frivolity were the blue-checked gingham curtains at the window and a matching blue gingham tablecloth.

"Those are Maggie's touches," Kirsten said. "Her family would be strictly oilcloth."

Paul smiled. "How about a swim before lunch," he said, looking out of the windows at the inviting lake.

"Okay, but be warned, that water is always frigid."

Kirsten put their picnic basket and the scotch cooler up on the table. They had planned to spend the entire day on the mountain and had brought enough food not only for lunch but also for dinner in case they wanted to stay and see the sunset. Paul put his knapsack on the bed, pulling out of it a couple of towels and his swimming trunks.

"Oh, you won't need those," Kirsten said. "It's absolutely isolated up here. Unless you're shy in front of me."

Paul said nothing but picked up the towels, following her down to the lake. A small dock extended beyond the shoreline. Kirsten, still in her jeans and T-shirt, walked out on it to stick a toe in the water. "Cool as ever," she said.

Paul looked at the lake. It was so clear that all the trees could now be seen in double, upside down, making the water as verdant as the land.

"But cold or not, I'm going in." She quickly pulled off her clothes and then stood poised for a dive at the edge of the dock. "I feel so silly, but after all that, I can't seem to get my courage up."

Paul stared at her. The sight of this beautiful naked girl suddenly pulled him back to the past where that same body, younger, more childish, less full, had also stood before him. He had wanted that body then and he desperately wanted it now.

She finally dove into the water and he took off his clothes, leaping in after her. His dive was deep but he never came close to seeing the bottom. This lake seemed to go down endlessly, a great water-filled hollow which could have extended to the bottom of Mt. Mohecan itself. What was extraordinary too was the absolute clarity of the water. There were no reeds, no water lilies, no sign of a fish or a tadpole. It had the texture of water which cascades down the sides of mountains, cleansed and purified along the way.

"Brrr, I'm turning blue." Kirsten climbed back up on the dock and grabbed a towel, rubbing her hair. "At least the sun is warm," she said, walking off the dock and stretching out on the grassy bank.

Paul joined her, wrapping himself up in the other towel and lying down next to her. He ran his fingers down her back. "You know, I'll never forget your body. I remember every inch of it from when I painted you."

Kirsten turned toward him. "Those were lovely days, weren't they? At least, for a while."

"You know, I was in love with you," he said.

"You were? And you never told me? And there I was, in love with you and thinking it was all one-sided."

"I guess we had what they call a breakdown in communication," he smiled.

"Well, let's not have one again," she said, reaching up to him and pulling him gently down toward her.

He kissed her softly and began to stroke her body, feeling her cool skin grow warm beneath his touch. She moved closer to him, putting her arms around his neck and kissing his cheek, his throat, his ear.

"Paul," she whispered.

He began to feel himself growing hard against her. He was as aroused now as he had ever been, and he began to believe that maybe he could make love to her after all. He must have believed that before, he thought, or he probably would not have come here with her.

"I love you," she said.

He looked at her beautiful face, her eyes now looking into his. He loved her too, he knew. He felt her soft stomach against his and ran his fingers along the curve of her hips, across her smooth thighs, and on the velvet skin between her legs. And then, in a sudden plunge much like the one he took on entering the lake, he entered her. How soft, how moist she was, how warm, as warm as the noon sun on his back. Slowly, he began to move, to perform that ancient, rhythmic dance. It must have been this, he thought, that inspired those waltzes of Ravel that he and Kirsten had listened to together. And now, just as that music had reached its crescendo, so did the two of them.

Afterward, they lay quietly in the sun, Kirsten's head resting on his shoulder, her fingers playing on his thigh. "Shall I get the lunch?" she asked.

"Later," he said. Her touch had made him ready to make love to her again. This time, surer of himself, the pleasure became even more intense for him and he knew it must have for her as well. They made love all that afternoon, stopping briefly to swim and to eat some of the picnic lunch.

"What do you think about staying the night?" Paul asked.

"That's exactly what I planned we'd do. Didn't you notice the cornflakes in with lunch and dinner?"

They both laughed.

There was no doubt that Paul was in love with Kirsten. He had never felt so good about himself, so pleased that he was who he was. The first time he had made love to Isabel, he had discovered both a set of sensations and a power in himself that were new and exciting to him. But now in love with Kirsten, he knew that what he had felt for Isabel, what he still felt, was not love at all. It was gratitude, it was affection, and perhaps most important of all, a sense of affinity. Isabel had begun as his analyst, ending up his soul mate. Kirsten, once his best friend, had finally become his lover. And this discovery of love must have been what Isabel had been preparing him for when she insisted that they separate. Wise as she was, she understood just what he was feeling, just what was right for him, even before he himself knew. He had to tell her what had happened, he had to call her in New York and tell her all about Kirsten.

As usual, Isabel was difficult to reach by phone, but when Paul finally did get in touch with her, she sounded warm and very glad to hear from him—and especially after he told her the reason for his call.

"But go easy," she had warned. "Don't rush things. You don't want to risk getting hurt."

She seemed to be talking more slowly than usual, choosing her words more carefully. There was something disappearing between them, retreating somehow. It unsettled Paul for a few minutes after they hung up. Then he thought about her warning. Kirsten hurt him? It was as hard to conceive as Paul hurting her. And not only because he would never do anything to harm her in any way but because she seemed so healthy, so resilient. Had she been a member of the Kingman family, she never would have felt the way Paul did about them, overwhelmed by her relatives, intimidated by them. The idea of Kirsten interacting with his uncles, aunts, cousins, his father and mother fascinated him, and he was anxious to see them all together. Kirsten's reaction was one thing, his family's would be another. The Kingmans might be less than cordial to the daughter of a local farmer. But, in any case, they all did have to meet sometime.

He carefully broached the subject with her. Perhaps the best thing would be to spend an afternoon or evening with only his parents, saving the rest of the family for later. Perhaps the very best thing of all would be for her to come and have dinner at William and Barbara's one night. She went white at the suggestion. Was the idea of his family really so terrifying? he asked. His father could be very gallant to pretty young women. Finally, she agreed to come. She would have to meet his parents someday, she said, she might as well get it over with now.

Barbara said she was delighted that Paul had asked a friend to dinner. And a girl friend at that. He could, though, she hinted, have done a little better than a local farm girl. And he certainly could have selected a different night to have invited her over. After all, Foster Richardson and Megan Evans had been asked to dinner that very night more than a week ago. Paul offered to make it another time, but then his mother, on second thought, said perhaps it was best that Kirsten come that evening after all. With Foster Richardson there, raconteur that he was, there would be no awkward silences, no problem at all in keeping the conversation going.

Foster certainly was in top form that night. An architect who some thirty years ago had decided to leave his native New York, he had made his summer home in Shropshire his permanent one. He had been quite sure he could make a living what with the growing interest in renovating the old colonial farmhouses indigenous to the Shropshire area as well as the current rage for transforming such farm outbuildings as barns into weekend homes. Professionally, at least, things had gone well for him. But Foster's wife, unable to adjust to the long lonely winter evenings in the country, had returned to New York, reluctantly divorcing the agreeable and attractive man. At sixty, Foster was still remarkably good-looking, with shaggy straight gray hair, a perpetual tan, and a youthfully slim and muscular body.

Foster's dinner partner that evening and the evident cause of his high spirit was Megan Evans, a Welsh novelist who since her arrival in the United States some five years before had become the darling of the New York literary world. Her name was continually popping up in *Women's Wear Daily*, in Suzie's column, and on *Vogue*'s "People Are Talking About . . ." page. Her remembrances of a Welsh girlhood during World War II had won a National Book Award last year, and about that time, she had bought the Pearson cottage on Lovelane which Foster had renovated for her.

Megan, who was six feet tall, with short-cropped hair, bright blue eyes, and a big broad smile, was, though far from delicate, a strikingly handsome woman. Like Foster, she was extremely animated and filled the room with her hearty laughter as she sat entertaining her hosts with her large fund of Dylan Thomas stories. How Thomas had slipped her a Mickey at the Ram's Head Tavern in Cardiff when she was a mere green thing, how he'd fallen off a podium at a lecture at Wolverhampton just as the rector of St. Mary's had introduced him, how he'd seduced every girl between the ages of eighteen and thirty in the village of Swansea, where he'd been raised.

Was she one of them? Only Foster would have had the nerve to ask what everyone was wondering.

She smiled. "I didn't grow up in Swansea. So there."

The party seemed to be going well, Barbara thought. Mary's ducks were crisp, her wild rice firm, perhaps the asparagus were a bit stringy but the watercress salad made up for it. And Foster, as usual, was a darling, keeping the conversation going, getting Megan Evans to tell all those stories about Wales. They were a bit raunchy and maybe that was why William looked so strained all evening. He hardly even glanced at Paul's friend, which was surprising, considering what Kirsten Cooper looked like. She certainly was pretty—Paul seemed to have inherited his father's taste in women. She was, though, a little quiet for William's taste, although perhaps she was just uncomfortable this evening, having dinner with a different sort of people than she was evidently used to. Paul, however, his mother was surprised to see, was far more friendly and open than she had ever seen him be before. And it was obviously this girl's doing. Barbara found herself liking Kirsten because of this. Perhaps with her Paul could finally break his dependency on his analyst, perhaps he could finally be whole enough to stop being a burden on his family and a source of contention between William and herself. William may not have said so, but she always suspected that he blamed her for Paul's failings. She wasn't Phi Beta Kappa like every other member of the family, she wasn't even a college graduate, her husband had often pointed out. You couldn't consider a finishing school like Finch a real college. And Barbara's accomplishments, she knew, were limited to giving dinners and parties. He would have liked her, she knew, to have done something, maybe written a book as this Megan Evans had. But then, would Megan Evans be able or willing to entertain William's family, friends, and colleagues the way he demanded, to run his household precisely as he wanted it run. No, he could never have married a Megan Evans. Still, Barbara thought with a chill as she saw William exchanging glances with her, he could easily have an affair with one.

Thank God it was over, Kirsten thought, after Paul had dropped her off at the farm. It hadn't gone badly at all. William had been cordial, if a little distant, but the important thing was that no one could have suspected anything at all. She was his son's friend, he was the doctor who had set her broken wrist, and that was all as far as the world was concerned. She was, she told herself, a far better actress than any of them suspected.

But even more surprising than the ease of the deception was the spirit of welcome she had sensed coming from Paul's mother. She had assumed that Barbara would have found her lacking in the aristocratic finish a Kingman girl friend would be required to possess. Instead, Barbara's handshake and smile when she said good night and her invitation for Kirsten to visit again soon were obviously genuine expressions of warm feelings. This cordiality gave Kirsten a new pang of guilt. She had been crazy to have slept with William, and she could only hope that her mistake would not end up having the unimaginably cruel consequence of forcing a break with Paul.

Paul had been in such a good mood all that evening. He told her later that it was the first time he had felt so comfortable with his parents, so accepted by them. Now, since she was obviously such a great success with his father and mother, she would have to meet the other Kingmans. And what better occasion than the annual Labor Day Square Dance at the club. She hesitated, but finally agreed to go.

Kirsten had never been to the club's side of the lake before, her swimming having always been done at the town beach directly across from it. She could remember hearing the music and seeing the lights of the square dance when she was a teen-ager, parked by the lake in cars full of beer and kids from the local high school. But she had never even driven down the dirt and stone road which led to the large wooden clubhouse. Close-up, as she saw it now, it looked different, less imposing, revealed in all its cultivated shabbiness. The downstairs, she discovered as Paul escorted her through, was a series of unpainted, unstained wooden rooms marked "Boys Under Twelve" or "Women." The adult changing rooms were divided into tiny cubicles, while the children's, offering no such gesture of modesty, had long wooden benches which were covered with soggy towels and even soggier bathing suits.

The upstairs room was huge and rectangular, the furniture all pushed to one side, evidently to make room for the dancing. There was a Ping-Pong table in one corner, covered with a checkered cloth, and serving as a buffet to hold doughnuts, cider, pitchers of beer, and paper cups. Kirsten looked around at the people, most of whom looked familiar. She had seen them in the grocery store or at the vegetable stand she used to set up every summer outside her father's farm. Now, as she walked next to Paul, many of them came over to say hello. Was it being with a Kingman that brought out everyone's friendliest nature? Or was it that she was no longer just a local girl but a model they saw on television? Whatever, she felt good about it and mainly because Paul was so obviously pleased at her reception.

"Hey, gorgeous, remember me?" A slender young woman was standing next to Paul. He introduced her to Kirsten as Peggy Flynn.

"Belle Chevelle," Peggy commented when she saw Kirsten. "My God, are you a Kingman too? Or are there others here as well?"

"No, she doesn't have that distinction," Franklin, standing next to Peggy, said, "but she certainly has others." He eyed Kirsten approvingly. "You're all grown-up these days," he said, smiling at her.

Kirsten saw Paul tense and put her arm in his.

"Are you and Gorgeous going together or something?" Peggy asked. "You make a great couple and that'd make a sweet item for my program. Since none of you Kingmans have done anything spicy enough, I guess I'll have to go for the sugar."

"I don't know if even the sugar will please old Uncle Ernest, Peg," Franklin said. "I remember him telling me that people shouldn't be in the news except when they were born, got married, died, or won the Nobel Prize."

The sound of violins made everyone quiet. The musicians, a group of middle-aged men dressed in blue jeans and plaid shirts, were in the corner tuning their fiddles as the caller turned on the amplifier. Most of the dancers, assembled now, were fairly young children—those who might have been the owners of the soggy bathing suits scattered about the dressing rooms marked "Boys" or "Girls Under Twelve." All of the teenagers seemed to be outside on the darkened porch which overlooked the lake, but when the music started, a few of them started coming inside.

"Virginia Reel," the caller announced, and Kirsten felt a tap on her shoulder. It was William, who had evidently just come in, and she was startled.

She greeted him and then Barbara, who was right behind him. William seemed to want to tell her something, but the music was so loud she couldn't quite get what he was saying. They all moved to the edge of the room where it was quieter.

Did she like square dancing? No, she shook her head in answer to Barbara's question. It might sound weird but she had never really gotten her left sorted out from her right. She could when she thought about it, of course, but in square dances, which were complicated anyway and offered little time for contemplation, she was lost, always crashing into the next couple or into her partner. Paul laughed. Square dancing was not his favorite pastime either, and they stood, with the senior King-mans, watching Posie and Abbie, Margo's little girls, do a do-si-do, the one with her father, the other with her grandfather.

Clara came over to William. "I wish Ernest would stop. Can't you persuade him as a doctor that he ought to give up some of these activities?" Ernest's face was a bright red.

"He wouldn't pay a bit of attention," William told his sister-in-law. "Clara, have you met Paul's friend, Kirsten Cooper?"

"John Cooper's girl? I didn't know you knew Paul. You're the image of your poor dear mother. I remember when we first bought our house in Shropshire what a lovely-looking girl she was." Clara smiled at Kirsten and then at Barbara and William.

"Promenade right," the caller cried, and stamped his foot in rhythm to the squeaking violins. "Now swing your partner and promenade left."

"Hey there, Paul," Whitney Craig called out, "we need one more couple to make up our square."

Paul looked at Kirsten, who shook her head. "You go," she said, "I'll watch."

Peggy Flynn appeared from nowhere and grabbed Paul's arm, and Whitney propelled them both into his square, which also included a smiling beribboned Allison, an extremely unsteady, sweaty Mitch, a cool-looking Phillip, and an immaculate Pat, both of whom miraculously seemed unaffected by the heat and exertion.

As Kirsten stood watching them all skipping, Sebastian joined them and then, after a quick introduction, took a reluctant Barbara into the square which included Frederica and Franklin, Jonathan and the nurse-maid, Jenny. And Kirsten found herself alone with William.

"Can we go outside?" he asked. "It's so hot in here."

She nodded and he led her down the back stairs, out onto the dock. The water was inky now, except where it reflected the colored lights of the Japanese lanterns hung on the balcony above their heads.

"I wanted to talk to you," he began. "Now there, don't look so worried."

"Do I? I guess it's just that I care so much for Paul, I don't want anything to go wrong."

"That's just what I wanted to hear you say, that you really cared for him. And of course, you thought I'd object."

"Well, it is an awkward situation, isn't it?"

He nodded. "Do I dare ask you something?"

"What?"

"Are you two sleeping together?"

"I really don't see what right you have to ask me that."

"I suppose I don't have any right, but believe me, I have my reasons."

"You mean because I slept with you?"

"No, honestly, Kirsten, that has nothing to do with it at all. Just tell me, it's important."

The tone of his voice persuaded her—it was somehow important to him, very important. "Yes, I am," she told him and added softly, "I love him, William."

"And I'm glad you do, sincerely glad. You're obviously good for him, he seems so happy with you." William's voice was warm, almost paternal. She knew he really meant what he was saying.

"Funny, I was so terrified of your reaction. I was sure you'd be horrified and not only because of what happened between us but because I was sure you'd feel I wasn't good enough for him to take seriously. After all, he's a Kingman and I'm a Cooper."

"I'm sorry if I've given the impression that I'm such a snob, that my family as a whole has given that impression. I think you'll find that quite the contrary, every one of the Kingmans is ready to welcome you in every way."

"Yes, they have been extraordinarily warm already, everyone from Aunt Clara to Uncle Sebastian."

William smiled. "That 'uncle' and 'aunt' sound so odd coming from you. I promise," he said as he took her arm and led her back up toward the dance floor, "you won't ever have to call me 'father,' though from now on, you will have to think of me that way."

Kirsten woke up in the middle of the night. She had felt so relieved when she had gone to bed, feeling that there was no way now to spoil her relationship with Paul. But all her fears and anxieties must have asserted themselves while she was asleep because when she awoke, she knew that she could no longer keep her past with William a secret from Paul. She knew herself too well, she could not live with such dishonesty. She would have to tell him and before she left Shropshire. And, when the very next morning her agent called to tell her that that departure was coming sooner than she had thought, Monday morning in fact, she knew the time had come.

* * *

What was it she wanted to tell him? Paul wondered as he drove up the Old Avon Road toward Butternut Farm. It was a crisp September morning and the touch of fall in the air was sharpened by a golden leaf appearing here and there among the foliage of the tall oak trees that lined the road and by the screeching of a kingfisher, the huge, white-collared, long-beaked bird that came to Shropshire only at summer's end. The cows were out to pasture feeding on the last of the summer's tender green grass. Evidently, they had already eaten their morning's fill for, as Paul turned up the dirt road that led to the Cooper's house, he saw them lying in the field, lazily chewing their cud.

Kirsten was waiting for him at the door of the farmhouse as he drove up, a beige fisherman's sweater thrown over her shoulders, her hands in the pockets of her jeans, her silvery blond hair tied up in a ponytail.

"Let's walk," she suggested, taking his arm and leading him toward the orchard where the apple trees were heavy with fruit just ready to be picked.

She reached up and found him a bright red McIntosh. "Here, Adam," she said, tossing it to him, "a bit of knowledge from Eve."

He smiled and then bit into it—the apple was cool and tart.

"I love it here this time of year," she said, breathing deeply, clearly savoring the cool, fresh air. "But vacation's over. I just got a call from my agent and I have to be back in New York tomorrow."

"That was hardly worth my rushing over here for. After all, I can go back with you. You're really the only thing that's keeping me in Shropshire at this point."

"No, that wasn't what I wanted to talk to you about." Her tone suddenly became very serious. Oh, God, he thought. What was it? Was she going to tell him it was over?

"You don't want me to go back with you, is that it?"

"Paul, that isn't it at all." She took both his hands in hers. "Look, I love you and I've never said that to anyone before. I really do love you. But I've got something to tell you, and after I do, you may not want to go back with me. You may never want to see me again."

She let go of him and sat down on the grass, motioning for him to join her.

"I really don't know how to begin," she said. "I really don't even know how it happened, but it started last year. It was the day I broke my wrist . . ."

At first, Paul couldn't quite register what she was telling him, for as she spoke he felt himself growing numb, distant. He had a sensation he remembered having several times before as a child when things became too much for him to understand or too much for him to handle. It was as though he were outside his own body, looking down at himself from a safe distance. No, not quite looking at himself because he was focusing on anything but himself—on the texture of the bark of the tree, on the shape of a cloud, on the way in which round blazes of sunlight broke into the canopy of the trees.

But as far away as he went, he couldn't escape her words. Yes, he heard everything that she was saying, although he would have given anything not to. And as she spoke, a picture kept forcing itself into his mind, a picture in a mirror. Hard as he tried, he couldn't make it go away. A naked man's body, his father's body, a woman's head buried between his strong thighs. Once Claudia Monteverde, now that woman was Kirsten. He shuddered.

"Paul?"

"Why you?" he said in a voice that sounded angrier than he intended. "Oh, God, why you?"

"I don't know—because—I don't know."

He looked at her now, the tears streaming down her face. She was so beautiful and he loved her beyond words, beyond anything he had imagined possible.

"I'm sorry. Forgive me," she said.

Forgive her? Forgive her for being like Claudia, like the blushing clerks in the local shops, like the women who stared at the dashing Don Juan who just happened to be his father. Here's a story, Isabel, about Don Juan's son, another one to add to all the others. How do you like this one?

Suddenly, uncontrollably, he started to laugh. Harder and harder until he felt himself choking and then the hysteria transformed itself into sobs.

"Oh, Paul." Kirsten put her arms around him and began to kiss his forehead, his cheek, his mouth. And now he was returning her kisses, holding her in his arms, holding on to her, until the tears subsided, and both sat in absolute quiet.

"I hate him," he said.

"*Him?* But you should hate *me*. I was the only one who knew about both of you. How can you blame him? Paul, he had no way of knowing what had happened with us in the past or what would happen with us in the future."

"That doesn't matter. It's part of everything—all the pain, all the hurt he's given me in the past, given me all my life."

"I don't think he ever wanted to hurt you," Kirsten said softly. "You're his son. He just wanted you to be something special, to be . . ."

"A Kingman."

"All right, a Kingman. Why blame him for that? It was the one way of being special he knew. He couldn't have found it easy either."

"Why are you apologizing for him, protecting him. Is it him you love or me?"

"How can you ask such a question?" Kirsten's voice was earnest. "Look, Paul, if he's guilty, I'm guiltier. It happened, that's all. But it's over and was over before we even started seeing each other again. And Paul, I know, he's happy for you, for us."

Suddenly, it struck him. Even though by some awful turn of events, Kirsten had been involved with both father and son, had slept with both of them, somehow, miraculously, the son had not failed her. In fact, even after knowing William, she could still fall in love with Paul, could want him in a way and feel for him in a way that she had never felt for his father. If before he had failed in everything, lost in everything, this time he had truly won. And it was the only victory that ever really mattered.

He turned to Kirsten suddenly and took her in his arms.

"I love you," he said. "I love you."

She smiled and kissed him, pressing her body close to his. Gently, softly, they lay back on the grass, its sweet smell mingling with the perfume of the apple trees. Above them, a rush of wings as a great flock of swans passed overhead.

"They mate for life," he told her.

"I know," she said.

And he felt her tremble beside him.

13

Isabel felt as if she would jump out of her skin. She threw down the copy of the New York *Times* with which she had tried to distract herself and started to pace the floor again. The air conditioner in her living room window put out a steady hum that somehow underscored the heavy silence of this humid September evening. Indian summer—it always sounded so pleasant, but of course it never was. She looked at her watch. He would be here in half an hour—that is, if he were on time; that is, if he were going to come at all. Maybe he just said he would come in order to get rid of her, to get her off the phone. No, that wouldn't be like William. He certainly had no qualms about saying that he was busy, not in the mood, would rather do something else. In fact, that was what he said almost every time she had called him since coming back from Wildwood, and she had only managed to entice him over twice during the past month. But if she hardly saw him, she thought about him constantly. And this obsession was beginning to show.

She failed to keep an appointment with the parents of her patient Gloria Hooten, the girl she had recently cured of anorexia. The Hootens, filled with gratitude now that their daughter was out of danger of starvation and could eat normally, had agreed to participate in a study the hospital was sponsoring about this puzzling disease and Isabel's amazingly successful tactics for dealing with it. Isabel, scheduled to conduct the first interview with the Hootens, totally forgot. Later, her attention lapsed so completely and obviously during Evan Wilcox's session that he interrupted his tirade against his wife to ask Isabel angrily if she was listening. He was, he said testily, paying her well for her attention. Another day she developed a splitting headache just as her patient Gordon Chandler arrived, and she had to ask him to cancel his hour. She grew irritable with Leslie Chester when she once again had to listen to the hysterical woman excuse her daughter Pinkie, blaming herself for the girl's blatant rudeness.

And it wasn't only in the context of the psychiatric session that her control was beginning to falter. She snapped at her secretary, Miss Lee. She rebuked the superintendent Otto with uncharacteristic harshness for neglecting to fix a dripping faucet. And though nothing she could pinpoint had occurred with Gerson Richler, his warm solicitude had so intensified in these last weeks that she realized he must have noticed something wasn't quite right with her.

She mustn't let William see this side of her, she thought now as she walked into the kitchen and started to heat some water for coffee. But no, it was too hot for coffee. Was the Schweppes in the refrigerator? No, she had forgotten. It would be warm, he would be annoyed. She put a six-pack in the freezer. Now, don't let me forget that, she said to herself. Maybe she should change. She walked into the bedroom and looked at herself in the full-length mirror on her closet door. She had on a mauve shirtwaist dress. The color was good on her, but the effect itself was too tailored, too efficient, not romantic at all. Would a peignoir have been a better idea? She could still put one on. But when she started to take her blue silk robe off its hanger, the doorbell rang. She jumped, her throat went dry, her palms grew damp, as she hurriedly walked to the front door.

William was somehow different tonight, more relaxed, lighter in mood, less irritable than he had ever seemed before. She poured him a drink. It was Schweppes and vodka he wanted—good that she had chilled the soda. He took it and sat down on the living room couch.

"Well, what was so very pressing that I absolutely had to be here tonight?"

"Is it really such a hardship?" she asked. "Do I really have to give you reasons?"

"No, but you certainly gave the impression on the phone that it was at least a matter of life and death. But"—he paused—"if you have nothing to tell me, I do have something to tell you."

"What is it?" What was he going to say? She was suddenly conscious of her own heartbeat.

"It's Paul, my prodigal son. He's finally decided to join the human race."

"I wasn't aware that he had left it."

"Well, you and I obviously have quite different views regarding acceptable patterns of behavior. In any case, Paul is in love. And with a beautiful woman, someone his own age, who if she lacks an impeccable pedigree"—his tone set the phrase within quotes—"at least seems quite acceptable to everyone in the family. And mainly because, without a degree in psychiatry, she has managed to transform that boy into a happy, alive human being."

"You say this as if you thought I would be jealous. Don't you realize I'm thrilled that Paul is doing so well, that this kind of relationship was precisely what I had in mind for him, what I tried to make possible for him."

"Well, then, you should be very happy."

"I am—I was—I told Paul myself—"

"You told him?" he interrupted. "You mean you're still speaking to him? I thought surely that was over."

"Oh, come, William, didn't you think he would call me with such wonderful news. You really don't have the slightest idea of what our relationship involves."

"I assure you, I know enough," he said curtly, standing up and putting his drink down on the coffee table.

"You're not going to leave?" She was panicked. "Please, William, don't go. I've hardly seen you. You know," she said softly, "we don't have to talk about Paul."

She went over and put her arms around his neck, pressing her body to his. She then ran her fingers down his muscular back, feeling knots of tension dissolve under her touch. Her hands were on his buttocks now, pressing the tight spheres toward her. Whether or not it was against his will, he was responding, she knew, for she felt his penis harden, pressing into her stomach.

"Stay with me, William, please stay."

He said nothing, but followed her into the bedroom, where he languidly stretched out on the bed, making no gesture to undress himself. She began to do it for him, and when he was naked, she took off her own clothes and lay down beside him. Suddenly, abruptly, he sat up and turned her over, pushing her face away from him. What was he going to do? She was terrified as she felt his strong hands grab her hips and raise them into the air. She wanted to cry out, to tell him to stop, that she didn't want him to take her in that way, in that part of her. But she didn't dare, he might just leave, and anything, anything at all, that he chose to do to her was better than that. She prepared herself for the searing pain that she knew would come—it would help, she knew, if she could relax, but she felt her muscles involuntarily tighten. She felt his fingers pulling at her, pushing her open, and then the thrust of his penis as he entered her. It was painful, but not the pain she had feared. It was her vagina he sought, after all, and the pain had simply been that of her own unreadiness and confusion.

He was pounding against her now—she could feel his thighs pressing against her. But with her face turned down into the pillow, she could see nothing. It struck her, with not a little horror, that someone else could have taken William's place and she would not have known the difference. And as if to assure herself that it was he, after all, she strained her neck to look up, catching his reflection in the full-length mirror on the closet door. It was William, of course, it was William, but a William she had not seen since the very first night he had come to her apartment. His face was contorted in rage—it was clear that he hated her, that he had turned her this way, taken this position, so as not to have to look at her. She felt the pillow beneath her face growing wet with her tears—tears William couldn't see and that she knew would have meant nothing to him anyway.

His body shuddered violently and then pulled away from her. Could he leave her like this? She turned toward him.

"You can't leave me now," she said hoarsely.

"Oh yes I can," he answered as he put on his clothes. "You don't quite understand, Isabel. Now that Paul is well, he's free of you. And that"—he paused, looking at her triumphantly—"makes me free of you too."

So she had lost him. She couldn't accept it. And remembering the nightmare of her life after Bryan, she felt a growing sense of dread at what awaited her after William. As cruel as it sounded, it would have been less painful to her if William had died. To lose him that way was simply to lose him. But this way, he remained always within reach, yet always out of grasp, a dashed hope, an impossible possibility.

She would go mad. As miraculous as Larsen's effect on her had been, she had always known that her stability remained tenuous. And maybe that was why in all those years between Bryan and now, she had never taken the risk of allowing herself an emotional involvement. She was not only losing William, she was losing herself as well.

She fell back on the still wet pillow and pulled the blankets around her, conscious once again of the groan of the air conditioners. They stood between her and the world, and so too did the blankets that she wrapped around herself. She felt herself falling deeper and deeper into the bed, burying herself in it, making herself disappear. Then she fell asleep, only to awaken the next morning still clinging to the pillow, not ready to relinquish the enveloping safety of the blankets. But somehow she managed to force herself to get up, get dressed, and get to work.

Gerson Richler parked his car in the lot adjoining the Marcy Avenue Neighborhood House. The most recently opened of the public health centers in the Bedford-Stuyvesant section of Brooklyn, it was the one which Sandy had been instrumental in establishing, and he was anxious to show off the facilities to his father. Just from the look of the building itself, Richler was impressed with his son's efforts. Three months ago, all this had looked like London during the blitz. The windows of what used to be a dry goods shop, an appliance store, and a bakery were shattered into bits and pieces of jagged glass. The upper stories were blackened first by fire and again by soot, and wherever possible, the building was covered with graffiti. The sidewalks were broken, weeds were working their way through the cracks in the concrete, and garbage littered the gutters. Today, in contrast, all was neat and clean. The street had been repaved, the building facade refaced, the windows had been replaced, and the trim and doors had been freshly painted. A large red and white sign that stretched across all three storefronts said, "Marcy Avenue Neighborhood House—All Welcome."

Richler looked around. There were a lot of doors, but no indication as to which was the main entrance. Well, that was something he would have to tell Sandy to take care of. If all were welcome here, they had to figure out how to get in. And what if it was an emergency? After two false tries, the third door opened, revealing a cheerful waiting room. Didn't he recognize that couch, that chair, that table? Of course, the old living room set from their summer home in Peekskill. He smiled, remembering a twelve-year-old Sandy curled up on that very couch, watching *Gunsmoke* on television. Leah always complained about Sandy watching such programs, and Richler had always assured her that there was nothing to be concerned with. Now where Sandy had sat was a boy about the same age, only this one was black and had his nose buried in a book. Leah would have approved of that. Next to the boy was another, this one a little younger, who could have been his brother and who had his arm in a cast. There was a pregnant woman, several babies with their mothers, an old man without a tooth in his head, and an old woman with a constant cough.

Sandy came up behind his father. "Hi, Papa. You found it all right, I see. Well, what do you think. Terrific, isn't it? Let me show you around."

Sandy took his father through a series of clean if sparsely equipped consultation rooms, examining rooms, exercise rooms, and a clinic with several white metal beds.

"Who sleeps here?" Richler asked. "You don't have hospital facilities, do you?"

"No, no. These are for the runaways, the kids who for one reason or another can't sleep home one more night." A phone rang, interrupting him, and Sandy excused himself for a moment.

Runaways, Richler thought. How could parents be so cruel that they drove their own children away? How could children hurt their parents by running away? How could families strike out at their own members? When someone was your own flesh and blood, you stood by them whatever they did, you loved them simply because they were yours, and you forgave them simply because you loved them. And there were some people who, even if they weren't your flesh and blood, inspired these feelings in you anyway. You loved them unquestioningly, you made them your family. In a sense, it was this family feeling that Sandy was extending to the runaways he was providing these beds for. In a sense, it was this family feeling that Richler extended to those he cared for and worked with. Maybe that was why he was so upset about Isabel, he thought.

"Have you seen Isabel lately?" he asked his son as they walked into Sandy's small office with its crayon drawings from younger, grateful patients, and its simple furniture. The porch set from Peekskill, Richler observed.

Sandy shook his head sadly. "No, I've called her and called her but she doesn't seem to have time for me. But what gets me is not that she's too busy for me but that she sounds funny, lifeless, not the old Isabel."

"That's it exactly. And she looks that way too. I'm really worried about her. She's going through something very difficult, and I wish she'd let someone help her."

"I wish she'd let me," Sandy said quietly, almost to himself.

If only she would let Sandy help, Richler thought as he drove back to Manhattan across the Williamsburg Bridge. And not only, he had to admit, because from the start the idea of Isabel and Sandy as a couple had struck him as a good one—Leah would adjust to it and surely learn to love her—but because Isabel, right now, seemed to be in desperate need of help.

Paul walked up Fifth Avenue at a brisk pace. He was due at Isabel's office at 11 A.M., and the weather was so clear, the air so fresh and invigorating, that he had decided against taking a bus or a cab up from the zoo where he had spent the early hours of the morning. He had been watching Kirsten at work, modeling a series of shots for a fashion feature in *Vogue* on fake furs, and the photographer, the witty Daniel Chu, had decided that the very best backdrop for someone in a false leopard skin would be an actual leopard looking on gratefully. Or that the most persuasive way to make a phony seal parka look appealing was to give it the pathos it would gain from being put next to a real-life seal.

Crew, model, and audience had met in the monkey house at 6:30 A.M. when the baboons and orangutans were still yawning and the gorilla snoring loudly. Patty Cake, the baby chimpanzee who had become famous the preceding winter for her broken arm widely publicized by the empathetic TV cameras, was the only one wide awake and was swinging happily from an inner tube, munching on an orange skin. Chu's stylist, a tiny birdlike woman, pinned Kirsten's outfit with clothespins, combed her hair, and put lip gloss on her lips between shots, while Chu himself kept selecting the locations, guiding his assistants as to where to set up the lights needed to supplement the early morning haze.

Paul stood watching, together with a zoo keeper and a guard, amazed as the morning went on and the zoo became more crowded with little children, their mothers or nursemaids, and a few elderly men and women, at the nonchalance everyone showed toward the crew of photographers and model. New York was one big fashion studio, he guessed, and the sight of a young woman, however beautiful, posed against one or another of its famous sites, was simply too ordinary to attract many onlookers.

But now it was 10:15, and if Paul wanted to walk the forty blocks or so up to the hospital, he had better leave now. He kissed Kirsten goodbye, much to the annoyance of the little stylist who flew at the model with a giant powder puff, and started walking. He felt good, very good, and he was anxious to communicate this to Isabel. He had always imagined in the past that should everything by some miracle turn out all right for him, what he would feel would be a kind of euphoria. He would be walking on air and, like the hero in a musical comedy, he would feel like singing and dancing, with the world, in turn, singing and dancing with him. But now that everything was, in fact, working out for him, it was nothing like that at all. What he felt instead of the almost childish delight he had imagined was a mellowness, a maturity, a sense of self-acceptance and self-assurance. Being happy was being able to handle things. It was being capable of running your own life, of controlling things around you. It was being able to take in stride some less than friendly remark like the one Margo had made about the fact that Kirsten hadn't a degree to her name, a statement that made the lack of a B.A. seem a sign of total illiteracy. Rather than send him into his usual defensive reaction, it merely struck him as silly, almost amusing. Paul also had no trouble declining his parents' pointed suggestion that he move back into his old room in their apartment, an invitation which reflected a view of him as less than self-reliant.

But most monumental of all, he told Isabel now as he sat across from her in her small office, had been the way he had dealt with Kirsten's shocking revelation that William had been her lover.

"At first, for a second, I hated her. I kept seeing her body entangled with his, seeing her the way I saw Claudia Monteverde going down on him," he said. "But then, it was over—the rage, that is, the resentment. Suddenly it seemed to me that if I wanted her, and I knew I did, I would have to accept the past and accept as well the fact that there was nothing I could do about it. What had happened, had happened, and all that I could hope for was that it really was over."

He paused, waiting for Isabel to comment on what he had just told her. But to his surprise, she sat there silently, and so he simply went on.

"I don't mean to say that I accept my father with open arms. In a way, I find him disgusting, pathetic, weak, self-indulgent—I can give you a string of hateful adjectives. But he is my father, and nothing I feel can change that. What has changed now is how I feel about myself. I can't any longer think of myself as failing to live up to him, because I don't think of him as someone that anyone, and certainly not I, would want to live up to."

Paul, waiting for Isabel's customary warm comments praising his positive viewpoint, his new maturity, his sudden emergence as a truly adult human being, paused again. But Isabel said nothing, and for the first time this day he looked at her closely, shifting his attention from his own reactions to hers. He saw, to his surprise, that she was shaking. Yes, there had been something funny about her that morning when he first came in. Her smile had been fleeting, her greeting somewhat distant, and her voice filled with a faint tremor. But he was too absorbed with all he had to tell her that day after such a long separation and so never really focused on her. He had noticed as he told her about his father and Kirsten that now and then she seemed to have trouble catching her breath, but he didn't give it any significance until now. Something must be terribly wrong.

"Isabel, what's the matter?" he said. Was she displeased with him in some way?

He reached out to hold her hand but she drew away. "Have I done something wrong?" he asked.

"No, no, Paul," she said. "I just don't feel quite right today. Maybe I'm coming down with something, a cold, I suppose, but I am pleased to hear about you and Kirsten."

"I've something more to tell you," he said. "We've decided to get married. I know it's not in style this season, but I guess we're both old-fashioned. Old-fashioned enough too for a honeymoon. And because of that, we've decided to wait until my SoHo show is over and Kirsten is finished with the reshooting of the television pilot she worked on last spring. And so, that'll make it December. A Christmas wedding in Shropshire, what do you think about that? Would you come? It would mean a lot to me."

"How wonderful," Isabel said in a hollow voice. "I'm really happy for you."

"You sure don't sound like you are. I don't understand. Am I misreading everything? Have I misunderstood something?"

"No, not at all. I am pleased that you are so well, so wonderfully well, and I'm happy for that and happy that because of it, you've been able to work things out with Kirsten. It must be this damned virus or the change in the season. That always happens to me, a cold whenever there's a change in the temperature."

She was the old Isabel again, and Paul felt a tremendous sense of relief. He was fine, she was affirming this, and when she smiled and told him he was dismissed, the therapy concluded, he felt as if he'd finally won all the prizes he'd never won before.

"We'll still see each other, won't we?"

She nodded with a warm smile as she stood by the door of the office, saying good-bye.

"And you'll come to the wedding, won't you?"

She nodded again, her face close to his, and he noticed how she looked. There were dark shadows under her eyes and she was so pale and thin. She really should see someone.

"Hey, Doctor, promise me you'll see a doctor, won't you?" He smiled, kissing her on the cheek.

When Paul left, Isabel asked Miss Lee to please hold her calls for the next half hour. There was no way, Isabel thought, that she could see or talk to anyone just now. It had taken so much out of her to keep from breaking down in front of Paul. The story about William and Kirsten had really shaken her, much more, it seemed, than it had shaken Paul, and it would have been cruel and destructive to allow Paul to imagine that her agitation had anything to do with him.

He really was in such good shape right now, and she had a professional pride in his well-being. Still, she couldn't help but feel a slight tinge of loss. If he had once been her lover, she had more than once been his mother, strange as that might sound. For like a mother, she had been the one to comfort him, to counsel him, to care for him. And now he was leaving her because he was beyond needing her. It was right that he should go, but, with all the ambivalence characteristic of parental feelings, she would miss him.

But it wasn't the loss of Paul that had set her on edge. It was the idea of William and Kirsten. Why had it upset her so much? She knew William had a compulsive need to go to bed with woman after woman. And remembering the sight of Kirsten in the restaurant in SoHo that night, she recognized how tempting such an exquisite young woman would be to him. She couldn't be jealous. Kirsten had come before her, and William, she knew only too well, wasn't the type to carry any image of one woman over with him into his affair with the next. What it was instead was simply the mention of William himself. She couldn't bear to think of him at all, whether with Kirsten, with anyone else, or by himself. These last few days she exerted a superhuman effort to keep pushing the idea of him away from her, only to have his image assert itself forcefully, interrupting her other thoughts. And Paul, with his tale of William and Kirsten, had given her obsession a new force. Paul's tale served to underscore something she knew all along but couldn't bear to confront—the fact that William, who had women before her, would have women after her, would probably be having a woman right now.

Suddenly, automatically, she dialed William's number. She recognized the cultivated voice of Mrs. Gregory, his nurse, who took her name and number with no hint of recognition, telling her that Dr. Kingman was just finishing up with a patient. Could he call her back in about five minutes? Of course. Except that five minutes later he did not call nor ten minutes later. She dialed his number again. The doctor hadn't called her back? How strange, said the nurse, she had given him the message. She'd connect her with him right now, but he was in with another patient. She certainly would repeat the message.

Whether she did or not, William did not return the call, and Isabel felt helpless. She remembered all those messages, all those unanswered messages she had left for Bryan Madison so many years before. She couldn't let it happen that way again. She'd fight back. She had to.

Grabbing her jacket and telling Miss Lee to cancel all her appointments, she ran from the hospital down the few streets to William's office. He had just left for New York Hospital, the nurse told her. He had an emergency operation to perform.

Isabel ran from the office and took a car east to the vast complex of buildings along the river which made up New York Hospital. Which entrance? The main one, she supposed, and the cab entered the circular driveway, past flower beds filled with the first chrysanthemums of the season and the last of the impatiens.

At the desk she asked for Dr. Kingman, and a round-faced black woman whose speech marked her as a West Indian connected her by phone to William's hospital office. Another West Indian voice told her he was in surgery. How long? It was impossible to say. Isabel decided to wait anyway and sat down in the lobby, outside the gift shop.

Two children sat facing her. They were evidently too young to be allowed upstairs to visit their sick relatives and were restlessly waiting for someone to come for them. Near them sat a very old woman, tears streaming down her face, here and there getting stopped by the wrinkles. A young couple, tears in their own eyes, were trying to comfort her. Isabel stared at them for a while and then got up to look in the gift shop. There was a rack of magazines, some paperbacks, boxes of candy, packages of handkerchiefs, some toys and plants. What was she doing in here? She did not want any of these things. She walked out and back to her seat.

The crying trio was gone and in their place was a tall woman; she must have been almost six feet, with short-cropped curly hair, bright blue eyes, and a large generous mouth. Suddenly the woman smiled and Isabel found herself looking to see just what or who had inspired it. It was William, and he was smiling back at the tall woman. Isabel found her stomach churn. She ran over to him, stopping him in his path.

"Why, Isabel, what are you doing here? Have you joined our staff?" he asked.

"No . . . I . . ." she stammered. She didn't know what to say, she realized with horror. Was she insane to be there like this, with nothing at all to say to him?

"Come meet a friend of mine. Megan Evans, Dr. Isabel Dunne, a psychiatrist from Mount Sinai. Megan is a writer. Have you read her *Memories of a Welsh Girlhood?* It's really quite amusing."

No, Isabel hadn't.

Megan forgave her. But only if Isabel would forgive Megan for her ignorance of psychiatry. Welsh people had far more trust in the healing power of song and poetry.

Isabel felt a sudden weariness come over her. She couldn't pretend any longer. "William, I have to talk to you, right now."

He looked startled, then furious. "Not now," he said. "I'm afraid Megan and I have to be off."

"No," Isabel insisted. "I must speak to you."

Would Megan excuse him for a moment? He and Dr. Dunne had a case in common that was causing some problem.

William grabbed Isabel by the arm and propelled her into a corner. "All right then, what is it?"

But again, she had nothing to say. Her body started to tremble.

"Isabel," she heard him say, "you're cracking up. I'm going to put you in a taxi. You are going home, and I never ever want to see or hear from you again."

Isabel was in a daze. She couldn't remember entering her apartment, taking off her clothes, getting into bed. She could hardly remember waking up. Did she sleep at all? Maybe, maybe not. It was all so unclear. What she knew was that somehow she managed to get back to Mount Sinai the next morning and that she was now sitting in her office, facing a distraught Emily Richmond.

"That bastard. That goddamn bastard. Just why does he think he can have everything? And he's got everything. He's got her, he's got the love of the children, he's got his work. And I have nothing, absolutely nothing. The children would rather be with him. Why not, he's more fun. He's all laughs, I'm all tears. You know something, I bore myself."

How sad Emily's voice was, Isabel thought. What a sad idea, to bore yourself. Did Isabel bore herself? Maybe. Perhaps.

"And besides, he's never alone. He doesn't know what it's like to be alone. He's got that girl, he's got his friends. I have no one and I'm always alone."

Emily had begun to cry. And her sobs grew louder and louder. How loud they were, Isabel thought, far more loud than she had ever heard them before. And then she knew why. It wasn't only Emily who was sobbing. It was Isabel as well.

The telephone rang. It had been ringing for a while and Isabel finally stretched out an arm to pick up the receiver. She was so tired that even this minimal gesture seemed somehow to require more energy than she was able to summon up.

"Isabel?" The voice was familiar, a warm voice. "It's Sandy. Where have you been? You've had me frantic."

"Right here," she said.

"And for two days you haven't answered the phone?"

"Has it been two days? I guess so then."

"Isabel, I'm coming over."

"No, no, Sandy. I can't see anyone."

"You *can't?*"

"No, I can't. I won't, I just won't." Her voice had become shrill, and she heard its grating sound as if it belonged to someone else, a patient perhaps. Someone very far away. Someone who wasn't herself.

"Isabel, are you still there?"

Yes, she was there, but she couldn't tell him that because somehow it just took too much effort to utter the words. She was too tired, much too tired, to say anything at all. She let the receiver slip out of her hand, and she pulled the covers around her.

When Isabel opened her eyes, she saw Gerson Richler sitting in a chair next to her bed, looking at her.

"Fine hours you keep," he said. "Do you know it's almost noon? Who do you think you are, some kind of movie star or something?"

She wanted to smile at what was so evidently an effort to be cheerful, but she couldn't make her face assume the right expression. It was as if her muscles were frozen.

"Movie star or not, you're getting the royal treatment. Do you know I haven't made a house call in forty years?"

Again she tried to smile and again she couldn't.

"And now I know why I haven't made any," he went on. "It's freezing in here. Don't they ever send the heat up?" He began rubbing his arms. "No wonder you won't get out of bed. I wouldn't either if my apartment were so cold."

"Gerson?" she asked tentatively, for as soon as she had uttered the name, she thought she had made a mistake. It wasn't Gerson Richler, it was Arne Larsen. No, it wasn't. It was Bishop O'Connor. What was she supposed to say? What was it that she used to say? She remembered now. Forgive me, Father, for I have sinned. Yes, that was it. Forgive me, Father . . .

But it couldn't be Bishop O'Connor or Arne Larsen either. Both the bishop and Arne were dead.

"Gerson?" she asked again.

"Yes, Isabel. It's me," Gerson Richler said softly. "I thought for a moment you thought I was someone else, someone you wanted to forgive you?"

"Yes, that's it, forgive me. Forgive me, Father, for I have sinned, oh, forgive me, Father, forgive me, Father." She began to say the words in a toneless voice, repeating them over and over again like a record caught in a groove.

"Can I forgive you, Isabel? Will you let me forgive you?"

"You?" she asked. His offer caught her up short. "You? But you're not my confessor, you can't hear my confession."

"Why not, Isabel? What is a confessor that I am not? What should I do? I'll turn my head. I'll look away if that's what you want, if that's what a confessor does."

"A confessor gives penance. A confessor gives absolution." Her voice was becoming shrill. "A confessor saves your soul."

"I do that all the time. Let me be your confessor."

For a moment she did not seem to comprehend what he had said. Her eyes seemed glazed, lifeless. Then slowly, without expression, she began to speak. At first the voice was timid, almost like a small child's. But then her tone grew bolder, clearer. She was making her confession at last, tears streaming down her face all the while.

She told him about Bryan, about the child she did not have, about the children she could not have. She told him about Paul, about how she had led him, not really out of passion, not really out of desire except the desire to make him whole, to become her lover. And she told him about William, about how hearing of him through Paul's words, seeing him through Paul's eyes, she had fallen in love first with the idea of William and then with William himself. She told him about Wildwood, about Paoli long before that, about her estrangement from Dorchester and about her fears of Shropshire as well. Where could she go? With whom did she belong? Who was she?

She was sobbing and he was sitting on the bed, cradling her, patting her head and telling her that everything would be all right.

"All right? How can it be?" she cried. "I have to be punished. I've sinned and I must do penance."

"You've done enough penance. You've had enough pain. It's finished with, Isabel. It's over."

His voice was so warm that it made her warm. Yes, all these years had been an act of contrition. Her exclusive devotion to career had been her Hail Marys, her self-denial in all else had been her Our Fathers.

"Are you listening to me?" he went on.

She nodded.

"What I want you to understand is that everything you've done, whether or not I agree with it, or would do it myself, or would tell others to do, I can accept. And not because it's wrong or right but because it's part of you." He paused, as if to give her a moment to digest what he had said. And then, in that voice which in its heavy rhythms and cadences seemed almost chantlike, went on to ask the pointed, perfect questions that sounded out all those feelings which lay just below the surface, that pulled together and clarified the disparate insights, giving them unity and significance. Little by little, the picture she had of herself altered, becoming more well defined, no longer sullied and sinful.

"Then I'm forgiven?" she asked softly, timidly.

"Yes, of course, you're forgiven. Isabel, it's over. What has happened has happened and now, no one is judging you, no one is testing you."

How much she wanted to believe him. How much she wanted it to be true. How much she wanted the world to be as infinitely loving and accepting as he. But she knew otherwise.

"No, Gerson, others wouldn't forgive me. You forgive me because you're kinder than others, more gentle than others, more fatherly."

"Isabel, I tell you. Many people would feel as I do. Your own father would, if he were alive."

"My father? My father?" Something in her awoke. It was a memory, a picture. Was it real? She would never know. But the faceless man now had a face, much like Isabel's own, with sparkling blue eyes and curly red hair. And it came close to her, that face, smiling and full of love. He had loved her, after all. And at that age, way back then, he could not have loved her for what she had accomplished, for her good grades or gold stars. He loved her for her alone. An incredible feeling of well-being came over her. Yes, Gerson was right. Her father who loved her would have forgiven her.

Isabel reached out and took Richler's hand.

"You know, you're a good doctor."

He smiled. "I know."

14

How BEAUTIFUL SHROPSHIRE WAS, Isabel thought as she drove now over the covered bridge and into the small neat village that was Shropshire Center. A tall Christmas tree stood before her in the tiny village green, its sparkling lights reflected and repeated in the small square windows of a grocery store, a wineshop, a hardware store. The snow was banked deep on the side of the road, its thick crust of white forming a perfect bed for a red barn she could see standing at the top of a nearby hill, for the huge conical evergreens that dotted the landscape. It was so beautiful, she thought, that it looked like a make-believe place, a child's dream of Christmas.

And the wedding, in the small white church at the edge of the green, its staid New England interior decked now with sweet-smelling branches of evergreen, with red-berried holly, with white-flowered mistletoe, was a child's dream of a wedding too. Paul, dark and slim, in an appropriately dark suit, stood next to Kirsten, fair and tall in a simple white dress, as both faced the young minister. From the balcony where an usher had seated her with the other latecomers—was he Franklin or Phillip? she wondered—she could see the pews below, and she knew that among them were not only William but Ernest and Clara and Sebastian and Natalie and Barbara and all the Kingman cousins who, if she did not know exactly what they looked like, were as vivid to her as if they had been her own family.

The minister spoke the final words of the ceremony, the organ burst into the Triumphal March from *Lohengrin,* as Paul kissed Kirsten, and the young couple were enveloped by swarms of well-wishers. Isabel, having no wish to push her way into that crush, decided to save her congratulations until the reception at William and Barbara's. She followed the crowd around her down the stairs and then the line of cars, all of which, going in a single direction, were obviously on their way to the Kingman home. The traffic moved slowly now that the snow had begun to fall.

William's home was just as she had pictured it. It was a huge white classically New England house with the large fan-shaped front door, shutters at each of its dozens of windows, porches jutting out here and there, added over the centuries to please each new generation's wives, dormer windows on the third floor, and chimneys signaling each of the several fireplaces. From inside she could hear laughter, music, the sound of people who knew each other well and were enjoying themselves and, for a moment, she regretted that she had ever come. But no use feeling this way. She had come, and now that she had, she would go in. Besides, the snow was getting heavier.

The large center hall was filled with people who spilled over into the living room to the right, the study to the left, and the dining room. Little children were darting in and out among the adults. Which were Margo's? Which was Allison's? A muscular-looking elderly man in a shiny blue suit and with the largest, strongest hands Isabel had ever seen came over and introduced himself. He was Kirsten's father. Was she Dr. Dunne? Paul had mentioned her, and he recognized her right away from a painting he had seen of her at Paul's show. Wasn't that Paul a terrific artist that he could paint someone so well that you could spot them just like that? And the critics seemed to like him too. They'd sure written up some good words about the boy's work. He had a real future, didn't she think so? She did, Isabel assured Mr. Cooper.

Had she met anyone yet? There were a lot of fancy people here. A United States senator, the governor was going to drop in later, there was a Supreme Court justice and even that television reporter. What was her name? Peggy Flynn? Well, he could at least introduce her to the Kingmans.

How accurately Paul had described everyone. If Natalie Kingman Rush, that sharp-featured woman with the equally sharp-featured husband, could recognize her, as had Mr. Cooper, from Paul's paintings, she could recognize Natalie from Paul's stories. Only this Natalie was less frightening than she was somehow comical—so spartan, so efficient, so tautly wound that she almost exaggerated herself into a caricature.

And here, of course, was sweet round-faced Clara, who blushed violently on meeting Isabel. She knows about Paul and me, doesn't she? Isabel thought, and she will never get over the shock. And there were

Frederica and Mitch. Their marriage certainly wasn't going to last to next Christmas, she thought, overhearing them bicker loudly at the bar as Mitch eagerly grasped at the drink that had just been poured for him. Allison's marriage might not make it either, Isabel noted. Her husband, Jonathan, certainly didn't seem surprised when that plump young woman, with those two little girls in tow, now familiarly brushed her hand against his trousers. And those were unmistakably Phillip and Franklin, two very ambitious-looking young men, laughing with no little effort at something said by the imposing-looking man they flanked who Isabel guessed must have been Senator MacIntyre.

"Isabel?" It was Paul. "I'm so glad you came. Come meet Kirsten."

She was beautiful and obviously in love. How happy she was for both of them, Isabel told them. And she truly was. Had she met any of the other famous folk? Paul asked, smiling. Most of them, she told him, but not the fabulous Ernest. He would take care of that, and in a moment there she was, being introduced to the famous Nobel Prize winner himself. He was the only one that Paul somehow hadn't managed to paint quite correctly. He wasn't quite so tall, his head not quite so huge, his appearance not quite so godlike as Paul had suggested. Apparently, Paul had always seen him through his father's eyes.

"How are you?" a familiar voice whispered in her ear. She turned around. How handsome he looked in his dark blue suit.

"Fine, I've been fine. And you?"

William shook his head. "I've missed you, you know."

"Really? Whatever happened to the Welsh girlhood?"

"It turned out to be not so memorable after all."

She smiled.

A delicate, beautiful, somewhat nervous woman interrupted them. This, of course, was Barbara. "Dr. Dunne? I just wanted to thank you for all the help you've given our son. You, probably more than anyone, have made all this possible."

"You give me too much credit," Isabel said, "but I'm delighted about Paul." They chatted on, Barbara obviously the only Kingman who had not been let in on the truth of Isabel's affair with Paul.

Finally, Isabel excused herself. "I really must leave. It's a long drive back to New York and a slow one in this weather."

"You're not going to try to drive back tonight," Barbara said. "It can be treacherous. I insist you spend the night."

"No." Isabel shook her head hurriedly, she couldn't do that.

William had an idea. If Dr. Dunne felt uncomfortable staying with them, and he did understand that—it was going to be both crowded and noisy at their home for quite a few more hours, from the looks of it— why not allow them to put her up at the Shropshire Inn? It was only a few miles down the road and very pleasant.

Isabel was about to protest again, but William would have none of it. And the snow was heavy and somewhat frightening, she could see that now.

He would telephone for the reservation, he said. When he returned a few minutes later, Barbara had gone off to check on the caterers.

"It's all set," William smiled, "and I'm sure to be able to get away by eleven. I'll call you first," he whispered.

It was a slow drive down to the inn, even though the road was straight and had recently been plowed. But the snow kept falling so heavily that there was practically no visibility at all. One mistake, she thought, and the car would skid right off the road.

She was exhausted when she got to the inn, and she ran herself a warm bath. The water relaxed her as she lay back now, thinking about the wedding. So this was the world that had so intimidated her all these years, the world that whether it was in Shropshire or in Paoli or in Wildwood or anywhere else produced the Bryan Madisons and the William Kingmans and all the rest of that special nobility.

What amazed her was that despite what she had always believed, she wasn't out of place at all. For though in one way or another they might have been different from her, they certainly were no better. Yes, it was good that she hadn't set foot in this world until now. The young Isabel, the scholarship girl, would never have been able to feel this way. And the Isabel of even just a few months ago had too much of the frightened sensibility of that girl to feel any differently. Now, however, she had changed. After all, if they had achieved, so had she. If fact, considering from where she had started, her achievements were greater. Gerson was right. She was more in control now, more contented, above all happier with herself than she had ever been.

She got out of the tub and, throwing a large towel around her, lay back on the double bed. The phone rang. And rang again. But Isabel did not answer it.